Spartan Gold

Clive Cussler is the author or co-author of thirty-eight previous books, including twenty Dirk Pitt® novels, most recently *Arctic Drift*; eight NUMA® Files adventures, most recently *Medusa*; and six *Oregon* Files books, most recently *Corsair*. He has written three works of non-fiction and a historical adventure series, which began with *The Chase*. He lives in Arizona.

Grant Blackwood is a US Navy veteran and the author of the *Briggs Tanner* series. He lives in Colorado.

Spartan Gold

CLIVE CUSSLER
with GRANT BLACKWOOD

MICHAEL JOSEPH
an imprint of
PENGUIN BOOKS

MICHAEL JOSEPH

Published by the Penguin Group

Penguin Books Ltd, 80 Strand, London WC2R 0RL, England

Penguin Group (USA) Inc., 375 Hudson Street, New York, New York 10014, USA

Penguin Group (Canada), 90 Eglinton Avenue East, Suite 700, Toronto, Ontario, Canada M4P 2Y3
(a division of Pearson Penguin Canada Inc.)

Penguin Ireland, 25 St Stephen's Green, Dublin 2, Ireland (a division of Penguin Books Ltd)

Penguin Group (Australia), 250 Camberwell Road,
Camberwell, Victoria 3124, Australia (a division of Pearson Australia Group Pty Ltd)

Penguin Books India Pvt Ltd, 11 Community Centre,
Panchsheel Park, New Delhi – 110 017, India

Penguin Group (NZ), 67 Apollo Drive, Rosedale, North Shore 0632, New Zealand
(a division of Pearson New Zealand Ltd)

Penguin Books (South Africa) (Pty) Ltd, 24 Sturdee Avenue,
Rosebank, Johannesburg 2196, South Africa

Penguin Books Ltd, Registered Offices: 80 Strand, London WC2R 0RL, England

www.penguin.com

www.penguin.com

First published in the United States of America by G. P. Putnam's Sons 2009
First published in Great Britain by Michael Joseph 2009

2

Printed in Great Britain by Clays Ltd, St Ives plc

A CIP catalogue record for this book is available from the British Library

ISBN: 978-0-718-15608-4

ACKNOWLEDGMENTS

We would like to thank the following people for graciously offering their expertise:

Yvonne Rodoni Bergero, Stanford Society, Archaeological Institute of America; Martin Burke; Christie B. Cochrell, exhibits manager, Stanford University Press; K. Kris Hirst, Archaeology Section, About.com.

Dr. Patrick Hunt, director of the Stanford Alpine Archaeology Project 1994–2009 & National Geographic Society Hannibal Expedition 2007–2008, Stanford University; Tom Iliffe, professor of Marine Biology, Texas A&M University; D. P. Lyle, M.D.; Katie McMahon, reference librarian, Newberry Library, Chicago; Connell Monette, assistant professor, Al Akhawayn University in Ifrane, Morocco; Eric Ross, associate professor, Al Akhawayn University in Ifrane, Morocco; Jo Stoop; Stephen Toms; Tim Vandergrift, Wine Writer and Technical Services Manager, Winexpert Ltd.

And last, but far, far from least: Janet, for her hints and insights.

PROLOGUE

A gust of wind whipped snow around the legs of the horse known as Styrie and he snorted nervously, sidestepping on the trail before the rider clicked his tongue a few times, calming him. Napoleon Bonaparte, Emperor of the French, pulled up the collar of his greatcoat and squinted his eyes against the sleet. To the east he could just make out the jagged sixteen-thousand-foot outline of Mont Blanc.

He leaned forward in his saddle and stroked Styrie's neck. "You've seen worse, old friend."

An Arabian Napoleon had captured during his Egyptian Campaign two years earlier, Styrie was a superb warhorse, but the cold and snow disagreed with his disposition. Born and bred in the desert, Styrie was accustomed to being peppered by sand, not ice.

Napoleon turned and signaled to his valet, Constant, who stood ten feet behind, holding a string of mules. And behind him, trailing for miles down the winding trail, were the forty thousand soldiers of Napoleon's Reserve Army, along with their horses, mules, and caissons.

Constant untied the lead mule and hurried forward. Napoleon handed over Styrie's reins, then dismounted and stretched his legs in the knee-deep snow.

"Let's give him a rest," Napoleon said. "I think that shoe is bothering him again."

"I'll see to it, General." At home, Napoleon preferred the title of First Consul; while on campaign, General. He took in a lungful of air, settled his blue bicorne more firmly on his head, and gazed up the granite spires towering above them.

"Lovely day, isn't it, Constant?"

"If you say so, General," the valet grumbled.

Napoleon smiled to himself. Constant, who'd been with him for many years, was one of the few underlings he allowed a small measure of sarcasm. After all, he thought, Constant was an old man; the cold went right through his bones.

Napoleon Bonaparte was of medium height with a strong neck and broad shoulders. His aquiline nose sat above a firm mouth and a square chin, and his eyes were a piercing gray that seemed to dissect everything around him, human and otherwise.

"Any word from Laurent?" he asked Constant.

"No, General."

Général de Division, or Major-General, Arnaud Laurent, one of Napoleon's most trusted commanders and closest friends, had the day before led a squad of soldiers deeper into the pass on a scouting mission. However unlikely they were to encounter an enemy here, Napoleon had long ago learned to prepare for the impossible. Too many great men had been toppled by the mere act of assumption. Here, though, their worst enemies were the weather and terrain.

At eight thousand feet, the Grand St. Bernard Pass had for centuries been a crossroads for travelers. Straddling the borders of Switzerland, Italy, and France, the pass's home, the Pennine Alps, had seen its share of armies: the Gauls in 390 B.C., on their way to trample Rome; Hannibal's famous elephant crossing in 217 B.C.; Charlemagne in A.D. 800, returning from his coronation in Rome as the first Holy Roman Emperor.

Laudable company, Napoleon thought to himself. Even one of his predecessors, Pepin the Short, king of France, had in 753 crossed the Pennines on his way to meet Pope Stephen II.

But where other kings have failed in greatness, I will not, Napoleon reminded himself. His empire would grow beyond the wildest dreams of those who'd come before him. Nothing would stand in his way. Not armies, not weather, not mountains—and certainly not some upstart Austrians.

A year earlier, while he and his army were conquering Egypt, the Austrians had brashly retaken the Italian territory annexed to France in the Campo Formio treaty. Their victory would be short-lived. They would neither expect an attack this early in the year, nor would they imagine any army attempting to cross the Pennines in winter. With good reason.

With its towering walls of rock and snaking gorges, the Pennines were a geographic nightmare for solitary travelers, let alone an army of forty thousand. Since September the pass had seen thirty feet of snow and temperatures that routinely dipped below zero. Drifts, standing as tall as ten men, loomed over them at every turn, threatening to bury them and their horses. Even on the sunniest of days fog cloaked the ground until midafternoon. Windstorms frequently arose without warning, turning a calm day into a howling nightmare of snow and ice that left them unable to see a yard in front of their feet. Most terrifying of all were the avalanches—cataracts of snow, sometimes a half mile wide, that roared down the mountainsides to entomb anyone unlucky enough to be in their way. So far God had seen fit to spare all but two hundred of Napoleon's men.

He turned to Constant. "The quartermaster's report?"

"Here, General." The valet pulled a sheaf of papers from inside his coat and handed it to Napoleon, who scanned the figures. Truly, an army fought on its stomach. So far his men had consumed 19,817 bottles of wine, a ton of cheese, and 1,700 pounds of meat.

Ahead, down the pass, there came a shout from the outriders: "Laurent, Laurent . . . !"

"At last," Napoleon murmured.

A group of twelve riders emerged from the blowing snow. They were strong soldiers, the best he had, just like their commander. Not a one rode hunched over, but all were erect, chins held high. Major-General Laurent trotted his horse to a stop before Napoleon, saluted, then dismounted. Napoleon embraced him, then stepped back and gestured to Constant, who hurried forward and handed Laurent a bottle of brandy. Laurent took a gulp, then another, then handed the bottle back.

Napoleon said, "Report, old friend."

"We covered eight miles, sir. No sign of enemy forces. The weather improves at the lower elevations, as does the depth of the snow. It will only get easier from here."

"Good . . . very good."

"One note of interest," Laurent said, placing his hand on Napoleon's elbow and steering him a few feet away. "We found something, General."

"And would you care to elaborate on the nature of this something?"

"It would be better if you saw it for yourself."

Napoleon studied Laurent's face; there was a glint of barely contained anticipation in his eyes. He'd known Laurent since they were both sixteen, serving as lieutenants in the La Fère Artillery. Laurent was prone to neither exaggeration nor excitability. Whatever he'd found, it was significant.

"How far?" Napoleon asked.

"Four hours' ride."

Napoleon scanned the sky. It was already midafternoon. Over the peaks he could see a line of dark clouds. A storm was coming. "Very well," he said, clapping Laurent on the shoulder. "We'll leave at first light."

———

As was his custom, Napoleon slept five hours, rising at six A.M., well before dawn. He had breakfast, then read the overnight dispatches from his demi-brigade commanders over a pot of bitter black tea. Laurent arrived with his squad shortly before seven and they set out down the valley, following the trail Laurent had broken the day before.

The previous night's storm had dumped little new snow but fierce winds had piled up fresh drifts—towering white walls that formed a canyon around Napoleon and his riders. The horses' breath steamed in the air and with every step powder billowed high in the air. Napoleon gave Styrie his head, trusting the Arabian to navigate the path, while he stared, fascinated, at the drifts, their facades carved into swirls and spirals by the wind.

"A bit eerie, eh, General?" Laurent asked.

"It's quiet," Napoleon murmured. "I've never heard quiet like this before."

"It is beautiful," Laurent agreed. "And dangerous."

Like a battlefield, Napoleon thought. Except for perhaps in his bed with Josephine, he felt more at home on a battlefield than anywhere else. The roar of the cannons, the crack of musket fire, the tang of black powder in the air . . . He loved all of it. And in a matter of days, he thought, once we're out of these damned mountains . . . He smiled to himself.

Ahead, the lead rider raised a closed fist above his head, signaling a halt. Napoleon watched the man dismount and trudge forward through the thigh-deep snow, his head tilted backward as he scanned the drift walls. He disappeared around a curve in the trail.

"What's he looking for?" Napoleon asked.

"Dawn is one of the worst times for avalanches," Laurent replied. "Overnight the winds harden the top layer of snow into a shell, while the powder underneath remains soft. When the sun hits the shell, it starts to melt. Often the only warning we have is the sound—like God himself roaring from the heavens."

After a few minutes the lead rider reappeared on the trail. He gave Laurent the all-clear signal, then mounted his horse and continued on.

They rode for two more hours, following the snaking course of the valley as it descended toward the foothills. Soon they entered a narrow canyon of jagged gray granite interlaced with ice. The lead rider signaled another halt and dismounted. Laurent did the same, followed by Napoleon.

Napoleon looked around. "Here?"

His major-general smiled mischievously. "Here, General." Laurent unhooked a pair of oil lanterns from his saddle. "If you'll follow me."

They set off down the trail, passing the six horses ahead of them, the riders standing at attention for their general. Napoleon nodded solemnly at each soldier in turn until he reached the head of the column, where he and Laurent stopped. A few minutes passed and then a soldier—the lead rider—appeared around a rock outcropping to their left and plodded back through the snow toward them.

Laurent said, "General, you might remember Sergeant Pelletier."

"Of course," Napoleon replied. "I'm at your disposal, Pelletier. Lead on."

Pelletier saluted, grabbed a coil of rope from his saddle, then stepped off the trail, following the path he'd just carved through the chest-high drifts. He led them up the slope to the base of a granite wall, where he turned parallel and walked another fifty yards before stopping at a right-angle niche in the rock.

"Lovely spot, Laurent. What am I looking at?" Napoleon asked.

Laurent nodded to Pelletier, who raised his musket high above his head and slammed the butt into the rock. Instead of the crack of wood on stone, Napoleon heard the shattering of ice. Pelletier struck four more times until a vertical gash appeared in the face. It measured two feet wide and almost six feet high.

Napoleon peered inside, but could see nothing but darkness.

"As far as we can tell," Laurent said, "in the summer the entrance is choked with brush and vines; in the winter, snowdrifts cover it up. I suspect there's a source of moisture somewhere inside, which accounts for the thin curtain of ice. It probably forms every night."

"Interesting. And who found it?"

"I did, General," replied Pelletier. "We'd stopped to rest the horses and I needed to . . . well, I had the urge to . . ."

"I understand, Sergeant, please go on."

"Well, I suppose I wandered a bit too far, General. When I finished, I leaned against the rock to collect myself and the ice gave way behind me. I went a little ways inside and didn't think much of it until I saw the . . . Well, I'll let you see it for yourself, General."

Napoleon turned to Laurent. "You've been inside?"

"Yes, General. Myself and Sergeant Pelletier. No one else."

"Very well, Laurent, I will follow you."

The cave's entrance continued for another twenty feet, narrowing as it went until they were walking hunched over. Suddenly the tunnel opened up and Napoleon found himself standing in a cavern. Having entered ahead of him, Laurent and Pelletier stepped aside to let him through, then raised their lanterns, shining the flickering yellow light on the walls.

Measuring roughly fifty by sixty feet, the cavern was an ice palace, the walls and floor coated in it, several feet thick in some places; in others, so thin Napoleon could see a faint shadow of gray rock beneath. Glittering stalactites hung from the ceilings, so low they merged with the floor's stalagmites to form hourglass-shaped ice sculptures. Unlike the walls and floor, the ice on the ceiling was roughened, reflecting the lantern light like a star-filled sky. From somewhere deeper in the cave came the sound of dripping water, and more distant still the faint whistling of wind.

"Magnificent," Napoleon murmured.

"Here's what Pelletier found just inside the entrance," Laurent said, moving toward the wall. Napoleon walked over to where Laurent was shining his lantern on an object on the floor. It was a shield.

Roughly five feet tall, two feet wide, and shaped like a figure 8, it was made of wicker and covered in leather painted with faded red and black interlocking squares.

"It's ancient," Napoleon murmured.

"At least two thousand years is my guess," Laurent said. "My history isn't what it used to be, but I believe it's called a *gerron*. It was used by Persian light infantry soldiers."

"Mon dieu . . ."

"There's more, General. This way."

Winding his way through the forest of stalactite columns, Laurent led him to the rear of the cavern and another tunnel entrance, this one a rough oval four feet tall.

Behind them, Pelletier had dropped the coil of rope and was knotting one end around the base of a column under the glow of the lantern.

"Going down, are we?" Napoleon asked. "Into the pits of hell?"

"Not today, General," Laurent answered. "Across."

Laurent aimed his lantern into the tunnel. A few feet inside was an ice bridge, not quite two feet wide, stretching across a crevasse before disappearing into another tunnel.

"You've been across?" Napoleon asked.

"It's quite sturdy. It's rock beneath the ice. Still, you can't be too safe."

He secured the line first around Napoleon's waist, then his own. Pelletier gave the knotted end a final tug and nodded to Laurent, who said, "Watch your footing, General," then stepped into the tunnel. Napoleon waited a few moments, then followed.

They began inching their way across the crevasse. At the halfway point, Napoleon looked over the side and saw nothing but blackness, the translucent blue ice walls sloping into nowhere.

At last they reached the opposite side. They followed the next tunnel, which zigzagged for twenty feet, into another ice cavern, this one smaller than the first but with a high, arched ceiling. Lantern held before him, Laurent walked to the center of the cavern and stopped beside what looked like a pair of ice-covered stalagmites. Each one was twelve feet high and truncated at the top.

Napoleon stepped closer to one. Then stopped. He narrowed his eyes. It wasn't a stalagmite, he realized, but a solid column of ice. He placed his palm against it and leaned his face closer.

Staring back at him was the golden face of a woman.

CHAPTER 1

GREAT POCOMOKE SWAMP, MARYLAND
PRESENT DAY

Sam Fargo rose from his crouch and glanced over at his wife, who stood up to her waist in oozing black mud. Her bright yellow chest waders complemented her lustrous auburn hair. She sensed his gaze, turned to him, pursed her lips, and blew a wisp of hair from her cheek. "And just what are you smiling at, Fargo?" she asked.

When she'd first donned the waders he'd made the mistake of suggesting she looked like the Gorton's Fisherman, which had earned him a withering stare. He'd hastily added "sexy" to the description, but to little effect.

"You," he now replied. "You look beautiful—Longstreet." When Remi was annoyed at him she called him by his last name; he always responded in kind with her maiden name.

She held up her arms, coated to the elbows in slime, then said with a barely concealed smile, "You're crazy. My face is covered in mosquito bites, and my hair is flatter than paper." She scratched her chin, leaving behind a dollop of mud.

"It simply adds to your charm."

"Liar."

Despite the look of disgust on her face, Sam knew Remi was a trouper without peer. Once she set her mind on a goal, no amount of discomfort would dissuade her.

"Well," she said, "I have to admit, you do look rather dashing yourself."

Sam tipped his tattered Panama hat at her, then went back to work, scooping mud from around a length of submerged wood he hoped was part of a chest.

For the past three days they'd been plodding through the swamp, searching for that one clue that might prove they weren't on a wild-goose chase. Neither of them minded a good goose chase—in treasure hunting it came with the turf—but it was always better to catch the goose in the end.

In this case, the goose in question was based on an obscure legend. While the nearby Chesapeake and Delaware bays were said to be home of nearly four thousand shipwrecks, the prize Sam and Remi were after was land based. A month earlier Ted Frobisher, a fellow treasure hunter who'd retired not long ago to concentrate on his antique shop in Princess Anne, had sent them a brooch with an intriguing provenance.

The pear-shaped gold and jade brooch was said to have belonged to a local woman named Henrietta Bronson, one of the first victims of the notorious outlaw Martha "Patty" (a.k.a. Lucretia) Cannon.

According to legend Martha Cannon was a tough, ruthless woman who in the 1820s not only stalked the wilds of the Delaware-Maryland border with her gang, robbing and murdering the wealthy and poor alike, but who also ran a hostel in what was then called Johnson's Corners, today Reliance.

Cannon would lure travelers into her establishment and feed, entertain, and tuck them in to bed before murdering them in the middle of the night. She would drag the bodies into the basement, take anything of value, then stack them in the corner like cordwood until she'd accumulated enough to warrant a wagon trip to a nearby forest, where she would bury them en masse. Horrific as that was, Cannon would later commit what many considered her most heinous crimes.

Cannon established what many local historians had dubbed a "reverse underground railroad," kidnapping freed southern slaves and keeping them bound and gagged in the inn's many secret rooms and its makeshift earthen dungeon before sneaking them in the dark of the night to Cannon's Ferry, where they would be sold and loaded onto ships headed down the Nanticoke River bound for Georgia's slave markets.

In 1829, while plowing a field on one of Cannon's farms, a worker uncovered several partially decomposed bodies. Cannon was speedily indicted on four counts of murder, found guilty, and sentenced to prison. Four years later she died in her cell by what most agreed was suicide by arsenic.

In subsequent years both Cannon's crimes and her ultimate demise grew in myth, ranging from the claim that Cannon had escaped from prison and went on murdering and robbing far into her nineties, to tales that have her ghost still roaming the Delmarva Peninsula, waylaying unsuspecting hikers. What few people disputed was that Cannon's loot—of which she'd reportedly spent only a fraction—had never been recovered. Estimates put the treasure's present-day value somewhere between $100,000 and $400,000.

Sam and Remi had of course heard the legend of Patty Cannon's treasure, but lacking solid leads they'd consigned it to the "someday" file. With the emergence of Henrietta Bronson's brooch and an exact datum with which to begin their search, they'd decided to tackle the mystery.

After a detailed study of the Pocomoke's historical topography and mapping Cannon's alleged hideouts in comparison to where the brooch had been found, they'd narrowed their search grid to a two-square-mile area, most of which lay deep within the swamp, a labyrinth of moss-draped cypress trees and brush-choked bogs. According to their research this area, which in the 1820s had been dry ground, had been home to one of Cannon's hideouts, a tumbledown shack.

Their interest in Cannon's treasure had nothing to do with the money—at least not for their own benefit. Upon first hearing the story, Sam and Remi agreed if they were ever lucky enough to find the treasure, the bulk of the proceeds would go to the National Underground Railroad Freedom Center in Cincinnati, Ohio, an irony they felt sure would outrage Cannon if she were still alive. Or, if they were lucky, it would outrage her ghost.

"Remi, what was that poem . . . the one about Cannon?" Sam called. Remi had a near-photographic memory for details, both obscure and pertinent.

She thought for a moment, then recited:

"Hush your mouth
Go to sleep
Old Patty Ridenour take you back deep
Got a gang of seven
Taking slave and free
Riding day and night
On her coal-black steed."

"That's it," Sam replied.

Around them the exposed roots of the cypress trees jutted from the water like disembodied talons of some great winged dinosaur. The previous week a storm had blown across the peninsula, leaving behind mounds of branches like hastily constructed beaver dams. Overhead, the canopy was alive with a symphony of squawks and buzzes and fluttering wings. Occasionally Sam, a part-time bird-watcher, would isolate a trilling and announce the bird's name to Remi, who would humor him with a smile and a "That's very nice."

Sam found the exercise helped his "by ear" piano playing, something he'd picked up from his mother. For her part, Remi had a nice touch with the violin, which she put to good use during their frequent impromptu duets.

Despite his engineering background, Sam was an intuitive, right-brain thinker, while Remi, a Boston College–trained anthropologist/historian, was firmly grounded in logical, left-brain thinking. While the dichotomy made them a balanced, loving pair, it also led to vigorous debates, ranging in topic from what had started the English Reformation to which actor made the best James Bond to how to best play Vivaldi's concerto *Summer*. Most often the debates ended in laughter and an ongoing but good-natured disagreement.

Bent at the waist, Sam probed underwater with his fingers, sliding along the wood until he touched something metal . . . something with a U-shaped hasp and a square body.

A padlock, he thought, visions of an ancient barnacle-encrusted hasp swirling through his mind. "Got something," he announced.

Remi turned toward him, muddy arms hanging by her sides.

"Hah!" Sam pulled it from the water. As the mud slid off and plopped back into the water, he saw the glint of rust and silver, then some raised letters. . . .

M-A-S-T-E-R L-O-C-K.

"Well?" Remi said, her voice tinged with skepticism. She was used to Sam's sometimes premature excitement.

"I've found, my dear, a vintage Master padlock, circa 1970," he replied, then hefted from the water the piece of wood it had been attached to. "Along with what looks like an old gatepost." He dropped it back into the water and then straightened up with a groan.

Remi smiled at him. "My intrepid treasure hunter. Well, it's more than I've found."

Sam looked at his watch, a Timex Expedition he wore only on expeditions. "Six o'clock," he said. "Shall we call it a day?"

Remi ran her cupped hand down her opposite forearm, shedding a layer of goop, and gave him a broad smile. "Thought you'd never ask."

They gathered their packs and hiked the half mile back to their skiff, which they'd tied to a grounded cypress stump. Sam cast off and pushed the boat into deeper water, wading up to his waist, while Remi yanked the engine's starter cord. The motor growled to life and Sam climbed in.

She turned the bow into the channel and throttled up. The nearest town and their base of operations was Snow Hill, three miles up the Pocomoke River. The B&B they'd chosen had a surprisingly decent wine cellar and a crab bisque that had put Remi in culinary heaven at the previous night's supper.

They motored along in silence, lulled by the soft gurgle of the motor and gazing at the overhanging canopy. Suddenly Sam turned in his seat, looking to the right.

"Remi, slow down."

She throttled back. "What is it?"

He grabbed a pair of binoculars from his pack and raised them to his eyes. Fifty yards away on the bank there was a gap in the foliage—another hidden inlet among the dozens they'd already seen. The entrance was partially blocked by a tangle of branches piled up by the storm.

"What do you see?" she asked.

"Something . . . I don't know," he muttered. "I thought I saw a line in the foliage . . . a curve or something. Didn't look natural. Can you get me over there?"

She turned the rudder and aimed the skiff at the mouth of the inlet. "Sam, are you hallucinating? Did you drink enough water today?"

He nodded, his attention fixed on the inlet. "More than enough."

With a soft crunch, the skiff's nose bumped into the mound of branches. The inlet was wider than it looked, nearly fifty feet across. Sam looped the bow line around one of the larger limbs, then slipped his legs over the gunwale and rolled into the water.

"Sam, what're you doing?"

"I'll be right back. Stay here."

"Like hell."

Before she could say more, Sam took a breath, ducked underwater, and disappeared. Twenty seconds later Remi heard a splash on the other side of the branches, followed by Sam sucking in a lungful of air.

She called, "Sam, are you—"

"I'm fine. Be back in a minute."

One minute turned into two, then three. Finally Sam called through the foliage, "Remi, can you join me, please?"

She could hear the mischievous lilt in his voice, and thought, *Oh, boy.* She loved her husband's adventurous impulses, but she'd already started imagining how good a hot shower was going to feel. "What is it?" she asked.

"I need you to come here."

"Sam, I just now started to dry off. Can't you—"

"No, you're going to want to see this. Trust me."

Remi sighed, then slipped over the side into the water. Ten seconds later she was treading water beside him. The trees on either side of the inlet formed an almost solid canopy over the water, enclosing them in a tunnel of green. Here and there sunlight stippled the algae-filmed surface.

"Hi, nice of you to come," he said with a grin and a peck on her cheek.

"Okay, smarty-pants, what are we—"

He rapped his knuckles against the misshapen log he had his arm draped over, but instead of a dull thud she heard a metallic gong.

"What is that?"

"Not sure yet. Part of it—can't be sure what part until I get down there and get inside."

"Part of what? Get inside what?"

"This way, come on."

Taking her by the hand, Sam sidestroked deeper into the inlet and around a corner, where the course narrowed to twenty feet. He stopped and pointed to a vine-covered cypress trunk near the bank. "There. You see it?"

She squinted, tilted her head left, then right. "No. What am I looking for?"

"That branch sticking out of the water, the one that ends in a T shape. . . ."

"Okay, I see it."

"Look harder. Squint. It helps."

She did, narrowing her eyes until slowly what she was seeing registered on her brain. She gasped. "Good Lord, is that a . . . It can't be."

Grinning from ear to ear, Sam nodded. "Yep. It is. That, my dear, is a submarine's periscope."

CHAPTER 2

SEVASTOPOL, UKRAINE

Hadeon Bondaruk stood at the floor-to-ceiling windows of his study and stared out at the Black Sea. His study was dark, lit only by dimmed ceiling lights that cast soft pools into the corners of the room. Night had fallen over the Crimean Peninsula, but to the west, over the Romanian and Bulgarian coasts, backlit by the last remnants of the setting sun, he could see a line of storm clouds moving north over the water. Every few seconds the clouds would pulse from within, shooting veins of lightning across the horizon. It would be here within the hour, and God help those foolish enough to be caught afloat in the midst of a Black Sea storm.

Or, Bondaruk thought, God not help them. No matter. Storms and disease and yes, even war, were nature's way of culling the herd. He had little patience for people who didn't have the sense or strength to protect themselves against the violence of life. It was a lesson he'd learned as a boy, and one that he'd never forgotten.

Bondaruk had been born in 1960 in a village south of Ashgabat, Turkmenistan, high in the Kopet Dag Mountains. His mother and father and their parents before them had been farmers and shepherds living in that gray geographic area between Iran and what was then the Soviet Union, and like all natives of the Kopet Dag they were tough, self-reliant, and fiercely independent, claiming neither country as their own. However, the Cold War had other plans for Bondaruk and his family.

With the Iranian Revolution of 1979 and the deposition of the Shah, the Soviet Union began to pour more troops into the border area north of Iran, and Bondaruk, then nineteen, saw his village's independence stripped away as Red Army bases and antiaircraft missile sites began cropping up in their once peaceful mountain home.

The Soviet troops treated the Kopet Dag natives like backward savages, moving through villages like a scourge, taking food and women, shooting livestock for sport, and rounding up "Iranian revolutionary elements" for summary execution. Never mind that Bondaruk and his people knew little of the outside world and world politics. Their Muslim religion and proximity to Iran made them suspect.

A year later a pair of tanks appeared on the outskirts of the village, along with two companies of Red Army soldiers. A squad of soldiers had been ambushed nearby the night before, the commander told Bondaruk and the villagers. Eight men, their throats slit and their clothes, weapons, and personal belongings stripped from them. The village elders had five minutes to produce those responsible, lest the entire community be held responsible.

Bondaruk had heard stories about Turkmen resistance fighters in the countryside being aided by Iranian commandos but to his knowledge none of the villagers were involved. Unable to produce the guilty parties, the village chieftain pleaded with the Soviet commander for mercy and was shot for his trouble. Over the next hour the tanks rained shells down on the village until it was in ruins and burning. In the commotion, Bondaruk was separated from his family and he and a handful of boys and men retreated higher into the mountains, far enough away to be safe from the soldiers, but close enough that they could watch through the night as their home was razed to the ground. The next day they returned to the village and began looking for survivors. More dead than alive were found, including Bondaruk's family, who had taken shelter in the mosque only to have it collapse and crush them alive.

Something inside him changed, as though God had pulled a dark curtain on his old life. He gathered up the strongest and most eager villagers, men and women alike, and they all took to the mountains as partisans.

Within six months Bondaruk had risen not only to a position of leadership among his fighters, but also to that of a legend among the rural Turkmen people. Bondaruk's fighters would strike in the night, ambushing Soviet patrols and convoys, then disappear back into the Kopet Dag like ghosts. Within a year of his village's destruction, Bondaruk had a bounty on his head. He'd come to the attention of the Soviet leadership in Moscow, which was now embroiled in not only a tense standoff with Iran and a full-blown war in Afghanistan but also a guerrilla conflict in Turkmenistan.

Shortly after his twenty-first birthday Bondaruk received word that Iranian intelligence operatives had put out the word that his Kopet Dag fighters had an ally in Tehran, if only he would sit down and listen, which he did in a small café outside Ashgabat.

The man Bondaruk met turned out to be a colonel in the elite Iranian paramilitary organization known as the Pasdaran, or the Guardians of the Revolution. The colonel offered Bondaruk and his fighters weapons, ammunition, training, and essential supplies for his war against the Soviets. Wary, Bondaruk had probed for a loophole in the deal—that one condition that would simply change the heel on their necks from that of the Soviets to the Iranians. There was no condition, he was assured. We are of common ancestry and faith and cause. What more of a bond did they need? Bondaruk accepted the offer and over the next five years Bondaruk and his fighters, under the guidance of the Iranian colonel, slowly wore down the Soviet occupiers.

As satisfying as that was for Bondaruk, it was his relationship with the colonel that had the most effect on him. The colonel, it seemed, had been a teacher of Persian history before he'd been called to serve the revolution. The Persian Empire, he explained, stretched back nearly three thousand years and at its height had encompassed the Caspian and Black Sea basins, Greece, North Africa, and much of the Middle East. In fact, Bondaruk was told, Xerxes I, Xerxes the Great, who had invaded Greece and crushed the Spartans at the Battle of Thermopylae, was born in the very same mountains Bondaruk called home and was said to have fathered dozens of children in the Kopet Dag.

This was a thought that was never far from Bondaruk's mind as he and his guerrillas continued to harass the Soviets until finally, in 1990, over a decade after they'd entered the Kopet Dag, the Red Army withdrew from the border. Shortly after that the Soviet Union collapsed.

With the fight over and no inclination to go back to being an ordinary shepherd, Bondaruk, aided by his Iranian colonel friend, moved to Sevastopol, which had, with the collapse of the Soviet empire, become the Wild West of the Black Sea Basin. Once there, his natural leadership ability and comfort with brutality and swift violence secured him a place first in the Ukrainian black market and then in the Ukrainian Krasnaya Mafiya, or Red Mafia. By the time he was thirty-five, Hadeon Bondaruk was in control of virtually every organized criminal enterprise in Ukraine and a millionaire many times over.

With his position and power and wealth secure, Bondaruk turned his attention to an idea that had been lingering in the back of his mind for many years: Had Xerxes the Great truly been born and raised in the Kopet Dag Mountains, in his very homeland? Had he and Xerxes, as boys separated by centuries, walked the same paths and marveled at the same mountain vistas? Could he himself be descended from Persian royalty?

The answer did not come easily, taking five years, millions of dollars, and a dedicated staff of historians, archaeologists, and genealogists, but by the time he turned forty Hadeon Bondaruk was sure of it: He was, in fact, a direct blood descendant of Xerxes I, ruler of the Persian Achaemenid Empire.

From there Bondaruk's curiosity quickly grew into an obsession with everything Persian; he used the full force of his wealth and influence to assemble a collection of Persian artifacts, from the drinking cup used at the wedding celebration of Cyaxares to a stone dais used for Zoroastrian rituals during the Sassanid Dynasty to the jewel-encrusted *gerron* shield carried by Xerxes himself at Thermopylae.

And his collection was nearly complete. Save one glaring omission, he reminded himself. His personal museum, which lay in the bowels of his mansion, was a marvel he shared with no one, partially because no one was worthy of its glory, but mostly because it was not yet complete.

Yet, he now thought. Soon he would remedy the issue.

As if on cue the door to his study opened and his valet entered. "Pardon me, sir."

Bondaruk turned. "What is it?"

"A call for you. Mr. Arkhipov."

"Send it through."

The valet left, gently closing the door behind him. A few moments later the phone on Bondaruk's desk trilled. He picked it up. "Tell me you are calling me with good news, Grigoriy."

"I am, sir. According to my sources, the man runs an antique shop in the area. The website where he posted the picture is a well-established forum for antique dealers and treasure hunters."

"And has anyone shown any interest in the shard?"

"Some, but nothing serious. So far the consensus is that it's simply a broken piece of bottle, nothing more."

"Good. Where are you?"

"New York, waiting to board my flight."

At this Bondaruk smiled. "Always taking the initiative. I like that."

"It's why you pay me," the Russian answered.

"And if you manage to secure this piece there'll be a bonus in it for you. How do you plan to approach the man, this antique dealer?"

The Russian paused for a moment and Bondaruk could almost see that familiar cruel smile curling Arkhipov's lips.

"I find the direct approach is always best, don't you?"

Arkhipov knew about directness and results, Bondaruk thought. The former Russian Spetsnaz was smart, ruthless, and relentless. In his twelve years in Bondaruk's employ, Arkhipov had never failed in a mission, no matter how dirty.

"I do," Bondaruk replied. "I'll leave you to it, then. Just take care that you're discreet."

"I always am."

Which was true. Many, many of Bondaruk's enemies had, as far as the authorities could determine, simply vanished from the face of the earth.

"Call me as soon as you have word."

"I will."

Bondaruk was about to hang up when another question popped into his head. "Just out of curiosity, Grigoriy, where is this man's shop? Anywhere close to where we'd predicted?"

"Very close. A small town called Princess Anne."

CHAPTER 3

SNOW HILL, MARYLAND

Sam Fargo stood at the bottom of the stairs, leaning against the banister, legs crossed at the ankles and arms folded across his chest. Remi was running late as usual, having decided at the last minute her black Donna Karan dress was going to be a bit much for the restaurant and returned to their room to change clothes. Sam checked his watch again; he wasn't so much worried about their reservation as he was about his empty belly, which had been grumbling loudly ever since they'd gotten back to the B&B.

The lobby of the hostel was quaint almost to a fault, done in Americana shabby chic and decorated with landscape watercolors done by local artists. A fire crackled in the fireplace and over hidden loudspeakers came the faint strains of Celtic folk music.

Sam heard the stairs creak once and looked up in time to see Remi coming down the stairs in a pair of cream Ralph Lauren trousers, a cashmere mock turtleneck, and a russet-colored shawl draped over her shoulders. Her auburn hair was up in a loose ponytail, a few strands touching her delicate neck.

"I'm sorry, have I made us late?" she asked, taking his offered arm as she reached the bottom of the stairs.

Sam stared at her for a few seconds without replying, then cleared his throat. "Looking at you, I fear time has come to a standstill."

"Oh, shut up."

The squeeze on Sam's biceps belied her words and told him that, corny line or not, his compliment had been appreciated.

"Are we walking or driving?" she asked.

"We'll walk. It's a beautiful night."

"Plus you run less risk of another ticket."

On the way into town Sam had let their rented BMW have a bit too much head, much to the annoyance of the local sheriff, who'd been trying to eat his bologna sandwich lunch behind a roadside billboard.

"That, too," Sam agreed.

There was a slight spring chill in the air, but not enough to be uncomfortable, and from the bushes along the sidewalk came the croaking of frogs. The restaurant, a locally owned Italian affair complete with a green-and-white-checkered awning, was only two blocks away, and it took only five minutes. Once they were seated they took a few minutes to peruse the wine list, settling on a Bordeaux from the French region of Barsac.

"So," Remi said, "how sure are you about this?"

"You mean about the you-know-what?" Sam whispered conspiratorially.

"I think you can say the word, Sam. I doubt anyone cares."

He smiled. "The submarine. I'm pretty sure. We'll have to get down there, of course, but I can't imagine it's anything else."

"But what's it doing here? All the way upriver."

"That's the mystery we'll have to solve, won't we?"

"And what about Patty Cannon?"

"She can wait a couple days. We'll ID the sub, put Selma and the others onto unraveling the mystery, then get back to our sociopathic murderous slave runner."

Remi gave it a few moments' thought, then shrugged. "Why not. Life is short."

Selma Wondrash was the drill sergeant–like head of Sam and Remi's three-person research team back in San Diego. Selma was widowed, having lost her husband, an air force test pilot, in a crash ten years earlier. They'd met in Budapest in the early nineties, she a university student, he a fighter jock on leave. Despite having lived in the United States for fifteen years, Selma had never entirely lost her accent.

After finishing her degree at Georgetown and becoming a citizen, she went to work for the Library of Congress's Special Collections Directorate until Sam and Remi lured her away. More than a research chief, Selma had proved herself a superb travel agent and logistics guru, getting them to and from destinations with military efficiency.

While Sam and Remi loved the research aspect of their field, Selma and her team were rabid about it, living for that buried fact, that elusive lead, that unsolvable riddle that always seemed to crop up in the course of a job. More times than they could count, Selma and her team had kept an investigation from going far astray.

Of course, "job" wasn't quite the right word for what Sam and Remi did. For them it wasn't about a paycheck but rather the adventure, and the satisfaction of seeing the Fargo Foundation flourish. The foundation, which split its gifting between animal protection, nature conservancy, and underprivileged and abused children, had grown in leaps and bounds over the last decade, the previous year donating almost five million dollars to a variety of organizations. A hefty part of that money had come from Sam and Remi personally and the rest of it from private donations. For better or worse their exploits attracted a fair amount of media attention, which in turn attracted wealthy, high-profile donors.

The fact that Sam and Remi got to do what they loved was a boon neither of them took for granted, having both worked hard to reach this place in their life.

Remi's father, now retired, had been a private contractor who'd built custom summer homes along the New England coast; her mother, a pediatrician with a series of bestselling child-rearing books. Following in her father's footsteps, Remi had attended his alma mater, Boston College, emerging with a master's in anthropology and history, with a focus on ancient trade routes.

Sam's father, who'd died a few years earlier, had been one of the lead engineers on NASA's Mercury, Gemini, and Apollo programs and rare-book collector, a love affair he'd passed on to Sam at an early age. Sam's mother, Eunice, lived in Key West, where, despite being almost seventy, she ran a charter boat specializing in snorkeling and deep-sea fishing.

Like Remi, Sam had followed in his father's footsteps, if not in his choice of education, then in his vocation, earning a summa cum laude engineering degree from Caltech, along with a handful of trophies for lacrosse and soccer.

While in his final months of study at Caltech Sam was approached by a man he would later find out was from DARPA, the Defense Advanced Research Projects Agency, where the government developed and tested the latest and greatest toys for both the military and intelligence communities. The offered salary had been far below what he could have earned in the civilian world, but the lure of pure creative engineering combined with serving his country made Sam's choice an easy one.

After seven years at DARPA Sam retired with the vague notion of bringing some of his own wild ideas to reality, and moved back to California. It was there, two weeks later, that Sam and Remi met at the Lighthouse, a jazz club on Hermosa Beach. Sam had wandered into the club for a cold beer and Remi was there celebrating a successful research trip looking into rumors of a sunken Spanish ship off Abalone Cove.

Though neither of them had ever called their first meeting a case of "love at first sight," they'd both agreed it had certainly been a case of "pretty damned sure at first hour." Six months later they were married where they'd first met, in a small ceremony at the Lighthouse.

At Remi's encouragement Sam dove headfirst into his own business and they struck pay dirt within a year with an argon laser scanner that could detect and identify at a distance mixed metals and alloys, from gold and silver to platinum and palladium. Treasure hunters, universities, corporations, and mining outfits scrambled to license Sam's invention and within two years the Fargo Group was seeing an annual net profit of three million dollars, and within four years the deep-pocketed corporations came calling. Sam and Remi took the highest bid, sold the company for enough money to see themselves comfortably through the rest of their lives, and never looked back.

"I did a little research while you were in the shower," Sam said. "From what I can gather, I think we may have a real find on our hands."

The waiter came, deposited a basket of warm ciabatta and a saucer of Pasolivo olive oil, and then took their orders. To start they ordered calamari with red sauce and porcini mushrooms. For entrées, Sam selected a seafood pasta with pesto-sautéed bay scallops and lobster, while Remi chose a stuffed shrimp-and-crab ravioli in basil white cream sauce.

"What do you mean?" Remi asked. "Isn't a submarine a submarine?"

"Good Lord, woman, bite your tongue," Sam said, feigning shock.

Where Remi's forte was anthropology and ancient history, Sam loved World War II history, another passion he'd inherited from his father, who'd been a marine during the United States' island-hopping campaign in the Pacific. The fact that Remi had little interest in who exactly sank the *Bismarck* or why the Battle of the Bulge was so important was something that never ceased to amaze Sam.

Remi was an anthropologist and historian without peer, but she tended to take an analytical approach to things, while for Sam history had always been stories about real people doing real things. Remi dissected; Sam dreamed.

"Apologies for the gaffe," Remi said.

"Forgiven. Here's the thing: Given the size of the inlet, there's no way it can be a full-sized submarine. Plus, that periscope looked way too small."

"A mini sub, then."

"Right. But there was a lot of growth on the periscope. A few decades' worth, at least. And one more thing: As far as I know, commercial subs—for surveys or mapping or whatever—don't have periscopes."

"So it's military," Remi said.

"Has to be."

"So, a military mini submarine, twenty-some miles up the Pocomoke River . . . " Remi murmured. "Okay, I admit it. You got me. I'm officially intrigued."

Sam smiled back at her. "That's my girl. So, what do you say? After dinner, we drive over to Princess Anne and see what Ted has to say. He's forgotten more legends about this area than most people will ever know. If anyone might have some hunches about what this thing is, it's going to be him."

"I don't know. . . . It's getting late and you know how Ted hates visitors."

Ted Frobisher, for all his genius and well-hidden softheartedness, wasn't exactly people-oriented. His shop thrived not on his interpersonal skills, but on his breadth of knowledge and business acumen.

Sam said, smiling, "A little surprise will do him good."

CHAPTER 4

After dessert, a tiramisu so good it left them temporarily speech-less, they walked back to the B&B, grabbed the BMW's keys from the room, and set off for Princess Anne, heading northwest up Highway 12 to the outskirts of Salisbury before turning south-west onto Highway 13. The evening's earlier clear skies had given way to low rain clouds and a fine, steady mist fell on the BMW's windshield.

Remi frowned. "It feels like you're going too fast." She enjoyed the BMW, but not the latent race-car-driver urge it brought out in her husband.

"Dead on the speed limit. Don't worry, Remi. Have I ever crashed?"

"Well, there was that time in Mumbai—"

"Oh, no. If you'll recall, the tires were almost bald and we were being chased by a very angry man in a very big dump truck. Plus, I didn't crash. I just got . . . sidetracked."

"That's one way of putting it."

"An accurate description, I'd say."

"Okay, then, there was the time in Scotland. . . ."

"Okay, that was my fault."

"Don't feel bad, Sam. That peat bog did jump right in front of us out of nowhere."

"Very funny."

"You got us out of it, though, and that's what counts."

And he did. Using a short coil of rope, the car jack, a stump and a branch for leverage, and some well-applied basic physics.

They drove in silence, watching the darkened countryside slide by until finally the lights of Princess Anne appeared a half mile down the road. Named after the daughter of King George II, the town—or hamlet, as many locals demanded it be called—boasted a population of 2,200 souls, not counting the students who called University of Maryland Eastern Shore their home. During their first trip here years ago, Sam and Remi had agreed if not for the cars on the streets and the electric lighting, it would take little effort to imagine you'd been transported back to Maryland's prerevolutionary days, so quaint were parts of the hamlet of Princess Anne.

Sam took Highway 13 into the middle of town, then turned east onto Mount Vernon Road, which he followed for a mile before turning north onto East Ridge Road. They were now on the outskirts of Princess Anne. Frobisher's shop, whose second floor served as his apartment, was set a quarter mile back from the road down a long driveway bordered by maple trees.

As Sam reached the turn-in, a black Buick Lucerne sedan pulled out of the driveway and passed them, heading south to Mount Vernon Road. As the BMW's lights washed over the passing car's windshield, Sam caught a glimpse of Ted Frobisher sitting in the passenger seat.

"That was him," Remi said.

"Yeah, I know," Sam muttered distantly.

"What is it?"

"Don't know . . . Something about his face didn't seem right."

"What're you talking about?"

"He looked . . . scared."

"Ted Frobisher always looks scared. Or annoyed. Those are his only two expressions, you know that."

"Yeah, maybe," Sam muttered, swinging the BMW into a precise Y-turn, backing into the driveway, then heading after the Lucerne.

"Oh, boy," Remi said, "here we go."

"Just humor me. Probably nothing."

"Fine. But if they pull into an IHOP, promise me you'll turn around and leave the poor man alone."

"Deal."

The Lucerne did not pull into an IHOP, nor did it stay on the main road for very long, turning south onto Black Road after only a few miles. The streetlights had long since disappeared, leaving Sam and Remi driving in pitch blackness. The earlier drizzle had turned to a steady rain and the BMW's windshield wipers beat out a rhythmic squeaking thump.

"How's your night vision?" Sam asked her.

"Good . . . why?"

In response, Sam turned off the BMW's headlights and accelerated, closing the distance to the Lucerne's taillights.

Remi looked at her husband, her eyes narrowed. "You're really worried, aren't you?"

He nodded, jaw clenched. "Just a feeling. Hope I'm wrong."

"Me, too. You're scaring me a little, Sam."

He reached over and gave her thigh a squeeze. "Now, have I ever gotten us into trouble—"

"Well, there was the time—"

"—without getting us back out again?"

"No."

"Do we have a signal?" he asked.

Remi pulled out her cell phone and checked the reception. "Nothing."

"Damn. We still have that map?"

Remi rummaged through the glove compartment, found the map, and opened it. After thirty seconds she said, "Sam, there's nothing out here. No houses, no farms—nothing for miles."

"Curiouser and curiouser."

Ahead, the Lucerne's brake lights flashed once, then again, then turned right and disappeared behind some trees. Sam pulled up to the turn and slowed just in time to see the Lucerne's taillights turn again, this time left into a driveway about a hundred yards down the road. He turned off the engine and rolled down the passenger window. Through the trees they could see the Lucerne's headlights go out, followed by the sound of a car door opening then closing, followed ten seconds later by another.

Then a voice: "Hey . . . don't!"

Frobisher's voice. Clearly agitated.

"Well, that settles it," Sam said.

"Yep," Remi said. "What do you want to do?"

"You drive to the nearest house or wherever you can get reception and call the police. I'm going to—"

"Oh, no, you're not, Sam."

"Remi, please—"

"I said no, Sam."

Sam groaned. "Remi—"

"We're wasting time."

Sam knew his wife well enough to recognize the tone in her voice and the set of her mouth. She'd planted her feet and that was that.

"Okay," he said, "but no stupid chances, okay?"

"That goes for you, too."

He grinned at her and winked. "Am I anything but the epitome of caution?" Then: "Don't answer that."

"In for a penny—" Remi started.

"In for trouble," Sam finished.

CHAPTER 5

Headlights still off, Sam slowly steered the BMW up the road, trying to avoid potholes, until they were within fifty yards of the driveway, then shut off the engine.

Sam said, "Will you please wait in the car?"

Remi frowned at him. "Hi, it seems we haven't met." She stuck out her hand for him to shake. "I'm Remi Fargo."

Sam sighed. "Point taken."

They had a brief strategy/what-if/worse-case-scenario talk, then Sam gave her his sport coat and they climbed out.

They stepped off the road into the drainage ditch, which was shielded by high grass on either side. It ran up to the driveway, where it was funneled into a culvert.

Hunched over, pausing every few steps to listen, they followed the ditch to the driveway, then climbed up the bank and began picking their way through the trees. After twenty feet the trees began to thin out and they found themselves at the edge of a clearing.

The space was immense, perhaps two square acres filled with hulking tubular shapes, some the size of garages, some the size of compact cars, lying at angles like a child's set of pick-up sticks. As

Sam's eyes adjusted to the darkness he realized what he was seeing: a boiler junkyard. How and why it was here, in the middle of the Maryland countryside, he didn't know, but here it was. Judging from their size he guessed the boilers had come from a variety of sources— locomotives, ships, and factories. The falling rain pattered the leaves around them and pinged softly on the steel of the boilers, sending echoes through the trees.

"Well, this is the last thing I was expecting to find here," Remi whispered.

"Me, too." And this told them something about Ted's assailant. Either he knew this area well or he'd done some homework before coming here. Neither thought gave Sam much comfort.

The Buick Lucerne was parked in the middle of the clearing, but there was no sign of either Frobisher or the car's driver. Clearly they'd gone deeper into this maze of boilers. *But why come here?* Sam wondered. The first answer that came to mind chilled him. What Ted's abductor had planned for him was unknown but one thing seemed certain: The man wanted privacy. Or a place to leave a body. Or both. Sam felt his heartbeat quicken.

"We can cover more ground if we split up," Remi suggested.

"Forget it. We don't know who this guy is or what he's capable of."

He was about to step out from the trees, when an idea formed in his head. A Buick Lucerne. Buick . . . GMC. He pulled Remi back into cover and said, "Wait here, be right back."

"What—"

"Just stay put. I'm not going far."

He took one last look around, watching for the slightest move- ment, then, seeing nothing, dashed out and headed for the Lucerne. He reached the driver's-side door, crouched down, then said a quick prayer and tried the door handle. It clicked open. The dome light popped on. He clicked the door shut again.

Damn! At least there was no "keys in the ignition" chime.

Nothing to do but risk it.

Sam opened the door, slid inside, shut the door behind him, then waited for thirty seconds, occasionally peeking over the dashboard.

Nothing was moving. He began looking around the car's interior and found what he was looking for almost immediately. Set into a panel on the dashboard was a button labeled OnStar. Sam pushed it. Twenty seconds passed, then a voice came over the radio speakers.

"This is Dennis at OnStar, how may I assist you?"

"Uh, yeah." Sam grunted. "I've been in a crash. I'm hurt. I need help."

"Sir, do you know your location?"

"Uh . . . no."

"Stand by, sir." Five seconds passed. "All right, sir, I have your location near Black Road, west of Princess Anne in Maryland."

"Yeah, that sounds right."

"I've alerted the 911 dispatcher in your area. Help is on the way."

"How long?" Sam croaked, doing his best injured-driver impression.

"Six to seven minutes, sir. I'll stay with you. . . ."

But Sam was already moving, slipping back out of the car and shutting the door behind him. Using his pocketknife he punched a hole in the left rear tire's valve stem. He then crawled around to the opposite side, repeated the process on the other tire, then sprinted back to the trees and rejoined Remi.

"OnStar?" Remi asked with a smile.

Sam kissed her on the cheek. "Great minds."

"How long until the cavalry arrives?"

"Six, seven minutes. It'd be great if we were gone before then. I'm not in a question-and-answer mood."

"Me neither. I'm in a warm brandy mood."

"Ready for a little hide-and-seek?"

"Lead on."

They had little hope of following any footprints in the mud so he and Remi dashed across the clearing and began picking their way through the paths and tunnels formed by the boiler graveyard. Sam found two pieces of rebar and gave the shorter one to Remi and kept the longer one for himself. They'd gotten only fifty feet or so when they heard a faint voice through the falling rain.

"I don't know what you're talking about . . . what piece?"

It was Ted.

A male voice said something in return, but neither Sam nor Remi could make out the words.

"That thing? It was a piece of a bottle. Nothing important."

Sam turned his head, trying to catch the sound and narrow in on where it was coming from. Using hand gestures, Sam pointed ahead and to the left, under an arch formed by a boiler that had half collapsed against its neighbor. She nodded. Once they were through the arch the voices became more distinct.

"I want you to tell me exactly where you found it," the unidentified man was saying. The voice was accented, either eastern European or Russian.

"I told you, I don't remember. It was somewhere on the river."

"The Pocomoke River?"

"Right," Ted replied.

"Where?"

"Why are you doing this? I don't understand what—"

There was a slapping sound, something hard striking flesh. Ted grunted, followed by a splash as he obviously fell over in a mud puddle.

"Get up!"

"I can't!"

"I said, get up!"

Sam signaled for Remi to wait as he crept ahead, pressed himself against the wall of the boiler, then slid ahead until he could see around the curve.

There, in a space between a pair of pickup truck–sized boilers, was Ted Frobisher. He was on his knees, arms bound behind his back. His assailant stood a few feet in front of him, a flashlight in his left hand, a revolver in his right. He was pointing the gun at Ted's chest.

"Tell me where you found it and I'll take you home," the man said. "You can forget all about this."

There's a lie if ever I've heard one, Sam thought. Whoever this man was he hadn't brought Ted all the way out here only to take him back home and tuck him safely into bed. *So sorry about all this, have a nice night.* . . . Whether or not the man got what he'd wanted, Ted's fate was sealed unless they acted quickly.

Sam thought for a few seconds and formulated a rudimentary plan. He would have preferred a more elegant solution, but they had neither the time nor the resources for that. Besides, simple was often the most elegant. He slid back along the boiler and returned to where Remi was waiting.

He sketched out the scene he had witnessed, then his plan.

"Sounds like you're getting the most dangerous part," Remi said.

"I have absolute confidence in your aim."

"And my timing."

"That, too. I'll be right back."

Sam disappeared into the trees for half a minute, then returned and handed her a rock about the size of a grapefruit.

"Think you can climb that one-handed?" he asked, nodding at the rusty maintenance ladder rising up the side of the nearest boiler.

"If you hear a big thump in the dark you'll have your answer." She leaned forward, curled her fist around his shirtfront, and drew him in for a quick kiss. "Listen, Fargo: Try to look harmless and for God's sake be careful. If you get killed I'll never forgive you."

"That makes two of us."

Sam hefted his piece of rebar and took off at a half sprint, heading back the way he came, then veered right and began circling around. He stopped to check his watch. Six minutes had passed since his OnStar call. He couldn't wait any longer.

He tucked the rebar into the waistband at his back, then took a calming breath and started walking until he came around a boiler and the pool of light from the flashlight appeared in the darkness. Sam stopped and called out.

"Hey, there, howdy, is everything okay?"

The stranger whipped around, shining his flashlight in Sam's eyes. "Who are you?"

"I was just driving by," Sam said. "I saw the car. Thought maybe somebody broke down. Hey, how about not shining that in my eyes?"

In the distance came the faint sound of sirens.

Gun raised, the man spun back to Ted, then back to Sam.

"Whoa, fella, what's the gun for?"

Sam raised his hands and took a careful step forward.

"Don't move! Stay right there!"

"Hey, I'm just trying to help." Breath held, Sam took another step forward, closing the gap to fifteen feet.

Be ready, Remi. . . .

He raised his voice to make sure he could be heard over the rain and said, "If you want me to leave, no problem. . . ."

Remi took her cue, and to his right Sam saw a shadow arcing out of the dark sky from atop the boiler. The stone seemed to hang for an impossibly long time, then landed with a sickening crunch on the man's right foot. Remi's aim was dead-on. Though a head shot would have made things much easier, it would have also likely killed the man, a complication they didn't need.

Even as the man groaned and stumbled backward, Sam was moving, drawing the rebar from his waistband with his left hand as he charged ahead. Arms windmilling, the man was trying to regain his balance and had almost succeeded when Sam's perfectly timed upper-cut caught him squarely in the chin. The gun and flashlight flew up and away, the former landing with a plop in the mud, the latter rolling toward Ted. From the corner of his eye Sam saw Remi appear behind Ted. She lifted him to his feet and together they started running.

The stranger was lying on his back, half sunken in the mud, groaning. *Tough customer,* Sam thought. That uppercut should have solidly shut off his lights. Sam switched the rebar to his right hand.

The sirens were coming closer now, not two minutes away.

Sam picked up the flashlight and cast it around until he spotted the man's pistol half buried in the mud a few feet away. Using the tip of his shoe, Sam pried it free, slipped the top of his foot beneath it, and kicked it far into the trees.

He turned back and shined the light into the man's face. The man stopped moving, eyes squinting against the glare. His face was lean and weathered and he had small, mean eyes and a nose that had clearly been broken many times over. The white line of a scar ran from the bridge of his nose across his right eyebrow and ended just above his temple. *Not just tough,* Sam now thought. *But cruel, too.* The eyes told him that much.

Sam said, "Don't suppose you'd care to tell me who you are or why you're here, would you?"

The man blinked rapidly, clearing away the cobwebs, then focused on Sam and spat out a word. *Russian,* Sam thought. Though his Russian was passable for tourist purposes, he didn't recognize the word. Still, it was a safe bet it had something to do with either his mother, some form of carnal knowledge, or both.

"That had a distinctly unfriendly sound to it," Sam said. "Let's try this one more time: Who are you and what's your business with our friend?"

Another curse, this one a full sentence.

"Didn't think so," Sam said. "Well, better luck next time, pal."

With that he leaned forward and swung the rebar in a tight arc, tapping the man behind the ear with what he hoped was just enough force. Rebar wasn't the most delicate of weapons. The man grunted and went limp.

"Here's hoping we never meet again," Sam said, then turned and started running.

CHAPTER 6

"Here, Ted, drink this," Sam said, handing Frobisher a snifter of warm brandy.

"What is it?" Frobisher grumbled. Surprising neither Sam nor Remi, Ted's adventure in the boiler graveyard had done nothing to improve his disposition. Then again, Ted wouldn't be Ted if he were sunny.

"Just drink it," Remi said and gave his hand a pat.

Frobisher took a gulp, scrunched up his face, then took a second gulp.

Sam put another log on the fire, then joined Remi on the love seat. Frobisher sat opposite them in a wingback chair, wrapped in a flannel blanket and fresh from a hot shower.

After leaving Frobisher's mystery man lying in the mud, Sam had sprinted back to the BMW, which Remi had turned around and pulled up to the driveway. His decision to leave before the police had been an instinctive one: Though they'd done nothing wrong, being embroiled in a police investigation would also entangle them with Frobisher's attacker. Sam's gut told him the more distance they put between themselves and the man, the better.

With Sam back in the car they'd sped back down Black Road, then headed west on Mount Vernon Road. Thirty seconds later they saw flashing lights come around the corner behind them and pull onto Black Road. At Sam's direction Remi did a quick U-turn, pulled over to the shoulder, and doused the headlights, waiting until the emergency responders—a police cruiser and a fire truck, it appeared—reached the boiler graveyard. She then pulled out and headed back toward Princess Anne. Forty minutes later they were back in their room at the B&B.

"How do you feel?" Sam asked Frobisher.

"How do you think I feel? I've been kidnapped and assaulted."

Frobisher was in his mid sixties and bald save a monk's fringe of silver. He wore a pair of Ben Franklin half-glasses; behind them, his eyes were a pale, watery blue. Other than being wet and cold and shaken up, the only leftover from his ordeal was a badly bruised and swollen right cheek where the man had pistol-whipped him.

"Kidnapped and assaulted is better than kidnapped, assaulted, and killed," Sam observed.

"I suppose," he replied, then grumbled something under his breath.

"What was that, Ted?"

"I said, thanks for rescuing me."

"I bet that hurt to say," Remi replied.

"You have no idea. But I mean it. Thanks. Both of you." He drained the last of his brandy, then held out the snifter for more. Remi obliged.

"So what happened?" Sam asked.

"I was dead asleep and I woke up to someone pounding on my door. I asked who it was through the door and he said, 'Stan Johnston, from down the road.' He said Cindy—his wife—was sick and their phone wasn't working."

"Is there a Stan Johnston?" Sam asked.

"Of course there's a Stan Johnston. The next farmhouse to the north."

This meant something, Sam knew. Judging from the attacker's accent it seemed reasonable to assume he wasn't a local, which meant he'd planned out his raid of Ted's house, going as far as finding out the names of his neighbors for use in his ploy.

During his time at DARPA Sam had had enough interaction with case officers from the CIA's Clandestine Service to know how they thought and how they worked. Everything Frobisher's attacker had done screamed "professional." But a professional for whom? And to what end?

"So you opened the door . . ." Remi prompted Frobisher.

"So I opened the door and he rushes in, pushes me to the floor, and shoves that gun in my face. He starts asking questions, shouting at me—"

"About?"

"Some shard of glass. It was nothing, the punt from a wine bottle. He wanted to know where it was, so I told him. He tied up my hands with some kind of tape, then went into the shop, rummaged around—broke God knows what in the process—then came back with the piece and started asking where I'd found it."

"Where did you find it?"

"I don't remember exactly. I really don't. It was on the Pocomoke, somewhere south of Snow Hill. I was fishing and—"

"You fish?" Sam asked, surprised. "Since when?"

"Since forever, you idiot. What, you think I just sit around the shop all day fondling plates and doodads? As I was saying . . . I was fishing and I snagged something. It was a boot, an old leather boot. The shard was inside it."

"You still have the boot?"

"What am I, a garbage man? No, I threw it back. It was an old rotted boot, Sam."

Sam raised his hands, palms out, in a calming gesture. "Okay, okay. Go on. He started shouting questions at you and . . ."

"Then the phone rang."

"That was me."

"He asked if I was expecting anyone and I said yes, thinking he would leave. He didn't. He dragged me to the car and drove me out to that place, whatever it was. That's it. The rest you know."

"He had it on him," Sam muttered. "I should've searched him."

"How many times do I have to say this, Sam? The piece was nothing. There was no label, no writing—just some kind of weird symbol."

"What kind of symbol?"

"I don't remember. There's a picture on my website. I posted it, thinking someone might know what it was."

"Remi, do you mind?" Sam asked.

She was already up, retrieving their laptop, which she set on the coffee table and powered up. Thirty seconds later she said. "Here, is this it, Ted?" She turned the laptop for him to see.

He squinted at the screen, then nodded. "Yep, that's it. See, it's nothing."

Sam scooted closer to Remi and looked at the picture. As described, it looked like the concave bottom, or punt, of a green wine bottle. In the center of the punt was the symbol. Remi zoomed in until they could make it out:

Sam said, "That doesn't look even remotely familiar. You?"

"No," Remi replied. "And this doesn't mean anything to you, Ted?"

"No, I already told you."

"No strange phone calls or e-mails about it? No one showed any curiosity?"

Frobisher groaned. "No, no, and no. When can I go home? I'm tired."

Sam said, "Ted, I don't think that's a good idea."

"What? Why?"

"He knows where you live—"

"Ah, he was just some nut. Probably high on something. It's just a piece of wine bottle, for God's sake, and he has it. It's over."

I doubt it, Sam thought. And neither did he think the man was a nut or a druggie. For whatever reason, someone felt this punt, this odd piece of green glass, was very important. Important enough to kill for.

Forty-five miles away, Grigoriy Arkhipov lay unmoving beneath the low-hanging branches of a tree, his face covered in mud, eyes tracking the movements of the Somerset County sheriff's deputy as the tow-truck driver finished hooking up the Lucerne. In some primitive part of his brain Arkhipov wanted to move, to *act,* but he quashed the urge and concentrated on remaining still. It would have been so easy—not to mention satisfying—to take the deputy and the tow-truck driver by surprise, dispatch them, then take one of their vehicles and disappear into the night, but he knew that would cause him more trouble than the pleasure was worth. A murdered police officer would bring down a manhunt, including roadblocks, random stops, and even perhaps the FBI, none of which would help him on his mission.

He'd been awoken from the blow to his head by the glare of white light and the nearby warbling of sirens and had opened his eyes to find himself staring into a pair of headlights. He'd stayed still, certain he'd see figures running toward him, but when no one came he slowly rolled onto his belly and started crawling away, behind the boilers and into the trees where he now lay.

Don't move, he commanded himself. He would stay here, stay invisible, and wait for them to leave. The rental car had been secured with a false driver's license and a sanitized credit card, neither of which would lead the police anywhere. The rain had turned the junkyard into a morass, so there were no signs of a struggle to pique the police's curiosity. At this point all they had was an abandoned car and what they would likely decide was a prank OnStar call from some teenagers.

Now, that had been a clever trick, Arkhipov thought, as was their ambush of him. Humiliating, yes, but the professional in Arkhipov appreciated the ingenuity of the thing. The sheer nerve of it. His foot throbbed with pain, but he didn't dare check it until he was alone.

The mud had absorbed part of the stone's impact, but his two small-est toes were probably broken. Painful but not debilitating. He'd experienced much worse. In the Spetsnaz, a broken bone rarely even warranted medical treatment. And Afghanistan . . . the mujahideen were savage fighters who liked nothing better than to kill up close and personal, face-to-face and knife-to-knife, and he had the scars to remind him. Pain, Grigoriy Arkhipov knew, was a simple matter, a thing of the mind and nothing more.

So who were they, he wondered, these mysterious rescuers? Not your average good Samaritans, that much was certain. Their actions showed skill and courage. And resourcefulness. Friends of Frobisher's, the man had said. It had been a fleeting slip of the tongue that Arkh-ipov was only too happy to exploit. It would be enough. He would find them—hopefully before he had to report this incident to his employer.

Clearly they had close ties with the antique dealer. Why would they risk their lives otherwise? So, two plus two equals four. If Frobisher didn't want to cooperate and tell him where he'd found the shard, perhaps this other man and woman would be more accommodating.

And if not, well, he would simply settle the score and move on. Ingenious as they'd been in their ambush of him, he felt it only fair he find an equally novel way of repaying them.

CHAPTER 7

POCOMOKE RIVER

W hat do you think the chances are Ted will stay away?" Remi asked, giving the outboard motor's starter cord a tug.

Sam climbed into the skiff's bow and pushed off the dock with his leg. "I think I got through to him, but with Ted you never know. That shop is his life."

After questioning Frobisher for another half hour the night before and satisfying themselves they'd gotten the whole story, Sam had ordered a cot from the reception desk and put Ted, who was by then more than a little tipsy from three servings of brandy, to bed.

The next morning after breakfast they'd convinced him to take a vacation, then made some calls and found a beach house on Fenwick Island that belonged to a friend of a friend of a friend. It was unlikely anyone would trace Frobisher to there. Whether Ted would stay there, they didn't know, but short of tying him up it was the best they could do.

The question for them was whether to get any further involved.

Par for his personality and his solidly Libertarian ideals, Ted had dismissed their suggestion that he get the authorities involved. He had little love or use for the government and asserted the police would simply take a report and file it away, which Sam and Remi tended to agree with. They doubted Ted's abductor had left enough of a trail to follow.

While they mulled it all over, Sam had decided they'd continue with their original plan of identifying the mini sub trapped in the inlet, then return to their search for Patty Cannon's treasure.

Remi got the engine started, then brought the skiff about and pointed the nose downriver, the engine puttering softly in the cool morning air.

"What a difference a day can make," she said, staring up at the sky.

"Amen," Sam replied.

The previous night's rain had stopped just before dawn, giving way to a bright blue sky dotted with cotton-puff clouds. Along the riverbanks, birds chirped and flitted from branch to branch. The surface of the water, cloaked in a thin mist, was flat save a ripple here and there as a fish popped to the surface to catch an unwary fly or water bug.

"Say," Remi said, "have I already mentioned how proud I am of you?"

"For what? Finding us those croissants this morning?"

"No, you dummy. For last night. You were downright heroic."

"Yes, you mentioned it. Thanks. Don't forget, though, I had some fantastic help. Couldn't have done it without you."

Remi shrugged and smiled at the compliment. "You looked rather sexy, you know, all covered with mud and carrying that rebar around. Very cavemanish."

"Ugh-ugh."

Remi laughed.

"Sorry about your sweater, by the way."

Her cashmere turtleneck hadn't survived the previous night's adventure, having taken on the distinct and irreversible odor of wet goat.

"It's just a sweater. It's replaceable—which isn't true of every-thing," Remi said with an affectionate smile.

"Don't I know it," Sam said.

———

"I assume you've taken steps to make sure it doesn't happen again?" Hadeon Bondaruk asked.

Arkhipov clenched the phone tighter against his ear until his knuckles turned white. "Yes. Three of my best men are here now. I'm guessing they have an hour's head start on us."

"What are their names?" Bondaruk asked.

As Arkhipov had predicted, finding the identities of Frobisher's rescuers had been a relatively easy task.

After the deputy and the tow-truck driver had left, Arkhipov had half jogged, half limped up the road to the nearest farmhouse, where he found an old Chevy truck parked behind the barn with the keys in it. He drove back to Frobisher's shop and parked the truck behind the garage, then went inside and turned the house upside down, finding what he needed in ten minutes. Frobisher had only a few dozen names in his Rolodex, half of them businesses, the other half personal, and of these only eight were couples. A quick Google search gave him what he needed.

From Frobisher's house to the Princess Anne Greyhound station was a short five-minute drive. The truck he parked on a side street and the license plates he stuffed into a nearby trash can under some coffee grounds and a bucket of KFC chicken bones.

Twenty minutes later he'd recovered his backpack from the rental locker and was checked in to a nearby Motel 6 under a different driver's license and credit card.

"Sam and Remi Fargo," Arkhipov now told Bondaruk. "They're—"

"I know who they are. Treasure hunters, and good ones at that. Damn! This is a bad sign. Their being there can't be a coincidence. Clearly Frobisher figured out what he had and called them in."

"I'm not convinced of that. I've interrogated a lot of men in my time and I know what lying looks like. Frobisher was telling the truth, I'm certain of it."

"You might be right, but assume he was lying. Assume the Fargos are after the same thing we are, and act accordingly."

"Yes, sir."

"How soon do you leave?"

"The boat's ready now." Armed with the Fargos' names and particulars it had been simple work to track their credit card purchases to the boat rental shop in Snow Hill. "It won't take long to catch up to them."

———

Sam had carefully marked the inlet's position on the map so they found it with little trouble. The previous night's rain had piled up even more branches at the mouth of the inlet. It now looked like a hunting blind, a patchwork of crisscrossing branches and leaves, both dead and still-green alike. Remi steered the skiff alongside the pile, then tied the painter line to one of the sturdier branches. They let the boat drift until the painter line was taut and Sam was sure it would hold, then Remi slipped into the water and onto the bank. Sam swam around to the side, handed up to her the two duffel bags containing their gear, then accepted her hand and climbed onto the bank himself.

With a duffel bag over each shoulder, Sam led the way through the tall grass and shrubbery along the bank, veering inland twenty feet until they reached the edge of the inlet. To their left through the undergrowth they could just make out the branch pile and the river's main channel beyond it. As it had the day before, the inlet had an eerie quality to it, a tunnel of green that felt somehow separated from the rest of the world.

Of course, Sam conceded, part of that feeling probably had something to do with the algae-draped periscope jutting from the water only a few feet in front of them, like the neck of some primordial sea serpent.

"A little spooky, isn't it?" Remi whispered, crossing her arms as though warding off a chill.

"More than a little," Sam agreed, then dropped the duffel bags and rubbed his hands together in anticipation. "Never fear, the Fargos are here."

"Just promise me one thing," Remi said.

"Name it."

"After this, a vacation. A real vacation."

"The destination is all yours, Mrs. Fargo."

———

The first order of business was to get down there and determine the general condition of the submarine, look for any markings they might use to identify it, and hopefully find an entrance. This last goal Sam hadn't yet shared with Remi, knowing she would forbid his entering the wreck, which was admittedly the prudent course. But Sam was confident that between his diving skills and Remi's reliability they'd have no trouble handling anything that came up.

To that end they'd brought along a dive mask, a pair of truncated swim fins, waterproof flashlights with extra batteries, four coils of nylon towing-grade rope, and three ratchet blocks to secure the sub in position lest it slip during Sam's inspection. If they even got that far.

Additionally, the day before he'd asked Selma to FedEx him a trio of Spair Air emergency pony tanks, each of which contained enough air for roughly sixty breaths, or two to five minutes.

"I know that look on your face, Fargo," Remi said. "You want to go inside, don't you?"

"Only if it's safe. Trust me, Remi, I got my adrenaline fix last night. I'm not going to take any stupid chances."

"Okay."

Sam slid down the bank into the water, then stroked over to where the periscope rose from the water. He grabbed ahold of it, gave it a tug and several shakes. It seemed solid. Remi tossed him two ends of rope, both of which he secured around the periscope. Remi took the other ends, secured each of them to a ratchet block, then each of those to nearby trees. Sam climbed back out and together they cranked the ratchets until the lines were taut. Sam gave each one a tug.

"It's not going anywhere. Okay, I'm going to have a quick look around. Three minutes, no more."

"Do you want me to—"

"Shhh," Sam whispered, a finger to his lips.

He turned his head, listening. Five seconds passed and then faintly, in the distance, came the sound of a boat engine.

"Coming this way," he said.

"Just fishermen."

"Probably." But after last night . . .

One thing that had been nagging at Sam was the proximity of their submarine to where Ted had said he'd found the punt shard. It was unlikely the two were connected, but not so unlikely that Ted's assailant might choose to search this area of the Pocomoke.

He crouched beside one of the duffel bags, rummaged around, and came up with a pair of binoculars. With Remi on his heels, he ran back along the bank to where they'd tied off the skiff. They dropped to their knees in the high grass and Sam aimed the binoculars upriver.

A few seconds later a powerboat appeared around the bend of the river. It contained four men. One at the wheel, one on the bow, and two sitting on the afterdeck. Sam zoomed in on the driver's face.

Scarface. "It's him," he muttered.

"You've got to be kidding," Remi replied.

"I wish I was."

CHAPTER 8

"The skiff!" Sam rasped softly. "Come on!"

He slid belly first down the bank and into the water. A quarter mile upstream Scarface had turned the powerboat into the mouth of another inlet, which the man in the bow was scanning through a pair of binoculars. Sam heard Scarface's voice echo over the water, followed by another voice saying, *"Nyet."*

Great, more Russian heavies.

Sam stroked over to where he'd secured the skiff's painter line, quickly undid the knot, then swam back and grabbed the bow cleat. He glanced over his shoulder. Scarface was bringing the powerboat about and turning their way.

"Sam . . ."

"I see them."

He wrapped the painter around one fist then accepted Remi's help up the bank. "Pull," he whispered. "Pull hard!"

Together they heaved on the painter. The skiff's bow bumped against the bank, then began inching up the slope.

The powerboat was three hundred yards away. The men's attention seemed focused on the opposite shore, but Sam knew that could change at any second. One stray glance and they were finished.

"Pull, Remi."

Again they heaved back on the painter. Sam spread his legs and dug his heels into the soil, pulling until the tendons in his neck bulged. The skiff's nose appeared over the lip of the bank, but now free of the water and subject to gravity the electric motor began fighting them. The skiff slipped backward a foot.

"One more good pull," Sam said. "On three. One . . . two . . . three!"

The skiff arced up and over the lip and slid onto level ground. In lockstep Sam and Remi backpedaled, dragging the skiff deeper into the grass.

"Down, Sam."

Remi dropped to her belly, followed a split second later by Sam. They went still, tried to slow their breathing.

"Think we made it?" Remi whispered.

"We'll know shortly. If things go bad, I want you to run as fast as you can. Head for the forest and don't look back."

"No, Sam—"

"Shhh."

The powerboat's engine was growing louder by the second, seemingly headed straight for their spot.

Then, Scarface's voice: "Anything?"

"Nothing. What are they in, anyway?"

"A skiff, about twelve feet long."

"Can't be on this side," the voice said. "There's nothing here. Got to be the other one. Plenty of side channels to hide in there."

"Yeah."

The engine noise began moving off, fading across the water until Sam and Remi could only hear its distant echo.

"They've moved into another channel," Sam said, rising to his knees and peeking over the top of the grass. "Yep. Don't see them. They're gone."

Remi rolled onto her back and let out a sigh. "Thank God."

Sam lay down beside her. She laid her head onto his shoulder.

"What do you say?" he asked. "Stay or go?"

She didn't hesitate. "We've come this far. Be a shame to leave the mystery unsolved."

"That's the woman I love," Sam said.

"What, reckless and misguided?"

"No, courageous and determined."

Remi sang softly, " 'You say potayto, I say potahto . . .' "

"Come on, back to work."

Sam spit into his mask, dipped it into the water, then settled it onto his head. Remi stood on the bank, arms on her hips, face etched with worry.

"Just going to have a look around," he assured her. "I'll save the air in case we can get inside. This won't happen, but if it shifts in my direction while I'm down there, just start working those ratchet blocks until it tips back. If I don't come up within, say, four to six hours, you can start worrying."

"Comedian."

"Hold the fort, I'll be back."

Sam clicked on his flashlight, took a deep breath, and ducked beneath the surface. Left hand extended, he finned downward. Within only a few feet the algae-filled water turned a deep green and visibility dropped to only a few feet. Sediment and bits of plant life swirled in the flashlight's beam, leaving Sam feeling like he was trapped inside a nightmarish snow globe.

His hand touched something solid, the hull. He kept going, letting his hand trail over the curve of the hull until finally the bottom appeared in his flashlight beam. The keel was perched atop a jumble of sunken logs, precariously balanced but stable enough that Sam felt a flood of relief knowing the sub wasn't likely to roll over on him. He felt the ache in his lungs turn into a burning, so he finned for the surface.

"Everything okay?" Remi asked once he'd caught his breath.

"Yep. Good news. She's sitting upright, more or less. Okay, going again."

He ducked back under, this time estimating the hull's diameter as he skimmed past it. At the keel, he turned aft. At about the midpoint he encountered a bracket of some sort jutting from the hull and running lengthwise. For a moment what he was seeing didn't register on his brain. He'd seen this before . . . one of the pictures from his earlier research. When the answer came, Sam felt a knot form in his belly.

Torpedo rack.

He stopped swimming and cast the flashlight along the bottom, seeing it with new eyes. Was one of those seemingly harmless sunken logs something else altogether?

He kept swimming aft until his flashlight picked out the tapered cigar end of the sub, and jutting from its side a horizontal plane. When he drew even with it he righted himself and let himself rise alongside the hull until the last piece of the puzzle came into view. Rising from the back of the hull was another tube, about eighteen inches tall and about shoulder-width in diameter.

Entry hatch.

Sam popped back up to the surface and stroked over to the bank, where Remi helped him out. He shed his fins and mask and took a moment to gather his thoughts.

"Well?" she said.

"There's a manila folder in one of the duffels. Could you grab it for me?" She was back with it in half a minute. Sam flipped back and forth through the loose pages for a couple minutes, then plucked one of the sheets out and handed it to Remi.

"*Molch*," she read. "What in God's name . . ."

Her words trailed off as she kept reading.

Sam said, " 'Molch' means 'Salamander.' It was a class of midget torpedo submarine produced by Nazi Germany in 1944."

Built for the Kriegsmarine by A. G. Weser, a company in Bremen, the Molch was the brainchild of Dr. Heinrich Drager. Measuring thirty-five feet long, three feet from deck to keel, and six feet from beam to beam, the Molch was designed to carry one crew member and two G7e torpedoes on port and starboard racks to depths of 120 feet and distances up to fifty nautical miles at a maximum submerged speed of three knots, a moderate walking pace.

As an offensive weapon the Molch, like most of Germany's other midget subs, was largely unsuccessful: it was hard to steer, almost impossible to dive, and with a range so limited it was dependent upon auxiliary vessels for support and deployment.

"Are you sure, Sam?" Remi asked.

"I'm sure. Everything fits."

"How in the world did it end up here?"

"That's the part that doesn't fit. According to everything I've read, these things only saw action in Holland, Denmark, Norway, and the Mediterranean. There are absolutely no records of Molches being deployed this far west."

"How many of these things were there?"

"Almost four hundred, and most of those were lost, either sunk or vanished. They were death traps, Remi. Only crazy men volunteered for midget-sub duty."

"You said a one-man crew. You don't think . . ."

"Won't know until I get in there."

"And that other lovely word you used—torpedo."

"That's the dicey part. My hunch is it got pushed this far upriver by six-plus decades of storm surges. Probably both the torpedoes—if it was equipped with any to start with—were knocked off long ago."

"Well, that's some small comfort," Remi replied. "Except for the unlucky fisherman who manages to snag one someday."

"We're going to have to tell somebody about this—the coast guard or the navy. How they'll deal with it, I have no idea."

"One thing at a time."

"Right. Step one: Make sure it isn't sitting atop a pair of sixty-year-old live torpedoes."

CHAPTER 9

Using one of the Spair Air pony canisters, Sam inspected the bottom beneath the Molch from stem to stern, lightly tapping on each log with the tip of his dive knife and praying he didn't get a metallic clank in reply. Their luck held; all he heard was the soft thump of rotten wood.

Given the appearance of the logs near the top of the heap, many of which still showed some remnants of bark, Sam suspected the Molch had been deposited here recently, pushed by the storm out of the main channel and into this inlet. If so, any torpedoes she'd been carrying were likely lost somewhere in the main channel of the Pocomoke, between here and the bay, some twenty miles to the south.

A sound theory, but a theory nonetheless, Sam reminded himself.

He finished his survey of the bottom, then moved on to his next task. Though he'd seen no external damage to the Molch's hull it didn't mean she wasn't flooded, and if so they were out of luck. Small as it was compared to its counterparts, the Molch was still no lightweight, weighing in at eleven tons. Add to that the volume of water her interior could hold and this midget submarine might as well be the *Titanic* for all the good their ropes and ratchet blocks would do them.

Moving from the aft end forward, Sam tapped along the hull every few feet with his knuckle, listening to the echoes. They were hollow. Damn, could they be this lucky . . . ?

He returned to the surface and climbed back onto the bank.

"Good news, bad news," Sam said. "Which do you want first?"

"Good."

"I'm ninety percent sure the torpedoes aren't down there and ninety-nine percent sure she's not flooded."

"And the bad?"

"I'm only ninety percent sure the torpedoes aren't down there."

Remi thought it over for a moment, then said, "Well, if you're wrong, at least we'll go together—and in spectacular fashion."

———————

Sam spent the next hour rigging the lines to the sub, checking and rechecking their placement, the angles, and the anchor points for the three ratchet blocks, which they'd spread out in a fan shape along the bank, each secured to the base of a full-grown tree. Sam had hooked the other ends to the Molch's bow cleat, around the entry hatch, and then around the propeller shaft.

Twice during their preparations they again heard the rumbling of a boat engine and each time crawled through the grass to their vantage point overlooking the river. The first boat turned out to be a father and son trolling for pike. The second boat, just five minutes later, was Scar-face and his crew heading back upriver toward Snow Hill. As before, they slowed at the mouth of each inlet on the opposite shore, Scarface steering while one of the others knelt on the bow and scanned the waterway with binoculars. After ten minutes of this they disappeared around the bend. Sam and Remi waited another five minutes to make sure they had truly moved on, then got back to work.

Even with the sub full of air, rolling her was going to take just the right amount of force, applied in just the right way. Sam scratched out the calculations on his notepad, figuring the force vectors and buoyancy variables until certain they were as ready as they were going to get.

"We'll know as soon as it slides off the logs," Sam said. "If it sinks, it's over. Opening the hatch will just flood it. If it floats, we're still in the game."

They rehearsed their plan one more time, then took up their positions, Sam at the center ratchet block, Remi on the stern block.

"Ready?" Sam called.

"Ready."

"As soon as you see it drop off the logs, start cranking."

"Shall do."

Sam started cranking slowly on the ratchet, one every second or so, listening to the line thrumming with tension and the groaning of steel. Thirty seconds and forty cranks later there came a soft crunching sound from the water and then, as if moving in slow motion, the Molch's periscope began swinging toward them.

There was another muffled crunch and Sam could see in his mind's eye the logs beneath the keel cracking. He felt a faint shudder beneath his feet, then the line went slack.

"Go, Remi, fast as you can!"

Together they began working the ratchets. After ten seconds Sam's line went taut again. He sprinted to the bow ratchet block and cranked it until the line was shivering with tension. Sam glanced over to Remi and saw her line was also vibrating.

"Okay, stop!"

Remi froze.

"Start walking backward into the grass, then lie down on your belly and wait till I give you the all clear."

If any of the lines parted under the strain they would snap back with lethal force.

Sam walked forward, hand lightly trailing over the line, feeling it tremble. He reached the lip of the inlet and looked down.

"Gotta love physics," Sam whispered.

The Molch was lying against the bank at a thirty-degree angle, periscope poking into the tree branches and her slime-encrusted entry hatch jutting from the water.

Remi appeared at his shoulder. "Wow," she whispered.

"'Wow' is right."

They added a second line to the one around the hatch, then slowly let out the bow and stern blocks, doubled up those lines, and resecured them around trees closer to the bank. Using one of the lines for balance, Sam gingerly stepped onto the Molch's deck. It groaned, shifted, and dipped a few inches, but otherwise held.

"Would you like the honors?" Sam asked, nodding at the hatch.

"Sure."

"Here."

Sam tossed her the hammer and she grabbed it in midair, then stepped onto the deck and knelt beside the hatch. She gave each of the hatch's four dogging levers a solid rap, then set the hammer aside and tried them. They didn't budge. Three more times she repeated the process before each of the levers let loose in turn, sliding aside with a screech.

Remi took a breath, looked at Sam with wide-eyed anticipation, then lifted open the hatch. Immediately she wrinkled her nose and jerked her head back. "Oh, God, that's awful. . . ."

"I guess that answers the question of whether her crew's still aboard," Sam said.

"Yeah, there's no doubt about that," Remi replied, pinching shut her nose and staring into the open hatch. "He's staring me right in the eye."

The body was wearing a Kriegsmarine cap and a dark blue jumpsuit. Then again, the word "body" seemed a woefully inadequate description of what Sam and Remi were looking at.

Trapped inside the dry, airless interior of the Molch for sixty-four years, the corpse had undergone a transformation Sam could only describe as part liquification, part mummification.

"Pretty safe to assume he suffocated," Remi said. "Once he was dead the body would have started decaying, but without oxygen the process ground to a halt, leaving him . . . half-baked, if you will."

"Oh, that's lovely, dear. I'll carry the image always."

The position of the remains, which lay sprawled on the deck at the bottom of the ladder with one petrified arm draped over a rung, spoke volumes about the man's final hours or minutes. Trapped inside this darkened cylinder, knowing death was tightening its grip on him with every inhalation of oxygen, it seemed natural that he would have gravitated to his only exit, half hoping for some miracle that he knew in his heart would never come.

"I assume you won't mind staying up here while I poke around," Sam said.

"Be my guest."

He clicked on the flashlight, then slid his legs into the hatch, probed with his foot until it found a rung, then started downward. A few feet from the bottom, Sam stepped off the ladder, opposite the body, and used his arms to lower himself to the deck.

Immediately Sam felt a gloom wash over him. He wasn't particularly claustrophobic, but this was different somehow. Not high enough to allow him to straighten up and barely wider than his outstretched arms, the interior had a dungeonlike feel to it. The bulkheads, painted in a dull gray, were festooned with cables and pipes, all seemingly going everywhere and nowhere at once.

"How is it?" Remi called down.

"Disgusting is the only word to describe it."

Sam knelt down beside the corpse and began carefully checking the pockets. All were empty save the breast pocket, inside which he found a wallet. He handed this up to Remi, then turned and moved forward.

According to what few descriptions of the Molch's interior he had been able to find, the front section of the bow held the craft's main battery and behind this, between a pair of trim ballast tanks, an operator's seat with rudimentary controls for steering, navigation, speed, power, and trimming, as well as a primitive hydrophone for detecting enemy vessels.

Under the operator's seat Sam found a small toolbox and a leather holster containing a Luger pistol and a spare magazine. These he pocketed.

Bolted to the bulkhead beneath each trim tank was a rectangular footlocker. In one he found a half dozen water jugs, all empty, and twice that number of empty food tins. In the other footlocker he found a leather satchel and a pair of hard-backed black leather journals. He slipped them into the satchel, then took one last look around. Something caught his eye: a piece of fabric sticking out from behind the footlocker. He knelt down and saw that it was a burlap sack; inside was a hinged wooden box the size and shape of a loaf of bread. He tucked the sack under his arm and returned to the ladder, then handed all the items up to Remi and climbed up. At the top, he stopped and looked back down at the corpse.

"We'll make sure you get home, Captain," he whispered.

Back on deck, Sam held the line steady to make Remi's leap back to the bank easier. As he braced his feet, his toe bumped the burlap sack. From inside came the muted tinkle of glass.

Curious now, they both knelt down on the deck. Remi opened the sack and slid out the box, which was devoid of markings. Gingerly she pried open the brass latch and swung open the lid, revealing a sheaf of what looked like aged oilskin. Remi peeled back a flap.

For a long ten seconds neither of them spoke, gaping at the object catching the sunlight. Remi murmured, "It can't be. Can it?"

It was a bottle, a green glass wine bottle.

Sam didn't reply, instead using his right index finger to lift the end a few inches out of the box, revealing the punt.

"Good Lord . . . " Remi murmured.

The symbol etched into the glass was all too familiar:

CHAPTER 10

LA JOLLA, CALIFORNIA

That poor man," Remi said. "To die like that . . . I can't imagine."

"I don't want to imagine," Sam replied.

They were stretched out on chaise lounges in the solarium surrounded by potted palms and flowing ferns, the midday sun highlighting every tone of the Tuscan flagstone tiles. It was one of their favorite rooms in the house, not an easy choice by any measure.

Sitting atop the cliffs overlooking Goldfish Point and the indigo waters of the Pacific, the Fargos' home and base of operations was a four-story, twelve-thousand-square-foot Spanish-style house with vaulted maple-beamed ceilings and enough windows and skylights to keep their maintenance man busy for eight hours every month.

The upper floor held Sam and Remi's master suite and below this, one flight down, were four guest suites, a living room, a dining room, and a kitchen/great room that jutted over the cliff. On the second floor a gymnasium containing both aerobic and circuit-training exercise equipment, a steam room, a HydroWorx endless-lap pool, and a thousand feet of hardwood floor space for Remi to practice her fencing and Sam his judo.

The ground floor sported two thousand square feet of office space for Sam and Remi and an adjoining workspace for Selma, complete with three Mac Pro workstations coupled with thirty-inch cinema displays and a pair of wall-mounted thirty-two-inch LCD televisions. Mounted on the east wall was Selma's pride and joy, a fourteen-foot, five-hundred-gallon saltwater aquarium.

Sam told Remi, "We can always hope he went quickly and peacefully."

The man in question, the poor soul they'd found sprawled at the bottom of the Molch's ladder, now had, thanks to the journals they'd found aboard, a name: Manfred Boehm. *Korvettenkapitän* (Commander) Manfred Boehm. One of the journals had turned out to be the Molch's log; the other, Boehm's private diary dating back to the early days of World War II.

Armed with rough translations courtesy of some software, Sam and Remi had dived headfirst into what quickly began to feel like the last will and testament of both Boehm and his submarine, which they soon learned had a given name: the *UM-34*—Underwater Boat, Molch type, thirty-fourth constructed.

Sam had been concentrating on the *UM-34*'s log, trying to piece together where it had come from and how it had ended up trapped in an inlet on the Pocomoke River, while Remi worked through Boehm's diary, learning about the man beyond the uniform and rank.

After packing up the skiff and leaving the Molch behind, they'd thought it wise to avoid Snow Hill and Maxine's Bait 'n' Boat, assuming Scarface and his friends would be lurking about awaiting their return. Instead, they'd motored ten miles downriver and put ashore just south of Willow Grove, where Highway 113 and the Pocomoke ran closest to one another. From there they'd first called for a Pocomoke City taxi, then Maxine's. Sam kept his explanation vague and short, offering a generous tip for troubling them to come down and collect the skiff. His final call went to the B&B's manager, who agreed to ship their belongings back to California.

Five hours later they were at Norfolk International Airport boarding a plane bound for home.

The bottle from the *UM-34* they'd immediately turned over to Selma upon their return, but they'd heard nothing from her on the matter since she'd locked herself and her assistants, boyfriend and girlfriend Pete Jeffcoat and Wendy Corden (both of whom had heard all the Peter Pan jokes they'd cared to), in the workshop for a marathon sleuthing session that wouldn't end until they had an answer.

On the outside, Pete and Wendy were stereotypical twenty-something Californians—tan and lean with easygoing smiles and blond hair highlighted by the sun—but intellectually there was nothing conventional about them, each having graduated from the University of Southern California in the top percentile, Pete with a B.A. in archaeology and Wendy with a degree in social sciences.

Whatever Sam and Remi had discovered, there was no doubt the insect symbol on their bottle was a perfect match for the one on Ted's shard, nor was there any doubt about the bottle's general provenance. The writing on the label was French. Handwritten French, no less.

The questions seemed to be piling up quickly: What was the connection between the two pieces? What did the symbol mean? Had both bottles started out aboard the *UM-34*, and if so how did they get separated? And finally, what about these bottles was worth killing over?

What to do about the *UM-34* itself and the remains of Boehm had been nagging at Sam's and Remi's consciences since leaving Maryland. Though somewhat of a gray area, it could be argued the submarine was in fact an archaeological site, which in a sense made them grave robbers. They consoled themselves by promising that once they were done with their investigation all of Boehm's possessions would be returned to their rightful owner, whether that be the German government or Boehm's surviving family or descendants.

Wanting to put as much distance between themselves and the *UM-34*, which it now seemed clear was what Scarface was after, they had called their lawyer, who assured them the submarine would be found by a responsible party and that the proper authorities would be alerted to the possible presence of torpedoes lying along the bottom of the Pocomoke.

"He had a wife and son," Remi said without looking up from the diary's pages. "Frieda and Helmut, in Arnsburg, outside Düsseldorf."

"That's fantastic. Then the chances are better than fair he's got family there. If so, we'll find them."

"How's the log coming?"

"Slowly. I'll have to start mapping some of these coordinates, but it looks like the *34* was attached to an auxiliary mother ship Boehm called Gertrude."

"Gertrude? Did the Kriegsmarine name their—"

"No, it has to be code."

"Secret codes, lost submarines, and mysterious wine bottles. Sounds like a suspense novel."

"Maybe when we've solved the whole puzzle . . ."

Remi laughed. "I think our plates are full enough."

"Someday we'll have to write all this down, you know. It would make a great book."

"Someday. When we're old and gray. I talked to Ted, by the way. He's sitting tight."

"Thank God. What did you decide? Did you ask him about the sub?"

"No."

Frobisher clung to his well-ordered cocoon of a life and his run-in with this mystery assailant was all the adventure he could handle. Besides, Sam knew Ted: Once the sub's discovery hit the airwaves he would wonder, given their proximity, if the shard and sub were connected. He would contact them if he had anything of value to add.

"Here, listen to this," Remi said, her finger tracing along the page: "'Wolfi gave me two fine bottles of wine today, two of three he brought along. He said we would celebrate together at the end of the mission.'"

"Wolfi," Sam repeated. "Do we know who that is?"

"No. I've been skipping around. I'll start looking. Here's more:

'Wolfi said I deserved two since I had the harder task.' I wonder what it was."

"Don't know, but at least we know where Ted's shard came from. Somewhere along the line Boehm lost one of the bottles."

The intercom on the wall above Remi's head crackled to life.

"Mr. and Mrs. Fargo?" Despite repeated attempts, they'd yet to get Selma to call them by their first names.

Remi reached up and pushed the Talk button. "Yes, Selma."

"I, uh, have something. . . . Well, I've found . . ."

Sam and Remi exchanged curious glances. In their ten years working with Selma they'd never heard her sound anything but decisive and curt.

"Is everything all right?" Remi asked.

"Uh . . . well, why don't you come down and I'll try to explain."

"We're on our way."

They found Selma sitting on a stool at the center worktable, eyes fixed on the bottle of wine before her. Pete and Wendy were nowhere to be seen.

Selma's appearance was a mixed metaphor. She wore her hair in what Remi had dubbed a "modified sixties bob," while her horn-rimmed glasses, which she wore on a chain around her neck when not in use, were straight from the 1950s. Her default fashion usually involved khaki pants, sneakers, and a seemingly endless supply of tie-dyed T-shirts. Selma didn't drink, didn't smoke, didn't swear, and had only one addiction: herbal tea, which she drank by the potful. One cabinet of the workroom was devoted to her tea, most of which had names neither Sam nor Remi could pronounce.

Sam asked her, "Where are Pete and Wendy?"

"I sent them home early. I thought you'd want to hear this in private. You can decide later if you want to tell them."

"Okay . . . " Remi replied.

"Please tell me you haven't found a bottle full of liquid Ebola," Sam said.

"No."

"Then what?"

"I'm not sure where to start."

"Wherever you'd like," Sam said gently.

She pursed her lips, thinking for a few moments, then said, "First of all, that symbol on the bottom, the bug . . . I've got no idea what it means. Sorry."

"It's okay, Selma. Go on."

"Let me back up. Let's talk about the box itself: The hinges and the latch are brass, and the wood is from a species of beech tree found in only a few places in the world. The biggest concentration is in the Pyrenees Mountains of southern France and northern Spain.

"As for the wrapping inside, that could be a discovery unto itself. It may be, depending on how all of this dates, the earliest European example of oilskin. It's calfskin—six layers of it—soaked in linseed oil. The outer two layers are dried out and slightly molded, but the interior four are in perfect condition.

"The glass is fairly remarkable as well—very high quality and quite thick, almost an inch, actually. Though I'm not inclined to test the theory, I'm fairly certain it could stand up to a fair amount of abuse."

"The label on the bottle: hand-tooled leather, glued to the glass as well as bound at the top and bottom by hemp twine. As you can see, the markings on the label were etched direcly into the leather, then filled in with ink—a very rare ink, in fact. It's a mixture of *Aeonium arboreum 'Schwartzkopf'*—"

"English, please," Remi said.

"It's a type of black rose. The ink is a mixture of its petals and crushed beetle—a spitting beetle native only to the islands in the Ligurian Sea. As for the details on the label itself . . ." Selma pulled the bottle closer, waited for Sam and Remi to come over, then turned on an overhead halogen task lamp. "You see this phrase . . . *mesures usuelles*—it's French for 'customary measurements.' It's a system that hasn't been used for a hundred fifty years or so. And this word here . . . *demis*—it means 'halves,' roughly the equivalent of an English pint. Sixteen ounces."

"Not much fluid for a bottle that size," Remi said. "Has to be the thickness of the glass."

Selma nodded. "Now, let's look at the ink itself: as you can see it's faded in places, so it'll take time to re-create the image, but do you see the two letters in the upper right- and left-hand corners, and the two numbers in the lower right and left?"

The Fargos nodded.

"The numbers represent a year. One and nine. Nineteen."

"Nineteen nineteen?" Remi said.

Selma shook her head. "*Eighteen* nineteen. As for the letters—*H* and *A*—they're initials."

"Belonging to . . . ?" Sam prompted.

Selma leaned back and paused. "Now, bear in mind, I'm not certain of this. I need to do some more research to make sure—"

"We understand."

"I think the initials belong to Henri Archambault."

Sam and Remi absorbed the name, then looked at one another, then back to Selma, who offered a sheepish grin and a shrug.

Remi said, "Okay, just so we're on the same page: We're talking about *the* Henri Archambault, correct?"

"The one and only," Selma replied. "Henri Emile Archambault— Napoleon Bonaparte's chief enologist. Unless I miss my guess, you've found a bottle from Napoleon's Lost Cellar."

CHAPTER 11

SEVASTOPOL

The ring-necked pheasant burst from the undergrowth and streaked across the sky, wings beating wildly in the sharp morning air. Hadeon Bondaruk waited, letting the bird get a good lead, then tucked the shotgun to his shoulder and fired. The pheasant jerked in the air, went limp, and started tumbling to the earth.

"Good shot," Grigoriy Arkhipov said, standing a few feet away.

"Go!" Bondaruk barked in Farsi.

The two Labrador retrievers who'd been sitting patiently at Bondaruk's feet leaped up and charged after the fallen bird. The ground around Bondaruk's feet was littered with no less than a dozen pheasant corpses, all of them having been torn to shreds by the dogs.

"I hate the taste of the things," Bondaruk explained to Arkhipov, using the toe of his boot to kick one away. "But the dogs love the exercise. What about you, Kholkov, do you enjoy the hunt?"

Standing a few feet behind Arkhipov, Vladimir Kholkov dipped his head to one side, considering. "Depends on the quarry."

"Good answer."

Kholkov and Arkhipov had served most of their time together in the Spetsnaz, Arkhipov the commander, Kholkov the loyal executive officer, a relationship that had continued into their civilian life as highest-bidder mercenaries. For the past four years Hadeon Bondaruk had been the undisputed highest bidder, making Arkhipov a wealthy man in the process.

After reporting to Bondaruk their failure to find the Fargos, Kholkov and Arkhipov had been summoned here, to their boss's vacation home in the foothills along the Crimean Peninsula. Though he'd arrived the afternoon before, Bondaruk had yet to mention the incident.

Arkhipov was afraid of no man—that much Kholkov had seen proven on the battlefield dozens of times—but they both knew a dangerous man when they saw one, and Bondaruk was as treacherous as they came. Though he'd never personally witnessed it, he had no doubt of Bondaruk's capacity for violence. It wasn't fear that put them on edge when they were around Bondaruk, but a hard-won and healthy caution. Bondaruk was unpredictable, like a shark. Placidly swimming along, paying attention to nothing and everything, ready to attack in the blink of an eye. Even now, as they talked, Kholkov knew his boss was keeping a soldier's eye trained on Bondaruk's shotgun, watching the movement of the barrel as though it were the mouth of a Great White.

Kholkov knew a little about Bondaruk's youth in Turkmenistan. The fact that his current boss had likely killed many dozens of his own countrymen—perhaps even men he knew—during the conflict along the Iranian border mattered very little to him. War was war. The best soldiers, the ones that excelled and survived, usually went about the work of killing the enemy with dispassion.

"It's easy to be a good shot with a good gun," Bondaruk said, cracking the breech and extracting the shell. "Custom-made by Hambrusch Jagdwaffen in Austria. Care to guess how old it is, Grigoriy?"

"I have no idea," Arkhipov replied.

"One hundred eighty years. It belonged to Otto von Bismarck himself."

"You don't say."

"It's a piece of living history," Bondaruk replied as though Arkhipov hadn't spoken. "Look down there." Bondaruk pointed southeast toward the lowlands along the coast. "You see that series of low hills?"

"Yes."

"In 1854, during the Crimean War, that's where the Battle of Balaclava was fought. You've heard of the poem by Tennyson—'The Charge of the Light Brigade'?"

Arkhipov shrugged. "I think we read it in elementary school."

"The actual battle has been overshadowed by the poem—enough that the average person today has no idea about the story. Seven hundred British soldiers—cavalrymen from the 4th and 13th Light Dragoons, 17th Lancers, and the 8th and 11th Hussars—charged a Russian position fortified by cannon. When the smoke cleared, less than two hundred of those soldiers were left alive. You're a military man, Vladimir. What would you call that? Foolish or courageous?"

"It's hard to know what was in the mind of the commanders."

"Another example of living history," Bondaruk said. "History is about people and legacies. Great deeds and great ambition. And great failures, of course. Come, both of you, walk with me."

Shotgun cradled in the crook of his arm, Bondaruk strolled through the high grass, casually blasting the occasional pheasant that popped up.

"I don't blame you for losing them," Bondaruk said. "I've read about the Fargos. They've got a taste for adventure. For danger."

"We'll find them."

Bondaruk waved his hand dismissively. "Do you know why these bottles are so important to me?"

"No."

"The truth is, the bottles, the wine inside, and where they came from aren't important. Once they've served their purpose you can smash them to pieces for all I care."

"Then why? Why do you want them so badly?"

"It's about where they can take us. It's what they've been hiding for two hundred years—and for two millennia before that. How much do you know about Napoleon?"

"Some."

"Napoleon was a shrewd tactician, a ruthless general, and a master strategist—all of the history books agree on that, but as far as I'm concerned his greatest trait was foresight. He was always looking ten steps ahead. When he commissioned Henri Archambault to create that wine and the bottles that held it, Napoleon was thinking about the future, beyond battles and politics. He was thinking of his legacy. Unfortunately, history caught up to him." Bondaruk shrugged and smiled. "I guess one man's misfortune is another man's good luck."

"I don't understand."

"I know you don't."

Bondaruk started walking away, calling to his dogs after him, then suddenly stopped and turned back to Arkhipov. "You've served me very well, Grigoriy, for many years."

"It's been my pleasure."

"As I said, I don't blame you for losing the Fargos, but I need your pledge that it won't happen again."

"You have it, Mr. Bondaruk."

"You'll swear to it?"

For the first time, Arkhipov's eyes showed a trace of uncertainty. "Of course."

Bondaruk smiled; there was none of it in his eyes. "Good. Raise your right hand and so swear."

After only a moment's hesitation, Arkhipov raised his hand to shoulder height. "I swear I will—"

Bondaruk's shotgun spun in his hands and the barrel spat orange flame. Arkhipov's right hand and wrist disappeared in a spray of blood. The former Spetsnaz stumbled backward one step, staring for a few moments at the gushing stump before letting out a moan and dropping to his knees.

Kholkov, standing a few feet behind and to the side, sidestepped, his eyes fixed on Bondaruk's shotgun. Arkhipov clutched feebly at the stump, then looked up at Kholkov. "Why . . . ?" he croaked.

Bondaruk strolled up to Arkhipov's side and looked down on him. "I don't blame you, Grigoriy, but life is about cause and effect. Had you worked more quickly with Frobisher, the Fargos wouldn't have had time to intervene."

Bondaruk shifted the shotgun again, leveled it with Arkhipov's left ankle, and pulled the trigger. The foot disappeared. Arkhipov screamed and toppled over. Bondaruk broke open the shotgun, loaded two more shells from his pocket, then methodically blasted off Arkhipov's remaining hand and foot, then watched his subordinate writhing on the ground. After thirty seconds Arkhipov went still.

Bondaruk looked up at Kholkov. "Do you want his job?"

"Pardon me?"

"I'm offering you a promotion. Do you accept?"

Kholkov took a deep breath. "I have to admit your management style gives me pause."

At this Bondaruk smiled. "Arkhipov isn't dead because he made a mistake, Vladimir. He's dead because he made a mistake that couldn't be fixed. The Fargos are involved now, and it is a complication we can't afford. You're allowed mistakes—just not irreversible ones. I'll need your answer now."

Kholkov nodded. "I accept."

"Wonderful! Let's have some breakfast."

Bondaruk turned and started walking away, his dogs trailing behind him, then he stopped and turned back.

"By the way, when we get back to the house you might want to check the American news sites. I heard a local man, a Maryland State Police officer, in fact, stumbled across a half-sunken German midget submarine."

"Is that so."

"Interesting, isn't it?"

CHAPTER 12

LA JOLLA

Y ou can't be serious," Sam said to Selma. "Napoleon's Lost Cellar isn't . . . It's just a—"

"Legend," Remi finished.

"Right."

"Maybe not," Selma replied. "First, let's talk a little history so we'ye got some context. I know you're both generally familiar with Napoleonic history, but bear with me. I won't bore you with his entire personal history, so we'll pick it up with his first command assignment.

"A Corsican by birth, Napoleon won his first acclaim at the siege of Toulon in 1793 and was appointed the rank of brigadier general, then General of the Army of the West, Commander of the Army of the Interior, then Commander of the French army in Italy. For the next few years he fights a series of battles in Austria, then returns to Paris a national hero. After spending a few years in the Middle East on his Egyptian Campaign—which was at best a marginal success— he returns to France and takes part in a coup d'état that ends up with him as the First Consul of the new French government.

"A year later he takes an army across the Pennine Alps to wage the Second Italian Campaign—"

Remi said, "The famous painting of him on the horse . . ."

"Right," replied Selma. "Sitting atop a rearing horse, chin set, arm pointed into the distance . . . The truth is a little different, though. First of all, most people think that horse's name was Marengo, but it was actually known at that time as Styrie; its name was changed after the Battle of Marengo a few months later. And here's the kicker: Napoleon actually did most of the crossing atop a mule."

"Not quite befitting his image."

"No. Anyway, after the campaign, Napoleon returns to Paris and is appointed First Consul for life—essentially open-ended benevolent dictatorship. Two years after that he proclaims himself Emperor.

"For the next decade or so he wages battles and signs treaties and so on until 1812, when he makes the mistake of invading Russia. It doesn't work out quite as he plans, and he's forced to conduct a winter withdrawal that all but decimates his Grand Army. He returns to Paris and over the next two years finds himself fighting Prussia and Spain, not only abroad, but on French soil as well. Soon after that, Paris falls. The Senate declares Napoleon's empire dead and in the spring of 1814 he abdicates his rule to Louis XVIII of the Bourbon line. A month later, Napoleon is exiled to Elba and his wife and son flee to Vienna—"

"Not Josephine, right?" Sam asked.

"Right. Pulling a page from Henry VIII's book, Napoleon divorced her in 1809 because she failed to give him a male heir. He married the daughter of the Emperor of Austria, Marie Louise, who managed to produce a son."

"Okay, go on."

"About a year after he was exiled Napoleon escapes, returns to France, and puts together an army. Louis XVIII flees the throne and Napoleon takes over again. This was the start of what historians call the Hundred Days Campaign—though it didn't even last that long. Not quite three months later, in June, Napoleon is routed by the British and Prussians at the Battle of Waterloo. Napoleon abdicates again and is exiled by the British to Saint Helena—a chunk of rock about twice the size of Washington, D.C., dead center in the Atlantic Ocean between West Africa and Brazil. He spends the remaining six years of his life there and dies in 1821."

"Of stomach cancer," Sam offered.

"That's the generally accepted theory, but there are a lot of historians who believe he was murdered—arsenic poisoning.

"So," Selma concluded, "that brings us back to the Lost Cellar: The myth dates back to 1852 and the alleged deathbed confession of a smuggler named Lionel Arienne, who claimed that in June of 1820, eleven months before Napoleon died, he was approached by an agent of Napoleon's at a tavern in Le Havre. The soldier—who Arienne simply referred to as 'the Major'—hired Arienne and his ship, the *Faucon*, to take him to Saint Helena, where they were to pick up cargo, then deliver it to a destination to be named after they left the island.

"According to Arienne, when they reached Saint Helena six weeks later they were met in a small cove by a lone man in a rowboat, who carried aboard a wooden case, roughly two feet long and a foot wide. With his back facing Arienne, the Major opened the case, inspected its contents, resealed it, then suddenly drew his sword and killed the man from the rowboat. The body was weighted with a length of anchor chain, then dumped overboard. The rowboat was scuttled.

"It was at this point in Arienne's telling of the story that the old smuggler was said to have simply died—in midsentence, no less— taking with him any clue as to the contents of the case or where he and the Major took it. And that might have been the end of it," Selma said, "if not for Lacanau."

"The name of Napoleon's private vineyard," Sam offered.

"Correct. While Arienne and the phantom Major were supposedly on their way to Helena, the vineyard at Lacanau—which the French government had generously allowed to remain as part of Napoleon's estate—was burned to the ground by person or persons unknown. The vines, the winery, all the casks—utterly destroyed. Even the soil was obliterated, dosed with salt and lye."

"As well as the seeds, right?" Remi said.

"Those, too. Actually the name 'Lacanau' was one of convenience. In fact, the Lacanau vineyard grapes came from seeds taken from the Corsican regions of the Ajaccio Patrimonio. Napoleon had Archambault cross-pollinate the seeds to create the Lacanau strain.

"Anyway, while he was still in power, Napoleon ordered the seeds for the Lacanau grape to be kept in secure repositories at Amiens, Paris, and Orléans. According to legend, while the fires were raging at Lacanau, the seeds mysteriously disappeared and were assumed destroyed. The Lacanau grape, which grew only in that coastal region of France, was gone forever."

Remi said, "For argument's sake let's say all of this isn't just a folktale. What we're getting at is this: From exile, Napoleon, via secret messenger or carrier pigeon or whatever, ordered Henri Archambault, his chief winemaker, to produce a final batch of Lacanau wine and have it delivered to Saint Helena, then he orders his loyalist operatives back in France to raze the vineyard, ruin the soil, then kidnap and destroy the seeds. Then a few months later he orders this . . . Major to sail to Helena and spirit—no pun intended—the wine away to points unknown." Remi looked at Sam and Selma in turn. "Have I got that right?"

"Sounds about right," Sam said.

The three of them paused for ten seconds, staring at the bottle on the table with new eyes.

"How much is it worth?" Remi asked Selma.

"Well, the story has it there were twelve bottles in the case the Major and Arienne took from Saint Helena, and it seems likely that one of the bottles is already broken. If the case were intact . . . I'd say nine or ten million dollars—to the right kind of buyer, of course. But the case isn't intact, so that really brings down the price. If I had to guess . . . I'd say each bottle would be worth between six and seven hundred thousand dollars."

"For a bottle of wine," Remi breathed.

"Not to mention the historical and scientific value," Sam said. "We're talking about a strain of grape that is in all likelihood extinct."

"So what do you want to do?" Selma asked.

"We have to assume Scarface is after the wine rather than the *UM-34*," Sam said.

"And he didn't strike me as a connoisseur," Remi added.

"Which means he's working for someone. I'll make some calls, pull in some favors, and see what we can find out. In the meantime, Selma, call Pete and Wendy and fill them in. Remi?"

"Agreed. Selma, you stay on the Lacanau angle. We need to know everything about it, about the bottle, about Henri Archambault— you know what to do."

Selma was jotting notes. "I'm on it."

Sam said, "When Pete and Wendy get here and they're up to speed, turn them loose on Napoleon and his mysterious Major. Anything and everything."

"Got it. There's one thing that's been nagging me, though. The crushed-beetle ink on this label came from the Tuscan Archipelago in the Ligurian Sea."

Sam realized what she was getting at. "Which is where Elba is."

"Which," Remi said, chiming in, "is where Napoleon spent his first exile. Six years *before* Arienne claims he and the Major arrived at St. Helena to pick up the wine."

"Either Napoleon had been planning this since Elba or he brought the ink with him to St. Helena," Sam said. "We may never know. Selma, get started on your end."

"Okay. And you two?"

"We've got some reading to do," Remi replied. "This bottle was aboard the *UM-34*, left there by Manfred Boehm. We find out where the *UM-34* and Boehm started, we find out where the bottle came from."

They worked on Boehm's diary and the *UM-34*'s log late into the night, Remi jotting notes she thought might help them better understand the man; Sam trying to retrace the *UM-34*'s course backward from its final resting place.

"Here," Remi said, straightening in her chair and tapping the diary. "This is what we've been looking for: Wolfgang Müller. Listen to this entry: 'August 3, 1944: For the first time as brothers in arms Wolfi and I ship out together tomorrow. I pray God we succeed and prove worthy of our commands.' "

"Brothers in *arms*," Sam repeated, "and the man with the other bottle. So Müller was also in the Kriegsmarine—Boehm the captain of the *UM-34*, Müller the captain of . . . what? Gertrude, perhaps? Boehm's mother ship?"

"Perhaps." Remi picked up her cell phone and called down to the workshop. "Selma, can you work your magic on something for us? We need anything you can dig up on a World War II Kriegsmarine sailor named Wolfgang Müller. In summer or fall of 1944 he might have commanded a ship of some kind. Right, thanks."

True to her reputation, Selma called back thirty minutes later. Remi put her on speakerphone.

"Found him," she said. "You want the short or long version?"

"Short for now," Sam replied.

"*Fregattenkapitän* Wolfgang Müller, born 1910 in Munich. Joined the Kriegsmarine in 1934. Standard promotions, no disciplinary action. In 1944 he was assigned to captain the auxiliary ship *Lothringen*. Home port was listed as Bremerhaven, her duty area the Atlantic. According to Germany's naval archive database, *Lothringen* was orginally laid down as a French ferry named *Londres*. The Germans captured it in 1940 and converted it into a mine layer. It was reassigned for 'special duty' in July of 1944, but there was no mention of the particulars."

"A mine layer?" Remi said. "Why would they—"

"By that time in the war the Germans were losing and they knew it—everyone but Hitler, that was," Selma said. "They were desperate. The kinds of auxiliary ships they would have normally used to transport the *UM-34* had either been sunk or converted into troop escorts.

"I also found a website entitled Survivors of the *Lothringen*, along with a fair number of blogs dedicated to the subject. It seems the *Lothringen* was attacked and disabled during a storm by a U.S. Navy destroyer in September of 1944 off Virginia Beach."

"About fifty miles south of Pocomoke Sound," Remi said.

"Right. Only about half the *Lothringen*'s crew survived the attack. Those who did spent the remainder of the war in a Wisconsin POW camp called Camp Lodi. The *Lothringen* was towed to Norfolk and sold to Greece after the war. As far as I can tell, there's no record of it ever being scrapped."

"What about Müller? Any idea what happened to him?"

"Nothing yet. Still looking. One of the *Lothringen* blogs, run by the granddaughter of a survivor named Froch, is sort of a diary in itself. The entries talk a lot about the weeks leading up to the attack. If we're to believe the account, the *Lothringen* spent about a month undergoing a refit at a secret German base in the Bahamas and frolicking with the native girls. Someplace called Rum Cay."

"Selma, did the *Lothringen* have facilities to do refitting?"

"Not even close. The best it could have done was simply strap the *UM-34* to the deck, cover it in a tarp to keep it hidden from prying eyes, then transport it across the Atlantic."

"That would explain why they didn't do whatever refitting was required at sea," Remi said.

"True, but why didn't they do the refit in Bremerhaven before they left? Maybe they were in a hurry. As I said, they were getting desperate by that point."

"Wait a second," Sam blurted out, then grabbed the *34*'s logbook and began paging through it. "Here, right here! At the beginning of his log Boehm mentions a place, but only by initials: R.C."

"Rum Cay," Remi murmured.

"Has to be."

"It fits," Selma agreed.

Sam looked questioningly at Remi, who smiled and nodded back. "Okay, Selma, time to put on your travel-agent hat. Get us on the next flight to Nassau."

"Will do."

"And a rental car," Sam added. "Something fast and sexy."

"I like your style," Remi said with a sly smile.

CHAPTER 13

NASSAU, BAHAMAS

Selma had donned her travel-agent hat with characteristic profi-
ciency, reserving them a pair of first-class seats on the last red-eye
out of San Diego heading east. Seven hours and one layover later
they touched down at Nassau International Airport shortly after
noon. They had less luck with their rental car, however, ending up
with a bright red Volkswagen Beetle convertible, which Selma swore
was the sexiest and fastest car in all of the Bahamas. Sam suspected
Remi had bribed their research chief, but said nothing until they
were pulling out of the parking lot and were passed by a Corvette
bearing an Avis sticker.

"Did you see that?" Sam said, glancing over his shoulder.

"It's for your own good, Sam," Remi said, patting him on the knee.
"Trust me." She put her hand atop her white sun hat to keep it from
whipping away and leaned her head back, basking in the tropical sun.

Sam grumbled something in reply.

"What was that?" Remi asked.

"Nothing."

Waiting for them at the Four Seasons Resort reception desk was a message:

Have information. Call landline ASAP.
—R

"Rube?" Remi asked.

Sam nodded. "Why don't you go to the villa? I'll see what he has to say, then join you."

"Okay."

Sam found a quiet corner in the lobby's seating area and hit speed dial on his satellite phone. Rubin Haywood picked up on the first ring.

"It's me, Rube."

"Hang on, Sam." There was a click, followed by a hissing squelch as Rube engaged what Sam assumed was some kind of encryption device. "How are you?"

"Great. Thanks for this. I owe you one."

"No, you don't."

Haywood and Sam went back twelve years, since Sam's early days at DARPA, having met at the CIA's Camp Perry training facility in the wilds of the Virginia countryside near Williamsburg. Haywood, a case officer in the CIA's Directorate of Operations, was going through covert operative training. Sam was there for the same purpose, but as part of an experimental program designed to put DARPA's best and brightest through the kind of real-world scenarios CIA officers experience in the field. The idea was simple: The better DARPA's engineers could understand what field work was really like—hands on and up close—the better they would be at creating gadgets and tools that met real-world challenges.

Sam and Rube had instantly bonded, their friendship cemented over the six long weeks of training, and they'd stayed in touch ever since, meeting once a year in the fall for a three-day hiking trip through the Sierra Nevada.

"Everything I'm going to tell you is unclassified—at least officially."

Sam read between the lines. After receiving his call, Rube had in turn made his own calls, tapping contacts and sources outside the government. "Okay. Your message said ASAP."

"Yeah. The name of the guy you call Scarface used a pretty heavily backstopped credit card attached to dummy accounts to rent the boat in Snow Hill, so it took a little digging. His name is Grigoriy Arkhipov. Ex–Russian special forces, spent time in both Afghanistan and Chechnya. He and his right-hand man, a guy named Kholkov, left the army in '94 and went freelance. Arkhipov you're familiar with, but I'll e-mail you a picture of Kholkov. If you haven't seen him around yet, you will. As far as we can tell they've worked for just one man since '05, a real nasty piece of work named Hadeon Bondaruk."

"I've heard the name."

"I'd be surprised if you hadn't," Rube replied. "He's the kingpin of the Ukrainian mafia and the toast of Sevastopol high society. He throws parties and hunt weekends at his estate several times a year and restricts his guest list to the überwealthy—politicians, celebrities, European royalty. . . . He's never been charged with a crime, but is suspected of dozens of murders—mostly other crime bosses and enforcers who for whatever reason made him mad. Other than rumors there's not much out there about his past."

"I love gossip," Sam said. "Let's hear it."

"Rumor is he commanded a cell of guerrilla fighters in Turkmenistan during that whole Russian-Iranian border mess. Moved around the mountains like a ghost, ambushing patrols and convoys, never leaving anyone alive."

"A real Samaritan."

"Yeah. So, what's your interest in him?"

"I think he's after the same thing we are."

"Which is?"

"Better you not know, Rube. You've stuck your neck out far enough already."

"Sam, come on—"

"Just leave it, Rube. Please."

Haywood paused, then sighed. "Okay, you're the boss. But listen: You've been lucky so far, but your luck could run out in a big hurry."

"I know."

"Will you at least let me help you? I know a guy down there you should see. You got a pen?" Sam grabbed a pad from the end table and took down the name and address Rube recited. "I trust him. Go see him."

"Will do."

"And for God's sake, take care of yourselves, you hear me?"

"I hear you. We've been through some tough scrapes together, Remi and I. We'll handle this one."

"How exactly?"

"Easy. We're going stay one step ahead of them."

———

Three hours later Sam pulled the Beetle off the coast road into a small gravel parking lot and eased to a stop beside a rusted Quonset hut topped by a windsock and bearing a faded hand-painted sign: AIR SAMPSON. Fifty yards to the right was another Quonset hut, this one larger, and through the sliding double doors they could see the nose of an airplane. On the other side of the hangar was a landing strip composed of crushed seashells.

"This is it?" Remi asked, eyes narrowed.

Sam checked the map. "Yep, this is it. Selma swears it's the best charter place on the island."

"If she says so."

"Are you really going to bring that thing?" she asked, nodding to the towel-draped object lying on the floor between Sam's feet.

After hanging up with Rube, Sam had gone to the villa and recounted the conversation to Remi, who listened carefully and asked no questions.

"I don't want to see you get hurt," she said finally, taking his hands in hers.

"And I don't want to see you get hurt. It'd be the end of my world."

"Then let's not get hurt. Like you said, we'll just stay one step ahead of them. And if things get too rough—"

"We'll call in the good guys and go home."

"Sure we will," she replied.

Before coming to the airstrip, after leaving the hotel they'd first followed Rube's address to a shoe-repair shop in downtown Nassau, where they found that the owner and Rube's contact, Guido, was expecting them.

"Rubin wasn't sure you would come," Guido said in slightly Italian-accented English. "He said you were both very stubborn."

"Did he now?"

"Yes, oh, yes."

Guido walked to the front door, flipped over the Out to Lunch sign, then led them into the back room and down a set of stone steps into the basement, which was lit by a single hanging lightbulb. Lying on a bench amid shoes in various states of disrepair was a snub-nosed .38-caliber revolver.

"You both have handled guns, yes?"

"Yes," Sam replied, answering for both of them.

In fact, Remi was a damned good marksman and had no fear of handling guns, but tried to avoid them if at all possible.

"Good," Guido answered. "No serial numbers on the gun. Untraceable. You may throw it away when you are done." He wrapped the gun in a towel along with a box of fifty bullets, then handed it to Sam. "One favor, if you don't mind?"

"Name it," Sam said.

"Don't kill anyone."

Sam smiled. "That's the last thing in the world we want to do. How much do we owe you?"

"No, please, nothing. A friend of Rubin's is a friend of mine."

Sam now asked, "You want me to leave it?"

"No, I guess not. Better safe than sorry."

They got out, collected their backpacks from the trunk, then went into the Quonset hut. A black man in his late sixties sat behind the counter on a lawn chair, a cigar jutting from his mouth.

"Well, hello there," he said, rising to his feet. "I am Sampson, owner, operator, chief bottle-washer." He spoke perfect Oxford English.

Sam introduced them, then said, "Not from around these parts, I take it?"

"Born in London. Came here ten years ago to live the good life. So, you're going to Rum Cay?"

"Right."

"Business or pleasure?"

"Both," Remi said. "Bird watching . . . photography. You know."

Sam handed over his pilot's license and filled out the required forms. Sampson looked over the forms, then nodded. "Overnight?"

"Probably."

"You've booked a hotel there?"

Sam shook his head. "We're roughing it. You should have gotten a delivery yesterday—tent, potable water, camping gear. . . ." Guided by one of her dozens of mental checklists, Selma had arranged a full load of gear for their trek, from the absolute necessities to the "what-ifs."

Sampson was nodding. "I did. It's already loaded." He pulled a clipboard off a nail on the wall, jotted a note, then returned it. "I've got you in a Bonanza G36, fueled and checked."

"Pontoons?"

"As requested. Head over to the hangar and Charlie will send you on your way."

They turned and headed for the door. Sampson called, "What kind of birds you hoping to spot?"

They turned back.

Sam shrugged and smiled. "Whatever is native to the island."

CHAPTER 14

RUM CAY, BAHAMAS

Comprising as the island did an area of less than thirty square miles, finding a hidden base on Rum Cay might at first glance appear a fairly straightforward task to uninitiated adventurers, but Sam and Remi had been down similar roads before and knew the coastline, uneven as it was with hundreds of coves and inlets, was in reality at least six times the island's gross circumference.

Originally known as Mamana by the local Lucayan Indians, the island was renamed Santa Maria de la Concepción by Christopher Columbus, finally gaining its modern name when Spanish explorers found a lone cask of rum washed up on one of its white sand beaches.

The island's only village of note, Port Nelson, lay on the island's northwest coast surrounded by groves of coconut trees. With a population that, according to the 1990 census, was somewhere between fifty and seventy souls—most of whom lived in Port Nelson—Rum Cay's primary, if anemic, industry was tourism, followed by pineapple, salt, and sisal, all of which have waxed and waned over the decades. Other settlements, long since deserted and overgrown, bore exotic monikers like Black Rock and Gin Hill. Formidable reefs, coral canyons, and plunging seabeds encircle the island, making it a favored destination for pirates of old—or so said the brochure Remi had picked up in Nassau.

"There's even a famous wreck," she said as Sam banked the Bonanza to the right, following the contour of the island.

However unlikely they were to spot their target from the air, both thought it prudent to at least circumnavigate the island to get a better feel for what lay ahead.

"Blackbeard?" Sam asked. "Captain Kidd?"

"Neither. The HMS *Conqueror*, Britain's first propeller-driven warship. Sank in 1861 in about thirty feet of water in a staghorn gully near Sumner Point Reef."

"Sounds like it may be worth a return trip here."

Rum Cay offered a few luxury resorts and even more beach cottage rentals. Judging by the azure waters, lush rolling hills, and relative seclusion, it struck Sam as the perfect get-away-from-it-all spot.

"There's the airstrip," Remi said, pointing out the window.

The 4,500-foot paved runway sat a couple miles from Port Nelson, a truncated white T amid a patch of forest that seemed determined to reclaim it. Sam could see antlike workers at the tarmac's edge, hacking at the foliage with machetes. Just east of the runway they could see Salt Lake, and a few miles north of that, Lake George.

Though Sam had no fear of using the airstrip, they had asked Selma to ensure whatever aircraft they rented was equipped with pontoons. Exploring the island by car would have taken weeks at least and required miles of cross-country bushwhacking. With the pontoons, they could hop around the island's shoreline, exploring interesting spots as they came across them.

Sam descended to two thousand feet, contacted Port Nelson Control, which verified their flight plan and permission, then banked around the northeast headland and turned south along the coast. As the least-inhabited part of the island, he and Remi thought it the best place to start their search. As the western half of the island was well explored and well populated—at least by Rum Cay standards—any discovery of the secret base would have been noted by now. Selma hadn't come across any such reports, so Sam and Remi took this as a good sign. Providing the secret base wasn't simply the concoction of some senile German Kriegsmarine.

"That looks like it'd make a good base of operations," Sam said, nodding through the windshield at a three-quarter moon cove with sugar-white beaches. The nearest structure, what looked like an abandoned plantation house, sat six miles inland.

Sam banked again, bleeding off speed and altitude as he went until they were two hundred feet off the waves, then lined up the Bonanza's nose on the beach. He did a quick visual check to make sure he hadn't missed seeing a reef, then eased the craft down, flaring at the last moment and letting the pontoons kiss the surface. He throttled back to idle, letting the plane's momentum carry them forward. The pontoons hissed as they contacted the shoal sand and they came to a gentle stop six feet onto dry land.

"Beautiful landing, Mr. Lindbergh," Remi said, unbuckling her seat belt.

"I like to think all my landings are beautiful."

"Of course they are, dear. Except for that time in Peru . . ."

"Never mind."

Remi climbed out onto the beach and Sam handed down their backpacks and the duffel bags containing their camping gear. Sam's satellite phone trilled and he answered.

"Mr. Fargo, it's Selma."

"Good timing. We just touched down. Hold on." Sam called Remi over and put the phone on speaker. "First things first: You're buttoned up?"

After learning the pedigrees of Bondaruk, Arkhipov, and Kholkov from Rube, Sam had ordered Selma, Pete, and Wendy to move into the Goldfish Point house and set the alarm system, which Sam had long ago tweaked to satisfy his engineer's mind; the system, he knew, would give a CIA black-bag team a run for its money. And, as luck would have it, the San Diego Commissioner of Police and Sam's thrice-weekly judo partner lived a half mile from them. Squad cars were on quick-response alert for their neighborhood.

"Safe and sound," Selma replied.

"How goes the battle?"

"We're getting there. Should have some interesting reading for you when you get home. First, some good news: I figured out what the bug is on the bottom of the bottle. It's from Napoleon's family coat of arms. On the right side of the coat is what looks like a bee. Though there's some debate about this among historians, most believe it isn't a bee at all, but a golden cicada—or at least that's what it was in the beginning. The symbol was first discovered in 1653 in the tomb of Childeric I, the first king of the Merovingian dynasty. It represents immortality and resurrection."

"Immortality and resurrection," Remi repeated. "A tad conceited—but then again we are talking about Napoleon."

"Let me get this straight," Sam said. "Napoleon's signature icon is a grasshopper?"

"Close, but not exactly," Selma said. "Different branch of the family tree. The cicada is more closely related to leafhoppers and spittlebugs."

Sam laughed. "Ah, yes, the royal spittlebug."

"Between the cicada and Henri Archambault's mark, there's no doubt the bottle's from the Lost Cellar."

"Good work," Sam said. "What else?"

"I also finished dissecting the translation of Manfred Boehm's diary. There's a line in there about 'the Goat's Head' . . . ?"

"I remember," Remi replied. Both she and Sam had assumed it had been a Rum Cay tavern Boehm and his shipmates had visited.

"Well, I massaged the translation a bit, using both High and Low German, and I think the Goat's Head is a landmark of some kind—maybe a navigation aid. Problem is, I did some digging and I couldn't find anything about a Goat's Head related to Rum Cay—or any of the other islands, for that matter."

"We'll keep our eyes peeled," Sam replied. "If you're right, it's likely a rock formation of some kind."

"Agreed. And last, I owe you guys an apology."

"For?"

"An error."

"Say it isn't so."

Selma rarely made mistakes and those that she did were almost always minor. Even so, she was a strict taskmaster—more so with herself than anyone else.

"I was slightly off in translating the abstract from the German naval archives. Wolfgang Müller wasn't the captain of the *Lothringen*. He was a passenger, just like Boehm. Another sub captain, in fact. He was assigned to the midget sub *UM-77*."

"So Boehm and Müller and their subs are aboard the *Lothringen*, which sails across the Atlantic, puts in at Rum Cay for resupply and refit—"

"That's the word the sailor—Froch—used in his blog, correct?"

"Correct. Refit."

"Then a week later, Boehm's boat, the *UM-34* ends up in the Pocomoke River and the *Lothringen* is sunk. Which begs the question, where is Müller's sub, the *UM-77*?"

"According to the German archives, it's listed as lost. According to U.S. Navy archives, they found nothing aboard the *Lothringen* when it was captured."

Remi replied, "Which means the *UM-77* probably went down on its own mission—something similar to Boehm's mission, I'm betting."

"I agree," Sam said, "but there's also a third possibility."

"Which is?"

"She's still here. It's the word 'refit' that got my attention. The *Lothringen* was what, one hundred fifty feet long?"

"About that," Selma replied.

"To refit a ship that big would have taken a fair-sized facility—something big enough that it would have been discovered by now. I'm beginning to think the refitting they mentioned was for the *UM-34* and the *UM-77*, and if we're right about their mission being top secret, they sure as hell weren't going to do that in the open—not with U.S. Navy PBY spotter planes flying out of Puerto Rico."

"Which means . . . ?" Remi asked.

"Which means we may have some spelunking in our future," Sam replied.

———————

They finished unloading the Bonanza, then staked her tie-downs deep into the sand and started looking for a campsite. Nightfall was only a few hours away. They'd get a fresh start in the morning.

"We've got a competitor," Remi said, pointing down the beach.

Sam shaded his eyes with his palm and squinted. "Well, that's not something you see every day."

A quarter mile away, nestled against the tree line along the cove's northern arm, was what looked for all the world like a Hollywood version of a tiki hut, complete with a thatched conical roof and plank walls. Hanging between the hut's two front posts was a hammock; in it was a figure, one foot dangling over the edge, rocking the hammock back and forth. Without looking up the figure raised a hand in greeting and called, "Ahoy."

Sam and Remi walked the remaining distance. In front of the hut was a fire pit surrounded by wave-worn logs for seating. "Welcome," the man said.

He looked distinguished if not a bit weathered, with white hair, a well-trimmed goatee, and twinkling blue eyes.

"Don't mean to intrude," Sam said.

"Nonsense. Wanderers are always welcome, and you two certainly look the part. Have a seat."

Sam and Remi dropped their gear in the sand and found seats on a log. Sam introduced themselves to their host, who simply said, "Happy to have you. In fact, I'm going to turn the estate over to you. Time to move on."

"Don't go on our account," Remi said.

"Nothing of the sort, dear lady. I've got a previous engagement in Port Henry. Won't be back for a couple days."

With that the man disappeared into the trees and emerged a few seconds later pushing a Vespa scooter. "There's a fishing pole, lures, pots, pans, and all that inside," he said. "Make yourselves at home. There's a trapdoor wine cellar. You're welcome to try a bottle."

Sam, strangely certain he could trust this stranger, said, "You haven't heard any legends about a secret base around here, have you?"

"A Nazi submarine base, yes?"

"That's the one."

The man put the scooter up onto its kickstand. He went inside the hut and came back out carrying what looked like a tray-sized square of sheet metal. He handed it to Sam.

"To carry our dinner?" Sam asked.

"That's a hydroplane, son. From a pretty small sub, too, by the looks of it."

"Where did you find this?"

"Liberty Rock, on the north side near Port Boyd."

"Sounds like the place to start looking."

"I found that in a lagoon. My guess is it washed out of an underground river. Here on the east side of the island they all flow south to north. Problem is, they're not strong enough to push anything heavier than that plane."

"No offense," Remi said, "but if you knew what this belonged to, why haven't you looked for it yourself?"

The man smiled. "I've done my fair share of exploring. I figured sooner or later someone would come along asking the right questions. And here you are." The man walked toward his scooter, then stopped and turned back. "You know, if I'd been a German sailor back then looking for a place to hide out, I would've loved to have stumbled across a sea cave."

"Me, too," Sam said.

"As luck would have it, Rum Cay is full of them. Dozens along this shore alone, most unexplored—most connected to underground rivers."

"Thanks. By the way, ever heard of anything called the Goat's Head?"

The man scratched his chin. "Can't say I have. Well, I'm off. Good hunting."

The man puttered off on the scooter and disappeared.

Sam and Remi were silent for a few moments, then Sam said, "I'll be damned."

"What?"

"We didn't even think to get his name."

"I don't think we need it," Remi said, pointing at the hut.

Beside the door was a wooden plaque. In hand-painted red letters it said, CASA DE CUSSLER.

CHAPTER 15

I could get used to this," Sam said, staring into the fire.

"I'll second that," Remi replied.

They'd decided to accept their host's invitation to spend the night at the hut. As the sun dipped toward the horizon Sam strolled the beach and gathered burnable driftwood while Remi used their host's collapsible bamboo fishing rod to snag a trio of snapper from the surf. By the time night fell they were lying against a log before a crackling campfire, their stomachs full of braised and sea-salted fish. The night was clear and black, with diamond-speck stars filling the sky. Aside from the *swoosh-hiss* of the surf and the occasional rustling of palm fronds, all was quiet.

Their host hadn't been joking about the wine cellar, which, though barely larger than a closet, sported two dozen bottles. They'd chosen a Jordan Chardonnay to complement Remi's catch.

They sat and sipped and watched the stars until finally Remi said, "You think they'll find us?"

"Who, Arkhipov and Kholkov? Not likely."

For the airline tickets, the hotel, and the rental car they'd used a credit card attached to a twice-removed Fargo Foundation expense account. While Sam had no doubt Bondaruk's hatchet men had the resources to eventually unravel the financial trail, it wouldn't happen, he hoped, before they were gone.

"Unless," he added, "they already have a lead that points them here."

"There's a cheery notion. Sam, I've been thinking about Ted. That Russian—Arkhipov—he was going to kill him, wasn't he?"

"I suspect so."

"Over wine. What kind of man would do that? If Rube's right, Bondaruk's filthy rich. What he'd gain from selling the Lost Cellar would be pocket change. Why is he willing to kill for it?"

"Remi, for him murder comes naturally. It's not a last resort; it's a ready option."

"I suppose."

"But you're not convinced."

"It just doesn't add up. Is Bondaruk a wine collector? A Napoleonophile, maybe?"

"I don't know. We'll check."

She shook her head, frustrated. After a few moments of silence, she asked, "So where do we start?"

"We have to make some assumptions," Sam replied. "First, that Selma's right about the Goat's Head being a landmark; and second, that Boehm and his team would have chosen the most uninhabited part of the island to set up shop. This coastline certainly fits the bill. At first light, we pile our gear into the dinghy—"

"Not the plane?"

"Don't think so. Boehm's vantage point would have been from the surface. From the air a goat's head could look like a duck's foot, or a donkey's ear, or nothing at all."

"Good point. Erosion's going to be a problem. Sixty years of weather could change a lot."

"True."

The Bahamian Archipelago was a spelunking and cave-diving paradise, Sam knew, and there were four general types of cave systems: blue holes, which came in both the open ocean and inshore variety and were essentially great tubes plunging hundreds of feet into the ocean or an island's rock strata; fracture-guided caves, which followed the natural fissures in the bedrock; solutional caves, which formed over time by rainwater mixing with minerals in the soil to dissolve the underlying limestone or calcium carbonate bedrock; and finally, garden-variety sea caves, formed along cliffs by thousands of years of pounding surf. While these systems rarely went any deeper than a hundred feet, they were also usually spacious and offered sheltered underwater entrances—precisely what one might look for when scouting for a spot to hide a mini submarine.

"You missed one," Remi said. "An assumption, I mean."

"Which is?"

"That all this isn't just a goose chase—or to be exact, a wild Molch hunt."

They woke at dawn, had a breakfast of wild grape, fig, and pigeon plums, all of which they found growing wild within a hundred yards of the hut, then piled their gear into the inflatable dinghy and set out. The trolling motor wasn't going to help them set any speed records, but it was fuel efficient and powerful enough to get through the reef line and to navigate the inshore tides. By the time the sun had lifted free of the horizon, they were tooling north along the coast, parallel to the reef line. The water was a crystalline turquoise, so clear they could see rainbow-hued fish skimming along the white sand bottom twenty feet below.

As Sam steered, staying as close to the shore as possible, which ranged from fifty to one hundred yards, Remi sat in the bow, alternately scanning the cliffs through her binoculars and taking shots with her digital SLR camera. Occasionally she would call for Sam to come about and make a repeat pass of a rock formation as she tilted her head and squinted her eyes and took more pictures before eventually shaking her head and giving him the okay to proceed.

The hours and the coastline slipped by until around noon they found themselves nearing the island's headland and Junkanoo Rock;

beyond that, on the northern shoreline, lay Port Boyd and the island's more populous western areas. Sam turned the dinghy around and they headed south.

"We've probably already passed dozens of sea caves," Remi said.

This was true. Many of the cliff faces they'd surveyed were shrouded in climbing vines and scrub foliage that jutted from every nook and cranny. From this distance they could be seeing a cave entrance and never know it. They had little choice, however. Slipping inside each reef break and checking every foot of every cliff would take years. More frustrating still was that most of their search had so far occurred during low tide, which should have given them the best chance to spot an opening.

Suddenly Remi sat up straighter and cocked her head, a posture Sam knew only too well: His wife had had a eureka moment.

"What?" he asked.

"I think we're going about this the wrong way. We're assuming Boehm used this Goat's Head as a navigation aid while test-driving the Molch before the mission, correct? They'd want to test out any refit work they'd done, wouldn't they?"

"I'd hope so."

"And close to shore, they wouldn't have risked grounding the sub by diving, which meant the Molch probably didn't roam too far. . . ."

The Molch's mothership, the *Lothringen*, would have been equipped with an advanced open-ocean navigation system, but not so the mini submarine, which would have relied on speed-distance dead reckoning and, quite likely, visual aids.

"Right again."

"So what if the only time Boehm would have to rely on a landmark was when he was coming back in—from a test dive."

"From offshore," Sam finished. "Inshore, a goat's head might not look like a goat's head, but from a mile or two out to sea . . ."

Remi was smiling and nodding.

Sam brought the dinghy about and pointed the nose toward open ocean.

Once they were about a mile out, they repeated their tour of the coastline, heading back the way they'd come, past their landing beach toward the southeastern tip of the island, Signal Point, and Port Nelson, where they turned around and headed north again.

By three thirty, tired, thirsty, and slightly sunburned despite their hats and repeated coatings of BullFrog sunscreen, they were a mile from the northern headland when Remi, who was studying the coast through her binoculars, held up a closed fist. Sam throttled down to an idle and waited. Remi turned in her seat and leaned back to hand Sam the binoculars.

"Take a look at that cliff." She pointed. "Bearing about two-eight-zero relative."

Sam aimed the binoculars and panned along the rock face.

"See the two banyan trees sitting next to one another?" Remi said.

"Hold on . . . okay, I see them."

"Imagine them sixty years ago, about a third their size with less branches. Add a little dimension to the rock . . ."

Sam made the illusive adjustment and looked again, but after ten seconds shook his head. "Sorry."

"Squint," Remi offered.

He did and suddenly, as if someone had flipped a switch, he saw it. Six decades of erosion had in fact softened the bump in the cliff, but there was no doubt: Combined, the outcropping and the twin banyans formed the vague profile of a goat's face topped by a pair of overgrown and tangled horns.

The question was, were they seeing what they wanted to see, the victims of self-suggestion, or was there really something there? One look at Remi's face told him she was wondering the same thing.

"One way to find out," he said.

The break in the reef was narrow, less than eight feet wide, and with high tide and churn, the top of the coral was submerged just enough to be invisible at a distance but close enough to the surface to rip the dinghy's rubber skin to shreds should Sam stray.

Remi sat in the bow, arms braced on the side walls as she leaned forward and peered into the water.

"Left . . . left . . . left," she called. "Okay, straighten out. Steady on . . ."

On either side of the dinghy, through the froth Sam could see dagger-edged coral just beneath the turquoise surface. He jinked the throttle and rudder, searching for that delicate balance between steerageway and power; not enough of the former and he couldn't avoid being pushed onto the coral; too much of the latter and he couldn't respond to Remi's signals.

"Good . . . hard right!"

Sam pushed the rudder over and the dinghy veered just as a wave broke on the reef and knocked the stern around. "Hold on!" He powered up and compensated.

"Left . . . a little more . . . more . . ."

"How far to go?"

"Ten more feet and we're through."

Sam looked over his shoulder. A swell was rising twenty feet behind them, building up on the reef's outer edge.

"Gonna get hit," Sam called. "Brace yourself!"

"Almost there . . . veer right, straight now . . . good. Give it all you've got!"

Sam cranked the throttle to its stops just as the wave broke under the dinghy's stern. Sam felt his belly lurch into his throat. For a brief second the prop lifted free of the water with a sputtering whine, then the dinghy was slapped back onto a calm lagoon.

Remi rolled onto her back, leaned against the bow, and let out a sigh. "I'll say it again, Sam Fargo, you sure know how to show a girl a good time."

"I do what I can. Welcome to Goat's Head Lagoon."

CHAPTER 16

Paradise, dead ahead," Sam said, straightening the dinghy's nose.

After spending the past eight hours first roasting in the hot sun and then navigating a shark's mouth of a reef break, the shaded lagoon felt like paradise. Roughly one hundred feet in diameter, it was sheltered to the north and south by curved thumbs of land choked with scrub pine and palms. The cliff, which rose thirty vertical feet from the water, was blanketed in vines, foliage, and overhanging banyan trees—the two most prominent ones forming the goat's horns. To the left of the cliff lay a crescent of white sand roughly the size of a standard house deck. With the sun on its downward arc toward nightfall, the lagoon was cast in deep shade. The water was glass calm. In the canopy came a symphony of squawks and buzzes.

"Not a bad place to spend the night," Remi agreed. "Not the Four Seasons, but it does have a certain charm. The question is, are we in the right place?"

"I don't know the answer to that, but one thing's for certain: We've got a cave." Sam pointed, then turned the rudder and steered toward the cliff face, throttling down as he drew alongside it.

The water here, moving in a barely perceptible clockwise rotation, gave off a faint iridescent shimmer, which generally indicated an out-flow of fresh water. Sam dug out his dive goggles from the duffel bag at his feet, pressed them to his eyes, and dipped his face into the water, which, despite being warmed by the sun all day, felt cool on his skin. Dozens of fish darted this way and that, squabbling over in-visible bits of nutrients being stirred up by the freshwater current.

Sam lifted his head out. He dipped his fingertip into the water and brought it to his lips. It tasted only about a third as salty as true seawater.

"Underground river?" Remi asked.

"Has to be," Sam replied, shaking the water from his hair.

Though it was an uncommon phenomenon, sea caves in this area did on occasion link up with both solutional and fracture-guided caves, which in turn joined underground inland streams.

"I'll have to look at a map. I think we're only a couple miles from Lake George. I wouldn't be surprised if this system dumps out there. Or even down to Salt Lake."

"Neither would I, but if you don't mind I'd prefer we put that adventure on our 'someday' list."

"Deal." Sam checked his watch. High tide was thirty minutes away. If they were going to explore the cave, they'd have to do it within the next hour lest they find themselves fighting the full force of the outflow. Ideally, they would enter at the end of the inflow, use the forty-five– to sixty-minute window of relatively calm current to explore the cave, then ride the outflow back out. The problem was, this was not a typical closed sea cave. The source of the underground river inside would create volatile currents that could either trap them inside or suck them into fracture tunnels that led into the bowels of the island. Neither option appealed to Sam.

He put the question to Remi, who replied, "I'd rather we wait, but I know that look in your eye: You want to go in."

"Better we find out now if we're on the right track. We've got seventy-five feet of rope. We tie one end to a banyan root out here, the other end to my weight belt. If I get into trouble, I can haul myself out."

"And if you bonk your head and are out cold?"

"Every sixty seconds I'll give the line three tugs. I miss one of those and you haul me out using the dinghy."

"Time limit?"

"Ten minutes, not a second more."

Remi considered this for a few moments, narrowed her eyes at him, then sighed. "Okay, Jacques Cousteau. Remember what I said, though: If you die, I'll never forgive you."

Sam smiled and gave her a wink. "Deal."

———

Ten minutes later he was suited up and sitting in the bow. Remi glided the dinghy to a stop against the cliff. Sam, moving carefully, stood up and tied a bowline knot around a protruding root, then sat down and secured the other end to the D-ring on his weight belt. Remi reversed the dinghy and stopped ten feet from the face, using minute throttle adjustments to keep them stationary.

Sam spit in his mask, rubbed the saliva around the inside, then dipped the mask into the water and slipped it on his head, the lower edge resting just above his eyebrows. Next he slipped on his fins, punched the regulator to test the airflow, then nodded to Remi.

"Luck," she said.

"I'll be back."

He settled the mask over his eyes and rolled backward into the water.

———

He let himself hang motionless for a moment, enjoying the sudden immersion and the striking clarity of the water that filled his vision. He waited for the bubbles and froth to fully clear, then tipped himself upright and did a pike dive for the bottom, already feeling the tug of the current. He let it take him, rolling onto his side so he could watch the sun-dappled surface for a few fleeting seconds before the lip of the cliff appeared and he slipped into darkness. He clicked on his dive light and cast it around.

The cave's entrance was a rough half circle, an arch ten to twelve feet wide and twenty feet tall. At low tide, its peak probably rose only a few inches above the lagoon's surface—that, combined with the foliage blanketing the rock face, rendered it all but invisible. If not for the Goat's Head clue, they would have never found it.

He finned downward, angling for the bottom, and let his fingers trail in the sand. After twenty or so feet, the bottom suddenly dropped away into darkness. He rolled back onto his side, shined his light upward, and saw the entrance arch had disappeared, replaced by surface reflection. He checked his watch and gave the line at his waist three solid tugs: All okay, Remi.

He was suddenly enveloped by cool water and he felt a new current take hold of him, this one pushing him to the right. He realized he was spinning ever so slightly, as though being pirouetted by an unseen hand. Whirlpool, he thought with a trickle of panic. The currents of the lagoon and the underground river were colliding, the cooler water slipping beneath the warmer water, creating a hydraulic tornado. Right now he was on the outer edge of the vortex, so the current was strong, but just manageable with fins—almost two knots, he estimated—but he knew it would grow stronger toward the center. He pointed himself toward what he hoped was a wall and scissored his fins once, twice, then broke the surface.

His outstretched hand touched rock and he grasped at it, his palm bumping over the surface before his fingers found purchase on an outcropping. He jerked to a stop, his legs trailing in the circular current. He gave the line three hard tugs, then checked his watch: two minutes down, eight to go. Aside from the soft gurgle of water rushing along the walls and some dripping sounds coming from deeper within the cave, it was eerily quiet.

Using his teeth, he pulled the glove from his free hand and held his fingertips up, instantly feeling the rush of cool air on his moist skin. This was a good sign. Though he judged the possibility remote, the cave's connection to an underground river brought with it the chance of pollutants, and while they would have seen signs of toxic-

ity in the outflow—a lack of fish, discolored rocks, dead sponges—
there was also the chance of gas buildup. The brisk airflow made this
unlikely. He pulled the regulator from his mouth and took a sniff,
then a breath. All okay. He gave the line another all-okay signal,
then put his glove back on and shined the light around.

Six feet above his head he got the first indication they were on
the right track: A cross-plank catwalk suspended from the ceiling by
rusted steel cables spanned the width of the cavern and ended at the
opposite wall above a makeshift wooden pier supported by wooden
pilings sunk into the sea floor. A second catwalk joined the first at its
midpoint and extended to the rear wall at a perpendicular angle. The
setup wasn't sophisticated by any means, but clearly someone had
put some effort into the structure, and judging by the rust on the
cables and the coating of slime on the wooden planking, it had been
quite a while ago.

The cavern was oval in shape, perhaps fifty feet wide with a vaulted,
stalactite-covered ceiling that rose twenty feet above Sam's head.
Panning the light along what should have been the back wall, he saw
only darkness. He'd imagined the juncture with the underground
river would feature a gushing cleft in the wall, but he now realized
this cavern was simply an antechamber. Aside from a narrowing of
the rear walls to a diameter of thirty feet, there was no discernible
separation between this cavern and the adjoining fracture-guided
system. Where and how far it went there was no telling.

*Was this catwalk and pier system enough to service a mini subma-
rine or two?* Sam wondered. It would depend on what kind and how
much work was required, he decided. This brought up another question: Why hadn't the work been done aboard the *Lothringen* while at
sea? A question for Selma.

The line at his waist began jerking violently, and though they'd
arranged no emergency signal from Remi's end, he instinctively knew
that was exactly what she was telling him.

He slipped the regulator back between his teeth, flipped over, and
dove, then scissored hard into the entrance, pulling himself hand over
hand along the line. As the light from the lagoon's surface appeared,

he angled toward the ceiling and rolled onto his back, using his fins to keep himself away from the rock. He slipped past the entrance's leading edge and broke the surface beneath a curtain of vines.

Suppressing the urge to call Remi's name, he looked around.

The lagoon was empty.

The dinghy was gone, along with Remi.

CHAPTER 17

His rising fear turned to immediate relief as he saw a hand emerge from the undergrowth along the bank across the lagoon. The hand was pointed toward him, palm out: Wait. A second later Remi's face emerged from the foliage. She tapped her ear, pointed toward the sky, and made a vertical twirling motion with her index finger. Ten seconds passed, then twenty. A full minute. And then he heard it: the thumping of a helicopter blade, faint and then moving closer. Sam poked his head out from beneath the vines and peered into the sky, trying to localize the sound.

Directly above his head, spinning rotor blades appeared over the edge of the cliff, followed a second later by a curved Plexiglas windscreen glinting in the setting sun. The lagoon's surface rippled with the downwash, a fine mist filling the air. Sam pulled his head back; Remi wriggled back out of sight.

For what seemed like minutes but was probably less than thirty seconds the helicopter hovered over the lagoon, then banked away and headed south along the coast. Sam waited until the thumping faded away, then ducked beneath the surface and stroked hard across the lagoon until his belly touched sand. He broke the surface to find Remi's outstretched hand before his face; he grabbed it and she helped him crawl into the underbrush.

"Is it them?" she asked.

"Don't know, but I'd rather assume so than be surprised. Plus, that's an expensive bird—a Bell 430, I think. Four million at least."

"Ideally suited for a Ukrainian mafia kingpin."

"And with room enough to seat a Russian henchman and eight of his best friends. Did they see you?"

"I'm not sure. The first time it passed over it was moving fast, but it swung around almost immediately, then made two more passes. They're either curious about this spot, or they know we're here."

"Where's the dinghy?"

Remi pointed off to the left and Sam could see a few inches of gray rubber jutting from the foliage. "I got it under cover as quickly as I could."

"Good." Sam thought for a moment. "Let's get into the cave. If they decide to land and look around, that's our best hiding spot." Ears tuned for any sign of the Bell's return, Sam shed his gear and handed it over to Remi, who started putting it on.

"What're you going to do?" she asked.

"You cross the lagoon and slip into the cave and wait for me. There's a clockwise current in there, so watch yourself. Take up the slack on the rope and stay close to the entrance."

"Three tugs from my end is emergency; two for all okay, stay put."

"Got it."

"I'll bring the dinghy over and try to get it inside. We'll wait until it's dark, then see what we can see."

Remi nodded, finished donning the dive gear, took one last look around, then crawled into the water and slipped beneath the surface. Sam watched her bubble trail cross the lagoon, then slip out of sight into the cave. Next he crawled through the underbrush to where Remi had hidden the dinghy. He went still and closed his eyes, listening, but heard nothing.

After stuffing all their loose gear into their two SealLine dry bags and securing them to the cleats, he tied the dinghy's eight-foot painter line around his belt, slipped into the water, and started breast-stroking across the lagoon. He was halfway across when suddenly from the direction of the beach he heard the pounding of rotors. Even as he looked over his shoulder, the Bell appeared over the tops of the palms and stopped in a hover above him. The door was open, and a figure in dark coveralls was leaning out and looking down at him. It wasn't Frobisher's kidnapper, Arkhipov, Sam realized immediately, but the other one, whose photo Rube had e-mailed to him— Kholkov. Nor was there any mistaking the stubby cylindrical object in Kholkov's hands: *compact submachine gun*.

He took a quick gulp of air, flipped over, and dove, his head disappearing beneath the surface just as the dinghy's side tube exploded with a *whoosh*. The water rippled above him and in the corners of his eyes he saw bullets arcing through the water leaving trails of froth in their wake. The dinghy trembled with each bullet impact, popping and hissing, then collapsed in on itself and slipped beneath the surface, the trolling motor dragging it down stern first.

Sam kicked his legs hard, arms spread wide as he pushed and pulled himself toward the cave entrance. The firing stopped for two seconds—Sam thought, reloading—then resumed, peppering the surface like hail, the bullets penetrating four feet before their thrust fell off and they fell harmlessly to the bottom. Everything went dark as he slipped beneath the rock arch. The *pop-pop-pop* of gunfire and the thumping of rotors became muffled.

He rolled over and kicked upward, hand groping for the ceiling. Rope . . . rope . . . come on. . . . He felt something brush his feet: the dinghy. Sinking toward the bottom, it had been caught by the cave's inflow. He felt a tug on his belt as the painter line went taut, felt himself being dragged along. He was distantly aware of muffled gunfire continuing outside. His fingers touched the rope; he drew his dive knife from its calf sheath and sawed through it. Then he was moving, being sucked inside.

Lungs aching, head pounding from oxygen deprivation, Sam fumbled, trying to knot the rope around the knife's haft. The knife slipped from his fingers, bumped off his chest. He caught it, tried again, managed to work a square knot, then kicked for the surface and broke into air. To the right, in the corner of his eye, he saw Remi clinging to the rock wall. He felt the vortex seize him, start pulling him along.

"Sam, what—"

"Gimme all the slack you got!"

Sam tossed the knife in a high arc that took it up and over the catwalk. As it plunged into the water he was already kicking that way, hand reaching for the rope. Suddenly he was jerked away from it, toward the wall, as the dinghy was pulled deeper into the circular current.

"Remi, the rope, throw it!"

"Coming!"

He heard splashing, saw her stroking behind him. The dinghy was full deadweight now. He was jerked beneath the surface; water gushed into his mouth and nose.

"Grab it!" Remi called. "Right in front of you!"

Sam felt something brush his cheek and he slapped at it. His fingers touched the rope and he closed his fist around it. He jerked to a stop.

He caught his breath, waiting for the sparkling behind his eyes to subside, then looked over his shoulder.

Remi was hanging half out of the water from the other end of the rope. The dive light dangled from her belt loop, casting dancing shadows over the walls.

"Nice toss," Sam said.

"Thanks. Are you okay?"

"Yeah, you?"

"Just barely."

They hung still for a few moments, getting their bearings, then Sam said, "I'm going to hoist you up to the catwalk. Tie off the rope and then I'll join you."

"Right."

Remi's triweekly ninety-minute power yoga and Pilates sessions showed their value in spades as she shimmied up the rope like a monkey, then rolled onto the catwalk. The planks gave a sharp *pop*, followed by a slow splintering sound. Remi froze.

"Spread yourself flat," Sam said. "Distribute your weight—slowly."

She did so and then, using her knees and elbows, put some test pressure on the boards until satisfied none were going to give way. "I think we're okay." She shed her fins, secured them to her belt, then tied off the rope.

"I've got the dinghy and all our gear hanging from my belt," Sam said. "I'm going to try to save it."

"Okay."

Between Remi's knot and him there was only twenty feet of exposed rope; the rest was trailing in the current. Sam reeled in ten feet of rope, fashioned a temporary waist harness, and then, working by feel alone, secured a closed clove hitch around his belt and the knotted end of the painter line. Right hand clenched around the line above his head, he pulled the release loop on the harness. With a wet zipping sound, the rope went taut. It lifted from the surface, trembled for a few seconds, then steadied.

"I think it'll hold," Sam called, then climbed the rope and rolled onto the platform beside Remi. She hugged him tightly, damp hair splayed over his face.

"I guess that gunfire answered our question," she whispered.

"I'd say so."

"You sure you're not hit?" Remi asked, eyes and hands probing his chest, arms, and stomach.

"I'm sure."

"We'd better get a move on. Something tells me they're not done yet."

While Sam knew Remi was almost certainly right, he also knew they had few options: go out the way they'd come in, find another way out, fight, or hide. The first option was a nonstarter—it would play right into their pursuers' hands; the second option, a huge question mark—this cave system could be a dead end for them, both figuratively and literally; the third, also a nonstarter. While they were armed with Guido the Shoemaker's snub-nosed .38 revolver,

Kholkov and his men were armed with assault rifles. The fourth option, to hide, was their only viable chance to get out of this.

The question was, how long would their pursuers wait before following them here? They had one thing on their side, Sam realized, checking his watch. The inflow period was ending; in a few minutes the current would start flowing out again, making entry difficult.

"So this is what passes for a makeshift secret Nazi submarine pen," Remi said, shucking off the remainder of her gear.

"Probably so, but there's no way of telling until we find—"

"No, Sam, that wasn't a question. Look."

Sam turned. Remi was shining the flashlight on the rock wall above the pier. Clearly homemade out of pounded tin and paint that had long ago lost most of its color, the four-by-three-foot rectangle was nonetheless recognizable.

"Kriegsmarine Nazi flag," Sam whispered. In his hurried survey of the cavern, he'd missed it. "The pride of home ownership, I suppose."

Remi laughed.

Taking it one careful step at a time, probing for weak spots as they went, they made their way across the catwalk to the pier; aside from a few nerve-wracking creaks and pops, the planking held firm. The cables, though coated in a thick layer of slimy rust, were similarly solid, bolted into the ceiling and rock walls by thumb-sized steel eyelets. Under the helpful beam of Remi's flashlight, Sam recrossed the catwalk, grabbed the rope, and returned to the pier, dragging the submerged dinghy along. Together they hauled it up onto the pier. While the dinghy itself was shredded, the motor and attached gas can had miraculously survived with only a few bullet scrapes. Similarly, of their two dry bags, one was riddled with a dozen or more holes, the other unscathed.

"We'll sort through this, see what we can salvage," Sam said.

They walked to the end to have a look at the rear wall. The second chamber was, as Sam had suspected, a fracture-guided system. While thousands of years of water erosion had smoothed the walls of the main cavern, the secondary chamber had jagged and wildly angled walls. At the juncture were two tunnels in the shape of a wide V, one tunnel slanting upward to the left, the other slanting downward to the right. Water sluiced from the left-hand tunnel, half its volume coursing into the main cavern, the other half disappearing down the right-hand tunnel.

"There's your river," Remi said.

"It can't have been here long," Sam replied. "Walls are too rough."

"How long, do you think?"

"No more than a hundred years, I'd say. Here, let me see the light. Grab my belt loop, will you?" Remi did as he asked, leaning backward as Sam leaned forward. He shined the light down the right-hand tunnel, then said, "Huh. Okay, reel me in."

"What?" Remi asked.

"The tunnel curves back to the right. Just around the corner I can see another pier and more catwalks."

"The plot thickens."

CHAPTER 18

Using what remaining rope they had—sixty feet of the original seventy-five—they set up a system to ferry themselves and their gear down the right-hand tunnel. Remi went first, with Sam giving her slack from a loop around the piling until she reached the next pier.

"Okay!" she called. "It's about thirty feet, I'd say."

Sam reeled in the line, then attached the motor, the dinghy (which they didn't want to leave for their pursuers to find, should they have any doubt about whether their quarry was still in the cave), the two dry bags, and the dive gear to the end. Once done, he played out the line until Remi called, "Okay, hold it." He could hear her grunting as she fished the gear from the water. "Tied off!"

From the entrance Sam heard a gurgling sound, then the tellale sputtering blow of a regulator breaking into air. He dropped onto his belly and went still, face pressed to the pier's planking. A flashlight clicked on and played over the walls and ceiling. In the ambient glow Sam could see the man's head; floating beside him was a bullet-shaped object—a battery-powered sea scooter, Sam realized. Combined with good fins and strong legs, a sea scooter could propel a 180-pound man at a speed of four or five knots. So much for the outflow advantage, Sam thought.

The man threw what looked like a grappling hook over the catwalk, gave the attached rope a tug, then shouted in Russian-accented English, "All clear, come on!" The man turned the scooter toward the dock and started across the cavern.

Sam didn't give himself a chance to think or second-guess, but gave the rope three emergency tugs, then rolled over the edge and lowered himself into the water. The current caught him and took him down the tunnel. A few seconds later the next pier came into view. Remi was kneeling on the edge, taking up the slack. Sam put his finger to his lips and she nodded and helped him onto the pier.

"Bad guys," he whispered.

"How much time have we got?"

"Only enough to hide."

Sam looked around. An E-shaped grid of catwalks spanned the cavern, connecting this pier to another against the opposite wall; both piers held stacks of wooden crates bearing the Kriegsmarine emblem.

Though almost twice as large as the first, this cavern was of the fracture-guided variety, which meant they would find no exit on the seaward side. Or would they? Sam thought, shining the light around. Hanging from the ceiling in the far corner was what he'd initially taken for an especially long stalactite. Under the flashlight's beam he could now see it was actually a desiccated tangle of roots and vines drooping nearly to the water's surface.

"A way out?" she asked.

"Maybe. The current's slower in here."

"Half a knot, no more," Remi agreed.

From the first cavern they heard a pair of voices calling to one another, then a third. A gunshot echoed down the tunnel, then another, then a ten-second burst.

"Shooting into the water," Sam whispered. "They're trying to flush us out."

"Look here, Sam."

He turned the light around and pointed it at the water where she was pointing. Resting just beneath the surface was a curved shape.

"Hull," Remi whispered.

"I think you're right."

"We might have just found the *UM-77*."

"Come on, we got some work to do."

Explaining his plan on the go, they wrapped the motor and the rest of their gear inside the riddled dinghy, cinched it shut using the painter line, then sank the bundle beneath the pier. Next they cut off a thirty-foot section of rope and started tying loops every few feet. Once that was done, Sam asked her, "Which part do you want?"

"You dive, I'll climb."

She gave him a quick kiss, then grabbed the rope and started half running, half creeping across the catwalk.

Sam took the flashlight, slipped off the pier, and dove.

———

He immediately realized this was not a Molch-class mini sub. It was far too small, at least six feet shorter and half the diameter of the *UM-34*. It was a Marder-class boat, he decided, essentially a pair of G7e torpedoes stacked atop one another, the upper one hollowed out and converted into a cockpit/battery compartment with an acrylic-glass viewing dome, the lower one a live, detachable torpedo.

Following the curve of the hull to the bottom, Sam could immediately see there was no torpedo attached, but only a cockpit tube lying on its side, the viewing dome half buried in the sand. He kicked down the length of the hull to the dome, laid the flashlight in the sand, and set to work on the unlatching bolts. They were frozen in place.

Time, Sam, time . . .

His lungs began to burn. He wrapped both hands around a bolt, braced his feet on the hull, and heaved. Nothing. Tried again. Nothing.

Through the water he heard muffled voices again, this time closer. He clicked off the flashlight, looked up, got his bearings, then kicked off the sub and swam toward the far wall. The pier's pilings appeared in the gloom and he slipped between them and turned right, following the wall. Clearing the pier, he let himself float upward and gently break the surface.

Across the cavern and down the adjoining river tunnel he could see lights dancing off the walls—Kholkov and his men at the end of the pier; they'd be coming here next. Ten feet to Sam's left the root/vine tangle hung just above the surface; close up it was even larger than he'd estimated, as big around as a fifty-five-gallon drum. He sidestroked to it, dug around a moment, and found Remi's rope. He started climbing.

A minute later and fifteen feet higher his reaching hand found Remi's foot, which was resting in a loop. He gave it a reassuring squeeze and got a wiggle in reply. He placed his foot inside a loop, did the same with his right hand, then got comfortable.

"Luck?" she whispered.

"No. Locked up tight."

"Now what?"

"Now we wait."

Their wait was short.

Kholkov's men moved fast, using generally the same ferry-rope system Sam and Remi had used to reach the second pier. Peering through the vines, Sam counted six men. One of them stalked down the pier, shining a flashlight over the crates, into the water, and down the catwalks.

"Where the hell are they?" he barked.

It was Kholkov himself, Sam realized.

"You four, flush them out!" Kholkov ordered; then he nodded at the other man and said, "You, with me!"

As Kholkov and one man searched the crates, the others lined up at the pier's edge and started firing short, controlled bursts into the water. After nearly a minute, Kholkov called, "Cease fire, cease fire!"

"There's something down there," one of the men called, shining his light into the water.

Kholkov walked over, looked a few moments, then pointed to two of the men. "That's it! Get your gear and have a look."

The men were back in five minutes, and five minutes after that they were diving under the water.

"Search the cavern first," Kholkov ordered them. "Make sure they're not hiding somewhere."

In a cloud of bubbles, the men disappeared beneath the surface. Sam watched their lights move over the bottom, under both piers, and along the walls, before finally both men resurfaced.

"Not here," one of them reported. "There's no place to hide."

Sam let out the breath he'd been holding. They'd missed the sunken gear.

"Perhaps they went down the river tunnel," the man standing beside Kholkov suggested.

Kholkov considered this for a moment. "You're sure there was nothing?" he asked the divers.

Both men nodded, and Kholkov turned to the man who'd suggested the river tunnel. "Take Pavel, rope yourselves off, and search the tunnel for any sign of them."

The man nodded, moved to the end of the pier, and began uncoiling a rope.

"Search the sub," Kholkov ordered the divers, who both replaced their regulators and dove.

Sam watched their lights move along the hull until they stopped at what he assumed was the cockpit dome. The lights wobbled and shifted and there came a faint clinking of metal on metal. After three more minutes, one of the men broke the surface and pulled the regulator from his mouth.

"It's a Marder," the man said. "The *77*."

"Good," Kholkov replied.

"The bolts are frozen, though. We need the crowbar."

One of the men on the pier kneeled beside a backpack and pulled out a crowbar. The diver swam over, took it, and dove again.

There were five more minutes of muffled metal-on-metal banging, then silence for a few moments, then suddenly a giant bubble
burst on the water's surface.

The minutes ticked by until finally both divers broke the surface
again. One of them gave a hoot and lifted an oblong object from the
water.

"Bring it!" Kholkov ordered. When they reached the pier he
knelt down and took the object, which Sam could now see was an
all-too-familiar loaf-shaped wooden box. Kholkov studied the box
for a full minute, turning it this way and that, peering closely at its
surface, before carefully lifting the lid and peeking inside. He closed
it and nodded.

"Good work."

From the river tunnel, a shout: "Help! Pull us in, pull us in!"

Several of the men rushed down the pier and began hauling the
rope hand over hand. After ten seconds a man appeared at the end of
it. Lights panned over him. He was semiconscious, half his face covered in blood. They pulled him onto the dock and laid him flat.

"Where's Pavel?" Kholkov demanded. The man mumbled something incoherent. Kholkov slapped him across the face and grabbed
his chin. "Answer me! Where's Pavel?"

"The rapids . . . the line got cut. . . . He hit his head. I tried to
reach him, but he was gone. One second he was there, then he was
gone. He's gone."

"Damn it!" Kholkov spun around, paced halfway down the
pier, then spun back. "Okay, you two carry him and get back to
the lagoon." He pointed to the other man. "You and I will set the
charges. If they're not already dead, we'll bury the Fargos alive! Get
moving!"

CHAPTER 19

Kholkov and his men left. Gesturing for Remi to follow, Sam scrambled down the rope, shifted his weight back and forth to get a swing going, then nodded to Remi, who jumped off onto the catwalk, followed by Sam. They knelt down together.

"You think he meant it?" Remi whispered.

"I doubt they have enough explosive to bury us, but they can certainly seal the main entrance. Did you check for an opening up there?" he asked, nodding at the tangle of roots.

She nodded. "It was nothing but a crack—no wider than a couple inches, and a good six feet to the surface."

"But you saw daylight?"

"Yes. Sun's going down."

"Well, exit or not, at least we'll have an air shaft—but they've got the damned bottle."

"One thing at a time, Sam."

"You're right. Let's get off this catwalk before the—"

As if on cue there came a *whump* from the main cavern, followed by two more in quick succession.

"Down!"

Sam pushed her to the ground and lay on top of her. A few seconds later they felt a gust of cool air wash over them. A cloud of dust billowed through the tunnel and filled the cavern, the heavier particles peppering the surface like rain. Sam and Remi looked up.

"Ah, alone at last," Remi murmured.

Sam grinned, stood up, brushed himself off, and pulled her to her feet. "You want to stay for a while?"

"No, thanks."

"Well, then we better get busy on our escape pod."

Remi put her hands on her hips. "What're you talking about?"

Sam unclipped the flashlight from his belt and shined it in the water, illuminating the sub's hull. "I'm talking about that."

"Explain, Fargo."

"I'll check to be sure, but chances are we can't go out the way we came, and no one knows exactly where we are, so we shouldn't count on rescue. That leaves one option: down the river."

"Oh, you mean down the river that killed one of Kholkov's men and sucked him into limbo? That river?"

"It goes somewhere. That tunnel is a good fifteen feet in diameter and the water's moving fast and steady. If it narrowed anywhere down the line we'd see backflow or signs of a higher tide line on the walls. Believe me, it dumps out somewhere—either aboveground in a lake or pond, or into another sea cave."

"And you're sure about this?"

"Reasonably."

"There's a subjective judgment if I've ever heard one." Remi chewed her lip for a moment. "What about this: You work your engineering magic with one of the tanks and blow a hole in the ceiling crack."

"Not enough power, and we might bring the whole roof down on us."

"True. Okay, we can wait for daylight then set the root tangle on fire. It'll be a smoke signal—" She caught herself and frowned. "Scratch that. We'd asphyxiate long before help arrived."

"You've done as much cave diving as I have," Sam said. "You know the geology. That river's our best chance. Our only chance."

"Okay. One problem, though: Our escape pod is full of water and sitting fifteen feet below the surface."

Sam nodded. "Yes, that's a problem."

———————

After checking to make sure the main cavern was in fact sealed, they returned to the secondary cave and got to work, first retrieving their gear from the bottom, then scrounging through the Kriegsmarine crates for any odds and ends that might be of use. In addition to a well-stocked toolbox of mostly rusted tools they found four lanterns and a dozen stubby votivelike candles that lit at the first touch from Sam's lighter. Soon the pier and surrounding water was dimly lit by flickering yellow light. While Remi sorted through their remaining gear and conducted an inventory of the toolbox, Sam stood at the edge of the pier, staring distantly into the water.

"Okay," Remi said. "We've got two air tanks, one two-thirds full, a second completely full; two flashlights, both working, charge unknown; my camera's shot but the binoculars are fine; the revolver is dry, but I can't vouch for the bullets; two canteens of water and some slightly soggy beef jerky; a first-aid kit; your Gerber Nautilus multitool; one dry bag that's in good shape, one that's Swiss cheese; and, finally, two cell phones that are dry, working, almost fully charged, but useless inside here."

"The motor?"

"I dried it out as best I could but we won't know until we try it. As for the gas tank, I didn't find any holes and all the valves are sealed, so I think it's fine."

Sam nodded and went back to staring at the water.

After ten minutes of this, he cleared his throat and said, "Okay, we can do it." He walked over and sat down beside Remi.

"Let's hear it," she said.

He started explaining. When he was done, Remi pursed her lips, tilted her head, and then nodded. "Where do we start?"

It started with a tense, claustrophobic crawl for Sam. He had no trouble with either confined spaces or water, but had no love for the two combined.

Wearing only his mask and a dive belt, he first did a series of practice dives to expand his lung capacity, then spent a full minute on the surface doing deep-breathing exercises to oxygenate his blood to its maximum.

He took a final breath, then dove to the bottom. Flashlight extended before him, he wriggled through the sub's dome hatch and turned aft. He knew from his cursory study of Kriegsmarine subs back in the Pocomoke, the nose section of a Marder-class boat held only a seat and some rudimentary steerage and diving controls. What he was looking for—the scuttle valves—would be in the tail section. Pulling and pushing himself along the interior piping, he felt the cylindrical walls close around him, felt the darkness and the water pressing him, crushing him. He felt the hot bloom of fear in his chest. He quashed it and refocused: *Scuttle valve, Sam. Scuttle.*

He shined his flashlight left, right, ahead. He was looking for a lever, a raised cylindrical fitting in the hull. . . . And then, suddenly, there it was, ahead and to the left. He reached out, grasped the lever, and heaved. Stuck. He drew his dive knife, wedged it between the lever and hull, then tried again. With a squelch and spurt of rust, the lever gave way. Lungs pounding, he turned to the opposite valve, repeated the process, then backed out and finned to the surface.

"You okay?" Remi called.

"Define okay."

"Not mortally wounded."

"Then, yes, I'm okay."

The next part of the plan took three hours, most of which they spent sorting and splicing the rope the Germans had left behind, about half of which was either completely rotted or so weakened Sam wasn't willing to trust it. They would get only one chance at what they were attempting, he told Remi. If they failed, they would have to turn to her signal fire idea and hope help would arrive before the smoke killed them.

After four hours, at nearly two A.M. according to Sam's watch, they were almost ready. They stood at the edge of the pier, studying their handiwork.

Two quadruple-braided lines, one secured to the sub's bow and the other to its stern cleats, rose from the water to the ceiling, where Remi, superb climber that she was, had threaded each through a catwalk ceiling eyelet. From there, each line dropped down again and was tied off to a cable under the catwalk planking. The vertical support cables were themselves connected, midpoint to midpoint, by a carefully constructed spiderweb of rope. To one of the cables—the farthest one from the lines secured to the sub—Sam had lashed one of their scuba tanks.

"So," Remi said. "Let's review: You shoot the tank, the blast sheers the cables, the catwalk drops, the sub pops to the surface, and the water drains out. Is that it?"

"More or less. The tank won't explode, but it'll take off like a rocket. If I've rigged it right, the torque should part the weakened cables. Beyond that, it's all math and chaos theory."

Estimating the weight of the sub and the water inside it, as well as the combined weight of the catwalks and the shearing limit of the cables, had given Sam a headache, but he was fairly confident in his process. Using the ancient and rusted but still-serviceable hacksaw they'd found in the toolbox he'd cut halfway through eleven of the eighteen vertical catwalk cables.

"And gravity," Remi added, curling her arm in his. "Win or lose, I'm proud of you." She handed him the revolver. "It's your mousetrap. You get the honors."

They climbed behind the protective bulwark of crates they'd assembled at the far end of the dock and made sure everything was snug around them, save Sam's firing slit.

"Ready?" he asked.

Remi cupped her ears and nodded.

Sam braced his gun hand on his opposite forearm, took aim, and pulled the trigger.

The gun's report was instantly overwhelmed by a *whump-whoosh*, a flash of light, the shriek of rending steel, and a thunderous splash.

Sam and Remi peeked their heads above the bulwark but for ten full seconds could see nothing but a fine mist filling the cavern. Slowly it cleared. They climbed out and walked to the edge of the pier and looked down.

"Never had any doubt," Remi murmured.

The Marder-class mini submarine *UM-77*, having spent the last sixty years of its life lying on the bottom of a sea cave, now sat perfectly upright on the surface, water gushing from its scuttles.

"Beautiful," was all Sam could say.

CHAPTER 20

With a reverberating gong that both Sam and Remi felt in their heads, the sub glanced over another boulder, tipped hard to port, then snapped upright and nosed over, plunging back into the river's main channel. Water sluiced over the acrylic dome, obscuring Sam's view for a few moments, then cleared. He clicked on the flashlight and shined it over the bow, but could see only rock walls flashing past on either side and whitewater crashing over the nose cone. The deadly seriousness of the experience notwithstanding, it was a lot like a ride at Disney World, Sam decided.

"You okay back there?" he called.

Remi, lying behind the cockpit seat, arms braced against the hull, shouted back, "Peachy! How long have we been going?"

Sam checked his watch. "Twenty minutes."

"My God, is that all?"

After recovering from the mild shock that their plan had actually worked, Sam and Remi had climbed into the water and hung from the sub's bow line, lifting the nose a few more inches off the surface and allowing the rest of the water to drain out. Remi had then crawled inside and closed both scuttles.

From there they'd had little work to do: check the sub for leaks and shore up the inside with a few carefully positioned planks from the catwalk. The fifty-gallon ballast tanks—a four-inch pipe running lengthwise down the port and the starboard side—were full and nicely balanced the sub.

Satisfied they were as prepared as possible, they'd caught four hours of sleep huddled together on the pier in a circle of lanterns. At dawn, they'd risen, eaten a breakfast of tepid water and damp beef jerky, then piled a few essentials into the sub and climbed aboard. Using a catwalk plank, Sam had paddled the sub to the mouth of the river tunnel, then closed the hatch and held on.

So far the sub's reinforced aluminum hull was holding up well, but they both knew geology was also on their side: While the tunnel walls were still jagged, the rocks and boulders in the channel itself had long ago been smoothed by erosion, leaving no sharp edges to rip the hull.

"Brace yourself!" Sam called. "Big rock!"

The sub's nose slammed squarely into the boulder, rose up and over the crest, then veered left. The current caught the tail section and spun it around, slamming the hull against the wall.

"Ouch!" Remi shouted over the rush.

"Okay?"

"Just another bruise for my collection."

"We'll get you a Swedish massage when we get back to the Four Seasons."

"I'll hold you to that!"

One hour turned into two as Sam and Remi rode the rapids, the sub caroming off the walls, vaulting over boulders, and tossing from one side to the other in the water. Occasionally they would find themselves in wider, calmer parts of the river, allowing Sam to open the dome and let in some fresh air to supplement the oxygen Remi was intermittently pumping into the space via their remaining scuba tank.

Almost like clockwork every few minutes the sub slammed into a jumble of boulders and they would find themselves beached, the sub either lying on its side or perched above the rapids, balanced like a teeter-totter. Each time either they would dislodge themselves by gently rocking from side to side until the sub slipped back into the channel or Sam would have to open the dome and push and lever them free using his plank paddle.

Nearing their third hour of travel, the sound of rushing water suddenly faded. The sub slowed and began spinning lazily.

"What's happening?" Remi called.

"Not sure," replied Sam.

He pressed his face to the dome and found himself staring up at a vaulted, stalactite-encrusted ceiling. He heard a scraping sound and looked left just in time to see a curtain of vines close over the dome like the swaying carpet arms inside an automated car wash. Sunlight burst through the dome, filling the interior with a yellow glow.

"Is that the sun?" Remi said.

"You bet it is!"

The hull scraped over sand, slowed, then came to a gentle halt. Sam peered ahead. They'd run aground in another lagoon.

"Remi, I think we have arrived."

He unlatched the dome and swung it open. Cool, salt-tinged air rushed through the hatch. He draped his arms outside, letting them hang, then leaned his head back and let the sun wash over his face.

He heard something off to his left, opened his eyes, and turned his head. Sitting on the sand ten feet away were a young couple wearing dive fins and scuba harnesses. Mouths agape and frozen in place, they stared at Sam. The man had a farmer's tan, the woman white-blond hair—Midwesterners on a tropical adventure.

"Good morning," Sam said. "Doing a little cave diving, I see."

The couple nodded in unison, saying nothing.

"Be careful you don't get lost in there," Sam offered. "It can be a little tricky getting back out. By the way, what year is it?"

"Leave the nice people alone, Sam," Remi whispered from the back.

CHAPTER 21

eaven," Remi murmured. "Absolute heaven."

True to his word, upon returning to their Four Seasons villa, Sam had, after they'd shared a long hot shower, ordered first a sumptuous lunch of seafood salad, hot sourdough bread, and a tropical fruit bowl, then a pair of masseuses, who'd spent an hour giving them a hot stone massage before moving to deep-tissue Swedish. Sam and Remi lay side by side on the veranda, the sheer curtains billowing around them in a light tropical breeze. Down the beach, the breakers gently washed in and out, nature's own lullaby.

Sam, hovering on the edge of sleep, simply muttered, "This is living."

The surprised couple they'd encountered upon their exit from the cave had in fact been Midwesterners—Mike and Sarah, from Minnesota and on their honeymoon. After three tries, they'd answered Sam's "Where are we?" question: on Rum Cay's northern coast between Junkanoo Rock and Liberty Rock. They had, by Sam's calculation, traveled some nine miles along the underground river.

Mike and Sarah had graciously offered to give them a ride—and a tow to the mini sub, to which Sam had grown quite attached—down the coast in their rented boat. Forty-two hours after first touching down at Rum Cay, Sam and Remi were back at their landing beach. Their host, the mysterious beachcomber, was nowhere to be seen, so they muscled the sub into the undergrowth and left a note on the hut's wall: *Please keep an eye on this. We'll be back for it.* Sam had no idea exactly what he had planned, but it seemed wrong to simply abandon it.

They then climbed aboard the Bonanza and headed for the main island and their hotel.

Massages complete, Sam and Remi lay still for a while, dozing, then got up and went back inside. Having already given Selma a "We're okay" text message, Sam now called her and put her on speakerphone. He gave her a quick rundown of their cave odyssey.

"Well, no one can accuse the Fargos of taking mundane vacations," Selma replied. "I may have an answer to one mystery—why it was Kholkov who came after you. Rube called: Grigoriy Arkhipov was found dead in a Yalta parking lot; his hands and feet were missing. Amputation by shotgun. Rube told me to—"

"Tell us to be careful," Sam finished. "We are."

"The question is, how did Kholkov find you?"

"We've been wondering that ourselves. Did you check our—"

"No credit checks on the account you used, and all our computers here are firewalled, so I doubt they got your itinerary that way. Same with your passport records; the government is tight with those."

Remi said, "That leaves airlines or . . ."

"Some lead they have that we don't," Sam finished. "But that begs the question, why hadn't they already raided the caves?"

"I'll keep working on it," Selma said, "but I don't think it came from our end."

"Until we know, we'll assume the worst and keep looking over our shoulders," Remi said.

"Good. So, about this submarine . . ."

"The *UM-77*," Sam offered.

"Right. You want me to get it back here?"

"We'd better," Remi replied, "or Sam is going to pout."

"It's a piece of history," he grumbled.

They'd agreed that once this was all over they would tell both the German and the Bahamian governments about the sub pens and let the two sort it out among themselves.

"And if no one wants it?" Remi had asked.

"We'll put it above our mantel."

Remi had groaned. "That's what I was afraid of."

Now, on the phone, Selma said, "I'll work it out. Might take a few days, but I'll get it back here. So: Kholkov got the bottle."

"Afraid so. Any news for us?"

"Yes, in fact, a few things I think you'll find interesting. Care to guess what else, besides the spitting beetle, is found only in the Tuscan Archipelago?"

Remi answered first. "Our black rose."

"Right again. We'll have to fill in the timeline, but it seems likely the ink was applied to the labels during Napoleon's stay on Elba."

"Or afterward with ink from there," Sam added. "Either way, it's another piece in the puzzle."

"Well, here's another one," Selma said. "Our bottle appears to be something of an onion wrapped in a riddle. The leather label is not one piece, but two layers pressed together. I managed to peel away the top layer without causing any damage."

"And?"

"There's no ink present, but more etchings—a grid of symbols, eight across and four down for a total of thirty-two."

"What kind of symbols?"

"You name it. Everything from alchemy to Cyrillic to astrology and everything in between. My guess: They're customized shape codes with no connection to their origin. Sam, you're probably familiar with shape code."

He was. During his training at the CIA's Camp Perry, they'd

spent three days on cryptographic history. "It's essentially a substitution cipher," he explained to Remi. He grabbed a pad and pen from the nightstand and quickly sketched three symbols:

Sam said, "Now suppose the first symbol represents the letter *c*; the second, *a*; the third, *t*."

"Cat," Remi said. "Seems pretty simplistic."

"It is, in a sense, but in another sense it's a virtually unbreakable code. The military uses a version of it, something called a one-time pad. The theory is this: Two people have an encoding/decoding book. One sends a message using shape codes, the other deciphers it by substituting letters for shapes. Without a book, all you've got is random symbols. To anyone else, they're meaningless."

"And we don't have a book," Remi said.

"Nope. Selma, can you send us—"

"On the way as we speak. It's not the original picture I took of the label, but Wendy used a vector drawing program to re-create some of the symbols. This'll be just a sample."

A moment later Sam's e-mail beeped and he called up the image:

"As for decoding it, I might have an idea about that—at least a place to start," Selma said. "You remember the mystery man, 'the Major' who hired the smuggler, Arienne, to sail to Saint Helena?"

"Of course," Remi said.

"I think I know who the Major is. I ran across an obscure German biography of Napoleon written in the 1840s. In 1779, when Napoleon was nine, he was sent to a French military school, Brienne-le-Château, near Troyes. There he met a boy named Arnaud Laurent and they became friends—all through École Royale Militaire college, then on to artillery school, and so on, all the way to Waterloo. According to the author, up until the mid 1790s, just before the First Italian Campaign, Laurent had been a step ahead of Napoleon in rank. It was said that in private or in close company Napoleon jokingly called Laurent 'the Major.' Napoleon had several confidants over the years, but none as close as Laurent."

"Is there an estate?" Sam asked. "An Arnaud Laurent library, by chance?"

"No such luck. There's not much out there on Laurent, but from what I gather, when he died in 1825, just four years after Napoleon, he was buried with what one article referred to as 'his most prized possession.'"

"Which, with any luck, will be a handy-dandy decoder ring," Sam said.

"Or book," Remi added. "Selma, where's he buried?"

"After his army was routed at Waterloo, Napoleon's surrender was accepted aboard the HMS *Bellerophon*, along with Napoleon's staff, which I'm guessing included Laurent, who was at the time his chief military adviser. Afterward the *Bellerophon* sailed to Plymouth, where after a two-week wait Napoleon was transferred to the HMS *Northumberland*—alone, with no staff—for the final voyage to Saint Helena. When Laurent died, his widow, Marie, asked the British for permission to have him buried on Saint Helena next to Napoleon, but they refused, so she did what she thought was next best thing: She had him laid to rest on Elba."

"Strange," Remi said.

"It's poetic," Sam replied. "Laurent's general, his best friend, had died in exile and been buried in exile. His widow had chosen a spot of . . ." Sam searched for the right word. "Symbolic solidarity."

Remi tilted her head at her husband. "That's beautiful, Sam."

"I have my moments. Selma, Napoleon's remains . . . weren't they moved from Saint Helena?"

"They were. Interesting story itself, really. In 1830 the Bourbons, who retook the throne after Napoleon's defeat at Waterloo, were themselves overthrown by the Orléans dynasty. They were a little more nostalgic over Napoleon, so they petitioned the British for permission to bring him home. After seven years of wrangling, the Brits agreed and the remains were fetched from Saint Helena and returned to Paris. His official grave is under the dome of Les Invalides.

"Laurent's grave is still on Elba—it's a crypt, actually. The trick is, how do you handle it? I assume you'd prefer to avoid breaking in and playing tomb raiders."

"Ideally," Sam said.

"Then you've got to get permission. And as luck would have it, Laurent has a granddaughter, five or six times removed, living in Monaco."

"Ah, Monaco in the spring," Sam murmured. "How can we say no?"

"We can't," Remi chimed in.

CHAPTER 22

Sam pulled their rented olive green Porsche Cayenne SUV down the lilac-lined driveway and stopped before a four-story, white stucco terra-cotta–roofed villa overlooking the waters off Point de la Veille.

As it turned out, Arnaud Laurent's distant granddaughter, Yvette Fournier-Desmarais, was embarrassingly wealthy, having inherited her late husband's interests in a number of Monaco businesses, including a half dozen beach resorts and motor sporting clubs. According to the gossip rags she was, at age fifty-five, Monaco's most eligible bachelorette and since her husband's death fifteen years earlier had been courted by an impressive collection of Europe's jet set, from princes to celebrities to captains of industry. She'd dated all of them, but none for longer than four months, and was rumored to have turned down dozens of marriage proposals. She lived alone in her villa with a modest staff and a Scottish deerhound named Henri.

Surprisingly, Sam and Remi had had little trouble arranging a meeting, first presenting their credentials and request to Ms.

Fournier-Desmarais's lawyer in Nice, who in turn agreed to contact his client. She'd e-mailed them directly within a day and insisted they come immediately.

They climbed out of the Porsche and walked into the front court-yard and along a path between a pair of bubbling fountains to the front door, twin slabs of mahogany and stained glass that rose four feet above their heads. Sam pressed the button on the wall and a soft chime sounded from within.

" 'A Marcia de Muneghu,' " Remi said.

"What?"

"The doorbell chime—it's 'A Marcia de Muneghu.' The March of Monaco. It's the national anthem here."

Sam smiled. "Read some guidebooks on the plane, did we?"

"When in Rome . . ."

The door opened, revealing a rail-thin middle-aged man in matching navy blue slacks and polo shirt. "Mr. and Mrs. Fargo, yes?" His accent was British. He didn't wait for a reply, but merely stepped aside and tipped his chin.

They stepped into the foyer, which was simply but tastefully done: light gray Egyptian slate on the floor and a soft Mediterranean blue plaster on the walls. A silver-framed mirror sat above a nineteenth-century English Sheraton painted demi-lune console table.

"My name is Langdon," the man said, shutting the door. "The mistress is on the veranda. This way, please."

They followed him down the hall, past the formal rooms to the private half of the house, then out a pair of French doors onto a mul-titiered deck made from polished burled walnut.

"You'll find her there," Langdon said, gesturing up a set of stairs that wound along the villa's outer wall. "If you'll excuse me . . ." Langdon turned and disappeared back through the French doors.

"My God, look at that view," Remi said, walking to the railing. Sam joined her. Below an embankment of rock outcrops, palm trees, and flowering tropical shrubs lay the breadth of the Mediterranean, a carpet of indigo stretching beneath a cloudless sky.

A female voice called, "It's a sight I never tire of either."

They turned. A woman in a plain white sundress and sunflower yellow broad-brimmed hat stood at the top of the steps. This was, they assumed, Yvette Fournier-Desmarais, but neither Sam nor Remi would have guessed her to be older than forty. Beneath the hat her face was tanned, but not baked, with barely perceptible laugh lines around a pair of hazel eyes.

"Sam and Remi, yes?" she asked, walking down the stairs, hand outstretched. "I'm Yvette. Thank you for coming." Her English was excellent, with the slightest trace of a French accent.

They shook her hand in turn, then followed her up the stairs and around the back to an open-air sunroom draped in gauze curtains and appointed in teak chairs and chaise lounges. A large, sleek brown and black dog sitting in the shade beside one of the chairs started to rise upon seeing Sam and Remi, but sat back down again at his mistress's soft, "Sit, Henri." Once they were all settled, she said, "I'm not what you expected, am I?"

Sam replied, "To be honest, no, Mrs.—"

"Yvette."

"Yvette. To be honest, no, you're not at all."

She laughed, her white teeth flashing in the sun. "And you, Remi, you were expecting someone more matronly perhaps, a French bejeweled snob with a poodle under one arm and a champagne flute in the other?"

"I'm sorry, but yes, I was."

"Oh, goodness, don't apologize. The woman I just described is more the rule than the exception here. The truth is, I was born in Chicago. Went to grade school there for a few years before my parents moved us back to Nice. They were simple people, my mother and father—quite wealthy, but with simple tastes. Without them, I might have ended up the stereotype you were expecting."

Langdon appeared up the stairs and placed a tray containing a carafe of iced tea and frosted glasses on the table between them. "Thank you, Langdon."

"Yes, ma'am." He turned to go.

"Have fun tonight, Langdon. And good luck."

"Yes, ma'am, thank you."

Once he was out of earshot, Yvette leaned forward and whispered, "Langdon's been dating a widow for a year now. He's going to ask her to marry him. Langdon is one of the best Formula One drivers in Monaco, you know."

"Really," Sam replied.

"Oh, yes. Very famous."

"If you don't mind me asking, why is he . . ."

"Working for me?" Sam nodded, and she said, "We've been together for thirty years, since I started dating my late husband. I pay him well and we like each other. He's not quite a butler, really, but more of a . . . what is the word . . . in American football he would be called a—"

"Free safety?"

"Yes, that's it. He wears many hats for me. Langdon was a commando before he retired—British Special Air Service. Very tough fellow. Anyway, we'll hold the wedding and reception here—providing she says yes, of course. You two should come, you really should. You don't mind iced tea, do you?" she asked, pouring for them. "Not really the beverage of the wealthy, but I love it."

Sam and Remi each accepted a glass from her.

"So: Arnaud Laurent . . . My great-great-great-something grandfather. You're interested in him, yes?"

"Very much," Remi said. "First, may I ask why you agreed to see us?"

"I've read about you, about your adventures. And your charitable work. I admire the way you live your lives. You know, at the risk of being crass, there are families here that are frighteningly rich, so much so that they couldn't spend all their money if they tried and yet they give none of it away. As far as I'm concerned, the tighter you cling to money, the tighter its hold on you. Don't you agree?"

"We do," Sam replied.

"So that's why I agreed to see you: I knew I would like you, and I was right, and I was also intrigued about how Arnaud fit into whatever quest you're on—you're on a quest, yes, an adventure?"

"More or less."

"Marvelous. Perhaps I can tag along sometime? Well, I apologize, I'm running at the mouth. Do you mind sharing with me the nature of your work?"

Remi and Sam exchanged glances, each reading the other's expression. Their instincts, which were more often right than wrong, told them they could trust Yvette Fournier-Desmarais.

Sam said, "We stumbled across a bottle of wine, very rare, that might be connected to Arnaud—"

"Napoleon's Lost Cellar, yes?"

"Well, yes. Maybe."

"That's fantastic!" Yvette said, laughing. "Wonderful. If anyone should find the cellar, it should be you two! Of course I'll help in any way I can. You'll do the right thing, I know. Back to Arnaud: In all fairness I should tell you you're not the first ones to ask about him. A man called my attorney a few months ago—"

"Did you get his name?" Sam asked.

"My attorney has it, but I don't remember. Something Russian, I think. Anyway, the man was quite insistent, even a little rude, so I chose not to see him. Sam, Remi, I can see from your faces this means something to you. Do you know who I'm talking about?"

"We might," Sam replied. "We've run into our own ill-mannered Russian and, given how far he's been willing to go, we're probably talking about the same person."

"You haven't had any unwelcome company?" Remi asked her.

"No, no. And I'm not worried. Between Langdon and his three cohorts—who are lurking around here somewhere—and the alarm system and Henri here, I feel completely safe. Not to mention I'm a fantastic shot with a pistol."

"Something you and Remi have in common," Sam said.

"Is that true, Remi, you're a marksman?"

"I wouldn't go that far—"

Yvette leaned forward and tapped Remi's knee. "When you can stay longer we'll go shooting, just us girls. There's a wonderful beach club in Menton not far from here; they have an indoor range. So, back to our Russian villain: He was very interested in Arnaud's crypt on Elba. I assume that's why you came to see me?"

"Yes," Remi said.

"Well, we told him nothing. I suspected he'd already been there and came away disappointed, which was why he was so badly behaved."

"What do you mean?"

Yvette leaned forward and lowered her voice to a conspiratorial whisper: "A few years ago there was some vandalism on Elba, just teenage children running amok, but it got me thinking. Given who Arnaud is, and how . . . zealous some Napoleonophiles can be, we decided to move Arnaud's sarcophagus."

"To where?" Sam asked. "Off the island?"

"Oh, no, it's still there. Arnaud wouldn't have approved of being taken off Elba. No, we found another graveyard with an empty crypt and moved him there. He's safe and sound. I assume you'd like my permission to peek inside his sarcophagus? That's why you've come, yes?"

Sam smiled. "I'm glad you said it. I wasn't sure of the etiquette when asking a relative if they'd mind us poking around their ancestor's remains."

Yvette waved her hand dismissively. "Not to worry. You'll be respectful, I'm certain. Anything you take, you'll return, yes?"

"Of course," Remi replied. "Though none of it might be necessary. We've been told Arnaud was buried with some personal effects. Do you happen to know what they were?"

"No, I don't, I'm sorry. I'm sure the only person who knew the answer to that was his wife, Marie. And I can assure you, the sarcophagus hasn't been opened since his death. So now I'll gladly tell you where to find the crypt, but on one condition."

"Name it," Sam said.

"You'll both stay for dinner."

Remi smiled. "We'd love to."

"Wonderful! When you reach Elba, you'll be in Rio Marina. From there you'll drive west on the SP26 into the mountains. . . ."

CHAPTER 23

ELBA, ITALY

H e let the beetle crawl up his finger and over the back of his hand
before he nudged it with his other finger into his palm. Sam rose
from his crouch alongside the dirt road and turned to Remi, who
was taking pictures of the ocean far below.

"History's a funny thing," he said.

"How so?"

"This beetle. For all we know it could be related to one Napoleon
himself used to make the ink."

"Has it spit on you?"

"Not as far as I can tell."

"Selma said the ink came from a spitting beetle."

"You're missing my point. Where's your sense of whimsy?"

Remi lowered her camera and looked at him.

"Sorry," he said with a smile, "forgot who I was talking to."

"I understand your point." She checked her watch then said,
"We'd better get moving. It's almost three. Daylight's burning."

Their dinner the night before with Yvette Fournier-Desmarais had gone late into the evening and well into three bottles of wine, by which time she had convinced them to cancel their hotel reservations and stay the night. They awoke the next morning and shared a veranda breakfast of coffee, croissants, fresh pineapple, and French scrambled eggs with leeks, fresh pepper, and mint before heading to the airport.

For reasons neither Sam nor Remi had been able to deduce, daily flights to and from Elba were restricted to one airline, Inter-Sky, which serviced only three cities, Friedrichshafen, Munich, and Zurich. The other two carriers, SkyWork and Elbafly, offered more departure points, but only flew three days a week, so from Nice they'd boarded an Air France flight to Florence, then a train to Piombino, then finally a ferry across the ten-mile stretch of sea to Rio Marina on Elba's east coast.

Their rental car—a compact 1991 Lancia Delta—paled in comparison to the Porsche Cayenne, but the air conditioner worked and the engine, small though it was, ran smoothly.

Per Yvette's instructions, they'd driven inland from Rio Marina, passing through one quaint Tuscan village after another—Togliatti, Sivera, San Lorenzo—winding their way through lush rolling hills and vineyards, higher and higher into the mountains, until stopping at this promontory overlooking the eastern side of the island.

If not for Napoleon's exile, Elba would not be the household name it was, which, as far as Sam and Remi were concerned, was a shame as it had its own unique story.

Over its long history Elba had seen its share of invaders and occupiers, from the Etruscans to the Romans to the Saracens, until the eleventh century, when the island fell under the aegis of the Republic of Pisa. From there it changed hands a half dozen times through sale or annexation, starting with the Visconti of Milan and ending in 1860 when it became a protectorate of the Kingdom of Italy.

Remi snapped a few more pictures then they got back in the car and continued on.

"So where exactly did Napoleon spend his exile?" Sam asked.

Remi flipped through her Post-it Note–marked Frommer's

guidebook. "In Portoferraio, on the northern coast. He had two homes, actually, the Villa San Martino and the Villa dei Mulini. He had a staff of somewhere between six hundred and one thousand, and took the title Emperor of Elba."

"Took the title, or was slapped in the face with it?" Sam asked. "After having had a good chunk of Europe under his thumb, 'Emperor of Elba' had to have been something of a letdown."

"True. Another fun fact: before leaving for Elba Napoleon tried to poison himself."

"No kidding."

"Apparently he kept it in a bottle around his neck—a cocktail of opium, belladonna, and white hellabore. Before leaving on the Russian Campaign he had it mixed up."

"He probably didn't want to fall into the hands of the Cossacks."

"Well, I can't say I blame him. They still don't like him. Anyway, he drank it but by then it was a couple years old and too weak. He spent the night writhing in pain on the floor, but survived."

"Remi, you're a font of knowledge."

She ignored him, still reading. "What none of the historians seemed to agree on is how exactly he escaped. There were both French and Prussian guards stationed all over the island and offshore there was a British man-o'-war on constant patrol."

"Tricky little devil."

———————

"Car behind us," Sam said a few minutes later. Remi turned and looked out the back window. A half mile down the mountain road a cream-colored Peugeot was rounding a curve. It disappeared from view for a few moments behind a hillside, then reappeared.

"He's in a hurry."

Since leaving the Bahamas both Sam and Remi had been hyper-vigilant to signs of pursuit, but had so far seen nothing. The problem with an island as small as Elba was that it had limited points of entry and Bondaruk's wealth could go a long way here.

Sam tightened his grip on the wheel, eyes alternating between the rearview mirror and the road ahead.

A couple minutes later the Peugeot appeared behind them and closed the gap until it was only a few feet off their bumper. Glare from the sun kept the occupants in silhouette, but Sam could make out two shapes, both male.

Sam stuck his arm out the window and waved for them to pass.

The Peugeot didn't move, glued to their tail, then abruptly it pulled out and started speeding up. Sam tensed his foot, ready to hit the brake. Remi glanced out the passenger window; there was the narrowest of dirt shoulders there, followed by a sharp drop-off. Five hundred feet below she could see goats grazing in a pasture; they looked like ants. Their passenger tire swerved a few inches right. Gravel peppered the side of the car. Sam eased left, back onto blacktop. "Buckled in?" he said through clenched teeth.

"Yep."

"Where are they?"

"Coming up right now."

The Peugeot drew even with Sam's door. Sitting in the passenger seat, a swarthy man with a handlebar mustache stared at him. The man nodded once, curtly, then the Peugeot's engine revved and it sprinted ahead and disappeared around the next bend.

"Friendly folks," Remi said with a loud exhale.

Sam relaxed his hands on the wheel, flexing his fingers to get blood flowing back into them. "How far left to go?"

Remi unfolded the map, her finger tracing along. "Five, six miles."

They reached their destination in the late afternoon. Perched on the slopes of Monte Capanello and surrounded by forests of Aleppo pines and juniper, the village of Rio nell'Elba, population nine hundred, sat under the shadow of the eleventh-century castle, Volterraio, and was to Sam's and Remi's eyes the epitome of a medieval Tuscan village, complete with narrow cobblestoned alleys, shadowed piazzas, and stone balconies overflowing with orchids and cascading lavender.

Remi said, "Says here Rio nell'Elba is the rock-hunting capital of Tuscany. They're still finding mines that date back to the Etruscans."

They found a parking spot across from the Hermitage of Santa Caterina and got out. According to Yvette, their contact, a man named Umberto Cipriani, was the assistant curator of the Museo dei Minerali, the Mining Museum. Remi got herself oriented on the map and they started walking, finding the museum ten minutes later. As they crossed the piazza Sam said, "Here, let me take your picture. Stand in front of the fountain."

She did as he asked, smiled for several shots, then rejoined Sam, who called up the images on the camera's LCD screen. "We should take another, Sam, I'm a little out of focus."

"I know. Look at what is in focus. Smile, look pleased."

Remi peered more closely at the image. Fifty feet behind her blurred figure she could see the hood of a cream-colored car jutting from the mouth of a shadowed alley. Behind the wheel a man stared at them through a pair of binoculars.

CHAPTER 24

Playing the carefree tourist, Remi smiled and pressed her face against Sam's as they looked at the LCD screen. "Our friendly tailgaters," she whispered through her smile. "A coincidence?"

"I'd like to think so, but the binoculars make me nervous. Unless he's an urban bird-watcher—"

"Or he's stalking an ex-girlfriend—"

"I think we'd better assume the worst."

"Do you see the other one around, the one with the mustache?"

"No. Come on, let's go in. Act casual. Don't look around."

They entered the museum, stopped at the welcome desk, and asked for Cipriani. The receptionist picked up the phone and spoke a few words in Italian, and a few moments later a portly man with thinning salt-and-pepper hair appeared in the doorway to their right.

"*Buon giorno,*" the man said. "*Posso aiutarla?*"

"You're up, Remi," Sam said. While they both spoke several languages, Italian had for some reason always flummoxed him; Remi was the same way with German, which came naturally to Sam.

"*Buon giorno,*" she said. "*Signor Cipriani?*"

"*Sì.*"

"Parla inglese?"

Cipriani smiled broadly. "I speak English, yes. But your Italian is very good. How can I help you?"

"My name is Remi Fargo. This is my husband, Sam." They all shook hands.

"I've been expecting you," Cipriani said.

"Is there somewhere we might speak in private?"

"Certainly. My office is this way."

He led them down a short hallway to an office with a window overlooking the piazza. They all sat down and Sam pulled Yvette's letter from his pocket and handed it across to Cipriani, who scanned it carefully, then handed it back.

"Forgive me . . . may I see some identification, please?"

Sam and Remi handed over their passports, then took them back when Cipriani was done. He asked, "And how is Yvette? Well, I hope."

"She is," Sam replied. "She sends her regards."

"And her cat, Moira, it is well?"

"It's a dog, actually, and its name is Henri."

Cirpriani spread his hands and smiled sheepishly. "I'm a cautious man, perhaps overly so. Yvette has entrusted me with this matter. I want to be sure I'm worthy of it."

"We understand," Remi said. "How long have you known her?"

"Oh, twenty years or more. She has a villa here, outside the castello. There were some legal issues in connection to the land. I was able to help her."

"You're an attorney?"

"Oh, no. I simply know people who know people."

"I see. You'll be able to help us?"

"Of course. You simply want to examine the crypt? You don't plan to move it?"

"No."

"Then it should be very simple. However, just to be safe, we should wait until it is dark. We Elbans are a nosy lot. Have you a place to stay?"

"Not yet."

"Then you'll stay with us, my wife and me."

Sam said, "We don't want to—"

"No imposition. You'll be my guest. We'll have some supper, then I'll take you to the graveyard."

"Thank you."

"May we use your office for a few minutes?"

"Of course. Take as much time as you need."

Cipriani left, shutting the door behind him. Sam pulled out their satellite phone and punched in Selma's number, then waited through twenty seconds of clicks and buzzes. Selma's voice came on the line: "Mr. Fargo. Everything okay?"

"So far. Any trouble there?"

"All's quiet."

"I need you to check a license plate for me. Could be tricky; we're on Elba. If you have trouble, call Rube Haywood." He gave her the number to Cipriani's office.

"Okay, I'll see what I can do. Be back to you shortly."

––––––––

She called back twenty minutes later. "Took some doing, but as it turns out the Italian DMV database isn't exactly what I'd call hacker-proof."

"Good to know," Sam said.

"The plate belongs to a tan Peugeot, correct?"

"That's it."

"Then I have bad news. It's registered to a Polizia Provinciale officer. The Provincial Police. I'm sending you the specifics right now."

Sam waited three minutes until the e-mail finally arrived, scanned the contents, then thanked Selma and hung up. He filled Remi in. "Either I've been speeding and haven't realized it, or someone's interested in us," he said.

"If it were official they would have stopped us at the ferry in Rio Marina," she replied.

"Agreed."

"Well, at least we got some warning."

"And we know what our other pursuer's face looks like."

At Cipriani's suggestion they spent an hour exploring Rio nell'Elba, but they did so warily, taking care to stay within the village limits and close to crowds. They saw no sign of either the Peugeot or its occupants.

Strolling arm in arm, Sam said, "Been thinking about what Yvette said—that she suspected Kholkov had already been here looking for Laurent's crypt. Bondaruk knew we'd come here eventually. It was a logical step."

"So he sits back and lets us do the heavy lifting," Remi replied.

"It's the smart move," Sam said.

At five thirty they returned to the museum to find Cipriani locking the front door and agreed to follow him home.

His cottage was less than a mile away, sitting behind an olive orchard. Signora Cipriani, portly like her husband and with flashing brown eyes, greeted them with smiles and double cheek kisses as they walked up. She exchanged some rapid-fire Italian with Umberto, who ushered them onto the porch and toward a cluster of chairs. A curtain of white clematis hung from the eaves, creating a cozy alcove.

"You'll excuse us for a moment," Umberto said. "My wife needs me in the kitchen for a moment."

Sam and Remi sat down and a few minutes later Umberto and his wife, whom he introduced as Teresa, reappeared with a tray and glasses. "You enjoy limoncello, I hope."

"We do," Sam said.

Limoncello was essentially lightly sugared lemonade cut by a healthy dose of vodka. "*Cento anni di salute e felicità,*" Umberto said, raising his glass. After they'd all sipped, he asked, "You know the toast—*Cento anni di salute e felicità?*"

Remi thought for a moment and said, "A hundred years of health and happiness?"

"Bravo! Drink up. We will eat shortly."

After supper they returned to the porch and sat in the dusk watching fireflies winking in the trees and sipping espresso. Inside they could hear dishes clinking as Teresa cleaned up. She'd adamantly refused Sam and Remi's offer to help, ushering them outside with flaps of her apron.

"Umberto, how long have you lived here?" Sam asked.

"All my life, and my family, going back . . . three hundred years? Yes, that's right. When Mussolini came to power my father and my uncles joined the partisans and lived in these hills for years. When the British finally landed here in 1944—"

"Operation Brassard," Sam said.

"Yes, that's right. Very good. When the British came my father fought alongside the Royal Navy Commandos. He even received a decoration for it. I was still in my mother's belly when the war ended."

"He survived the war?" Remi asked.

"Yes, but none of my uncles did. They were captured and executed by a Nazi death squad Hitler sent to quash the partisans."

"I'm sorry."

Cipriani spread his hands and shrugged: *What can you do.*

Sam pulled his cell phone from his pocket and glanced at Remi, who nodded. They'd already discussed this. "Umberto, does this name look familiar to you?"

Umberto took the phone, studied the screen a moment, then handed it back. "Oh, yes, of course. Carmine Bianco. First, let me ask: Where did you get this name?"

"There was a car following us today. It's registered to him."

"Bad business. Bianco is a police officer, but corrupt. He is in the pocket of the Unione Corse—the Corsican Mafia. Why would they be interested in you, I wonder?"

"We don't think it's them," Remi said. "We suspect they're doing a favor for someone else."

"Ah. Not that it makes a difference. Bianco is an animal. Was it just him in the car?"

Sam shook his head. "Another one: dark complected, handlebar mustache."

"He doesn't sound familiar."

"Why don't the police do something about this Bianco?" Remi asked. "You said he's corrupt. Can't they arrest him?"

"On the mainland, perhaps, but out here, and on Sardinia and Corsica things are not quite that simple. I think I know the answer to this, but have to ask: I don't suppose I could convince you to leave? Tonight, before Bianco does something?"

Sam and Remi looked at one another and instinctively knew each other's thoughts. Sam spoke for them: "Thanks, but we've got to see this through."

Umberto nodded somberly. "I thought as much."

Remi said, "We don't want to put you and Teresa in danger. If you'll give us directions to—"

Umberto was already rising. "Nonsense. Wait here." He went inside then returned a minute later carrying a shoebox. "You'll need this," he said, handing it over.

Inside Sam found a genuine World War II–era nine-millimeter Luger pistol along with two full magazines.

"My father liberated that from the Gestapo officer who executed my uncles. As my father told the story, the man no longer had any use for it."

Umberto smiled grimly at them and winked.

"We can't accept this," Sam said.

"Of course you can. When you're done here, you can return it. Besides, I have another. My father was an exceptionally good liberator. Come, we'll go now."

CHAPTER 25

The graveyard to which Yvette had had Laurent's remains moved had no name, Umberto told them, but it was hundreds of years old, dating back to when Elba was still a French protectorate. Nor was it on any map.

They took the Lancia and followed the main road to the outskirts of the village then turned north, heading higher into the mountains, now in complete shadow as the sun set. After ten minutes Umberto, who was riding in the backseat, said, "Stop the car, please."

"What's wrong?" Sam said.

"Just pull over, please."

Sam did so, shutting off the headlights and coasting to a stop. Sam and Remi turned around to see Umberto rubbing his forehead. "I've done something terrible," he murmured.

"What?"

"I'm leading you into a trap."

"What are you talking about?" Remi asked.

"This afternoon, while we were still in town, Bianco came to my home. Teresa called me. He threatened to kill us if we didn't help him."

"Why are you telling us this?"

"The gun. My father took that gun from a man who was threatening his family, his friends. He was afraid, too, I am sure, just like I am, but he fought back. I have to do the same. I'm very sorry."

Sam and Remi were silent for a few minutes, then Remi said, "You told us. That's enough. Are they waiting for us?"

"No, but they're coming." He checked his watch. "Thirty minutes, no more. I am to let you open the crypt and recover whatever you've come for, then they'll take it and kill you both, I imagine. And perhaps me as well."

"How many men?" Sam asked.

"I don't know." Umberto pulled a spare magazine for his own Luger from his pocket and handed it over the seat to Sam. "The bullets in yours are dummies."

"Thanks, but why give us a gun at all?"

"I wanted to gain your trust. I hope you can forgive me."

"We'll let you know in an hour or so. If you cross us—"

"You have my permission to shoot me."

"I'll hold you to that," Sam said, staring him in the eyes.

Remi said, "What about Teresa? Won't she—"

"She's already gone," Umberto replied. "I have cousins in Nisporto; they'll protect her."

"Well, we have the sat phone. Call the police. Umberto?"

The Italian shook his head. "They wouldn't get here in time."

"We can turn around or keep going and do our damnedest to get in and out before they get here."

"There are only two roads in and out of here," Umberto said, "and Bianco will have both watched. You can be sure of that."

Remi looked at Sam. "You're quiet."

"Thinking." The engineer in him was looking for an elegant solution, but he quickly realized he was overthinking the situation. Much like with their initial run-in with Arkhipov at the boiler graveyard, they had neither the time nor the resources for a sophisticated plan.

"Fortune favors the bold," he finally said.

"Oh, no. . . ."

"He who dares, wins," Sam added.

"I know what that means," Remi said.

"What?" Umberto asked. "What's happening?"

"We're going to make it up as we go along."

Sam started the car, put it in gear, and pulled out.

They found the graveyard in a weed-filled meadow surrounded on three sides by hillocks covered in pine and cork trees. Only an acre in size, it was surrounded by a waist-high wrought-iron fence that had long ago been overtaken by rust and vines. Befitting the evening's task, a low fog filled the meadow, swirling around the headstones and crypts. The sky was clear, showing a bright full moon.

"Okay, I'm officially creeped out," Remi said, staring through the windshield as Sam brought the car to a stop before the gate. He shut off the engine and doused the headlights. Somewhere in the trees an owl hooted twice, then went silent. "All we're missing is howling wolves," she whispered.

"No wolves on Elba," Umberto replied. "Wild dogs. And snakes. Many snakes."

The graveyard was arranged haphazardly with no regard to spacing or symmetry. Headstones jutted from the weeds at odd angles, some within a foot of its neighbor, while crypts of all shapes and sizes rose from the ground in various states of disrepair, crumbling or overgrown by foliage or collapsed altogether. In contrast, several crypts, freshly painted, were islands of manicured grass and flowers.

"They're not much for civil planning, are they?" Sam said.

"It's been here so long the government can't bring itself to intervene," Umberto replied. "The truth is, I can't remember the last time anyone was buried here."

"How many are here?"

"Many hundreds, I think. Some graves are deep, some shallow. The dead are stacked atop one another."

Remi asked, "Where's Laurent's crypt?"

Umberto leaned forward and pointed through the windshield. "That one, in the far corner, the one with the domed roof."

Sam checked his watch. "Time to find out how well the Lancia holds up to punishment."

He started the engine, did a Y-turn on the gravel drive, then spun the wheel and drove into the meadow, the tall grass scraping the car's underbody. He followed the fence line to the back of the grave-yard and coasted to a stop behind Laurent's crypt. He shut off the engine again.

"Where does that go?" Sam asked Umberto, pointing past Remi out the passenger window. A half mile away a pair of tire ruts disap-peared over the hill and into the trees beyond.

"I have no idea. It's an old mining road. It hasn't been used for seventy, eighty years—since before the war."

Remi murmured, "The road less traveled."

"Not for long," Sam replied.

He opened the door and climbed out, Remi and Umberto fol-lowing. To Remi he said, "Why don't you wait here? Slide into the driver's seat and keep your eyes peeled. We'll just be a minute."

He and Umberto walked to the fence and hopped over.

Compared to some of its neighbors, Laurent's crypt was small, not much bigger than a walk-in closet and barely four feet tall, but, walk-ing around to the front side, Sam saw that it was sunk into the ground a few feet. Three moss-covered steps led to a rough-hewn wooden door. Sam pulled his LED microlight from his pocket and shined it on the lock while Umberto used the key. In keeping with the fog, the hooting owls, and the full moon, the hinges moaned as Umberto swung open the door. He glanced back at Sam and smiled nervously.

"Keep an eye out," Sam said.

He walked down the steps and through the door and found himself facing a curtain of cobwebs. Under the blue-white glow of his flash-light, spiders scrambled across the webs and disappeared. Using his hand like a blade Sam slowly cut the curtain down the center; desic-cated flies and moths pattered on the stone floor. Sam stepped inside.

The space measured five feet deep and eight feet wide and smelled of dust and rat droppings. To his right he heard the faint scratching of tiny claws on stone, then silence. In the center the sarcophagus, which was devoid of either markings or adornment, stood on a three-foot-high platform made of red brick. He stepped around the sarcophagus to the rear wall, then placed the flashlight between his teeth and gave the lid a tentative shove. It was lighter than he'd anticipated, sliding a couple inches with a hollow grating sound.

Sam pushed the lid another few inches, then grabbed the projecting end and walked the lid around until it was sitting perpendicular to the sarcophagus. He shined his light inside.

"Nice to finally meet you, Monsieur Laurent," he whispered.

Arnaud Laurent, now nothing more than a skeleton, had been buried in what Sam assumed was the full dress uniform of a Napoleonic-era army general, complete with ceremonial sword. Lying between his black-booted feet was a wooden box the size of a large hardcover book. Sam carefully lifted the box free, blew off the layer of dust covering it, then knelt down and placed it on the floor.

Inside he found an ivory comb, a flattened musket ball speckled with a flaky brown substance Sam guessed was blood, a few medals in tiny silk pouches, an oval-shaped gold locket inside which he found a picture of a woman—Laurent's wife, Marie, he assumed—and finally, a palm-sized brown leather book.

Breath held, Sam gently opened the book at its midpoint and could see in the narrow beam of his flashlight a line of shapes:

"Bingo," he whispered.

He returned the other items to the box, returned it to its place between Laurent's feet, and was about to close the lid when his flashlight glinted off something metallic. Wedged between Laurent's boot and the wall of the sarcophagus was what looked like a thumb-sized steel chisel. Sam fished it out. It was a die stamp, he realized, a type of stone chisel. One end was flattened like the head of a nail; the other end was concave with a knife-edged border. He shined his flashlight into the indentation. It was the outline of a cicada.

"Thank you, General," Sam whispered. "I wish we could have met two centuries ago."

He pocketed the stamp, closed the lid, and stepped out.

Umberto was nowhere to be seen.

Sam walked back up to ground level and looked around. "Umberto?" he whispered. "Umberto, where are—"

At the cemetery's gate a pair of headlights flashed to life, pinning him in their glare. He held his hand before his eyes, squinting.

"Don't move, Mr. Fargo." A Russian-accented voice echoed through the graveyard. "There is a rifle aimed at your head. Raise your hands above your head."

Sam complied, then muttered out of the side of his mouth, "Remi, go, get out of here."

"That's going to be a problem, Sam."

Slowly, he rotated his head over his shoulder.

Standing beside the Lancia's driver's-side door, a revolver pressed against Remi's temple, was Carmine Bianco.

CHAPTER 26

Gun never wavering from Remi's head, Bianco stared at Sam with a smug barracuda's grin. The headlights went dark. Sam looked back toward the gate and could see two figures walking toward him. Behind them, the dark outline of an SUV.

"Remi, are you okay?" Sam called over his shoulder.

"Shut up!" Bianco barked.

Sam ignored him. "Remi?"

"I'm okay."

Kholkov walked up through the knee-high weeds and stopped ten feet away. To his right, Mustache held a scoped hunting rifle at his shoulder, its muzzle level with Sam's chest.

"You're armed, I assume?" Kholkov said.

"Seemed the prudent thing to do," Sam replied.

"Very carefully, Mr. Fargo, let's have it."

Sam slowly pulled the Luger from his pocket and dropped it on the ground between them.

Kholkov looked around. "Where's Cipriani?"

"Hog-tied and gagged in his barn," Sam lied. "After a little coaxing, he told us about your partnership."

"Too bad for him. At any rate, here we are. Give me the book."

"First call off Bianco."

"You have no leverage. Give me the book or at the count of three I'll order Bianco to shoot her. Then my friend here will shoot you and we'll take the book."

Ten feet behind and to Kholkov's left, a shadowed figure rose from the weeds alongside another crypt and started creeping forward.

Sam kept his eyes fixed on Kholkov. "How do I know you won't shoot us once you have the book?"

"You don't," said Kholkov. "As I said, you've got no leverage."

The figure stopped just beyond arm's reach behind the Russian.

Sam smiled, shrugged. "I have to disagree."

"What exactly is that supposed to mean?"

"I think he's referring to me," Umberto said.

Kholkov tensed, but didn't move a muscle. Mustache, however, started to spin toward Umberto, who barked, "He moves another inch and it'll be my pleasure to shoot you, Kholkov."

"Stop!" the Russian ordered.

Mustache froze.

Umberto said, "Sorry for the disappearing act, Sam. I saw them pulling in and only had a moment to decide."

"You're forgiven," Sam replied. Then to Kholkov: "Tell Bianco to give Remi the gun and join us."

Kholkov hesitated. Sam could see the muscles in his jaw pulsing. "I won't ask again," Sam said.

"Bianco, give her the gun and climb over the fence."

Bianco shouted something. While Sam's Italian consisted of little more than simple greetings, he felt certain his response was either scatological or carnal in nature, or both.

"Bianco, now!"

Without turning, Sam called over his shoulder, "Remi . . . ?"

"I've got the gun. He's climbing over the fence now."

"Kholkov, tell your mustachioed friend to take his rifle by the barrel and toss it over the fence into the trees."

Kholkov gave the order and the man complied. Bianco appeared on Sam's left and walked around to join Kholkov and Mustache.

"Now you," Sam told Kholkov.

"I'm not armed."

"Show me."

Kholkov took off his jacket, turned it inside out, gave it a shake, then dropped it on the ground.

"Shirt."

Kholkov pulled his shirttails from his waistband and slowly spun in a circle. Sam nodded at Umberto, who circled around Kholkov and backed across the open space, stopping to retrieve the Luger, which he handed over to Sam.

"Stronzo!" Bianco barked.

"What did he say?" Sam asked.

"He seems to think my mother and father were not married when I was born."

"I will kill you," Bianco spat. "And your wife!"

"Shut up. Now I recognize that one—the one with the mustache."

"Who is he?"

"A nobody. He's a petty thief, a thug." Umberto called to the man, "I know who you are! If I see you again, I'll cut off your nose!"

Sam said, "Kholkov, here's how this is going to work: You're all going to lie on the ground and we're going to leave. If you follow us, I'll burn the book."

"You're lying. You won't do that."

"Bad gamble. To save our lives, I'll do it without a second thought."

It was a lie, of course, and Sam knew that Kholkov knew it, too, but he was hoping to plant even a slight seed of doubt, enough to buy them some running room. He'd considered other options—tie them up, disable their vehicle, call the police, but his every instinct was telling him to put as much distance as possible between themselves and Kholkov, and to do it as quickly as possible. And were he a different man, there would be a fourth option: Kill them right now.

But he wasn't that kind of man and didn't want cold-blooded murder on his conscience.

Kholkov was a superbly trained soldier who knew more ways to kill than most chefs had recipes. Every minute he, Remi, and Umberto spent around these men increased the chances of the tables being turned.

"You won't get off the island," Kholkov growled, lying down.

"Maybe, but we're going to give it the old college try."

"Even if you do, I'll find you again."

"That's a bridge we'll cross when we get there."

Umberto said, "Sam, a favor if I might. I'd like to take Bianco along with us. I'll make sure he's no trouble."

"Why?"

"Let me worry about that."

Sam considered this, then nodded.

"Let's go!" Umberto ordered Bianco. "Hands up!"

Under Umberto's gun, Bianco started walking toward the fence. Once they were over it and standing beside the car, Umberto plucked Bianco's handcuffs from his belt, secured them around his wrists, frisked him, then shoved him in the backseat and climbed in behind him. Remi started the car, then opened the door for Sam and slid over to the passenger seat.

Sam got in the car, put it in gear, turned around, and headed around the fence toward the main road.

"How long do you think they'll wait?" Remi asked.

Sam glanced out the side window. Kholkov and Mustache were already on their feet and running back through the graveyard.

"About five seconds," he said and stepped on the accelerator.

CHAPTER 27

Sam sped down the fence line, heading for the main gate. In the corner of his eye he could see Kholkov and Mustache sprinting in the same direction, dodging headstones as they went, fog swirling in their wake.

"Gonna be close," Sam muttered.

"Where are you going?" Remi said. "You heard Umberto . . . Bianco will have the roads watched."

"How's your aim tonight?"

"What? Oh." She held up Bianco's gun as though suddenly remembering she had it. "Fine, why—"

"I'm going to make a quick pass by their SUV. See if you can get the tires. Umberto, are you sure you can handle him?"

In the backseat, Bianco was leaning in the corner wearing that same smug grin. Umberto reversed the Luger in his hand and smacked Bianco across the temple; he went limp and slid into the floor. "I am sure!"

The corner of the fence was coming up fast; thirty feet beyond that and to the right was the SUV. Kholkov had pulled ahead of Mustache and was seconds from reaching the gate.

"Get ready!" Sam called.

Remi rolled down her window, stuck the pistol out the opening, and braced her arm on the door. "You're going too fast!"

"Have to. Just do your best. If you can't get the tires, try for the windshield. Damn!"

Kholkov raced through the gate and skidded to a stop beside the SUV's driver's-side door. The interior dome light popped on.

Remi snapped off two shots. The bullets sparked on the SUV's quarter panel, but missed the tire. "Too fast!" Remi called.

"Windshield! Empty it!"

Remi squeezed off four shots, the gun's barrel spouting orange flame. Three spiderwebbed holes appeared in the SUV's windshield.

"Atta girl!"

Suddenly Kholkov appeared around the front of the car, dropping into a crouch, a gun coming up in his hands. Sam spun the wheel hard left. The Lancia's tail whipped around, the front tires spinning freely in the moist grass before finally finding purchase. Two metallic thunks echoed through the car as Kholkov's bullets hit the car's trunk. Sam accelerated again, straightening the car out and heading back into the meadow toward the hills.

"Everybody okay?" Sam asked.

Umberto peeked his head over the front seat, said, "Yes," then disappeared again. Remi nodded and said, "Sorry I couldn't get the tires. We were going too fast."

"No worries. You got the windshield; that'll slow them down. They'll either have to punch it out or drive with their heads out the side windows."

Remi turned in her seat and saw Kholkov and Mustache standing on the SUV's hood stomping on the windshield. "Option A," she said. The windshield collapsed inward; Kholkov and Mustache knelt down, dragged it out, and tossed it aside. Seconds later the SUV's lights popped on and it surged forward, speeding into the meadow.

"Here they come. With that four-wheel drive they'll—"

"I know," Sam muttered. "Hold on!"

The Lancia lurched sideways as the front wheels slipped into the mining road's ruts. Sam tapped the brakes, gave the wheel a jerk, felt the rear wheels follow, then punched the accelerator again. The Lancia surged up the hill. The road was narrower than he'd imagined, no wider than six feet. When they reached the crest the trees closed in around them, boughs scraping the car's sides and blotting out the sky. Headlights washed through the back window as the SUV started up the hill.

On the downslope now, Sam started to accelerate, but immediately tapped the brakes as the road veered right and deeper into the trees. Behind them the SUV's nose cleared the crest, went airborne, then slammed down again.

"He's going to miss it," Remi said.

She was right. Still bouncing from its impact, the SUV overshot the turn and skidded to a stop, its hood buried in the trees. Sam glanced in the mirror in time to see the SUV's brake lights pop on just before the Lancia plunged down another slope. Sam caught a fleeting glimpse of washboard ruts ahead and shouted, "Hold on." Wheels thumping and shock absorbers shrieking in protest, the Lancia bumped over the patch, then up another slope, down the other side, and onto a straightaway. Sam accelerated. Branches slapped at the windshield, pinecones bouncing over the hood and over the roof. The SUV reappeared behind them, its headlights bouncing wildly as Kholkov negotiated the washboard.

While more durable and powerful than the Lancia, the SUV was also two feet wider, a disadvantage Sam now saw was bearing fruit. Where the pine boughs had simply swiped at the Lancia, they were thrashing the SUV's hood and into the hole where the windshield had been. Branches were snapping off, jutting from the grille, and becoming entangled with the windshield wipers. The headlights fell back.

"Sam, watch out!"

He tore his eyes from the rearview mirror in time to see a boulder looming ahead. He spun the wheel hard right, sending the Lancia in a sideways skid. The boulder filled Sam's window. He stepped on the gas as the Lancia lurched forward, but not quickly enough. With a crunch, the rear quarter panel glanced off the boulder and the rear side window shattered. The impact spun the Lancia's tail around, off the road, and under the pine boughs. The side bumper smashed into a trunk and they jerked to a stop. The engine sputtered and died. Pine needles rained down on the windshield.

"There goes our deposit," Remi said.

"Everybody okay?" Sam asked. "Remi?"

"Fine."

"Splendid," called Umberto.

"Bianco?"

"Still napping."

Out Sam's window they saw the SUV's headlights filtering through the trees. He turned the ignition. Nothing.

"Still in gear," Remi said.

"Damn. Thanks."

He put the shifter into park and turned the ignition again. The engine chugged and wheezed but didn't catch. He tried again.

"Come on, come on. . . ."

Down the road the SUV was halfway down the straightaway and approaching the boulder.

The Lancia's engine caught, revved up, then coughed out.

"Cutting it close, Sam," Remi said, teeth clenched.

He closed his eyes, said a quick prayer, tried again. The engine caught. He shifted into drive, spun the wheel right, and accelerated back onto the road.

"Umberto, slow them down!"

"Okay!"

Umberto stuck his Luger out the window and squeezed off two shots, and then two more. The bullets thudded into the grille, shattering the driver's-side headlight. The SUV swerved left, heading straight for the boulder, then jinked right. The side mirror scraped the rock, shattered, and bounced away into the darkness.

The SUV's lights filled the Lancia's interior. Sam squinted and slapped the rearview mirror off-angle. He glanced over his shoulder and saw a hand holding a gun jut through the windshield gap.

"Down, get down!" he yelled. Remi slid to the floorboards.

The gun roared from the SUV, muzzle winking from the darkened interior. Umberto poked his head up over the seat, said, "I'll slow them down," then leaned out the side window with the Luger.

"No, don't!"

Two more shots. Umberto screamed and rolled back into the car. "I'm hit!"

"Where?"

"The forearm! I'm okay," he gasped.

"The hell with this," Sam muttered. "Brace yourselves!"

He stood on the brakes for a two count, then punched the gas again. The SUV skidded, swerved, then slammed into the Lancia's bumper. Sam had timed it well, accelerating just before the moment of impact. They pulled ahead of the SUV: twenty feet . . . thirty . . . four car lengths.

"Whoa!"

Abruptly, the trees disappeared from either side of them.

Remi popped her head up. "Oh, no!"

The Lancia's wheels thumped over a berm and they were airborne. Open space loomed in the windshield. The Lancia landed again and bounced, the tires spraying gravel.

"Shoulder!" Remi called.

"I see it," Sam replied and spun the wheel left. The Lancia went into a tail skid. He eased right, compensating, then straightened out. Out Remi's window a boulder-strewn embankment dropped several hundred feet into a ravine.

Engine roaring, Kholkov's SUV sailed over the berm and slammed onto the road.

"He's not going to make it," Remi said.

"Let's hope."

The SUV went into its own skid, but Kholkov overcompensated. The passenger-side rear tire crunched into the rocks along the shoulder and slipped over the edge. Carried by its own momentum, the rear third of the SUV's chassis scraped over the dirt, edging inch by inch over the precipice until it stopped, partially suspended in space.

Sam took his foot off the accelerator and let the Lancia coast to a stop. Fifty feet behind them the SUV was seesawing at the road's edge. Aside from the faint rhythmic groaning of stressed metal, all was quiet.

Remi sat up, looked around.

"Careful," Sam whispered.

"Are we going to help them?" she asked.

A hand emerged from the darkened interior of the SUV and grasped a windshield wiper. A muzzle flashed from within the cab.

A bullet thunked into the Lancia's bumper.

"The hell with them," Sam said and stepped on the accelerator.

"That's gratitude for you," Remi said. "We could have bumped them into that ravine."

"Something tells me we're going to wish we did."

CHAPTER 28

GRAND HÔTEL BEAUVAU VIEUX PORT, MARSEILLE, FRANCE

Even as Sam tipped the bellhop and shut the door behind him Remi was dialing the iPhone. Selma answered on the first ring. "Safe and sound, Mrs. Fargo?"

"Safe and sound," Remi replied as she sat on the bed and kicked off her shoes. "Now will you tell me why we're in Marseille?"

After leaving Kholkov and his mustachioed partner teetering on the precipice, they'd driven at the Lancia's best speed to Nisporto. Umberto, his forearm wrapped in his own shirt, used the sat phone to alert his cousin to their arrival.

Nisporto, a village of a few hundred people, sat in the nook of a V-shaped cove ten miles up the coast from Portoferraio. When they arrived, Umberto's wife, Teresa, and his cousins—all five of them—were waiting at the back door. While Teresa tended to Umberto's wound, which had missed hitting any bones or arteries, the cousins bundled the now-conscious Bianco into the garage. The mother of the house, Umberto's aunt Brunela, ushered Sam and Remi into the house and straight to the kitchen table, where she set about feeding them homemade pasta with onions, capers, olives, and red sauce. Thirty minutes later Umberto reappeared, his arm bandaged.

"We've put you in some danger," Sam said.

"Nonsense. You've helped me redeem my honor. I think my father would have been proud."

"I think he would, too," Remi said, leaning over and kissing him on the cheek. "Thank you."

Sam asked, "Do we want to know what you're going to do with Bianco?"

"Here and in Corsica, he's untouchable. On the mainland . . ." Umberto shrugged. "I'll make some calls. I think with the right evidence, real or otherwise, the Carabinieri will be happy to embrace him. As for the other one, his partner . . . he's a coward. We'll be fine, my friends. Now, finish eating and we'll see about getting you off the island."

Knowing Bondaruk's influence and Kholkov's thoroughness made the Marina di Campo Airport too risky, they'd enlisted Umberto's cousin Ermete, who ran a charter fishing boat, to ferry them back to Piombino on the Italian mainland. From there they'd returned to Florence, checked into the Palazzo Magnani Feroni, and called Selma, who'd directed them to e-mail her the photographed symbols from Laurent's codebook then head straight to Marseille. The next morning they dropped the book itself into an overnight envelope for San Diego, then headed to the airport.

"Why all the mystery? Remi now asked Selma. Sam sat down on the bed and Remi put the phone on speaker.

"No mystery," Selma replied. "I was hashing out some details, but I knew you'd want to be in Marseille one way or the other. By the way, Pete and Wendy are working on the symbols right now. It's fascinating stuff, but the book's condition is the big question—"

Sam said, "Selma."

"Oh, sorry. Remember Wolfgang Müller, captain of the *UM-77*? I found him."

"Him? You mean—"

"Yep, he's still alive. Took a lot of legwork, but it turns out he was aboard the *Lothringen* when it was captured. After the war he was shipped back to Germany by way of Marseille. He got off the boat, but didn't take the train home. He lives with his granddaughter. I've got their address. . . ."

The next morning they got up and walked to a café, Le Capri, a few blocks away on Rue Bailli de Suffren overlooking the Vieux Port, or Old Port, which was filled with sailboats of all shapes and sizes, their sails dancing in the offshore breeze. The bright morning sun glinted off the water. At the mouth of the port, rising from the north and south shorelines, were the forts of Saint Jean and Saint Nicholas. Above these on the hillsides stood the Abbaye de Saint Victor and the churches of Saint Vincent and Saint Catherine. Farther out, in the Bay of Marseille proper, lay the four-island archipelago of Frioul.

Sam and Remi had been to Marseille three times together, the last a few years earlier on their way to the Camargue up the coast. Every May some twenty thousand gypsies from western and eastern Europe gathered there to celebrate their *gitane* heritage.

They finished breakfast and hailed a taxi, giving the driver an address in the Panier, a cluster of medievalesque neighborhoods filled with tightly packed pastel-painted houses sandwiched between the town hall and the Vieille Charité. Wolfgang Müller lived in a two-story butter yellow, white-shuttered apartment on Rue de Cordelles. A blond woman in her mid twenties answered the door when they knocked.

"*Bonjour,*" Sam said.

"*Bonjour.*"

"*Parlez-vous anglais?*"

"Yes, I speak English."

Sam introduced himself and Remi. "We're looking for Monsieur Müller. Is he at home?"

"Yes, of course. May I ask what this is about?"

They'd already discussed this and decided honesty was the best course. Remi replied, "We'd like to talk to him about the *UM-77* and the *Lothringen.*"

The woman cocked her head slightly, her eyes narrowing. Clearly her grandfather had told her about his time in the war. "One moment, please." Leaving the door open, she walked down a hall and disappeared around the corner. They heard muffled voices for a minute, then she reappeared. "Please, come in. My name is Monique. This way, please."

She led them into the front room, where they found Müller sitting in a rocking chair in front of a muted television tuned to France's version of the Weather Channel. He wore a gray cardigan buttoned up to his throat, and his lap was covered in a blue and yellow argyle blanket. Completely bald, his face heavily wrinkled, Müller watched them through a pair of placid blue eyes.

"Good morning," he said in a suprisingly strong voice. He gestured with a trembling hand to a floral-patterned couch across from him. "Please. Can I offer you some coffee?"

"No, thank you," Remi answered.

"Monique tells me you found Ilsa."

"Ilsa?" Sam asked.

"It's what I named the *77*. After my wife; she died in the Dresden bombings a few months after we left Bremerhaven. You found her in the cave, in Rum Cay?"

Remi nodded. "We were doing some exploring and came across the entrance. We found her sitting on the bottom, in almost pristine condition."

"She's still there?"

Sam smiled. "Well, no, not exactly. There was a . . . problem. We used her as what you might call an escape raft."

"I don't understand."

"The main entrance collapsed. We rode the *77*—"

"Ilsa."

"Rode Ilsa down the underground river and out through another cave."

Müller's eyes went wide and he smiled. "That's astounding. I'm glad she was put to good use."

"We've arranged to have her transported back to the U.S. If you'd like, we'll have her shipped—"

Müller was shaking his head. "That's kind of you, but no. Keep her; take good care of her." He smiled and shook his finger at them. "Something tells me you didn't come all this way just to tell me that."

"We also found the *UM-34*."

At this Müller leaned forward. "And Manfred?"

"Captain Boehm was still aboard her." Sam recounted their discovery of the sub, leaving out any mention of Bondaruk or Kholkov. "The authorities are salvaging her right now."

"*Mein Gott* . . . We'd always worried about the weather. Those boats weren't meant for open ocean." Müller's eyes went distant for ten seconds, then he blinked and refocused on them. "Manfred was a good friend of mine. It always pained me that I never knew what happened. Thank you."

"The reason we're here is the wine," Remi said.

"The wine? Oh, the bottles . . . yes, we were going to celebrate with them after the mission was over. Are you telling me they survived?"

Remi nodded. "One aboard the *34*, and one aboard Ilsa."

"And the third? Did you find that one? As Manfred had the harder of the two missions, I gave him two bottles."

"We found a shard near his sub's resting place. We're not sure how it got out of the sub."

Müller waved his hand. "The vagaries of war."

"Just out of curiosity," Sam said, "can you tell us about your mission? What were you and Boehm trying to accomplish?"

Müller frowned, thinking. After a few moments he said, "I suppose it doesn't really matter now. . . . It was an absurd task, really, concocted by the Führer himself. Manfred was supposed to sail up Chesapeake Bay and attack the navy base at Norfolk. At the same time, I was to attack the ammunition depot in Charleston, but Ilsa had a problem with her screw, so we were delayed. Before we could repair it, we were recalled to Bremerhaven. You know the rest, about the *Lothringen* and all that."

"You'd stopped at Rum Cay for refitting? What kind?"

"Bigger batteries to increase the boats' ranges. Another idiotic plan. Both Manfred and I knew the missions were suicide."

"Then why did you volunteer?"

Müller shrugged. "Duty. Indiscretion of youth. Neither of us were fond of Hitler or the Party, but it was still our country. We wanted to do what we could."

"We were hoping you might tell us more about the bottles," Remi said. "Where they came from."

"Why?"

"We're collectors. As it turns out, they were very old and very rare."

Müller chuckled. "I never knew. Well, I might have guessed they were important somehow. My brother Karl gave them to me before we shipped out from Bremerhaven. He told me he found them here, actually—he was in the army and was part of the occupation force."

"Where exactly did he find them?"

"Let me think. . . ." Müller scratched his head. "My memory isn't quite what it used to be. It was a castle . . . no, not a castle. A fort." He sighed in frustration, then his eyes lit up. "It was one of the islands in the bay. . . . Do you remember that book by Dumas—*The Count of Monte Cristo*?"

Both Sam and Remi had read it. In an instant they knew what Müller was talking about. "Île d'If?"

"Yes! That's it. He found them in the Château d'If."

CHAPTER 29

CHÂTEAU D'IF, FRANCE

Despite their love for Marseille, the Fargos had never managed to squeeze the Frioul Archipelago and Château d'If into their itinerary, an oversight they planned to correct that night with their own private tour. They doubted the château's staff would let them explore every nook and cranny of the island. Though neither of them knew exactly what they'd be looking for, or whether they'd recognize it if it appeared, the expedition seemed the next logical step in the journey.

From Müller's apartment they took a taxi to the Malmousque, a waterfront district overlooking the Friouls, and found a quiet café. They settled under the umbrella on the patio and ordered a pair of double espressos.

A mile offshore they could see Château d'If, a faded ocher-colored lump of rock fronted by sloping cliffs, vertical ramparts, and stone arches.

While the island itself covered just over seven acres, the château itself was a smaller square, a hundred feet to a side, made up of a three-story main building flanked on three sides by cylindrical turrets topped with crenellated cannon slots.

At the behest of King François I, Château d'If began its life in the 1520s as a fortress to defend the city against attacks from the sea, a purpose that was short-lived as it was converted into a prison for France's political and religious enemies. Much like San Francisco's Alcatraz, Château d'If's location and its deadly offshore currents gave it a reputation as escape proof, a claim that was shattered, at least fictionally, by Alexandre Dumas's *Count of Monte Cristo*, in which the character Edmond Dantès, after fourteen years of imprisonment, managed to escape d'If.

Sam read from the brochure he'd picked up at the Vieux Port tourist office: "'Blacker than the sea, blacker than the sky, rose like a phantom the giant of granite, whose projecting crags seemed like arms extended to seize their prey.' That's how Dantès described it."

"Doesn't seem so bad from here."

"Try being stuck in the dungeon for a dozen years."

"Good point. What else?"

"The prison operated by a strict class structure. Rich inmates could buy their way into private cells on the upper floors, with windows and a fireplace. As for the poor, they got the basement dungeons and the oubliettes—which are . . ."

"It's derivative of *oublier*—'to forget.' They were essentially trapdoored pits in the floor of a dungeon." Remi's French was also better than Sam's. "You go in and you're forgotten—left to rot."

The phone trilled and Sam answered it. It was Selma: "Mr. Fargo, I have something for you."

"Go ahead," Sam said. He put the phone on speaker so Remi could hear.

"We've deciphered the first two lines of symbols on the bottle, but that's it," Selma began. "The other lines are going to take some time. I think we're missing a key of some kind. Anyway, the lines spell out a riddle:

"Folly of Capetian, Sébastien's revelation;
A city under cannon;
From the third realm of the forgotten a sign that eternal
 Sheol will fail.

"We're working on solving it—"

"Done," Sam proclaimed. "It's talking about Château d'If."

"Pardon me?"

He recounted their meeting with Wolfgang Müller. "The fortress is where his brother found the bottles. I already had the answer; from there it was just a matter of working backward. 'Capetian' refers to the dynastic line King François I came from; he had the fortress built. 'Sébastien' is the first name of Vauban, the engineer who had to tell the government the fort was all but useless. For whatever reason, the architects had built it with the heaviest fortifications and gun embattlements facing not the open sea, and potential invaders, but the city—'a city under cannon.'"

"Impressive, Mr. Fargo."

"It's in the brochure. As for the second line, I don't know."

"I think I do," Remi said. "In Hebrew, 'Sheol' means abode of the dead, or underworld. The opposite—eternal Sheol—is everlasting life. Remember the cicada from the bottle . . . ?"

Sam was nodding. "From Napoleon's crest: resurrection and immortality. And the other part . . . 'the third realm of the forgotten'?"

"It's the French version of a dungeon: oubliette. To forget. Unless we're wrong, somewhere in the basement of the château is a cicada waiting to be found. But why a riddle at all?" Remi wondered. "Why not simply, 'go here, find this'?"

"That's where it gets really interesting," Selma replied. "From what I've been able to translate so far, Laurent's book is part diary, part decryption key. He makes it pretty clear the bottles themselves aren't the real prize. He called them 'arrows on a map.'"

"Arrows to what?" Remi asked. "And for whom to follow?"

"He doesn't say. We'll know more when I finish the translation."

Sam said, "Well, it seems clear Laurent was doing this on Napoleon's orders, and if they went to this much trouble to hide the bottles, whatever's at the end of the map has to be something spectacular."

"Which might explain why Bondaruk has no problem with murder," Remi replied.

They chatted for a few more minutes, then hung up.

"Uh-oh," Remi said out of the side of her mouth and pointing with her eyes. "Look who's here."

Sam turned around. Kholkov was walking across the patio toward them, hands stuffed into the pockets of his jacket. Sam and Remi tensed, ready to move.

"Relax, do you think I'd be stupid enough to shoot you both in broad daylight?" Kholkov asked, stopping before them. He pulled his hands from his pockets and held them up. "Unarmed."

"I see you escaped your little fender bender," Remi said.

Kholkov pulled out a chair and sat down.

Sam said dryly, "Please, join us."

"You could have easily bumped us off the edge," Kholkov said. "Why didn't you?"

"It occurred to us, believe me. If not for your trigger-happy friend, who knows?"

"I apologize for that. He overreacted."

"I don't suppose you'd care to explain how you've been tracking us," Remi said.

Kholkov smiled; there was none of it in his eyes. "I don't suppose you'd be willing to tell me why you've come here."

"You suppose correctly," Remi replied.

"Whatever you're selling, we're not buying," Sam said. "Your colleague kidnapped, tortured, and was seconds away from killing a friend of ours, and you've tried to kill us twice. Tell us why you're here."

"My employer is proposing a truce. A partnership."

Remi laughed softly. "Let me guess: We help you find whatever you're after and you'll kill us for it later rather than sooner."

"Not at all. We join forces and split the proceeds, eighty-twenty."

"We don't even know what we're after," Sam said.

"Something of great value—both historically and monetarily."

"And which of those interests Bondaruk most?" Remi asked.

"That's his business."

Sam and Remi had no illusions. Her prediction of Bondaruk's and Kholkov's plans for them was dead-on. Whatever Bondaruk's true motives and whatever the prize, there was no way they were going to let it fall into the Ukrainian's hands.

Kholkov added, "Let's just say the items involve a family legacy. He's simply trying to finish what was begun a long time ago. If you were to help bring that about, he'd be properly grateful."

"No deal," Sam said.

Remi added, "And you pass along a message for us: Nuts."

"You should reconsider," Kholkov said. "Have a look around."

Sam and Remi did so. Standing on the far side of the patio were three of Kholkov's men—all familiar faces from the Rum Cay cave.

"The gang's all here," Sam said.

"No, they're not. I have more. Wherever you go, we'll be there. One way or another, we'll get what we want. What you need to decide is whether you wish to live through this."

"We'll manage," Remi said.

Kholkov shrugged. "Your choice. I don't suppose you're stupid enough to have brought the codebook along with you, are you?"

"No," Sam replied. "And we're not stupid enough to have left it at the hotel, either, but you're welcome to have a look around."

"We already did. I assume it's already in Mrs. Wondrash's hands."

"Either that or it's in a safe-deposit box," Remi said.

"No, I don't think so. I think you have your people trying to decode it right now. Perhaps we'll pay them a visit. I've heard San Diego is beautiful this time of year."

"Good luck with that," Sam said lightly, fighting to keep his face impassive.

"You're talking about your security system?" Kholkov waved his hand dismissively. "That won't be any trouble."

"Clearly you're not familiar with my résumé," Sam said.

Kholkov hesitated. "Ah, yes, an engineer. Tinkered with the alarm system, have you?"

Remi added, "And even if you get past that, who knows what you'll find once you're inside? You said it yourself: We're not stupid."

Kholkov's brows furrowed, a flicker of uncertainty, but it was gone in a second. "We'll see. Last chance, Mr. and Mrs. Fargo. After this, the gloves come off."

"You have our answer," Sam replied.

CHAPTER 30

CHÂTEAU D'IF

A drizzle had begun to fall shortly before they left the hotel and now, as midnight approached, it had given way to a steady rain that pattered through the trees and gurgled down the rain gutters. The streets glistened under the hazy yellow glow of the streetlights. Here and there late-night pedestrians hurried down the sidewalks under umbrellas or folded newspaper or waited in clusters beneath bus shelters.

In the alley across from their hotel, Sam and Remi stood in the shadows and watched the lobby doors.

Down the block a gray Citroën Xsara sat at the curb, a pair of figures just visible in the dimmed interior. Earlier from the window of their hotel room Remi had gotten a look at the driver's face: he'd been with Kholkov at the Malmousque café. Whether there were more watchers around they couldn't tell, but they knew it was best to assume so.

After parting company with Kholkov at the café earlier that afternoon, they'd roamed the Malmousque, shopping and taking in the sights for a few hours. They saw neither Kholkov nor his men until they started back to the hotel, when two men on motorcycles fell in behind their taxi.

Despite their nonplussed reaction to Kholkov's threats, Sam and Remi had taken them seriously. Fearing their room was bugged, they found a quiet corner in the mostly deserted hotel bar and called Rube Haywood on the Iridium; he wasn't at CIA headquarters in Langley, but they reached him at home.

Sam put him on speakerphone and quickly explained the situation and their worries.

Rube said, "I know a guy in Long Beach—used to work for the Diplomatic Security Service. He runs his own shop now. Want me to have him send a couple guys to the house?"

"We'd be grateful."

"Give me ten minutes." He called back in five: "Done. They'll be there in two hours. Tell Selma they'll have IDs—Kozal Security Group. They'll ask for Mrs. French."

"Got it."

"Don't you think it's time to call it a day?" Rube asked. "You've seen how far these guys will go. Nothing's worth this."

"We don't even know what it is," Remi said.

"You get my point. I'm worried about you two."

"We appreciate that, Rube, but we're going to see this through."

Haywood sighed. "At least let me help you."

"What did you have in mind?" asked Sam.

"I've taken a second look at Kholkov. A few years ago he was in Chechnya; we think he was playing middleman for a black-market AK-47 dealer. Wouldn't take much to get his name slipped onto the Terrorist Watch List. A couple calls and I could put him on the radar of the DCPJ," he said, referring to the Direction Centrale Police Judiciaire, or Central Directorate Judicial Police, France's version of the FBI. "There's nothing they could arrest him on, but they might be able to detain him and his buddies for a while."

"Do it. Any breathing room you can buy us will help."

"The question is whether they'll be able to find him. Given his background, he's not going to make it easy for them."

Three hours later Rube had called back: The DCPJ had put out a bulletin for Kholkov, but he wouldn't know anything more for a few hours, if then. The French, Rube told them, were cagey about sharing information.

"I don't suppose you know a French version of Guido the Shoemaker–slash–Arms Dealer?"

"Sam, the French are rabid about their gun laws; you don't want to get caught with an unregistered one. But, I do know a guy named Maurice. . . ."

He gave Sam the phone number and they hung up.

Now Remi pulled up her jacket collar against the chill and huddled closer to Sam beneath the umbrella. "I don't see anyone else."

"Me neither. Shall we?"

With one last look around they stepped from the alley and started down the sidewalk.

Using the rudimentary tradecraft skills Sam had picked up at Camp Perry, they strolled the streets north of the harbor for an hour, doubling back on their path, stepping abruptly into cafés and then out the back door, and generally watching for any signs of pursuit. Satisfied they were alone, they hailed a cab and directed the driver to take them to Rue Loge on the Vieux Port.

As promised by the rental company's manager, at a slip in the northwest corner of the harbor they found waiting for them a gray eighteen-foot Mistral. Though essentially a motor whaleboat with a glassed-in pilothouse barely bigger than a phone booth, it was wide-beamed and sported a reliable and quiet Lombardi engine. It would, they hoped, serve their purposes.

Using the key the manager had messengered over, Sam undid the padlocked hawser and the lines while Remi started the engine. He jumped aboard and she throttled up, pointing the bow toward the mouth of the harbor.

———————

Ten minutes later the breakwater appeared off the bow. Astern the lights of Marseille, hazy in the rain, reflected off the rippled surface of the water. Working to keep up with the droplets streaming down the pilothouse windscreen, the single windshield wiper thumped softly.

Beside Remi at the wheel, Sam said, "I've been thinking about what Kholkov said." He saw her expression and quickly said, "Not about his offer—about what Bondaruk's interest is in whatever-it-is. He said it was a legacy. We know he's deadly serious about it, so maybe the answer's in his family history."

"Good point," Remi said, taking a buoy down the Mistral's port side. "We'll turn Selma loose on it. You're not, are you—having second thoughts, I mean?"

"Only as far as you're concerned."

Remi smiled in the darkness, her face dimly lit by the helm console's green lighting. "We've been through worse."

"Such as?"

"Well, for starters there was that time in Senegal when you insulted that shaman—"

"Forget I asked."

———————

Thirty minutes later Île d'If appeared, a white lump rising from the dark ocean a half mile off the bow. The château had closed at five thirty and aside from a lone navigation beacon pulsing red against the night sky, the island was completely dark.

"Doesn't look as welcoming at night, does it?" Remi asked.

"Not even close."

In preparation for their after-hours tour, they'd used Google Earth to scrutinize the island for hidden mooring spots that would shield them from not only Kholkov, should he and his men happen to follow, but also the Marseille harbor patrol. They'd found a promising spot on the island's seaward side.

Now Remi eased the Mistral to port. They spent a half hour circumnavigating the island, looking for other boats or signs of life.

Seeing nothing, they came about and proceeded along the northern shoreline. Ahead, the château's westernmost turret, the largest of the three, came into view above the battlement. Remi steered into the cove below it, throttled down, and let the Mistral glide to a stop at the base of the wall. Aside from a rain-churned surface, the water was flat calm here. Sam dropped anchor and used the boat hook to pull the Mistral closer to the rocks. Remi jumped over and followed, stern line in hand. He jammed the line beneath a basketball-sized rock.

Hand in hand they picked their way along the wall, hopping from rain-slick boulder to rain-slick boulder until they reached a particularly tall one they'd spotted on the satellite shots. Sam climbed atop it, positioned himself below a notch in the battlements used by archers, then leaped up and grabbed the wall's inner ledge. He chinned himself up and crawled atop the wall, then he helped Remi up and down the other side. He hopped down beside her.

"Thank God for bad architecture," he said.

If not for the fort's backward-facing fortifications, they would have needed an extension ladder to accomplish what they'd just done.

"Don't see anyone," Remi said. "You?"

Sam shook his head. In their research they'd found no mention of the island employing after-hours guards, but to be safe, they would proceed as if there were.

With Remi in the lead, they crept forward along the curved wall of the turret to where it met the straight western wall and followed this to the end. Beside them, the stone, having been warmed by the sun all day then soaked by the rain, smelled like chalk. Remi peeked around the corner.

"Clear," she whispered.

In Sam's pocket, the Iridium vibrated. He pulled it out and answered, keeping his voice a whisper. It was Rube: "Bad news, Sam. The DCPJ can't find Kholkov or his buddies. They know he entered the country on his own passport, but none of the hotels or rental car agencies have any record of him."

"Switched to a false passport," Sam guessed.

"Probably so. Bottom line, he's still out there. Be careful."

"Thanks, Rube. We'll be in touch."

Sam hung up and gave Remi the news. "We're not any worse off than we were before. Shall we?"

"Absolutely."

They continued along the southern wall and around the next turret to the château's side entrance, an arched breezeway that led into the courtyard.

"Freeze," Sam whispered. "Very slowly, crouch down." Together they dropped to their knees.

"What?" Remi whispered.

"Directly ahead of us."

A hundred yards away across the plaza stood two red-roofed outbuildings. The left-hand one, shaped like a truncated J, abutted the wall along the island's northern shoreline. Under the eaves they could see four windows, black rectangles in the gloom. They waited, staying perfectly still for a minute, and then two. After three minutes, Remi whispered, "You saw something?"

"I thought so. Guess I was wrong. Come on."

"Stop," she rasped. "You weren't wrong. There, at the far corner."

Sam looked where Remi had indicated. It took a moment for his eyes to pick it out, but there was no mistake. Barely visible in the darkness was the white oval of a man's face.

CHAPTER 31

They watched the face for a full minute; the man was all but a statue, occasionally rotating his head to scan behind and to the sides, but otherwise still.

"A guard?" Remi ventured.

"Maybe. But would a lazy guard trying to stay out of the rain stand that still? He'd be shifting or smoking or fidgeting." Moving with exaggerated slowness, Sam reached inside his rain jacket and pulled out a Nikon monocular. He aimed it toward the outbuilding and focused on the man's face. "Doesn't look like any of Kholkov's men we've seen."

"If it is them, how did they get here? We didn't see any boats."

"They're trained commandos, Remi. Skulking is what they do."

Sam scanned the grounds, taking his time, looking into shadows and darkened doorways, but seeing no one else. "Great Christmas present idea," Sam said. "A night-vision monocular."

"My pleasure."

"I don't see anyone else. Wait . . ."

The man under the eaves moved now, turning again to look over his shoulder. On the sleeve of his jacket was a patch, and on his belt a flashlight and key ring.

"I'm happy to report I'm wrong," Sam murmured. "It's a guard. Still, it would probably be best if we didn't get caught sneaking about a French national monument in the dead of night."

"True."

"When I say go, slowly move into the tunnel and stop about half-way. Don't go into the courtyard. And be ready to freeze."

"Right."

Sam watched the guard through the monocular until he looked away again. "Go."

Hunched over, Remi hurried into the corner, then along the wall and into the arch. Sam kept watching. It took another two minutes, but finally the man moved again and Sam was able to join Remi.

"My heart's pounding," she admitted.

"The joy of adrenaline."

They took a moment to catch their breath, then crept down the tunnel to the mouth of the courtyard, stopping just short of a two-inch-high step.

To the left of the door was a short wall and a wooden bench. To the right, a set of stone steps bordered by a wrought-iron hand-rail rose alongside the courtyard's inner wall then turned left and ascended to a turret, where it branched off into a walkway that wrapped around the courtyard. Sam and Remi scanned the walkway, pausing on each rectangular door or window, looking for movement. They saw nothing.

They scooted forward, gave the courtyard and walkway one more look, and were preparing to move when Sam saw, set back in the shadows, another archway beneath the steps.

Nothing moved. Aside from the pattering rain, all was quiet.

Eyes scanning the courtyard, Sam leaned in and whispered in Remi's ear, "When I say go, head straight up the steps and into the turret. I'll be right—"

Behind them a beam of light filled the tunnel.

"Remi, go!"

Like a sprinter coming off the blocks, Remi dashed out and started up the steps, taking them two at a time. Sam dropped to his belly and went still. The flashlight panned through the tunnel, then back out again, then went dark. Sam crawled over the step into the courtyard, then rose to his feet and joined Remi in the turret.

"Did he see us?"

"We'll know shortly."

They waited for a minute, then two, half-expecting to see the guard walk through the arch, but he didn't appear.

Sam looked around the darkened interior of the turret. "Are we in the right one?"

The brochure map had identified several entrances to the oubliette level, one of which was in this turret. "Yes, the next landing down, I think," Remi said, nodding at the spiral steps; another set led upward to the battlements.

They started down the steps, Remi in the lead. On the next landing they found a wooden trapdoor in the floor, secured to the stone lip by a padlocked latch. From his waistband Sam pulled a miniature crowbar. Given the predominantly stone construction of the château and recalling Müller's words about his brother finding the bottles "tucked away in a cranny," they'd guessed the tool would come in handy.

While the padlock looked new, the latch itself was anything but, having turned black and flaky by years of exposure to the salt air. Remi pointed her LED microlight at the latch, but Sam stopped her from turning it on. "Let's wait until we're out of sight."

It took thirty seconds of gentle work with the crowbar's tip to wriggle the latch free of the wood. Sam lifted the hatch, revealing a wooden ladder dropping into a dark shaft.

"Better let me test it," Remi said.

She sat down, slid her legs into the hole, and started downward. Ten seconds later she whispered up, "Okay. It's about twelve feet. Go easy. It's bolted into the stone, but the whole thing looks as old as the latch."

Sam climbed in, ducked down on the second rung, and shut the hatch behind him, leaving a gap wide enough for his fingers, which he used to flip the latch back into place; with luck, a passing guard wouldn't notice the tampering.

In complete darkness and working by feel alone, Sam started downward. The ladder creaked and shifted, the bolts rasping inside their stone holes. He froze. He held his breath for a ten count, then began moving again.

With a splintering crack, the rung parted beneath his lowermost foot. He lurched downward. He clamped his hands on the uprights, arresting his fall, but the sudden shift of his weight was too much for the ladder, which twisted sideways. With a shriek and a pop, the bolts gave way and Sam felt himself falling. He braced himself just before impact, slamming into the stone floor back first.

"Sam!" Remi whispered, rushing over and kneeling down.

Sam groaned, blinked rapidly, then pushed himself up onto his elbows.

"Are you okay?" she asked.

"I think so. Just bruised my pride a bit."

"And your tailbone."

She helped him to his feet.

Before them the ladder lay in a heap. The uprights were twisted away from one another, the rungs jutting at crazy angles.

"Well," Remi said, "at least now we know how we're not getting out of here."

"Always a bright side," Sam agreed.

Remi clicked on her LED and they looked around. Behind them was a stone wall; ahead, a passageway barely taller than Sam stretched into the darkness. Unlike the fort's outer walls, the stones here were dark gray and rough-hewn, showing chisel marks that were four hundred–plus years old. This was the upper dungeon level; there was one more below them, and below that, the oubliettes—"the realm of the forgotten."

Remi clicked off her LED. Hand in hand, they started down the passage.

When they'd gone twenty paces, Sam clicked on his LED, looked around, shut it off again. He'd seen no end to the passage. They kept going. After another twenty paces, he felt Remi's hand squeeze on his.

"I heard an echo," she whispered. "To the left."

Sam clicked on the LED, revealing a tunnel containing a dozen cells, six to a wall. For safety purposes the barred steel doors had been removed. They stepped into the nearest cell and looked around.

While these tunnels were gloomy in their own right, Sam and Remi found the tiny coalpit-dark cells a nightmare. The château's guides reportedly divided tour groups into threes and fours, then shut off the lights and had everyone stand in silence for thirty seconds. Though Sam and Remi had found themselves in similar situations before—most recently in Rum Cay—Château d'If's cells evoked a unique sense of dread, as though they were sharing the space with still-imprisoned ghosts.

"Enough of this," Sam said, and stepped back into the main passage.

They found the next tunnel farther down the passageway on their right. This one was slightly longer and contained twenty cells. Moving more quickly now, they repeated the process, passing cell tunnel after cell tunnel until they reached the end of the passageway, where they found a wooden door. It was closed but had neither latch nor lock. Beside the door a placard said in French, DO NOT ENTER. AUTHORIZED PERSONNEL ONLY.

"Why no lock?" Remi wondered aloud.

"Probably removed so wayward tourists can't accidentally lock themselves in places they shouldn't be."

He stuck his finger through the latch hole and gently pulled. The door swung open an inch. The hinges creaked. He stopped, took a breath, then pulled the door the rest of the way open.

Remi squeezed through the gap, then he followed, easing the door shut behind them. They stood still for a few moments, listening, then Remi cupped her hands around her LED and clicked it on. They were standing on a narrow, four-by-four-foot landing. To the right of the door was a ledge; at their backs, another cylindrical stairwell, this one leading only downward. Together they peeked over the ledge.

The LED's beam didn't penetrate any deeper than ten steps.

CHAPTER 32

ollowing the blue-white beams of their LEDs, they picked their way down the steps to the next landing. As above, they found a wooden door set into the wall, and beside it another Do Not Enter placard. Expecting the shriek of ancient hinges, Sam was surprised when the door swung noiselessly open. They stepped through.

Another tunnel, this one barely four feet wide and five feet tall, forcing Sam and Remi to duck. Spaced at four-foot intervals along each wall was a rectangular cell door, but unlike their counterparts on the upper level, these were equipped with what Sam and Remi assumed were the original vertically barred doors, each one standing open and tethered to an eyelet in the stone with a length of twine. Sam examined the nearest door under the glow of the LED and found the lock and latch were still present.

"Just when you thought it couldn't get any more depressing," Remi whispered.

Scanning the walls as they went, they started down the tunnel. After sixty or seventy feet they found a ten-foot-deep side tunnel set into the left-hand wall. At the end was a waist-high rectangular opening. They knelt down and Sam leaned into the opening. A few feet inside, a hatch was set into the floor; Sam shined his light into it. "Another ladder," he whispered. "It goes down about six feet. I think we've found the place."

"I'll go first," Remi said, then slipped feet first into the hatch and started down. "Okay," she called. "The ladder seems sturdy."

Sam climbed down and crouched beside her. This tunnel was narrower still: three feet wide and four feet tall. Stretching down the centerline was hatch after hatch after hatch, each one a steel-barred black square that seemed to swallow their flashlight beams.

"God almighty," Sam whispered.

"How many, do you think?" Remi asked.

"If this tunnel is as long as the ones above . . . Forty or fifty."

Remi was silent for a long ten seconds. "I wonder how long it took for someone to go insane down here."

"Depends on the person, but after a day or two your mind would start feeding on itself. No sense of time, no points of reference, no outside stimulus. . . . Come on, let's get this over with. What was the last line of the riddle . . . ?"

" 'From the third realm of the forgotten . . .' "

Careful of their footing, they walked down the wall to the third hatch. Under the beam of Remi's LED, Sam examined the grate. The hinges and latch had been removed and the bars were scabrous with corrosion. He touched one; flakes sloughed off and floated down into the oubliette. He gripped the bars, lifted the grate free, and set it aside.

The oubliette lay at the bottom of a narrow six-foot long shaft, while the cell itself was four feet to a side and three feet deep— neither wide enough for a prisoner to lie fully prone, nor tall enough to stand without being bent at the waist. "I better go," Remi said. "I'm smaller and I couldn't pull you back up."

Sam frowned, but nodded. "Okay." From his waistband he pulled the miniature crowbar. She took off her coat and laid it aside, then tucked the crowbar into her belt and let Sam lower her into the shaft, dropping the last couple feet on her own. On hands and knees she clicked on her light, stuck it between her teeth, and began examining the stone walls and floor. After two minutes of crawling around she suddenly murmured, "There you are. . . ."

"Spittlebug?"

"Yep, in all its glory. It's carved into the corner of this block. There's a good-sized gap here. . . . Hang on."

Remi worked the pry bar first into one gap, then the other, inching the block away from the wall. With a grunt, she pulled it free and shoved it aside, then dropped to her belly and shined the light into the hollow. "It goes back a couple feet. . . . Damn."

"What?"

Remi got to her knees and looked up the shaft at him. "It's bedrock. There are no other openings, no gaps. . . . There's nothing here, Sam."

Remi took another two minutes to make sure she hadn't missed anything, then pushed the block back into place. Sam reached down and lifted her up. She pursed her lips and puffed a strand of hair from her eyebrow. "I was afraid of that. Karl Müller found three bottles here. Something told me we weren't going to find the rest."

Sam nodded. "Whatever Laurent was up to, it doesn't seem likely he'd stash them all together."

"Well, it was worth a try. We know one thing for sure: Laurent did in fact use his cicada stamp."

"Come on, time to leave the party and find a way out."

They replaced the grate and walked down the tunnel away from the door, Remi pressed against one wall, Sam the other. Ten feet from the end, Sam suddenly stumbled backward into an alcove and landed on his butt with an *umph*.

"Sam?" Remi called.

"Looks like I found something."

He looked around. Only three feet deep, the rear half of the alcove's floor was taken up by a hatch, this one unbarred.

Remi walked around the oubliette between them and ducked

into the alcove with Sam, who shined his light into the hatch, then dropped through, followed by Remi. Sam clicked on his LED for a moment. Running perpendicular to the tunnel above, a crawl space stretched into the darkness.

On hands and knees they started crawling, Remi in the lead and Sam bringing up the rear. Not wanting to miss any side branches, every few feet they reached out and touched each wall.

After a full minute of crawling, Sam tapped Remi on the butt to call a halt, then clicked on the LED again. Ahead the tunnel stretched on.

"Did you notice the walls?" Remi whispered.

"Yes."

The crawl space's walls were not constructed of stone block but had rather been carved from the bedrock. Crawling as they were in a dark and cramped space, inches of travel felt like many feet.

After thirty more seconds of moving, Remi stopped. "Wall," she whispered. "Branch to the right."

They made the turn, then crawled another twenty feet to another turn, this one to the left. After another short straightaway and another two right and left turns, they found themselves at a ceiling hatch tall enough for Remi to stand in. She ducked back down and said, "There's a ledge, then a drop-off into some kind of room."

"Can you make it?"

"I think so." She boosted herself up and disappeared. Ten seconds later she called, "Okay."

Sam stood up, crawled over the ledge, and dropped down beside Remi, who was already surveying the room, which measured ten by ten feet. Like the crawl space, the walls and floor and ceiling were bedrock. Mounted on three walls were what looked like wooden gun cases, each one divided into vertical slots meant for, they assumed, either muskets or swords. In the wall to their left was a truncated arch.

"This must be original to the fort," Sam whispered. "Probably a last-ditch bolt-hole and armory for defenders."

"Which means there has to be another way out or in."

"Unless it got closed up when the château was converted to a prison."

"Don't even joke about that."

"One way to find out."

They ducked through the arch and into the tunnel beyond.

It was labyrinth. For the next hour they picked their way along the tunnel, into dead ends, through horseshoe hallways, and up and down stairs until Sam finally called a halt. Ahead the tunnel split yet again into three branches like spokes on a wagon wheel.

"What is this place?" Remi panted.

"I don't know that it has a name," Sam replied, "but I'm guessing it's still part of the last-ditch defense theory—attackers come down here, get trapped, then are ambushed by the defenders." He licked his finger and held it up. "There's air movement." He turned in a circle, trying to localize it, then shook his head. "Can't tell where it's coming from."

Remi wasn't listening. Eyes closed, she turned first this way, then that, her hands at her waist, fingers alternately left and right. "Retracing our steps," she finally whispered. "That way's the court-yard." She pointed down the left tunnel. "I think. If there's a hidden entrance, it's got to be there."

"Good enough for me," Sam said.

He took her hand and they set off again.

Time and again the tunnel branched off and each time Remi would stop, repeat her slow-motion, eyes-closed spin, then point.

After another hour their tunnel came to an abrupt dead end— or near dead end. Leaning against the wall was a wooden ladder; roughly hewn from what looked like red oak, the uprights and rungs were slightly crooked. They shined their lights upward. The ladder, well over thirty feet tall, ended at a wooden hatch.

"Smell that?" Remi said. "It's rain, Sam. We're close."

He nodded absently, eyes poring over the ladder. "This is ancient," he murmured. "It could be original. This could be hundreds of years old."

"That's wonderful, Sam, but right now all I care about is whether it'll take our weight."

He gave the ladder a twist, then put his weight on the bottom rung. It creaked, but held. "Give me the pry bar, will you?"

He tucked it into his belt and climbed up to the hatch. "It's locked," he called down.

He wriggled the pry bar under the edge and wrenched once, then again, then once more and the latch popped open. Sam threw open the hatch. Fresh air rushed through the opening and down the ladder.

"We're in one of the turrets," Sam whispered down.

He boosted himself up and out, then Remi followed. As her head cleared the opening, outside the door they heard the scuff of a shoe on stone. Sam helped Remi the rest of the way out and together they crept to the door.

Over the railing they could see a guard—the one from before, they assumed—strolling across the courtyard, flashlight panning left and right. The man turned around, shined his flashlight briefly over the walkways, then disappeared through the arch.

They gave him thirty seconds to move off a safe distance, then trotted down the walkway, left down the steps, then through the courtyard and into the tunnel they'd first entered.

Outside it was still raining and the temperature had dropped twenty degrees. The cold washed over them. They looked around to get their bearings; they were back where they'd started. Ahead, across the plaza, lay the red-roofed outbuildings. His progress marked by his flashlight, the guard was a hundred yards away and heading toward the reception area.

"Had enough prowling for one night?" Sam asked Remi.

"And then some," Remi replied. "Besides, knowing you as I do, I'm sure there's plenty of skulking left in our future."

"Safe bet."

Together they stepped out into the rain.

CHAPTER 33

GRAND HÔTEL BEAUVAU

An hour later, freshly showered and enjoying their second room-service Bombay Sapphire Gibson, Sam and Remi sat on their balcony and looked out over the Vieux Port. The lights of the city reflected off the water's surface in a mosaic of red, yellow, and blue that slowly rippled with the falling rain. In the distance they could hear the mournful howl of a foghorn, and closer in the occasional clang of a buoy.

The phone trilled. Sam checked the screen: It was Rube. As soon as they got back to the hotel he had called Haywood, given him a purposely vague recounting of the night's events, and asked him to call back.

Sam closed the balcony door, then answered and put the phone on speaker. "Rube, please tell us Kholkov and his merry band are in custody."

"Sorry, no. The French DCPJ can't find them."

"Wish I could say I was surprised."

"Me, too. Ready to quit and come home now?

"Not on your life."

"Remi?"

"No chance."

"Well, on the bright side, Kholkov's name and picture are everywhere. If he tries to leave the country through an airport, port, or train station, they'll pick him up."

"Then again," Sam said, "from what you told me it sounds like the Spetsnaz are trained to slip across borders. And he doesn't strike me as stupid enough to walk into an airport."

"True."

"What about Bondaruk?" Remi asked. "Any chance of digging into his family's skeleton closet and figuring out what's driving him?"

"Possibly. It turns out the Iranian Pasdaran colonel who was Bondaruk's handler during the border war ran into some trouble with the Ayatollah a few years later. We're not sure what the rigmarole was about, but the colonel—his name is Aref Ghasemi—escaped to London and started working for the British. He's still there. I've got someone reaching out to him."

"Thanks, Rube," Remi said, and hung up.

———

The next morning they slept in until nine and had breakfast on the balcony. The previous night's rain had disappeared, leaving behind a blue sky with scattered cotton-puff clouds. Over coffee they called Selma, who was awake despite it being nearly midnight in California. As far as they could tell, their chief researcher slept only five or so hours a night but never seemed the worse for it.

Leaving out the finer details, Sam told her about finding the Château d'If hiding place empty. Remi added, "The cicada was there, though, and it looked like a perfect match for Laurent's chisel stamp."

"That's better than nothing," Selma said. "I'm making some headway on deciphering lines three and four on the bottle, but as for the rest, zilch. And I think I know why: There's a third key."

"Explain," Sam said.

"Laurent's book is one key and the bottle we have is another—at least the first four lines are. I'm guessing the third key is another bottle. We need all three to cross-reference and decode the rest of the lines."

"This feels convoluted," Remi said.

"From our perspective, maybe, but we've got to make some assumptions: first, that Laurent intended to hide the twelve bottles from the original case individually, at scattered locations—his 'arrows on a map' to whatever's at the end of all this."

"We need to find a name for this thing," Sam said.

"Napoleon's Gold," Remi suggested with a shrug.

"Works for me."

Selma said, "Okay, Napoleon's Gold. I suspect he meant it to work like this: Find one bottle, decode it with the book, then follow the riddle to another bottle—"

Sam caught on: "Then use that label's code with the book and the first bottle to decode the next line—"

"And its riddle, which leads to yet another bottle . . . and so forth. The good news is—and this is another guess—I don't think there's any sequence to the code—in other words, Laurent designed it so any bottle would lead to another riddle."

Remi said, "If all this is right, why did he hide three bottles together at d'If?"

"No idea. We might find out down the road."

"We're ignoring the elephant in the room," Sam said. "We know for sure one of the bottles is lost—the shard from the Pocomoke proves that. Without that bottle, we could be missing the last riddle—the one that points us to Napoleon's Gold."

"I was thinking the same thing," Remi replied. "I guess we won't know until we reach the end."

"Selma, what are the chances the bottle Kholkov recovered in Rum Cay is doing them any good?" Sam asked.

"Slim. Unless they have a codebook, that is. And based on how he's been on your heels every step of the way, I'd say they're lost."

"Here's elephant number two," Remi said. "At some point we're going to have to get our hands on the Rum Cay bottle."

"Which means," Sam said, "a trip into the lion's den."

SEVASTOPOL

Two thousand miles east of Marseille, Hadeon Bondaruk sat at his desk, hands clasped before him. Spread across the burgundy leather blotter were a dozen high-resolution color photographs, each one highlighting a separate line of symbols. For the tenth time in an hour, he picked up a lighted magnifying glass and studied each photo in turn, focusing on the minute details of every symbol—the right angle of this square, the looping curve of a truncated omega, the tilt of a crescent moon . . .

Nothing. There was nothing!

He tossed the magnifying glass across the desk then swept his arm over the surface, scattering the photos.

Despite its monetary value, alone the bottle was worthless to him, and now that the Fargos had Arnaud Laurent's book, he had to assume they would quickly begin to unravel the code. As much as he wanted to blame Kholkov for the book's loss, Bondaruk had to admit he'd also underestimated the Fargos. They were treasure hunters—adventurers. Neither he nor Kholkov had anticipated they would be this much trouble. Or this resourceful. Perhaps they should have foreseen this. After all, it stood to reason the Fargos' escapades had landed them in enough dicey situations to have seasoned them.

Still, their resources couldn't hope to match his own. On Napoleon alone he'd spent hundreds of thousands of dollars. His researchers had dissected the man's life, from cradle to grave, had tracked down not only his every known descendant, but those of the dozens of friends and advisers and lovers Napoleon might have confided in, Arnaud Laurent included. Every book written about Napoleon had been scanned into their computer database and parsed for clues. Period artwork, from battle scenes to portraits to rough sketches, had been scoured for anything that might point the way—a symbol on a tunic button, a finger pointing at something in the background, a book on a shelf behind Napoleon's head. . . .

And for all that, for all the money spent and time invested, he had nothing but a useless bottle of wine and a pictograph of a damned insect.

His desk phone chimed and he picked it up. "It's me," Vladimir Kholkov said.

"Where have you been?" Bondaruk growled. "I was expecting your call last night. Tell me what's happening."

"We tracked them to Marseille yesterday afternoon. I met them and proposed a truce—and a partnership."

"You what? I didn't tell you to do that!"

"Proposing a truce and keeping a truce are two different things, Mr. Bondaruk. At any rate, they didn't budge."

"Where are they now?"

"Back in Marseille."

"Back? What does that mean?"

"I had to leave France; I'm in La Jonquera, on the other side of the Spanish border. The French police are looking for me. Someone put out a bulletin."

"The Fargos. It has to be. How would they do that?"

"I'm looking into it. It doesn't matter. If they leave, I'll know it."

"How?"

Kholkov explained, and Bondaruk said, "What about the book?"

"I had a man watching their house, but Fargo wasn't bluffing: They've got security. I think it would cause more trouble than it's worth. And since we'll know where they're going and when, we can let them do the hard work for us."

"Agreed."

Bondaruk hung up, strode to his window, and forced himself to take a calming breath. Kholkov was right: There was still time. The Fargos were ahead, but they had a long way to go and many hurdles to clear before they reached the end. Sooner or later they would make a mistake. When they did, Kholkov would be there.

CHAPTER 34

SEVASTOPOL

Sam pulled their rented Opel coupe off the dirt road and coasted to a stop a few feet from the cliff's edge. Sunset was an hour away and the sun was already dropping toward the western horizon, casting the surface of the Black Sea in tones of gold and red. Directly below them the palisades of Cape Fiolent plunged directly into the blue-green water and just offshore dozens of spires of jagged rock jutted from the water, each surrounded by a whirlpool of churning surf.

In the distance, a gull cawed, then went silent, leaving only the sound of wind rushing through Sam's open window.

"A little foreboding," Remi murmured.

"Just a tad," Sam agreed. "Then again, it does suit his reputation."

The "he" in question was Hadeon Bondaruk. Knowing that without another bottle with which to complete the next lines of the cipher, Sam and Remi had chosen the only course open to them: stealing Bondaruk's bottle.

It was a dangerous if not foolish idea, but their adventures had taught them a number of things, one of which Sam had dubbed the

Inverse Law of Power and Assumption of Invulnerability. Given Bondaruk's power and notoriety, who in their right mind would try to steal from him? Having reigned as Ukraine's mafia kingpin for so many years, Bondaruk, like many powerful men, had likely begun to believe his own press. Certainly he and his property were well guarded, but, like muscles that haven't been exercised for many years, there was a fair chance his security had grown lax—or at least that was the theory.

Of course, neither of them were ready to risk such a venture on guesswork alone, so they had asked Selma to do a feasibility study: Were there any exploitable weaknesses in Bondaruk's home security? There were, she found. One, he kept his antique collection on display at the estate, along with a small team of experts who maintained and supervised the pieces. Two, the estate itself was sprawling and steeped in history, a piece of which Selma felt certain might offer them a way in.

They climbed out of the car, walked to the edge, and gazed north. A mile away along the undulating coast, perched before a rock bridge jutting from the cliff face, was Bondaruk's hundred-acre estate, officially named Khotyn. The bridge, undercut by millennia of erosion, extended to a pillar of rock that rose from the ocean like a skyscraper.

Bondaruk's home was a five-story, thirty-thousand-square-foot Kievan Rus–style castle, complete with steeply pitched slate roofs, deep-set gabled windows, and onion-domed copper minarets, all surrounded by a low white-stuccoed stone wall and serpentine groves of evergreen trees.

Khotyn began its life in the mid-eighteenth century as home to a Crimean Khanate chieftain whose line had split from the Mongol Golden Horde in the sixteenth century to settle in the area. After a hundred years the chieftain's clan was ousted by Muscovite Russian forces led by a Zaporozhian Cossack hetman who claimed it as a spoil of war only to have it taken from him thirty years later by a yet more powerful hetman.

During the Crimean War, Khotyn was commandeered by

Tsar Nicholas II's most prominent Black Sea Fleet admiral, Pavel Stepanovich Nakhimov, to serve as a retreat, after which its role changed four times, first as a museum dedicated to the Siege of Sevastopol; then as a Wehrmacht headquarters during World War II; then again as a military summer house for Soviet high commanders after the city was liberated. From 1948 to the fall of the Soviet Union Khotyn fell again into ruin, sitting mostly abandoned until Bondaruk purchased it from the money-starved Ukrainian government in 1997.

Given the estate's rich history, Selma had had little trouble finding plenty of tantalizing research trails to follow, but in the end it was one of the basest of human motivations—greed—that gave away the chink in Khotyn's armor.

"Give me the story again," Sam told Remi as he stared at the estate through his binoculars.

"His name was Bogdan Abdank," Remi replied. "He was the Zaporozhian Cossack who took it over from the Mongols."

"Right."

"Seems Abdank was only a part-time Cossack. The rest of the time he was a smuggler—fur, gems, liquor, slaves—anything he thought he could sell on the black market, he trafficked. Problem was, there were plenty of other Cossack clans and Kievan Rus warlords who wanted to take over Abdank's action."

"But old Bogdan was crafty," Sam replied, warming to the subject.

"And industrious."

According to the online archives Selma was able to unearth in the National Taras Shevchenko University of Kiev, Abdank had used slave labor to dig into the cliffs and hills surrounding Khotyn a series of tunnels in which to hide his illicit goods. Cargo ships laden with Romanian sable or Turkish diamonds or Georgian prostitutes bound for the West would weigh anchor in the waters below Khotyn for offloading into launches, which would then disappear into the night, ostensibly for further off-loading into the smuggler's tunnels beneath the mansion.

"So, more caves in our future," Remi said now.

"Looks like it. The question is, how familiar is Bondaruk with Khotyn's history? If the tunnels exist, does he know about them, and has he sealed them up?"

"Better still: Has he followed in Abdank's footsteps and put them to use?"

Sam checked his watch. "Well, we'll know shortly."

They had a contact to meet.

———————

As it turned out, Selma's research into Khotyn became something of a one-stop shopping trip, giving them not only a hint about how they might sneak into Khotyn, but also, hopefully, a road map of exactly how to go about it.

The archive curator at Taras Shevchenko University, a man named Petro Bohuslav, hated his work with a passion and he desperately wanted to move to Trieste, Italy, and open a bookstore. After some parrying, he'd made his pitch to Selma: For the right price he was willing to share a set of rare, as yet unarchived blueprints of Khotyn, as well as his personal knowledge of the grounds.

They found him in a mom-and-pop restaurant overlooking the Balaclava marina, a few miles down the coast. Night had fully fallen by the time they arrived and the interior of the café was dimly lit by hurricane lamps on each table. Soft kobza folk music played over loudspeakers hidden by hanging ferns. The air smelled of sausage and onions.

As they entered, a man in a corner booth lifted his head and studied them for five long seconds, then put his face back into his menu. A hostess in a bright red shirt and white blouse approached them. Sam smiled and nodded at the man and they made their way through the tables to the booth.

"Mr. Bohuslav?" Remi asked in English.

The man looked up. He had receding white hair and a bulbous drinker's nose. He nodded. "I am Bohuslav. You are Mr. and Mrs. Jones?"

"That's right."

"Sit, please." They did. "Something to eat? Drink?"

"No, thank you," Remi said.

"You want into Khotyn, yes?"

"We didn't say that," Sam replied. "We're writers doing a book on the Crimean War."

"Yes, your assistant told me. Tough woman, that one."

Remi smiled. "She is that."

"So, this book you are writing—it is about the Siege of Sevastopol or the war?"

"Both."

"You need special details. You are willing to pay?"

"Depends on the details," Sam replied. "And how special they are."

"First, tell me: You know who lives there now?"

Remi shrugged. "No, why?"

"A bad man bought Khotyn in the nineties. A criminal. His name is Bondaruk. He lives there now. Many guards."

"Thanks for the information, but we're not planning an invasion," Sam lied. "Tell us about you. How do you know so much about the place? Not just from the blueprints, I hope."

Bohuslav grinned, displaying a trio of silver front teeth. "No. More than that. You see, after the war, after we drove the Germans out, I was stationed there. I was a cook for the general. After that, in 1953, I moved to Kiev and worked at the university. Started as a janitor, then became research assistant in the history department. In 1969 the government decided to make Khotyn a museum, and they asked the university to head the project. I went with others from the department to do a survey. Spent a month there, mapping, taking photographs, exploring. . . . I have all my original notes and sketches and photos, you see."

"Along with the blueprints?"

"Those, too."

"The problem is," Remi said, "that was forty years ago. A lot could have changed in that time. Who knows what the new owner has done since you were there."

Bohuslav held up a finger in triumph. "Hah. You are wrong. This man, Bondaruk, last year he hired me to come to Khotyn and consult on restoration. He wanted help making it look more like Zaporozhian Cossack period. I spent two weeks there. Except for decoration, nothing has changed. I went almost anywhere I wanted, mostly without escort."

Sam and Remi exchanged oblique glances. Upon hearing about Bohuslav's offer from Selma, their first concern was that Bondaruk was setting a trap for them, but upon further contemplation they'd decided this was unlikely, primarily because of Sam's Inverse Law of Power and Assumption of Invulnerability, but also because of a suspicion that had been nagging at them since their journey had begun: Was Bondaruk, having had little luck unraveling the riddle on his own, letting them run free in hopes that they would lead him to what they'd dubbed Napoleon's Gold? It was possible, but still it didn't change their options: Keep going, or quit.

But, however unlikely the trap scenario, they were still curious about Bohuslav's motivation. The amount he was asking for—fifty thousand Ukrainian hryvnias, or ten thousand U.S. dollars—seemed a paltry amount given what Bondaruk would do to him should his betrayal be discovered. Sam and Remi suspected desperation, but about what?

"Why are you doing this?" Sam asked.

"For the money. I want to go to Trieste—"

"We heard. But why cross Bondaruk? If he's as bad as you say he is—"

"He is."

"Then why risk it?"

Bohuslav hesitated, his mouth twisting into a frown. He sighed. "You know about Pripyat, yes?"

"The town near Chernobyl," Remi replied.

"Yes. My wife, Olena, was there when she was younger, when the nuclear plant exploded. Her family was one of the last to get out. Now she has cancer—of the ovaries."

"We're sorry to hear that," Sam said.

Bohuslav gave a fatalist shrug. "She has always wanted to see Italy, to live there, and I promised her we would someday. Before she dies I'd like to keep my promise. I'm more afraid of breaking my promise to Olena than of Bondaruk."

"What's to keep you from simply turning around and selling us out to Bondaruk for a higher price?"

"Nothing. Except that I am not a stupid man. What would I do, go to him and say, 'I was going to betray you, but for more money I will not'? Bondaruk does not bargain. The last man who tried that—a greedy policeman—disappeared, along with his family. No, friend, I would rather deal with you. Less money, but at least I will be alive to enjoy it."

Sam and Remi looked at one another, then back to Bohuslav.

"I'm telling you the truth," he said. "You give me money, and I promise: You will know more about Khotyn than Bondaruk does."

CHAPTER 35

Leaning over the chart table under the dim red glow of the lamp above it, Remi used the compass and dividers to plot their current position. She used the pencil clamped between her teeth to jot a few calculations along the chart's margin, then circled a spot on the course line and whispered. "We're there."

In response, Sam, standing at the helm, throttled down the engines and turned off the ignition. The fishing trawler coasted through the fog, the water hissing along her sides until she slowed to a stop. Sam ducked out the pilothouse door, dropped the anchor overboard, then came back inside.

"It should be off our port bow," Remi said, joining him at the window. He lifted a pair of binoculars to his eyes and scanned the darkness off the bow, at first seeing only fog and then, faintly in the distance, a slowly pulsing white light.

"Nicely done," Sam said.

This point three miles off the lighthouse had been the critical waypoint for tonight's journey, and as their rented boat had not come equipped with a GPS navigation system, they'd had to rely on dead reckoning, using their course, speed, and the occasional recognizable landmark picked out by the short-range radar to guide their way.

"If only that were the hard part," Remi replied.

"Come on, let's get suited up."

The night before, after agreeing to Bohuslav's price and calling Selma to approve the money transfer to his account, they'd followed the Ukrainian to the Balaclava train station and waited in the car while he retrieved a leather satchel from one of the rental lockers. A quick scan of the satchel's contents seemed to confirm Bohuslav was on the level—either the sketches, notes, photos, and blueprints inside were genuine or they were dealing with a professional forger.

Back at their hotel in Yevpatoria, fifty miles up the coast from Sevastopol, they laid the contents of the satchel out on the bed and went to work, with Selma watching on via webcam. After an hour of cross-checking what they already knew about Bondaruk's estate, they were sure Bohuslav's material was the real deal. Every entrance, every stairwell, and every room in the mansion was accounted for, but more importantly so, too, were the rumors about Bogdan Abdank's smuggling tunnels. Khotyn was riddled with miles of them, starting in the cliff face below the mansion, where cargo was unloaded, and branching into myriad storage chambers and exits, some of which emerged from the earth almost a mile beyond the estate's grounds.

More surprising was the discovery that the Zaporozhian Cossack had not been the only one to take advantage of the tunnels. Every subsequent occupant, from the Crimean War's Admiral Nakhimov to the Nazis to the Soviet Red Army, had used them for a variety of purposes: ammunition depots, fallout shelters, private brothels, and in some cases as vaults for their own spoils of war.

However, the one piece of information they most needed was missing from Bohuslav's information—where precisely Bondaruk might be keeping his bottle from Napoleon's Lost Cellar.

"Of course, there's another possibility," Remi said. "Perhaps he's got it locked away somewhere else."

"I doubt it," Sam replied. "Everything about Bondaruk's personality suggests he's a control freak. He didn't get to where he is by leaving the important stuff to chance. Something he's this obsessed about he'd want to have close at hand."

"Good point."

"Assuming that's right," Selma said over the webcam, "there might be some clues in the blueprints. If he's a serious collector—and we know he is—then he's going to keep his most prized pieces in an environmentally controlled area—that means separate air-conditioning units, humidity-control systems, backup power generators, fire suppression. . . . And he'll probably have it separated from the rest of the mansion. Check Bohuslav's notes for any mention of those things."

It took an hour of work, picking their way through Bohuslav's chicken-scratched notes, which were written in both English and Russian, but finally Remi found a room in the mansion's western wing that was labeled SECURE UTILITY ROOM.

"The location fits," Selma said.

"Here's something else," Sam said, reading from another note: "'Denied access western side.' Add that to the secure utility room and we may have found our *X*."

Ironically, the mansion itself was laid out in the shape of a peace symbol, with the main portion of the house in the center, two wings radiating out to the southeast and to the northeast, and a third wing to the west, and all encircled by the low stone wall.

"The problem is," Remi said, "the plans show the smuggler's tunnels merge with the mansion in two places—at the stables a couple hundred yards north of the house and in the southeast wing."

Sam replied, "So we either have to hoof it—no pun intended—across the open ground to the west wing and hope we find a way in, or come up on the southeast wing and pick our way through the house and pray we're able to dodge the guards."

Surprising neither of them, Selma had found them a reliable equipment source in Yevpatoria, an old Soviet Red Army surplus store run by a former soldier turned body-shop mechanic. Their outfits for the evening were a pair of Cold War–era naval commando camouflage coveralls; their transport a five-foot rubber dinghy complete with a battery-powered electric trolling motor.

Suited up, their faces streaked with black face paint, they inflated the raft, affixed the motor to the transom, then lowered the raft over the side of the fishing boat, donned their backpacks, and climbed in. Remi pushed the trawler's gunwale and within seconds it disappeared in the fog. Sam turned the motor's ignition and it hummed to life. Sitting on the bow, Remi aimed her compass at the lighthouse, then lifted her hand and pointed into the fog.

"Damn the torpedoes," Sam said, and throttled up.

The trolling motor was quiet, but slow, pushing them along at three knots, barely a walking pace, so it was an hour before Remi, who had kept a steady fix on the lighthouse's pulsing beacon, raised her hand, calling a halt. Sam throttled down.

All was quiet save the waves lapping at the raft's sides. Fog swirled around them, obscuring all but a few feet of black water around them. Sam was about to speak when he heard it: in the distance, the muffled crash of waves. Remi looked at him, nodded, and pointed again.

Ahead lay their first hurdle. Given the nature of the Black Sea's currents they'd decided to approach from the south; while they wouldn't be fighting the tide, they would have to pick their way through the spires of rock that jutted from the bay beneath Bondaruk's estate, a dicey proposition in the dead of night, let alone in the fog. Worse still, assuming Bondaruk had guards posted on the cliffs, they'd decided against flashlights. On their side they had Remi's keen hearing and Sam's quick reflexes.

Moving at half throttle he aimed the raft's nose in the direction Remi had indicated for thirty seconds then throttled down. They listened. To their left and right, distantly, came the hiss of waves. Eyes closed, Remi turned her head this way and that, then pointed a few degrees left off the bow. Sam throttled up and kept going.

After twenty seconds, Remi's hand shot up. Sam let up on the throttle, keeping on just enough power to hold position. In the sudden quiet they heard the crash of waves, very close, to the right. Then more on the left. And behind. They were surrounded.

Suddenly dead on the bow, a towering rock wall veined with rivulets of whitewater appeared in the fog. The waves, stacking atop one another in the shoals beneath them, lifted the raft and shoved them forward.

"Sam!" Remi rasped quietly.

"Hold on! Drop flat!"

The spire loomed before the bow. Sam waited until the raft dropped into a trough, then twisted the throttle to its stops and pushed it hard right. The propeller bit down, shooting them toward the spire before veering away. The rock swept past on the left and disappeared in the gloom. Sam drove on for a ten count, then throttled down again. They listened.

"Closer on the right, I think," Remi whispered.

"Sounds closer on the left to me," Sam replied.

"Toss a coin?"

"No chance. Your ears are better than mine," he said, and steered left.

"Stop," Remi called ten seconds later. "Do you feel that?"

"Yeah," he replied, looking around.

The raft was moving sideways, and gaining speed. They felt their stomachs rise into their throats as the raft was lifted on another crest. Ten feet to the right they caught a glimpse of jagged rock and then it was gone, lost in the fog.

"Paddles," Sam called, and grabbed his from the floor of the raft. In the bow, Remi did the same. "Sharp eyes . . . " Sam muttered.

"Behind you!" Remi called.

Sam turned, paddle coming up in his hands like a spear.

The spire was right there, within arm's reach.

He slammed the tip of the paddle into the rocks, then leaned all his weight into it and pushed, but the wave was too powerful and the raft simply rotated around the pivot point the paddle created.

"Coming around," he called between clenched teeth.

"Got it!"

Remi was already moving, turning on her knees to face the other side, her paddle raised and ready. With a splintering *thunk* she slammed it into the rocks. The raft, its momentum slightly slowed, bounced off the rock and spun again.

Sam leaned back, dropping his center of gravity back into the raft, and reached for the throttle. His hand was halfway there when he felt his stomach rising again and heard the suddenly unmuffled whirring of the motor as the raft's tail end came out of the water.

He had only a fraction of a second to call "Remi" before he felt himself tossed into the air. Knowing the rock was close, but not how close, he turned his head, looking for it. Then out of the fog he saw it rushing toward his face.

CHAPTER 36

Seconds or minutes or hours later Sam felt his mind groping back toward consciousness. One by one his senses started to return, beginning with a feathery sensation on his cheek, followed by the distinct and familiar smell of green apples.

Hair, he thought, *hair brushing my face. Coconut and almonds.* Remi's shampoo.

He forced open his eyes and found himself staring into her upside-down face. He looked around. He was lying in the bottom of the raft, his head resting on her lap.

He cleared his throat. "Are you okay?" he asked.

"Am I okay?" Remi whispered. "I'm fine, you dummy. You're the one that almost drowned."

"What happened?"

"You slammed headfirst into the spire, that's what happened. I looked over just as you started to slip into the water. I threw you the line. You hadn't blacked out yet. I shouted at you to grab the line and you did. I reeled you in."

"How long have I been out?"

"Twenty, twenty-five minutes."

He squeezed his eyes shut. "My head hurts."

"You've got a gash in your hairline; it's pretty long, but not very deep."

Sam reached and probed with his fingertips, finding a stretchable bandage wrapped around the upper part of his forehead.

"How's your vision?" Remi asked.

"Everything's dark."

"That's a good sign; it's night. Okay, how many fingers am I holding up?"

Sam groaned. "Come on, Remi, I'm fine—"

"Humor me."

"Sixteen."

"Sam."

"Four fingers. My name is Sam and you're Remi and we're floating in a raft in the Black Sea trying to steal a bottle of wine from Napoleon's Lost Cellar from a mafia kingpin. Satisfied?"

She gave him a quick peck on the lips. "You're right on all counts except the raft part."

"What?"

"After I pulled you in, I beached us. I'm not sure where we are."

"You navigated through the rest of the spires? Heck, you should have been driving the whole time."

"Dumb luck and desperation."

"Sounds like a good name for a boat. How is it, by the way? The raft, I mean."

"No leaks that I could find. We're still seaworthy."

"What time is it?"

"Just after midnight. Feel up to having a look around?"

More remarkable even than Remi having picked her way through the spires without suffering so much as a scratch was that she'd found the patch of shale beach on which the raft now rested. Measuring no more than ten feet deep and twenty feet wide, the beach narrowed in both directions to stone paths no more than two feet wide.

Once Sam was on his feet and had shaken out the cobwebs, they first set out to the south, but found the way blocked by a rock wall after only a few hundred yards. To the north they fared better, walking almost a half mile before coming across a rickety wooden stairway set into the cliff. They climbed to the top and looked around.

Here, high above the ocean's surface, the brisk wind had driven the fog away, but far below, the ocean was still shrouded in mist. Using the compass, they got their bearings. Sam said, "Well, you either headed farther south of the estate or past it to the north. How long was it until you found the beach?"

"Twenty minutes. But I made several loops, I'm sure, so don't count on that."

"How was the current?"

"For the most part, choppy and almost dead on the bow."

"Probably headed south, then." Sam lifted the binoculars and started scanning. "Do you see the light—"

"In fact, I do. There it is," she replied and pointed. Sam looked down her outstretched arm. "Wait for it," Remi whispered.

A few seconds passed, then in the darkness a single white light pulsed.

"No more than two miles away," Sam said. "We're still in business."

Ten minutes later they were back in the water and motoring north, taking care this time to keep within hearing distance of the waves hissing against the cliff face. It was slack tide now and the swells were slow and rolling, but still Sam and Remi were keenly aware that somewhere to their left were the spires. Ebb tide or not, neither of them wanted to risk another run through the labyrinth.

After thirty minutes of travel, Sam throttled down and let the raft coast forward. Remi looked over her shoulder, a questioning look on her face. Sam held a cupped hand to his ear and pointed off the bow and whispered, "Boat."

The rumble of a high-powered engine at near idle echoed through the fog, seemingly crossing from left to right somewhere ahead of them. There came the squelch of a radio, then a tinny voice saying something neither Sam nor Remi could make out.

Ten seconds passed.

To their right, a spotlight glowed to life in the haze and began tracking over the water nearer the beach. After thirty seconds the light popped off and the boat began moving off, heading back the way Sam and Remi had come.

"Bondaruk's guards?" Remi whispered.

"Or a Ukrainian navy coastal patrol," Sam replied. "Either way, they're someone we don't want to run into. If it is part of Bondaruk's security, we can take it as a good omen."

"How's that?"

"If we'd been spotted, they would have sent more than one boat."

For the next hour they continued moving north along the coast while playing cat-and-mouse with the mystery patrol boat, which continued to move unseen through the fog around them, engines gurgling and spotlight occasionally glowing to life, scanning over the water, then disappearing again. Three times Sam had to use the trolling motor to circle slowly away from the panning light.

"It's on a schedule," Remi said. "I've been timing it."

"That will come in handy," Sam replied. "Do your best to keep track of it."

"It has to be Bondaruk's. If it were the navy, why would they be patrolling this same patch of water?"

"Good point."

After a few more minutes the boat's engine noise once again faded and Sam put the raft back on course and before long they saw the glow of lights to their right, high up on the cliff. Remi took a bearing on the lighthouse and said, "That's it. That's Khotyn."

With Remi perched in the bow, eyes scanning ahead, Sam steered toward shore. Remi's hand came up, pointing left. Sam veered that way and saw to their right the cliff face materialize out of the fog. He turned parallel to it and kept going.

The hum of the trolling motor changed its tone, echoing off stone walls as they slipped inside the bridge beneath the estate. From the drawings and blueprints of the island, they knew it was a cavernous open-ended tunnel, measuring eighty feet high and two hundred yards wide and running parallel to the shore for a hundred yards. Large enough to accommodate a medium-sized cruise ship.

"We have to risk a light," Sam whispered.

Remi nodded and pulled from her pocket a cone-nosed flashlight, which she clicked on and began playing over the passing rock.

"Now we see if Bohuslav is the real deal or a con man," Remi said. The words had no sooner left her mouth when she murmured, "Well, speak of the devil. Call me a believer. There, Sam, right under my beam. Back up, back up."

Sam eased up on the throttle, then reversed, inching backward until they drew even with the spot from Remi's flashlight.

Jutting from the rock face at chin height was what looked like a rusted railroad spike; a foot above it was another, then another. . . . Sam leaned his head back as Remi scanned the flashlight upward, revealing a ladder of staggered spikes.

CHAPTER 37

If they stick to their schedule they're already headed back this way," Remi said. "Four or five minutes away at most."

The presence of the patrol boat had dramatically changed the linchpin to their exit strategy: the raft. If they left it here it would almost certainly be found and the alarm would be raised, and there was no time to find a place to stash it, which left only one option.

They donned their backpacks and then Sam found a pair of hand-holds in the rock face and held the raft steady as Remi used his shoulders as a step stool to the first spike. Once she had ascended high enough to make room for him, he flipped open his Swiss Army knife and slit the raft's side tube from bow to stern, then gripped the spike and pulled himself onto the face as the raft sank below him with a soft hissing sound.

"Time?" Sam asked.

"Three minutes, give or take," Remi replied, and started climbing.

They were halfway to the top when Sam heard the rumble of the outboard engines to their right. As had the raft's trolling motor, the tone of the patrol boat's engines suddenly changed, echoing through the arch.

"Remi, company's arrived," Sam muttered.

"I've got a tunnel opening here," she replied. "It goes horizontally into the face, but I can't see how far—"

"Any port in the storm. Just go."

"Right."

The gurgle of the boat's engine was directly below them now, skimming along the face. Sam looked down. While the boat itself was invisible in the fog, he could see the mist cleaving before it like smoke around an object in a wind tunnel. The spotlight popped and began playing over the cliff, zigzagging upward.

"I'm in," Remi whispered from above.

Eyes alternating between the spikes above him and the rapidly ascending pool of light below him, Sam climbed the last few feet then suddenly felt Remi's hand on his own. He coiled his legs beneath him and pushed off while simultaneously pulling with his arms. He rolled into the tunnel and jerked his legs inside as the spotlight hovered over the opening for a moment then continued on.

They lay huddled together in the darkness, Sam trying to calm his breath as they listened to the boat make its way through the arch and the engine noise finally faded.

"Is this the place?" Sam asked, pushing himself up onto his elbows and looking around. The tunnel was roughly oval in shape, roughly five feet tall and six feet wide.

"I'd say so," Remi said, pointing.

Bolted to the ceiling at the mouth of the tunnel was a crisscross bulwark of thick tar-covered oaken beams supported by vertical timbers bolted to the walls. Dangling from the center of the bulwark was a rusted block-and-tackle pulley system linked by thick hawser rope to a hand-crank winch affixed to the uprights. A pair of narrow-gauge rails sitting atop wooden cross ties and crushed gravel ballast stretched into the darkness.

"Well, the winch isn't original, that's for sure," he said. "Unless, that is, Zaporozhian Cossack technology was way ahead of its time. See here . . . those bolts are precisely machined. This might go back to the Crimean War, but my guess is World War II. Just look at the

mitered joints . . . this thing could have lifted thousands of pounds."
He stepped up to the mouth of the tunnel and peered over the edge.
"Ingenious. See how they placed this, just above this natural bulge in
the face? Even in daylight it would've been invisible from the water."

"I see it."

"Wow, look at this—"

"Sam."

"What?"

"I hate to stifle your imagination, but we've got a bottle of wine
to steal."

"Right, sorry. Let's go."

Having used Google Earth to draw up their own overhead sketch
of Bondaruk's estate, complete with angles and distances, as well as
annotations from Bohuslav's notes, they kept track of their steps as
they headed into the tunnel.

Under the moving beam of their flashlights Sam could see signs of
limited blast work along the walls, but it appeared most of the tunnel
had been carved out the old-fashioned way, by hammer, chisel, and
backbreaking labor.

Here and there on the floor were wooden toolboxes, coils of
half-rotted rope, rusted pickaxes and sledgehammers, a pair of
half-rotted leather boots, canvas coveralls that partially disintegrated
when Remi nudged them with her shoe. . . . Attached to the right-
and left-hand walls every ten feet were oil lamps, their glass globes
black with soot, their bronze reservoirs and handles covered in a scabrous green patina. Sam tapped one with his index finger and heard
sloshing inside.

After fifty yards of walking, Remi stopped, studied the sketch,
and said, "We should be just under the outer wall. Another hundred
yards or so and we should be directly under the main house."

She was off by only a few yards. After another two minutes they
reached a widened intersection, the tunnel and tracks continuing
straight as well as to the right. Five old-fashioned ore carts sat in a

line against the left-hand wall, while a sixth sat on the north-south tracks.

"Straight ahead to the stables, and right to the east wings," Sam said.

"I think so."

He checked his watch. "Let's check out the stables first and see what we can see."

After another half mile or so of walking, Remi stopped suddenly and placed her index finger to her lips and mouthed, *Music*. They listened in silence for ten seconds then Sam leaned in and whispered in Remi's ear, " 'Summer Wind' by Frank Sinatra."

She nodded. "I hear voices. Laughing . . . singing along."

"Yeah."

They continued on and soon the tunnel came to a dead end at a set of stone steps leading upward to a wooden trapdoor. Sam lifted his head and sniffed. "Manure."

"Then we're in the right place."

The music and laughter were louder now, seemingly coming from directly above their heads. Sam placed his foot on the lowermost step. At that moment, there came the thunk of a footfall on the trapdoor. Sam froze. Another foot joined the first, followed by two more, these lighter, somehow more delicate. Through the gaps in the trapdoor shadows moved, blocking and unblocking the light.

A woman giggled and said in Russian-accented English, "Don't, Dmitry, that tickles."

"That's the idea, my *lapochka*."

"Ooh, I like that. . . . Stop, stop, what about your wife?"

"What about her?"

"Come on, let's get back to the party before someone sees us."

"Not until you promise me," the man said.

"Yes, I promise. Next weekend in Balaclava."

The couple moved off and moments later there came the banging of a wooden door. Somewhere above a horse whinnied, then silence.

Remi whispered, "We've managed to stumble into one of Bondaruk's damned parties. Talk about bad luck. . . ."

"Maybe good luck," Sam replied. "Let's see if we can make it work for us."

"What do you mean?"

"Chances are decent that Bondaruk is the only one who knows what we look like."

"Oh, no, Sam."

He grinned. "Remi, where are your manners? Let's mingle."

Once certain there was no one about, Sam climbed the steps, lifted open the hatch, and had a look around. He turned back to Remi. "It's a closet. Come on."

He climbed up and held the hatch for Remi, then closed it behind her. Through the open closet door was another space, this one a tack room dimly lit by theater-style lights along the baseboards. They stepped through and out the opposite door and found themselves on a gravel alleyway bordered on both sides by horse stalls. Overhead was a high vaulted ceiling with inset exhaust fans and skylights through which pale moonlight filtered. They could hear horses snorting softly and shuffling in the stalls. At the far end of the stable, perhaps thirty yards away, was a set of double barn doors. They walked to them and peeked out.

Before them lay an acre-sized expanse of lush lawn surrounded by chest-high hedges and flickering tiki torches. Multicolored silk banners fluttered on cross wires suspended over the lawn. Dozens of tuxedoed and evening-gowned guests, mostly couples, stood in clusters and strolled about, chatting and laughing. Waiters in stark white uniforms moved through the crowd, occasionally pausing to offer hors d'oeuvres and cocktails. The source of Sinatra's "Summer Wind," pole-mounted loudspeakers strategically placed around the lawn, now emitted a soft jazz number.

To Sam and Remi's right they could see the upper floors of Bondaruk's mansion, its onion-domed minarets silhouetted against the dark sky. To the left, through an entrance gap in the hedges Sam could see a gravel parking lot packed with several million dollars' worth of Bentleys, Mercedeses, Lamborghinis, and Maybachs.

"We're underdressed," Remi muttered.

"Severely," Sam agreed. "I don't see him, do you?"

Remi moved closer to the gap and scanned the throng. "No, but with the torchlight it's hard to tell."

Sam shut the door. "Let go check out the southeast wing."

———

They went back through the tack room trapdoor, retraced their steps down the tunnel, and took the east branch. Almost immediately they found side tunnels spaced at twenty- to thirty-foot intervals along the north wall.

"Storage chambers and other exits," Sam said.

Remi nodded, shining her flashlight on her sketch. "Bohuslav has these marked, but there's no description of where they go."

They shined their flashlights into the darkness, but could see nothing past ten feet. Somewhere in the distance they could hear wind whistling.

"I don't know about you, but I vote we avoid another dungeon-like maze if we can."

"Amen."

They kept walking and after a few hundred yards found themselves standing before another set of stone steps.

This time Remi took the lead, crouching beneath the trapdoor and listening until certain the way was clear. She lifted the hatch, peeked out, then ducked back down again.

"It's pitch-dark. I can't tell where we are."

"Let's go up. We'll see if our eyes adjust."

Remi climbed through the hatch, then stepped aside so Sam could join her. He eased the hatch shut and carefully reached out, trying to measure the space. It was roughly four by four feet square. After thirty seconds of standing still their eyes slowly began to adjust and they could make out a thin rectangle of light to their left. Sam crept to the wall and pressed his eye to the gap. He pulled back, frowned, then looked again.

"What?" Remi asked.

"Books," he whispered. "It's a bookshelf."

He felt along the wall and found a recessed wooden latch. He lifted it up, placed his palm against the wall, and gently pushed. Soundlessly the wall swung away from them on hidden hinges, revealing a foot-wide gap. Sam stepped into it and leaned out. He jerked his head back and had no sooner swung the bookcase shut again when a man's voice said, "Olga, is that you?" Footsteps padded across a rug, paused, then padded in another direction. "Olga . . . ?" Silence for a few seconds, then the sound of water running. The water shut off. Footsteps again, then a door opening and shutting.

Sam pushed the bookcase open again and peeked out. "All clear," he whispered to Remi. Together they stepped out and shut the bookcase behind them.

They were in a bedroom. Measuring twenty feet on a side, with an adjoining bathroom, the space was furnished in heavy walnut furniture, a massive four-poster bed, and well-worn expensive Turkish rugs.

"What now?" Remi asked.

Sam shrugged. "Let's spruce up and join the festivities."

CHAPTER 38

"You're serious, aren't you?"

"Don't I look serious?"

"Yes. That's what worries me."

"Why?"

"Because it's nuts, that's why."

"There's a fine line between nuts and ingenious."

"And an even finer line between ingenuity and idiocy."

Sam chuckled. "I didn't see any security guards at the party, did you?"

"No."

"Which means they're focused on the perimeter—on keeping people out; the guests have all been vetted and probably frisked. There were sixty or seventy people out there and I didn't see anyone checking invitations. You know the rule: 'Look like you belong and you belong.'"

"That sounds more like a Sam Fargo-ism than a rule."

"I like to think they're one and the same."

"I know you do."

"As for the guards, it's unlikely they'd know us from the King and Queen of England. You think it's even crossed Bondaruk's mind that we'd try to invade his home? No chance. His ego is too big for that. Fortune favors the bold, Remi."

"Another Fargo-ism. And what if the man himself appears?"

"We'll avoid him. We'll keep our eyes on the guests. Given Bondaruk's reputation, they'll be our best early-warning system. When he's near they'll part like a school of fish in shark-infested waters."

Remi sighed. "How sure are you about this?"

"About what part?"

"All of it."

Sam smiled and gave her hand a squeeze. "Relax. Worst case, we walk around, get the lay of the land, then come back here and plan our next step."

Chewing her lip, she thought about it for a moment, then nodded. "Okay, let's see if Olga is my size."

The fit wasn't perfect, but with a few safety pins Remi found in the bathroom she was able to tuck and gather the black V-necked evening gown until only a fashion designer would be able to tell it hadn't been fitted for her. Remi did the same for Sam's classic black tuxedo, cinching the waistband and gathering the shirt at the small of his back with a pin. With their faces washed, hair combed, and camouflage coveralls and backpacks safely stashed inside the bookcase, they gave one another a once-over, stuffed Sam's pockets with a few essential items, then left.

Arm in arm, they started down the hall, which like the bedroom was decorated in somber dark wood, heavy rugs, tapestries, and landscape oil paintings. They counted doors as they walked but stopped after they reached thirty; assuming the room they'd just left wasn't an aberration, it seemed clear this was Bondaruk's guest wing.

"One problem," Remi muttered as they reached the end of the hall and stepped into a high-ceilinged room flanked by a pair of brown granite spiral stairways. The rest of the space was divided into seating areas of well-worn leather chairs and divans. Here and there

sconces cast soft pools of light on the walls. Arched doorways to
their right and directly ahead led to other parts of the house.

"What problem?" Sam asked.

"Neither of us speaks Russian or Ukrainian."

"True, but we do speak the international language," he replied as
another couple entered the room and strolled toward them.

"Which is?"

"A smile and a polite nod," he replied, giving both to the passing
couple, who returned the greeting. Once they were out of earshot
Sam said, "See there? Magical."

A waiter appeared before them holding a tray of champagne flutes.
They each took one and the waiter disappeared.

"And if someone tries to strike up a conversation?" Remi asked.

"Have a coughing fit. It's the perfect excuse to slip away."

"So, which way do we go?"

"West. If his collection is here, that's where we'll find it. You have
the sketch?"

"In my cleavage."

"Mmm."

"Behave yourself."

"Apologies. Okay, let's see how close we can get to the secure
utility room before we see signs of security. I haven't seen any cameras yet, have you?"

"No."

Another couple approached. Sam and Remi raised their glasses,
smiled, and kept going. "I just had a thought," she said. "What if
we run into Olga and her husband and they recognize their own
clothes?"

"Well, that would be a problem, wouldn't it?"

The next room they entered was what Bohuslav had called in his
survey the "Sword Room"; upon entering they instantly realized the
name was woefully inadequate. Measuring seventy by forty feet, the
walls were painted a flat black and the floor covered in black rough-cut
slate. In the center of the room was a rectangular glass case lit from
within by recessed spotlights in the floor. Smaller than the room by

only a few feet and bordered by bloodred carpet runners, the case was filled with no fewer than fifty ancient edged weapons, from axes and swords to pikes and daggers, each resting on its own marble pedestal bearing a placard written in both Russian and English.

Eight or ten couples circulated around the room, staring in fascination at the case, their faces lit from below as they pointed at different weapons and murmured to one another. Sam and Remi joined them, but were careful to remain quiet.

History buff that he was, Sam immediately recognized many of the weapons: the famous claymore, the Scottish two-handed broadsword; a *bardiche*, a Russian poleax; a short, curved French falchion; a *shamshir*, a Persian saber; an ivory-handled Omani *khanjar*; the Japanese *katana*, the samurai's weapon of choice; the classic Roman short sword known as the *gladius*.

Still others were new to him: a British Mameluke saber; a Turkish yataghan; a Viking throwing ax known as the *Mammen*; a ruby-inlaid Moroccan *koummya*.

Remi leaned in close and whispered, "Not very original, is it?"

"What's that?"

"A murderer having a knife collection. It would have been so much more interesting if this case were filled with porcelain dolls."

They reached the far end of the case, rounded the corner, and paused to admire a gleaming, sickle-shaped Egyptian *khopesh*. From the other side of the case there came a murmuring of voices. Through the length of the glass case Sam and Remi could see couples stepping aside as a figure entered the room.

"The shark has arrived," Remi murmured.

"And here I am without my bucket of poison chum," Sam said.

Speaking in lightly accented English, Hadeon Bondaruk's deep basso voice filled the room: "Good evening, ladies and gentlemen. I can see by your expressions you find my collection fascinating."

Shoulders back, hands clasped behind his back like a general inspecting a line of soldiers, Bondaruk strolled down the side of the case. "The tools of war often have that effect. As so-called civilized people we try to pretend we're not captivated by death and violence, but it's in our genetic makeup. In our hearts we're all Neanderthals fighting for survival."

Bondaruk stopped and looked around as though daring anyone to disagree with him. Seeing no challengers, he continued walking. Unlike his guests, he wore not a tuxedo, but a pair of black trousers and a matching black silk shirt. He was a lean man, with sharp facial features, glittering black eyes, and thick black hair tied into a short ponytail. He looked ten or fifteen years younger than his reported age of nearly fifty.

He paid no attention to his guests, all of whom respectfully stepped aside at his approach, the men watching him warily, the women studying him with expressions that ranged from outright fear to curiosity.

Bondaruk stopped and tapped the glass before him. "The kris dagger," he said to no one in particular. "The traditional weapon of the Malay. Beautiful, with its wavy blade, but not very practical. More for ceremony than for killing." He walked on, then stopped again. "Here's a fine piece: the Chinese *dao*. Perhaps the best melee weapon ever produced."

He continued on, stopping every few feet to hold forth on another weapon, offering either a brief history lesson or his personal impression of the weapon's efficacy. As he neared the end of the case, Sam casually stepped backward, drawing Remi along with him until they were standing with their backs to the wall. Bondaruk, his face reflected in the glass, turned the corner and stopped to admire a six-foot-tall halberd. He stood less than six feet away now.

Remi tightened her hand on her husband's forearm. Sam, his gaze fixed on Bondaruk, tensed himself, ready to charge the moment Bondaruk turned toward them. That he would recognize them wasn't in doubt; whether Sam could subdue him and turn him into a human shield was the question. Without that advantage the guards would swarm them inside of a minute.

Finally Bondaruk said, "The halberd: Leave it to the British to come up with a weapon that is both ugly and purposeless."

The guests chuckled and murmured their agreement, then Bond-

aruk walked on, turning the corner and beginning his strolling lecture down the opposite side of the case. After a few more comments,
Bondaruk strode to the door, turned to the crowd, nodded curtly,
then disappeared.

Remi let out her breath. "Well, he's got a presence, I'll give him
that."

"It's cruelty," Sam muttered. "He wears it like a cape. You can
almost smell it on him."

"I got the same odor from Kholkov."

Sam nodded. "Yes."

"I thought for a moment there you were going to go for him."

"For a moment I thought so, too. Come on, let's find what we
came for before I change my mind."

CHAPTER 39

The farther west through the mansion they walked the fewer party guests they encountered. While the mansion and its wings were laid out as a peace symbol, the main portion of the house was an octagon with sitting rooms, parlors, dens, and libraries surrounding a central foyer. After twenty minutes of wandering they found themselves in a darkened conservatory filled with potted palms and hanging-trellis half walls overflowing with flowering vines. Through the arched glass ceiling they could see diamond-speck stars against the black sky. To their left, through the floor-to-ceiling glass walls, was a long porch surrounded by hedges.

Set into the northwest wall was a single door. They made one circuit through the conservatory to check for cameras and to make sure they were alone, then headed to the door. It was locked.

Sam was reaching into his pocket for his pick set when a voice behind them said, "Excuse me, sir, may I ask what you're doing?"

Sam didn't give himself a chance to think, but simply reacted on instinct. He turned on the man and barked in what he hoped was passable Russian-accented English, "Finally! Where have you been? Do you know the humidity-control sensors have been going off in there?"

"Pardon me—"

"You are security, yes?"

"Yes, sir. However—"

"Mr. Bondaruk told us to come straight here, that someone would meet us. We've already been standing here for what, dear, five minutes?"

Remi didn't miss a beat, nodding firmly. "At least that."

The guard narrowed his eyes at them. "If you'll wait just a moment I'll confirm—"

"Fine, do what you must, but let me ask you this: Have you ever seen what condensation can do to a nine-hundred-year-old *bardiche* with a Mongolian red maple handle? Have you?"

The guard shook his head, his portable radio halfway to his mouth.

Sam said, "Here, look at this palm—this is a perfect example of what I'm talking about . . . do you see the leaves?" He took a step forward and to the guard's left, pointing at a nearby palm tree. Already distracted by his own radio, the guard reacted with natural curiosity, turning his head to look at what Sam had indicated.

In that fleeting moment Sam reversed direction. Spinning on his right heel, he swept his left foot in a short arc, hooking the man's right ankle and kicking it out from under him. Even as the guard stumbled backward Sam was spinning again, this time with a perfectly timed uppercut that caught the man squarely on the chin. He was unconscious before he hit the floor.

"Wow," Remi breathed. "And here I thought your judo was just a hobby."

"It is. It just happens to be a very practical hobby. Next one's yours, by the way."

"Find me a foil and you've got a deal. Mongolian red maple? Is there such a thing?"

"I have no idea."

Sam knelt down, scooped up the man's radio, then frisked him, finding a Glock nine-millimeter pistol in a hip paddle holster, a set of handcuffs, a hotel-style card key, and a key ring. This he tossed to

Remi, who began trying keys in the door. Sam rolled the guard onto his belly, cuffed his hands behind his back, gagged him with his own tie, then dragged him by the collar into the corner and rearranged a few potted palms so he would be harder to spot.

"Got it," Remi said, turning and holding up one of the keys.

"Did you check the door?"

She nodded. "Didn't see any alarm wires. The striker plate and latch look pretty standard."

"Well, we'll know for sure in about five seconds," Sam said, then inserted the key into the lock and turned the knob. Silence. No whooping alarms, no blaring Klaxons.

"Still could be a silent alarm," Remi said.

"True. Hurry, over there."

They sprinted to the corner and ducked down with the guard's body. One minute passed. Two minutes and still there were no pounding footsteps or loudspeaker announcements.

"It can't be this easy," Remi said. "Can it?"

"No chance. No turning back now. Unless you want to, that is?"

"Me?" she replied with a smile. "I'm just starting to enjoy myself."

"That's my girl."

On the other side of the door they found a ten-foot-long corridor painted in pure white and lit by recessed overhead fluorescent lights. At the far end of the corridor was another door, this one made of heavy steel and controlled by a wall-mounted card reader.

"Very tricky," Sam said. "See that quarter-sized clear screen above the reader?"

"Yes."

"It's a biometric thumbprint scanner."

"Which means there's probably a security control center somewhere."

"I agree. It looks like we need our friend. Wait here."

Sam stepped out the first door then reappeared dragging the guard behind him. He handed Remi the card key, then together they hoisted the man up so Sam could wrap his arms around his waist and Remi had access to his cuffed hands.

"We might get as few as two chances at this before we trip something and attract some more company," he said.

"Swipe first, then the thumbprint?"

"Right. I think."

"Great."

Sam spread his legs wider for leverage, then shuffle-walked the man's limp form to the reader. Remi swiped the card, then grabbed the guard's thumb and pressed it to the scanner.

The reader emitted a squelchy beep.

"Strike one," Sam said.

"I'm nervous."

"Second time's the charm. Hurry, this guy's getting heavy."

She took a break, then tried again.

The reader let out a soft, welcoming chime, followed by a metallic snick as the lock disengaged.

"Open it just an inch before the lock reengages," Sam said, backing away and laying the guard down. "Be right back." He dragged the guard back out the first door, then returned.

"See anything?" Sam asked.

Remi eased the door open another inch, pressed her eye to the gap for a few seconds, then pulled back and whispered, "No cameras that I can see."

"Let's go."

Remi opened the door and they stepped through. The room was circular, with gray-painted walls and navy blue carpet. Pot lights in the ceiling cast pools of light on the floor. Directly ahead of them, at the ten o'clock and two o'clock positions on a clock face, were two card reader doors. They each took a door, Sam left, Remi right, and checked for wires. They found none.

Repeating their earlier swipe/thumb process, they first checked the left-hand door. Inside was a small landing and a set of steps that descended fifteen feet to a burgundy-carpeted corridor lit by soft baseboard lights.

They checked the right-hand door. "It's a square alcove, about ten by ten feet," Remi whispered, pulling it open an inch. "Straight

ahead is another door—a latch but no lock that I can see. The wall to
the right is glass from waist height to the ceiling. On the other side is
what looks like a control room—a couple computer workstations and
a radio console. There's another door, behind the workstations."

"Lights?"

"Dark except for the glow of the computer monitors."

"Cameras?"

She peeked again, this time dropping into a crouch and cran-
ing her neck. She pulled back again and nodded. "Only one that I
can see—a blinking green light near the ceiling in the right-hand
corner."

"Is it fixed?"

"No, rotating."

"Good for us, bad for them."

"How so?"

"In a space that small they should have gone with a fixed camera
and a fish-eye lens. No blind spots to hide in. Watch it, count how
long it takes to make a complete pan."

She did so. "Four seconds."

Sam frowned. "Not a lot of time. You have a preference?"

"No."

"Let's go left first."

They dragged the guard through the door, dropped him on the
landing, then descended the steps, hunched over so they could scan
the corridor ahead. They saw no blinking green camera lights. They
kept going.

After thirty feet the corridor ended at an oaken door bearing a
gold plaque embossed in Cyrillic lettering. While neither of them
read Russian, the style of the plaque suggested its context: PRIVATE.
KEEP OUT. The knob, too, was gold. Sam tried it. Unlocked. He
swung it open.

Another circular room, this one thirty feet in diameter and pan-
eled in polished and center-cut burled walnut. The floor was covered
in what looked to be a handwoven Turkish rug.

"That's a Dosemealti," Remi whispered.

"Pardon me?"

"The rug. It's a Dosemealti—they're woven by Yoruk nomads. Extremely rare and extremely expensive. I read an article about them last month. In every square yard of that thing are almost two hundred thousand hand-stitched knots."

"Impressive."

"Yes, but something tells me it's not the prize of this room."

"No kidding."

Spaced every few feet along the curved walls were gleaming glass cases, each containing yet another piece of militaria displayed on a marble pedestal. The room was dark save a single halogen lamp mounted inside each case. Unlike the Sword Room, however, the decor here made it clear this collection was for Bondaruk's eyes only. Any remaining doubt about this was quashed by the high-backed leather chair sitting in the exact center of the room.

"It has a distinctly thronelike feel, doesn't it?" Sam asked.

"Exactly what I was thinking."

They split up, each strolling along a wall, studying each piece in turn. "Here's something called a *gerron*," Sam said over his shoulder, stopping before a case displaying a tall, oval shield made of wicker and leather. "Used by Persian troops."

"I've got a Persian sword over here," Remi replied from across the room. "An *akinakes*, it's called. It was carried by Persian Immortals of the Achaemenid Dynasty."

"Looks like we have a theme going. I've got a *sagaris* over here. A Persian battle-ax—also from the Achaemenid Dynasty."

They continued their tour, each reading aloud from the placards as they went. Shields, spears, daggers, long bows . . . all from the ancient Persian Achaemenid Dynasty of Xerxes I.

"I think someone's got a fetish," Remi said as they met back near the door.

"I agree," Sam replied. "Unless I miss my guess, we may have just found the Bondaruk skeleton we've been looking for."

"Maybe, but that begs the question: What does any of this have to do with Napoleon's Lost Cellar?"

They made their way back to the blue-carpeted rotunda. Remi crouched by the right-hand door, pulled it open, and took another peek. "Nothing's changed."

"Okay, here's what we're going to do," Sam said, then quickly explained. "Once I go in, if the camera stops panning, close the door and find a place to hide. It might mean they've seen something and guards are on the way."

"What about you?"

"You worry about you. I'll be right on your heels."

They switched places at the door. Sam waited until the camera had panned fully to the right, then dropped to his belly and slithered through the door. He rolled right until his back touched the wall, then crawled along it to the next door.

Now he could hear the faint whirring of the camera's pivot motor. Remi, once again kneeling beside the door, tapped the floor twice with her fingernail: *Camera away.* Slowly, Sam turned his head until he could see through the glass. He checked the ceiling and walls above the computer workstations for cameras; he saw none. Out of the corner of his eye he saw the camera panning back toward him. Remi tapped her fingernail once—*Camera coming*—and he ducked down.

Five seconds passed. Remi tapped twice. Sam reached up and tried the doorknob. It was unlocked. He rolled left and got to his knees, careful to keep his head below the glass. He waited until Remi gave him the all-clear double tap again, then turned the knob, pushed open the door, crawled through, and shut it behind him. Three seconds later he was standing pressed against the wall below the camera. He gave her a thumbs-up. Fifteen seconds later she was through both doors and standing beside him.

The control room was twice as big as the alcove. Under the half-glass wall was a long white melamine desk holding two computer towers and twenty-four-inch LCD displays. Fifteen feet down the wall against which they stood was the other door.

Sam tapped his ear, pointed to the camera, then to himself: *Might have microphone; will check.* Remi nodded her understanding.

Synchronizing his movements with the camera's panning, Sam ducked first left, then right, rising up on his tiptoes so he could get a clear view of the camera.

"No sound," he told Remi. "I'll check the door. You say go."

They waited, watching the camera pivot above their heads.

"Go."

Sam slid left down the wall, checked the doorknob, found it unlocked, then slid back. "Our luck is holding," he said.

"That's what makes me nervous."

The camera's panning speed didn't leave them enough time to open the next door, peek through, then either pull back or keep going.

"We'll have to take our chances and risk it," Sam said.

"I know."

"Ready?"

She took a deep breath, let it out, then nodded.

They watched the camera, waiting for it to swing fully away, then dashed down the wall, opened the door, and stepped through.

CHAPTER 40

They were greeted by the blinding glare of white light. Before their eyes could adjust, a Scottish-accented voice said, "Hey, who are you? What are you—"

Hand held before his eyes, Sam jerked the Glock up and pointed it toward the voice. "Hands up!"

"Okay, okay, for God's sake, don't shoot me."

Their eyes adjusted. They were in a laboratory clean room, painted all white save the floor, which was covered in white antistatic, antimicrobial rubber tiles. In the center of the space was a twelve-by-six-foot worktable surrounded by rolling stools. On the shelves and tables was, Sam estimated, a quarter-million dollars' worth of restoration equipment, including autoclaves, glass-fronted refrigeration units, two Zeiss stereomicroscopes, a polarized fluorescence microscope, and a handheld XRF (X-ray fluorescence) device. On the table's Formica surface rested what looked like pieces from Bondaruk's war collection—a broken spear handle, a double-sided ax head, a tarnished and bent Civil War cavalry sword. A triangle of articulated stainless steel halogen lamps shined down from the ceiling.

The man who stood before them was short and bald save a fringe of orange hair above his ears. He was dressed in a knee-length white lab coat. From behind a pair of thick, black-rimmed glasses his eyes were comically magnified.

"Well, that's a familiar sight," Remi said, pointing.

Projected on one of the monitors was a piece of cracked leather bearing a grid of symbols.

"Eureka," Sam muttered. Then he said to the man, "Who are—"

Even as the words left Sam's mouth the man spun and began sprinting toward the far wall—heading for, Sam realized, the red mushroom-shaped panic button mounted there.

"Stop!" Sam shouted, to no effect. "Damn it!"

Behind him, Remi was moving. She leaped forward, snatched the spear handle from the table, and hurled it sidearm. It spun through the air in a flat arc and smacked the man behind the knees. Arm already outstretched for the button, he grunted and pitched forward. His head slammed into the wall with a dull thud just below the button. He slid face-first to the floor, unconscious.

Sam, eyes wide, his gun still raised, stared at her. She looked back at him and offered a shrug and a grin. "I used to toss a baton when I was a kid."

"It shows. Bet you're hell in a horseshoe pit."

"Hope I didn't kill him. Oh, God, I didn't kill him, did I?"

Sam walked over, knelt down, and rolled the man onto his back. Protruding from his forehead was a purple egg-shaped lump. Sam checked for a pulse. "He's just down for a long nap. He'll have a headache for a few days but nothing else."

Remi was standing before the monitor displaying the symbol grid. "You think it's the bottle from Rum Cay?" she asked.

"I sure hope so. If not, that means Bondaruk's got more than one bottle. Look around, see if it's here."

They checked the humidity-control cabinets, the refrigerators, and the drawers beneath the worktable, but found no sign of either the bottle or the label.

"It's probably a digital image," Remi said, studying the monitor. "See the edge there, on the left? It looks color enhanced."

"As much as I'd like to get the bottle away from Bondaruk, this might be all we need. See if you can print—" Sam stopped talking and cocked his head. "You hear that . . . ? Oh, crap." He pointed.

In the corner, partially hidden from view by a cabinet, was a wall-mounted video camera. It stopped panning, the lens aimed directly at them.

"Company's coming," Remi said.

"Quick, check the keyboard, see if you can print us a screen capture of the label!"

As Remi started tapping on the keyboard, Sam sprinted to the corner, grabbed the feed wire beneath the camera, and jerked it loose. Next he ran to the door, flipped off the lights, and returned to Remi, who said, "Got it!" and tapped a key. The laser printer's lights blinked green and it hummed to life.

From the control room they heard a door bang open, then shut, then open again. Footsteps clicked on linoleum, then went silent.

"Down," Sam whispered, then dropped onto his belly and pulled Remi with him. "Stay here and grab that printout." He crawled down the short side of the table and peeked his head out.

At the door, the knob was slowly turning. He extended the Glock and took aim.

The laser printer started rhythmically humming.

"Printing," Remi whispered.

The door burst open, revealing a figure silhouetted by the control room's LCD monitors. Sam fired once. The bullet struck the man in the calf just below the knee. He screamed and toppled forward. His weapon—a compact Heckler & Koch MP5 submachine gun—bounced across the rubber floor and landed a few feet from Sam. In the control room he heard a hushed voice bark something—a curse, Sam assumed from the tone—in Russian. The man Sam shot was whimpering and crawling back toward the door.

"Got it!" Remi called. "Detail's perfect. We can use it."

"Come around," Sam whispered. She crawled around the corner and tapped his ankle. "Here." Sam turned, handed her the Glock, and said, "When I say go, fire three shots through the door. Aim for the glass wall."

"Okay."

Sam got to his knees, took a breath. "Go!"

Remi popped up and started firing. Glass began shattering. Sam somersaulted out from behind the table, veered left, grabbed the MP5, then scuttled back to cover.

"What're they waiting for?" Remi asked.

"Reinforcements or better weaponry would be my guess. We need to get out of here before either arrives."

As if on cue, a hand appeared around the edge of the door and hurled something. The object bounced off the side of the table, hit the rubber floor, then came to a spinning rest.

"Down, Remi!" Sam shouted.

Moving on instinct and on the faith that he'd correctly identified the thrown object, Sam stood up, took a bounding leap, and soccer-kicked the object back toward the door. As it reached the threshold it exploded. Blinding white light and a deafening boom filled the lab. Sam stumbled backward and collapsed behind the table.

"What in God's name was that?" Remi said, shaking her head to clear it.

"Flash-bang grenade. Special forces and SWAT teams use them to distract the bad guys. A lot of sound and light, but no shrapnel."

"How did you know?"

"Discovery Channel. At least now we know one thing—they're trying to avoid any shooting in here."

"How about a little distraction of our own?" Remi said, pointing with the Glock.

Sam looked. On the wall opposite the panic button was a paperback-sized Plexiglas box housing a yellow mushroom bearing a pictograph of a water droplet. "That'll do."

"Two shots, if you will."

"Ready."

"Go."

Remi popped up and opened fire. Sam charged to the wall and slammed the butt of the MP5 sideways into the Plexiglas box, ripping it from the wall. He jerked the lever down. From unseen loudspeakers a computer-generated female voice made an announcement first in Russian, and then in English:

"Warning. Fire suppression system activated. Evacuate area immediately. Warning. Fire suppression system activated."

Sam rushed back behind the table. "Rain's coming, Remi. Protect that printout!"

"Already tucked away."

"Cleavage?"

"Safer. Found a ziplock Baggie."

To the right, in the corner of his eye, Sam saw movement in the doorway. He spun, let loose a quick three-round burst. A monitor in the control room exploded in a shower of sparks, then started smoking. He dove behind the table again.

With a whir, silver nozzles descended from the ceiling. There was a one-second delay followed by a *pop-hiss*. The nozzles exploded into cones of water.

Sam peeked his head around the corner of the table in time to see a figure run through the alcove and disappear through the door.

"Let's go before the cavalry arrives," Sam rasped over the rush of water.

"Wait, I'm checking my ammunition. . . . I've got nine shots left. Ready when you are."

"When I go, put three more shots through the doorway, then follow me. Stay directly behind me, got it?"

"Yep."

"Go!"

Sam got up and charged. As he passed the end of the table, he reached out with his right hand and snagged one of the rolling stools. Ten feet from the door, he pushed it ahead of him, then gave it a kick.

At that moment a figure appeared in the doorway. The stool, already tipping over and spinning, crashed into the man's legs. Arms flailing, he stumbled backward into the still smoking computer monitor. Sam was through the door in three more paces. He reversed the MP5 across his body and slammed it squarely into the center of the man's face. With a sickening crunch his nose shattered. He went limp and slid off the table, legs still entangled in the stool.

Sam picked up the fallen man's MP5 and handed it to Remi.

"What now?" she asked, flipping her sopping hair away from her face.

"Nothing complicated. We run for our lives."

They went through the first door, into the alcove, then through the card-reader door and into the corridor beyond, where the trapped water had risen to ankle depth. The overhead fluorescent lights had gone dark.

Remi asked, "You have a plan, right?"

"Wouldn't call it a plan. A sketch, maybe."

"Good enough for me."

He turned to her and took her free hand in his own. "Are you ready for this? You may have to do something you don't want to do."

Remi smiled. Water ran down her cheeks and over her lips in rivulets. "Like shoot someone? No worries; they started it."

"That's my girl. Okay, we go on three. Stay low and head left for cover. If it moves, shoot it."

"Gladly."

Sam grabbed the knob. "One . . . two . . ."

CHAPTER 41

. . . Three!"

Crouched down, Sam threw open the door.

Except for moonlight filtering through the ceiling, the conservatory was dark and, separated as it was from the lab area, not raining. Water from the corridor gushed out and began spreading across the floor.

Sam and Remi waited, watching. Silence. Nothing moved.

Remi whispered, "Where are they—"

A flash-bang thunked into the wall beside the door and landed at their feet. Sam kicked it away with his heel and slammed the door shut. From the other side came a bang; white light flashed through the cracks.

Sam opened the door an inch and was this time greeted by the sound of pounding footsteps and the sight of flashlights jostling their way toward them across the conservatory.

"Mind if I borrow that?" Sam asked and took Remi's MP5. "When I start shooting, you head right. Take out a window and go for the patio."

"And you?"

"I'm going to bring down the house. Go!"

Sam pushed the door open, angled both MP5s at the ceiling, and opened fire. Hunched over, Remi charged toward the patio, the barrel of her Glock flashing orange and bucking in her hand.

Knowing the glass itself was probably reinforced, Sam aimed for the support joints near the peak. With a reverberating, elongated cracking sound, the joints gave way. The first plate of glass collapsed inward and tumbled downward, followed by another, then another, crashing through the palm trees and cleaving trellis walls as they went. Voices started shouting in Russian, but almost immediately changed to screams as the first pane struck the floor. Shards of glass shot across the conservatory like shrapnel, ripping through foliage and peppering the walls.

Sam, already moving, saw all this out of the corner of his eye. Remi's shots had struck true, shattering one of the wall panes. She was already crouched on the patio, waving for him to hurry. He felt a pluck at his sleeve, then a trio of stings on his face. He put his head down and his arms up, kept running, and leaped through Remi's opening.

"You're bleeding," Remi said.

"Maybe I'll end up with a dueling scar. Come on!"

He handed her back one MP5, then turned and ran for the hedges. Arms held before him like a wedge, he bulldozed through the tangle of branches into open air, then reached back in and pulled Remi through. On the other side of the hedge they could hear the shattering of glass every few seconds as the remainder of the conservatory roof continued to collapse. Voices, some in English and some in Russian, called to one another. Similarly, from the main house and what Sam and Remi guessed was the party area, came a cacophony of voices from Bondaruk's guests.

Sam and Remi crouched down in the grass to catch their breath and get their bearings. To their right, fifty yards away, was the estate's cliff-side wall; behind them lay the west wing, the main part of the mansion, and the east wings; directly ahead, a hundred feet away, stood a line of closely set pine trees fronted by barberry bushes.

Sam checked his watch: four A.M. A few hours before dawn.

"Let's steal one of the cars," Remi said, taking off her shoes, snapping off their high heels, then settling them back on her feet. "We drive like hell for Sevastopol and find someplace with lots of people. Bondaruk wouldn't dare do anything in public."

"Don't count on it. Besides, that's too obvious. By now they've got the perimeter locked down. Don't forget: The only way he'll know it's us is from the camera footage or by putting our pictures in front of the guy back in the lab. Right now all he knows is all hell is breaking loose. Better we maintain that mystery."

"How?"

"Retrace our steps. The last place they'll check is the way we came in."

"Back through the tunnel? And then what, swim for the boat?"

Sam shrugged. "I hadn't gotten to that part yet. Still, I think it's our best chance."

Remi gave it five seconds of thought, then said, "Smuggler's tunnel it is—unless we spot a helicopter or a tank somewhere along the way."

"You find me a tank, Remi Fargo, and I'll never drive over the speed limit again."

"Promises, promises."

Of all the unknowns about Bondaruk's estate, two were of the greatest concern to Sam and Remi: One, did Bondaruk have guard dogs? Two, how many gunmen did he have, either on the property or in reserve, ready to come when called? Though they didn't know the answer to either of these questions, they decided to assume the worst and get out while confusion still reigned and before their host had a chance to muster whatever hounds—human or canine—he had at his disposal.

Hunched over, they sprinted in bursts to the end of the hedges, paused to make sure the way was clear, then dashed across an open patch of lawn to the line of barberry bushes. Sam took off his tuxedo jacket and gave it to Remi, then dropped to his belly and wriggled through the thorny branches and onto the narrow strip of grass before the pine grove. Remi joined him a few moments later and started to take off his jacket.

"Keep it," he said. "Temperature's dropping."

She smiled. "Always the gentleman—Sam, your arms."

He looked down. The barberry thorns had shredded his shirt-sleeves; the white material was streaked and dotted with blood. "Looks worse than it is, but this shirt is going to get us caught."

They crawled a few feet into the pine trees. Sam dug into the earth, grabbed a handful of dirt, and began rubbing it over his shirt-front, sleeves, and face. Remi did his back, then her own arms and face. Sam couldn't help but smile. "Looks like we've been to the cocktail party from hell."

"Not far off. Look . . . there."

A hundred yards east across the lawn they saw a trio of flashlights appear around the corner of the house and begin moving along the wall toward them.

"Hear any dogs?" Sam asked.

"No."

"Let's hope it stays that way. Come on."

They moved deeper into the trees, ducking under and sidestepping low-hanging branches until they came across a narrow, north-south game trail. They took it, heading north toward the stables. The pine grove was untouched old-growth, a hundred or more years old, which was both a curse and a blessing: While the intertwined boughs frequently forced them to crawl and crab-walk, it also provided perfect cover. Several times as they stopped to catch their breath they watched as guards moved along the other side of the tree line not thirty feet away, but so dense was the foliage that their flashlight beams penetrated only a few feet.

"Eventually they'll send someone in," Sam whispered, "but with luck we'll be long gone before that."

"How far to the stables?"

"On a straight line, a quarter mile, but this grove zigzags, so it's probably double that. Ready?"

"Whenever you are."

For the next twenty minutes they picked their way along the game trail, pausing every dozen paces to look and listen. Frequently they saw flashlights or shadowed figures moving around the estate grounds, sometimes hundreds of yards away, sometimes so close that Sam and Remi had to lie flat, not daring to breathe or move as the guards scanned the trees before moving on.

Finally the grove began to thin around them and soon the game trail opened into a clearing of grass across which they could see the south wall of the stables. Sam wriggled ahead, did a quick reconnaissance, then returned to Remi. "The party lawn is off to our right. The guests are gone but all the cars are still in the parking lot."

"Bondaruk's probably got them inside, lined up for interrogation," Remi muttered.

"Wouldn't be surprised. I didn't see any posted guards—except for one, and as bad luck would have it he's standing at the corner of the stables right beside the entrance."

"Any chance of taking him out?"

"Not unless I can levitate. His head's on a swivel. I wouldn't get halfway across the clearing before he heard me. I do, however, have an idea." He explained.

"How far?" she asked.

"Sixty, seventy yards."

"Over the stable roof, no less. It's a long shot, if you'll pardon the pun."

They spent a few minutes rummaging around the trees until they had a pile of a half dozen golfball-sized stones. Sam picked up the first one, crab-walked to the edge of the clearing, waited for the guard to look away, then popped up and hurled the stone. It sailed in a high arc over the stable roof. Sam popped back down and scurried back.

Silence.

"Miss," Remi whispered.

Sam grabbed another stone and repeated the process. Another miss. Then a third, and then a fourth. He picked up the fifth stone, shook it in his hand like a pair of dice, then held it before Remi's lips. "For luck." She rolled her eyes, but dutifully blew on the stone.

He crawled out, waited for his moment, then hurled the stone.

Two seconds passed.

From the parking lot came the sound of breaking glass, followed by the rhythmic honking of a car alarm.

"You sank someone's battleship," Remi said.

The alarm had an immediate and dramatic effect, starting with the guard at the stable door, who turned and sprinted toward the parking lot. Voices from other parts of the estate began shouting to one another.

Sam and Remi bolted for cover and sprinted for the wall, reaching it in under ten seconds. Bent at the waist now, they slid down its length to the corner. Ahead of them they saw five or six guards rush headlong across the party area and through the hedges.

"Go," Sam rasped. They stepped out, around the corner, and through the door into the stables.

They weren't two steps inside when a massive dark form rose up before them. Sam pushed Remi left then rolled right. The horse, a jet-black Arabian stallion standing at least sixteen hands high, reared up, its hooves clawing the air before Sam. It let out a deep-chested snort then slammed back to the ground, galloped down the alleyway, and disappeared into an open stall door.

Behind Sam the door opened. The guard saw Remi first and wheeled on her, his MP5 coming up. Before he could utter a word, Sam was there, driving a right cross into his temple. He stumbled sideways and fell to the ground. As Remi scooped up his gun, Sam closed the door and dropped the crossbar into place. Outside they could hear boots pounding on gravel.

"So much for a stealthy exit," Sam muttered.

"At this point I'll settle for any exit at all," Remi replied.

They turned and sprinted for the tack room.

CHAPTER 42

They had just reached the entrance to the tack room when the pounding on the stable door began. Instinctively Sam and Remi spun, looking back. "How long, do you think?" she asked, then followed Sam into the closet. They knelt beside the trapdoor.

He said, "Thirty seconds before they start shooting, another thirty for them to smarten up and find something to slip into the jamb and pop up the latch. Two minutes, no more."

"That plan you mentioned—"

"Sketch."

"Whatever. Let's hear it."

He took ten seconds to explain. Remi said, "We could just make a run for it."

"One big problem: If they're faster than I give them credit for we'll be caught on the cliff. They'll pick us off like pigeons. My way we'll at least have some cover and maybe even turn them back."

"Good point. Okay."

"I'll handle the heavy stuff; you gather the supplies. If we do it right it should be enough to slow them down—maybe even turn them back."

"Ever the optimist."

Sam ducked back into the tack room, grabbed the desk chair, and carried it back into the closet. He closed the door and jammed the chair beneath the knob. Remi already had the trapdoor open and was climbing down. Sam followed and shut it behind him.

Guided by their flashlights, they set to work, Sam jogging back to the intersection, where he began manhandling ore carts away from their place along the wall and onto the tracks, while Remi ran down the tunnel toward the cliff entrance.

Distantly there came the chatter of automatic weapons fire.

"Good guess!" Remi called from the darkness.

"I was kind of hoping to be wrong—by three or four hours," he replied, shoving a second cart into place. A minute later he had the third one seated on the tracks. Remi ran out of the darkness carrying a handful of oil lanterns. She hurled two or three into each cart, making sure they landed with enough force to start leaking oil into the bottoms of the carts.

The gunfire from above ceased. "They're using their brains now," Sam said.

Together they sprinted back down the tunnel, snatching lanterns as they went until they had a dozen more, then returned and tossed them into the ore carts.

"Kindling," Remi said, and they took off again. They grabbed anything that would burn, from wooden toolboxes to boots and coveralls to coils of dry-rotted rope, then returned to the carts and divided the haul into three piles, which they dumped into the three carts.

"You feel that?" Remi asked.

Sam looked up and for the first time noticed a cool breeze blowing in from the cliff entrance. "That's good luck for us."

Using his Swiss Army knife he cut a trio of wicks from the coveralls, then knotted each one at the bottom and together they soaked the knotted ends in the oil at the bottom of the lead cart.

Remi asked, "Do we wait or—" From the direction of the tack room hatch there came the sound of pounding. "Forget I asked," she finished.

Using his lighter Sam lit each of the three wicks as Remi held them. Once certain they were fully caught, she handed two to Sam, who tossed them into the first two carts. Remi tossed hers into the closest cart and they backed away.

Nothing happened.

"Come on . . . ," Remi muttered.

"I was afraid of that. Oil might be too sludgy."

Down the tunnel there came the sound of splintering wood, followed by a door banging open.

Sam stared at the carts, his jaw pulsing with anger. "Damn it!"

With a *whoosh*, one of the carts burst into flames and oily black smoke began gushing from the top. The second and third cart ignited and within seconds a thick cloud of smoke roiled near the ceiling. Pushed by the breeze, it began surging through the intersection and into the side tunnels.

Sam and Remi, coughing, eyes watering from the peripheral exposure, backed away from the carts. "If that doesn't slow them down nothing will," Sam said.

"Can we finally leave this party?" Remi asked.

"After you."

They sprinted down the tunnel and skidded to a stop at the entrance. Outside, the fog had lifted and the erosion bridge was dimly lit by moonlight. Waves lapped and hissed at the cliff face. Despite the breeze, the smoke cloud was moving down the tunnel toward them and with it came the faint sounds of coughing and retching.

"When we reach the water, we'll let the tide take us. It should be running north to south along the coast. Balaclava's only about three miles down the coast. We'll go ashore there."

"Right."

"Still have the printout?"

Remi patted her dress at the waistline. "Safe and sound."

Sam eased up to the edge and peered down. A bullet smashed into the rock beside his head. He jerked back and they dropped flat.

Remi gasped. "What—"

"There's a patrol boat down there," Sam muttered. "They're sitting right below the spikes."

"We're trapped."

"Like hell we are. Come on."

He pulled Remi to her feet and they began sprinting back down the tunnel. "Care to fill me in?" Remi said.

"No time. You'll get it. Just stay on the tracks."

With each step the smoke thickened until even their flashlight beams did them no good. Hand in hand, they kept running, heads down and eyes slitted against the fumes.

"Almost there," Sam called and stretched his free hand before him.

The retching and coughing were louder now, seemingly all around them. A voice shouted something in Russian, followed by a rasped reply in English: "Back . . . go back . . . !"

Sam tripped and fell, taking Remi down with him. They got back to their feet and kept going. His groping hand bumped into something hot and he jerked it back. He dropped to his knees and pulled Remi down beside him. Somewhere close by, multiple boots crunched on gravel. A flashlight beam cut through the smoke, then disappeared.

"What's going on?" Remi whispered.

In response, Sam gave the ore cart a quick rap with his knuckles. "Take off the coat." She did so. Sam shoved his hands into the sleeves from the outside in, then twisted the body of the jacket into a ball. "Oven mitts," he explained.

Now Remi caught on: "Depth charge?"

"You got it."

"Clever boy."

"Once I get it rolling, you push me from behind."

"Okay."

Hunched over, Sam moved around to the other side of the cart, planted his feet wide, then placed his gloved hands against the steel side and shoved. The cart didn't budge. He tried again. Nothing.

He heard a metallic *click-click*, then Remi's whispered voice: "Wheel brake was on. Try again."

Sam took a deep breath, set his jaw, and shoved. With a steel-on-steel shriek, the cart lurched forward. The crack of a gunshot echoed down the tunnel, but Sam ignored it and kept going. He passed Remi and she fell in behind him, hands pressed against his lower back. The cart quickly picked up speed. Pushed by the breeze, the flames and smoke streamed backward over their heads like a comet's tail.

Suddenly the smoke thinned out. The tunnel entrance loomed before them, not twenty feet away. "Braking," Sam shouted and leaned backward, digging his heels into the gravel ballast. Remi, her hands tight around his belt, did the same. Their combined weight began to slow the cart. The opening rushed toward them. Ten feet . . . five feet . . . Sam made a quick mental calculation, decided the momentum was right, then let go. They stumbled backward together, landed in a heap, and looked up just in time to see the flaming cart tip ever so gently over the lip of the entrance.

There were three seconds of silence, then a thunderous crash.

Sam and Remi crawled on hands and knees to the entrance and looked over the edge. Already half engulfed in flames, the patrol boat was listing heavily to port as water bubbled up through a crater in the afterdeck. After a few seconds a pair of heads bobbed to the surface; one began swimming away, but the other remained motionless. The boat dipped stern first below the surface and slid from view.

"I think that's called a bull's-eye," Remi said, then dropped to her belly and let out an exhausted sigh. Sam did the same. Above their heads black smoke spewed from the tunnel and began drifting away through the bridge.

"Well," Sam said, "I'd say we've thoroughly worn out our welcome. Shall we call it a night?"

"Yes, please."

CHAPTER 43

MONACO

Yvette Fournier-Desmarais's hazel eyes stared over the rim of her poised coffee cup as she listened intently to Sam recount their adventure on Elba. He'd left out any mention of Umberto's near betrayal of them to Kholkov.

"After that," Sam finished, "we drove to Nisporto, then made our way back to the mainland."

"Amazing," Yvette said. "You two certainly know how to live up to your reputations."

It was early morning and the three of them sat on the patio of Yvette's villa overlooking Point de la Veille. The sun sparkled off the flat calm waters of the Mediterranean.

After watching Bondaruk's patrol boat sink into the depths below the erosion bridge Sam and Remi had climbed down the spike ladder and slipped into the water. They found a pair of orange kapok life jackets that had escaped the boat's demise, latched on to them, and let the current carry them south along the coast. As the sun rose over the horizon they drifted along, watching plumes of black smoke gather over Bondaruk's estate and listening as the sirens of the fire engines grew louder. Several times to the north they saw more Bondaruk patrol boats, but the crews focused their attention on the cliffs beneath the estate.

An hour after they went into the water they found themselves off the beaches north of Balaclava and they paddled ashore and made their way into town, and two hours after their phone call to Selma they were sitting in the back of a limousine and on their way to Kerch, a hundred miles up the coast on the Sea of Azov. Waiting there was a courier who upon Selma's orders had gathered their passports, credit cards, and luggage from their hotel in Yevpatoria. An hour after that they were aboard a private charter headed for Istanbul.

Knowing they were in a holding pattern until Selma could decipher the printout they'd stolen from Bondaruk's lab, and knowing they needed a safe place to regroup, they'd called Yvette, who'd happily and immediately dispatched Langdon, her ex-SAS bodyguard, aboard her Gulfstream to collect them.

"Well, in all fairness I have to tell you: Umberto confessed everything," Yvette now said. "He was quite ashamed of himself."

"He redeemed himself," Remi said. "In spades."

"I agree. I told him that if the Fargos forgave, so did I."

Sam asked, "I'm curious: What happened to Carmine Bianco?"

"Who?"

"The Corsican mobster–slash–Elban cop."

"Ah, him . . . I believe he's now the guest of the Italian government. Something about attempted murder."

Sam and Remi laughed.

"So," Yvette said, "Laurent's diary is proving helpful?"

"And a challenge," Remi replied. "The code he used is complex and layered, but if anyone can puzzle it out, it's Selma." As soon as they'd arrived at the villa they faxed the printout to Selma.

Langdon appeared with a fresh carafe of coffee and refilled everyone's cups. Sam asked, "So, Langdon, what's the answer?"

"Pardon me, sir?"

"Did she have the good sense to say yes?"

Langdon cleared his throat and pursed his lips.

Yvette said, "Oh, for goodness' sake, Langdon . . ." To Sam and Remi: "He's so reserved, so proper. Langdon, you're allowed to share good news, you know. Go on, tell them."

Langdon allowed his mouth to form the barest of smiles and said, "Yes, sir, she agreed to marry me."

"Congratulations."

Remi raised her coffee cup. "To the groom to be."

The three of them toasted Langdon, whose face turned a deep shade of red. He nodded his thanks and murmured, "Madam, if there's nothing else . . ."

"Go on, Langdon, before you have a stroke."

Langdon disappeared.

"Unfortunately, this means I'll be losing him," Yvette said. "He'll be a kept man now. A gigolo, if you will."

"Not a bad job if you can get it," Sam said.

Remi lightly punched him on the biceps. "Mind your manners, Fargo."

"I'm just saying, there are worse jobs out there."

"Enough."

They chatted and drank coffee until Langdon returned thirty minutes later. "Mr. and Mrs. Fargo, Mrs. Wondrash is calling for you."

They excused themselves and followed Langdon down to the study. Yvette's MacBook Air sat open on a mahogany desk overlooking the garden. Langdon had already arranged a pair of club chairs before the laptop. Once they were seated, he left and closed the door behind him.

The laptop's screen displayed Selma's workroom back in La Jolla. "Selma, are you there?" Sam called.

Pete Jeffcoat's tanned face appeared before the camera. He smiled at them. "Hi, Sam. Hi, Remi."

"How're you, Pete?"

"Fantastic, couldn't be better." Pete's sunny attitude knew no bounds. He could not only turn lemons into lemonade, but he could turn them into a grove of lemon trees.

"And Wendy?"

"She's good. Getting a little stir-crazy, being all cooped up here. The bodyguard guys are great, but a little strict."

"It's for the best," Sam said. "Hopefully it'll be over soon."

"Sure, no worries, we're cool. Hey, here's the head honcho. . . ."

Pete disappeared from view and was replaced by Selma, who settled onto a stool in front of the camera, casually dunking a tea bag into a steaming cup. "Morning, Mr. and Mrs. Fargo."

"Morning, Selma."

"You want the good news or the bad news first?"

"Both at the same time," Sam replied. "Like peeling off a Band-Aid."

"Whatever you say . . . The printout you faxed did the trick. Very good image; high resolution. I used it to decipher the next lines of code. Here's the bad news: The riddle has us stumped. Maybe you'll have more luck with it." Selma grabbed her clipboard from the table and recited:

"Anguished House Fellows in amber trapped;
Tassilo and Pepere Gibbous Baia keep safe the place of Hajj;
The Genius of Ionia, his stride a battle of rivals;
A trio of Quoins, their fourth lost, shall point the way to Frigisinga.

"That's it," Selma said. "I've e-mailed it to your iPhones with the standard Blowfish encryption. We'll keep working on it, but it seems clear this one's a bit tougher than the last."

"I'd say so," Remi replied, already deep in thought.

Sam said, "Selma, the word in the last line—coins . . ."

"It's spelled Q-U-O-I-N-S."

"You're sure that's it?"

"We're sure. I triple-checked it myself, then had Pete and Wendy do the same. Why?"

" 'Quoin' is an architectural term. It has a couple meanings: It's a keystone of an arch or exterior cornerstone."

"But to what?" Remi said.

"That's the million-dollar question. We have to assume it's answered in the rest of the riddle."

"Unless it refers to any of its other meanings," Selma said. " 'Quoin' also relates to printing and naval warfare. The first is a device used to hold handset type in place. The second is a type of block used to raise and lower the barrel of a cannon."

"A block?" Remi said. "As in a wedge?"

"Yes, I think so."

"So it has something to do with cornerstones and wedges."

"If we take the meanings literally," Sam replied. "But if they're metaphorical they could mean anything—a wedge can either support or separate objects. Same with a cornerstone."

"We need the rest of the context," Remi agreed. "We'll get to work, Selma, thanks."

"Two more things before you go: I'm also deciphering Laurent's diary as we go along, and I think we've got the answer to a couple of our mini mysteries. First, I've found out why he and Napoleon bothered with a code and riddle instead of just a map with a big *X* on it.

"According to Laurent, Napoleon fell into a depression soon after he reached Saint Helena. He'd escaped exile on Elba only to get defeated four months later at Waterloo. He confided to Laurent that he thought his fate was sealed. He was sure he'd die in exile on Saint Helena."

"He was right," Sam said.

"It started him pondering his legacy," Selma continued. "He had one son, Napoleon Francis Joseph Charles—Napoleon II—by his second wife, Marie Louise. When Napoleon lost at Waterloo he abdicated the throne to junior, who ruled for about two weeks before the allies stormed Paris and dethroned him.

"Napoleon was heartbroken—and furious. He felt if his son had shown 'true Bonaparte character,' it wouldn't have happened. Never mind that the boy was four years old."

Sam said, "It couldn't have been easy for him to live up to his father's reputation."

"Impossible, I'd say. Anyway, Napoleon ordered Laurent to create a 'puzzle map' that would—and I'm quoting here—'confound our enemies, prove the new emperor's mettle, and point the way to the prize that would help return the Bonaparte name to greatness.'

"Unfortunately," Selma continued, "after the allies overthrew him, Napoleon II was bundled off to Austria, given the honorary title of Duke of Reichstadt, and kept a virtual prisoner there until he died of tuberculosis in 1832. As far as I can tell he never even tried to regain power—or even follow the map. Laurent isn't clear why, though.

"As for the second mini mystery—why Napoleon and Laurent chose wine bottles as their puzzle clues—according to Laurent's writings Napoleon himself ordered the Lacanau grape line destroyed—the seeds, the vineyard, everything—but it didn't have anything to do with his love of the stuff. His theory was the bottles would become instant collector's items—the wine Napoleon Bonaparte didn't want anyone else to have. If any of the bottles were unearthed from their hiding places they'd find their way into museums or private collections, where they'd remain safe until a Bonaparte descendant who knew their secret came along."

"So the father wasn't entirely confident in his son's 'mettle,' as he called it," Remi said. "He was hedging his bets."

"Seems so. When Napoleon abdicated for the second and final time, the First Napoleonic Law of Succession was in effect. It named Napoleon II as the legitimate heir to the throne; failing that, succession went to Napoleon's older brother, Joseph, and his male descendants, then to his younger brother, Louis, and his male line."

"None of whom bothered to follow the trail," Remi said.

"If they even knew about it," Selma replied. "We're still working on that part. Either way, it seems clear all the trouble Napoleon and Laurent went to was wasted. Until now, no one's even been aware of their grand plan."

"And now it's just us and Bondaruk," Sam said.

Remi said, "It's all very sad. In the end Napoleon was just desperate, pathetic, and paranoid, waiting for someone to restore the family name. And to think at the height of his power this was a man who held a good chunk of Europe under his thumb."

Sam said, " 'A tyrant is most tyrant to himself.' "

"Pardon?"

"It's a quote from George Herbert. A Welsh poet. I don't think he was talking about Napoleon, but it certainly fits. Selma, this 'prize' Laurent talked about . . . there was nothing else in the diary about it?"

"Nothing so far."

"The safe bet would be on money," Remi said. "Or something he could convert into money—a war chest the son could use to raise an army."

Sam nodded. "Enough for a new Bonaparte emperor to reconquer France and maybe Europe."

They signed off with Selma and headed back to the patio. They were halfway up the steps when Sam's phone chimed. He checked the screen. It was Rube Haywood. Sam put it on speaker.

"I think I found the skeleton in Bondaruk's closet," Rube said.

"We're all ears."

"The guy I sent to talk to Bondaruk's old Iranian handler—"

"Aref Ghasemi," Remi said.

"Right. At first Ghasemi was a little cagey, but he finally opened up. He pretty much confirmed he handled Bondaruk all through the border war with the Russians. The details are sketchy on this part, but somewhere along the way Bondaruk got the idea that he's a direct descendant of some ancient Persian king, a guy named—"

"Xerxes I," Sam finished.

"Yeah, that's it, how'd you know?"

Without going into too much detail Sam described the private Achaemenid Dynasty museum they'd found in the bowels of Bondaruk's estate.

"Well, there's your confirmation," Rube said.

"What was Ghasemi's take on this?" Sam asked. "Does he think Bondaruk could be from the Xerxes line?"

"He thought it was possible, but the thing you have to understand about Ghasemi is he's a slippery fish. The Brits don't buy anything he says without triple- or quadruple-checking it."

"That seems like an odd story to make up," Remi said.

"I thought so, too," Rube replied. "Either way, Bondaruk's spent millions researching this, so unless he's certifiably insane he may have found proof to support his claim—at least in his own mind."

Sam said, "Remi, remember what Kholkov told us in Marseille? About Bondaruk's goal?"

Remi closed her eyes, recalling the conversation, and Kholkov's words: "'. . . the items involve a family legacy. He's simply trying to finish what was begun a long time ago. . . .'"

"This Xerxes angle could be the key," Sam replied. "But what are the 'items'? Something Xerxes lost long ago?"

"Another project for Selma and the gang."

Rube said, "Whether his claim is true is irrelevant. He believes it, and it's driving everything he does. What he's after is a different story. Figure that out and you could be halfway home."

"So we're back to square one," Sam said. "What in the world do Xerxes and the Achaemenid Dynasty have to do with Napoleon's Lost Cellar?"

———

Sam awoke to the trilling of his iPhone. He rolled over. The red numerals of the LED display said 3:12 A.M. Sam grabbed the phone and checked the caller ID: BLOCKED.

He answered. "Hello?"

"I thought it was time we talked directly," a voice said. "Without intermediaries."

Still waking up, it took Sam a moment to place the voice. "You woke me up, Bondaruk. That's just bad manners. I don't suppose you'd like to tell me how you got my number?"

"Money is the great equalizer, Mr. Fargo."

"Money is just money. It's what you do with it that counts."

"Spoken like a true do-gooder."

Remi rolled over and sat up beside Sam. In answer to her questioning expression he mouthed, *Bondaruk.*

"What do you want?" Sam said.

"I'm curious: You were among the guests at my party, weren't you?"

"We were standing right behind you during your lecture in the Sword Room. We got the distinct impression you like to hear yourself talk."

"You're brave, both of you, I'll give you that much. You invaded my home, Mr. Fargo. If you were anyone else you'd—"

"Already be dead. Skip the threats and make your point. I'd like to get back to sleep."

"I'm giving you one last chance. We work together. When it's over, you get the bottles, I get what I'm after, and we part company. No harm done."

"Speaking of what you're after . . . It wouldn't have anything to do with your private Persian funland below the laboratories, would it?"

Bondaruk didn't answer.

"I thought so," Sam said. "Bondaruk, don't you think you're taking your Xerxes infatuation a little too far? It's not healthy."

"You're making a mistake, Mr. Fargo."

"It seems to us that you've been making all the mistakes. By the way, we know your people have been casing our house in San Diego. If any of them so much as touch a newspaper in the driveway half the San Diego County Sheriff's Department will fall on them like an avalanche."

"So noted. This is the last time I'll ask nicely."

"Thanks for the warning."

Sam hung up.

Remi said, "'Private Persian funland'? Very imaginative."

"I have my moments."

CHAPTER 44

A rmed with the next lines of the riddle and Yvette's broadband
Internet connection, Sam and Remi locked themselves in the
study and went to work. Yvette, ever the gracious host, ordered
Langdon to supply them with snacks and beverages, pens and paper,
a second laptop, dry-erase markers, and a four-by-six-foot dry-erase
board. On this they wrote the riddle in huge block letters:

> Anguished House Fellows in amber trapped;
> Tassilo and Pepere Gibbous Baia keep safe the place of Hajj;
> The Genius of Ionia, his stride a battle of rivals;
> A trio of Quoins, their fourth lost, shall point the way to Frigisinga.

They began by compiling a list of synonyms for each word
that easily lent itself multiple meanings. They counted sixteen:
"anguished," "House," "Fellows," "trapped," "Gibbous," "keep,"
"safe," "place," "Hajj," "Genius," "stride," "battle," "rivals," "trio,"
"point," "way."

From these they generated a list of dozens of words. Those they wrote on the board's opposite side in a spiderweb-like chart, branch leading to thread leading to question marks.

Next they turned their attention to words they felt had clear links to history—"amber," "Tassilo," "Baia," "Hajj," "Genius," "Ionia," "Quoins"—which they also placed on the board, in their own separate columns and lists. Once done they divided up the words and began scouring the Internet for historical references, which they plugged into briefs of each word.

Five of the words—"amber," "Tassilo," "Baia," "Hajj," "Ionia"— had links to well-known places, peoples, or things. Amber was a fossil resin used for jewelry; Tassilo was the given name of a long line of Bavarian kings; Hajj was the name of the yearly Islamic pilgrimage to the holy site of Mecca; Baia, which meant "mine," was the name of a commune in Romania on the Moldova River; and Ionia was a Greek island in the North Aegean Sea.

Unfortunately, like their list of synonyms, each of these historical references was in itself a web of facts and double meanings and cross connections.

Breaking only to eat and drink and refresh themselves in the study's attached bathroom, Sam and Remi kept at it through the morning into late afternoon until finally they decided on a different tack: to focus their attention on a single line of the riddle, hoping its solution would start a domino effect. They decided to try the second line.

"'Tassilo and Pepere Gibbous Baia keep safe the place of Hajj,'" Remi recited, absently tapping her temple with a pencil. "*Pepere* is easy. It's a French nickname for 'grandfather.'"

"Right. And unless we're missing some other significant reference to Tassilo, we can assume it's a reference to Bavaria—its history, its landmarks, its culture. Something Bavarian."

"Agreed. How about 'Gibbous Baia'?"

They'd already devoted two fruitless hours to Romanian history in hopes of stumbling across an epiphany about the Baia area.

"'Gibbous' means a moon that's between half and completely full."

"Are we sure about that part?"

"Yes, a gibbous moon is—"

"No, I'm asking if that's the only meaning."

Sam thought for a moment, then frowned. "I'd assumed so. Maybe I shouldn't have." He picked up and shoved books around the desk until he found the dictionary. He found the correct page, scanned the entry, then clicked his tongue. "Dumb, Sam. . . ."

"What?"

" 'Gibbous' also means 'humpbacked.' So Gibbous and Baia . . ."

Remi was already typing on the laptop. Though much of their in-depth references had come from library sites, their default starting point was good old Google. "Here . . . got something," she said after a few minutes of reading. "Put the two together and you get this: Baia is part of a phrase—'men of Baia.' It's a rough translation for the word 'Bavaria.' "

"So, the Humpback of Bavaria?" Sam asked.

"No, no . . ." Remi tapped the keyboard again and scanned the search results. "Gotcha! Okay, Tassilo III, the king of Bavaria from 748 to 787, was installed on the throne by Pepin the Short, father of Charlemagne and *grandfather* of Pepin the *Hunchback*."

"Now we're talking," Sam replied. "So Tassilo and the hunchback's grandfather, Pepin the Short, 'keep safe the place of Hajj.' "

"Problem is I can't find any connection between either of them, or Bavaria, to Mecca."

"It has to be a metaphor or a synonym," Sam replied.

"Yes, or maybe an Islamic artifact somewhere in Bavaria."

Sam, now on his own laptop, did a quick search. "Nope, nothing jumps out. Let's keep going. Try another line."

"We'll go back to the beginning: 'Anguished House Fellows in amber trapped.' We've already got the etymology and synonyms for 'anguished,' 'House,' 'Fellows,' 'amber,' and 'trapped.' So how do they all intersect?"

Sam plopped down in a chair and leaned his head back, squeezing the bridge of his nose between his index finger and thumb. "I don't know. . . . Something about the line is familiar, though."

"Which part?"

"I don't know. It's right there. I can almost see it."

They sat in silence for nearly a half hour, each wrapped in thought, their minds swirling with connections and possible connections.

Finally Remi looked at her watch. "It's almost midnight. Let's get some sleep and come back to it fresh in the morning."

"Okay. It's frustrating. I know I'm missing something, I just can't put my finger on it."

Four hours later as they lay asleep in Yvette's guest suite Sam bolted upright in bed and muttered, "There you are!" Remi, a light sleeper, was instantly awake: "What? What's wrong, Sam?"

"Nothing. I think I've got it."

In their pajamas they returned to the study, turned on the lights, and powered up their laptops. For twenty minutes Sam sat at the keyboard, typing and following links as Remi watched from the corner chair. At last Sam turned around and smiled.

"It's from a book I read in college—*The Days of the Upright* by a guy named . . . Roche. He talks about the origin of the word 'Huguenot.'"

"French Calvinists, right?" Remi asked. "Protestants."

"Right. Pretty big group from the sixteenth to eighteenth century. Anyway, there are a lot of explanations for where the word 'Huguenot' comes from. Some think it's a hybrid—from the German word *Eidgenosse*, meaning 'confederate,' and the name Besançon Hugues, who was involved in early Calvinist history.

"The etymology most historians subscribe to comes from the Flemish word *huisgenooten*, which was what some Bible students in Flemish France were nicknamed. *Huisgenooten* would gather secretly in one another's homes to study scripture. The name translates as 'House Fellows.'"

Remi stared at him for ten seconds before murmuring, "Sam, that's brilliant."

"What would have been brilliant is if I'd come up with it eighteen hours ago."

"Better late than never. Okay, so we're talking about Huguenots."

"Anguished Huguenots," Sam corrected.

Remi stood up and went to their whiteboard and used the dry-erase marker to circle their list of synonyms for 'anguished.' There were dozens. No obvious connection between them and Huguenots jumped out at them.

"So, let's talk about amber," Sam said, turning to the second part of the line. "'In amber trapped.' How do you get trapped in amber?"

They brainstormed this for a few minutes before Remi said, "Let's try this: What happens when something gets trapped in amber?"

"You die," Sam offered.

"Before that . . . Immobilized."

"Frozen in place."

"Right . . ." Head down, eyes closed, she paced back and forth. "Frozen in place . . . Like a snapshot."

Sam, his head resting against the chair's headrest, leaned forward. "Like a painting."

"Yes!"

He spun around in his chair and started typing on the laptop. "Painting . . . Huguenots . . ." He scanned the search results.

"Anything?"

"Massacre," he muttered.

"What?"

"'Massacre' could be, in a stretch, synonymous with 'anguished,' couldn't it?"

"Sure."

"Then how about this: a painting by François Dubois called *The Saint Bartholomew's Day Massacre*."

"What's the context?"

Sam scanned the article, then summarized: "France, in 1572 . . . from August to October of that year Catholic mobs attacked minority Huguenots throughout the country . . ." Sam leaned back in his chair and frowned. "Anywhere between ten thousand and a hundred thousand were killed."

"If that isn't anguish I don't know what is," Remi murmured. "Okay, so combine that with Bavaria. . . ."

Sam leaned forward and began typing again, this time using for his major search terms "Dubois," "Saint Bartholomew," and "Bavaria," in combination with "day" and "massacre."

"Might as well throw in our synonyms for 'Hajj,'" Remi said, then dictated from the whiteboard: "'Mecca,' 'pilgrimage,' 'Islam,' 'pilgrim' . . ."

Sam finished typing and hit Enter. "A lot of results," he whispered, scrolling through the page. "Nothing obvious, though."

"Let's start subtracting and mixing words from the search."

For the next hour they did just that, trying permutations of their search terms until finally, near sunrise, Sam found something interesting with the combination of "Saint Bartholomew," "Bavaria," and "pilgrim." He said with a grin, "Lightbulb just popped on."

"What?" Remi said, then leaned in and read from the screen:

"Saint Bartholomae's Pilgrim Church, Bavaria, Germany."

CHAPTER 45

SCHÖNAU, BAVARIA

U nbelievable," Sam whispered.

He and Remi stepped to the wooden railing of the overlook and stared at the vista below. Finally Remi murmured, "I don't think the word 'beautiful' even begins to capture this, Sam. Why did it take us this long to come here?"

"I have no idea," he whispered back, then lifted his Canon EOS digital camera and took a picture. They'd been to Bavaria before, but never this area. "Even 'breathtaking' doesn't seem to fit, does it?"

"Not even close. I can almost hear 'The Sound of Music.'"

Below them lay the emerald waters of the Königssee (King's Lake) Fjord. Measuring just over half a mile at its widest point and bracketed on both sides by thickly forested granite escarpments and jagged snowcapped peaks, the Königssee meandered its way from the village of Schönau in the north down to the Obersee, or Upper Lake, five miles to the south. Long ago severed from the Königssee by a landslide, the Obersee sat tucked away in its own oval valley surrounded by alpine meadows bursting with wildflowers and encircled by tumbling waterfalls, sights that attracted nature lovers and photography buffs the world over. A special boat service ran from Schönau to the Obersee's Salet docks.

Aside from the occasional wake from the handful of electric tour boats that soundlessly plied the Königssee, the lake's surface was perfectly calm, a sun-dappled mirror reflecting the greens and grays and ochers of the surrounding forests and cliffs. Everywhere Sam and Remi turned lay yet another perfectly composed alpine postcard.

Two-thirds of the way down the Königssee, where it narrowed to only a few hundred yards before widening again and curving southeast toward the Obersee, Saint Bartholomae's Pilgrim Church sat in a clearing of trees on the Hirschau Peninsula.

An architectural hybrid of sorts, half of Saint Bartholomae's Church was an old Bavarian ski lodge with white stucco exterior walls, steeply sloped gray shingle roof, and heavy wooden shutters painted in greens and yellows, while the other half was made up of a cluster of three red-roofed onion domes atop of which further rose two spires: one a windowless dome, the other, sitting nearer the water's edge, a more traditional steeple, with a sloped hip roof and shuttered slit windows.

"Is it ironic that Hitler also loved this place?" Remi asked, "or just a little scary?"

Berchtesgaden, the municipality in which the Königssee sat, was also home to Adolf Hitler's mountaintop retreat known as the Eagle's Nest.

"No one's immune to beauty," Sam replied. "Even him, it seems."

The question was, Sam and Remi knew, aside from the scenery, why exactly were they here?

Though they had deciphered only the first part of the latest riddle, they'd felt confident enough in their solution to immediately call Selma and ask her to arrange passage from Monaco to Bavaria. By midmorning, having thanked Yvette for her hospitality and promised to return and recount their exploration, they were on their way to the Nice airport, from there to Paris, and then to Salzburg, where they rented a car and drove the remaining thirty miles to Schönau am Königssee.

"What time does our boat leave in the morning?" Remi asked.

"Nine. Remind me to check the weather tonight." Even now in late spring the Königssee valley's weather was volatile, prone to days that could go from warm sunshine to brooding clouds to snow in the space of an hour. The savvy Königssee visitor was always armed with a spare sweater or Windbreaker.

Given Saint Bartholomae's location, there were only two ways to reach it, either by boat from Schönau or by hiking in through the surrounding mountain passes. While the latter option piqued their wanderlust they knew it would have to wait for their next visit. Time was not their friend now. While their infiltration of Bondaruk's estate had put them a step ahead, given how long the man had likely been pursuing the Lost Cellar, and given the scope of his resources, their lead could be short-lived. They'd seen no sign of Kholkov or his men, but still a touch of paranoia seemed warranted. Until they found whatever secrets Saint Bartholomae's held and were safely away, they'd assume they were being watched. Moreover, they would assume their invasion of Khotyn had enraged an already frustrated Bondaruk. Whatever restraint the man might have thus far shown was probably gone. What they couldn't predict was, given the lengths to which Bondaruk had already gone, what might he do now?

If the Königssee was the height of alpine beauty, Sam and Remi decided the nearest village, Schönau, epitomized the word "quaint."

Home to five thousand souls, Schönau, which sat astride the stone-strewn river that fed the Königssee, was a sprawling collection of homes and businesses, each one a Bavarian architectural gem that seemed more chalet than building. On the eastern side of Schönau's truncated S-shaped harbor, just south of a string of cafés, restaurants, and hotels, sat a curved line of boathouses whose styling seemed torn from the pages of a Vermont covered bridges coffee-table book.

Now, as Sam steered their car down the tree-lined road to Schönau, they could see the day's last tour boats gliding in and out of the boathouses, their wakes forming translucent fans atop the emerald water.

A few minutes later they pulled into the parking lot of the Hotel Schiffmeister. Fronted by white and red awnings and balconies bursting with red and white and pink flowers, the Schiffmeister's facade was painted in earth-toned rococo traceries of intertwined flowers and vines and spirals. As the valet saw to their car and the bellhop to their bags, they walked into the lobby and found the front desk. Minutes later they were being shown into their lakefront suite.

They each showered, wrapped themselves in the hotel's heavy terry cloth robes, then ordered coffee from room service and settled on the balcony overlooking the water. With the sun falling behind the mountains to the west, the lake was backlit in a golden hue and the calm evening air was growing chilled. On the streets and sidewalks below, tourists strolled along, looking in shop windows and taking pictures of the harbor.

Sam powered up his iPhone and tapped into the hotel's satellite Internet connection. "Something from Selma," he said, scanning their e-mail. With typical efficiency she had compiled a report on Xerxes I and the Achaemenid Dynasty, one a condensed version, the other more detailed. Sam forwarded both to Remi's iPhone and they spent the next thirty minutes learning about the ancient Persian king.

The eighth attested ruler of the Achaemenid Dynasty, Xerxes I took the throne at the age of thirty-five and wasted no time living up to his warlike reputation, first crushing a revolt in Egypt, then in Babylon, where he declared the Babylonian Empire abolished and promptly spirited away the golden idol of Bel-Marduk and had it melted down, effectively crushing the empire's spiritual foundations.

Two years later Xerxes turned his wrath on the Athenians, who had fallen afoul of the Achaemenid Dynasty at the Battle of Marathon, where they'd thwarted King Darius I's attempt to conquer all of Greece.

In 483 B.C. Xerxes began preparations for the invasion of Greece in dramatic fashion by creating a bridge to span the Hellespont, then by digging a navigable canal across the Athos Isthmus.

From Sardis, Xerxes and his army bulldozed north through Thrace and Macedonia before being stalled at Thermopylae by King

Leonidas and his Spartans, who despite a valiant effort were killed to a man. Now unhindered, Xerxes continued south down the coast to Athens, where he plundered the abandoned city. This would prove to be the zenith of Xerxes' invasion; shortly thereafter he lost much of his fleet at the Battle of Salamis, then most of his land force at the Battles of Plataea and Mycale in 479 B.C.

Leaving the army in the hands of one of his generals, Mardonius, Xerxes retired to Persepolis, in modern-day Iran, where he spent the remainder of his days dealing with political turmoil. He was eventually murdered by the captain of his guard, possibly at the behest of his own son, Artaxerxes I, who took the Achaemenid throne in 464 B.C.

"Oh, what a tangled web," Remi said as she finished. Sam, ten seconds behind her, looked up and replied, "Not a nice guy, Mr. Xerxes."

Remi smiled. "Are any of them?"

"Not often. Well, if we're looking to Xerxes' biography for clues about what Bondaruk's after, the first thing that strikes me is the Bel-Marduk idol from Babylon, but history says it was melted down."

"What if the history is wrong? What if he melted down a copy, made off with the original, then lost it somewhere?"

"Could be." Sam typed up a quick e-mail to Selma and sent it off. He got a "Checking on it" e-mail a few minutes later. "Okay, other possibilities?"

"It seems everything went downhill for Xerxes after his invasion of Greece. He surrendered control of the army, went home, loitered about for a few years, then was assassinated. Maybe he lost something on the campaign that in his own mind cursed his reign."

"And Bondaruk thinks recovering it will somehow balance the scales," Sam finished. "Put things right for the Xerxes line."

"As you said, the safe money is on Bel-Marduk, but history treats the Babylonian uprising as nothing more than an annoyance for Xerxes."

"How about the Egyptian revolt? It was roughly the same time."

Remi sighed. "It's possible. The problem with history—especially ancient history—is that often only the highlights get the attention. For all we know, buried in an ancient text in some library or museum vault there's a list of treasures stolen by Xerxes, along with their disposition."

"Great," Sam said with a smile. "Where do we start?"

"Take your pick: Cairo, Luxor, Istanbul, Tehran. . . . If we start digging today we'll be done in ten or twelve years."

"Not the best course, then. Okay, let's see if we can narrow things down: Xerxes ruled for twenty years. In that time he embarked on three major campaigns: Egypt, Babylon, and Greece. Of the three, Greece was the most important and, arguably, a turning point for his reign. Why don't we focus on the Greco-Persian war and see where that takes us?"

Remi considered this, then nodded. "Sounds good."

Sam's e-mail chimed and he read it. "From Selma," he explained. "The history around the melting down of Bel-Marduk is pretty firm. Plenty of supposedly firsthand accounts of the event, from both the Persians and the Babylonians."

"That settles it, then," Remi replied. "Greece it is."

They spent another hour researching the Greco–Persian War period of Xerxes' reign, then took a break, dining in the restaurant balcony overlooking the now darkened harbor. The combination of the altitude, the breathtaking scenery, and travel fatigue had left them famished. They tucked into the Bavarian fare with gusto, enjoying a meal of *kalte Braten*, cold thinly cut roasted pork with bread and horseradish; *Kartoffelsalat*, a potato salad in a vinegary marinade; and salmon trout fillets simmered in *Kristallweissbier* and enhanced with a Franconian Bacchus wine served in the traditional flattened bottle known as a *Bocksbeutel*. Finally they washed down the meal with mugs of ice-cold *Weizenbier*. Their below-room-temperature choice drew curious stares from a pair of Schönau townsfolk sitting at a nearby table, but Sam's one-word explanation—"Americans"— drew smiling nods and a free round.

Satiated and slightly tipsy, they returned to their room, ordered a pot of coffee, and got back to work.

"The point of the whole campaign seemed to be the sacking of Athens," Remi said. "It was the seat of Greek power."

"Thrace and Macedonia were just warm-up acts," Sam agreed. "He saved up most of his wrath for Athens. So, let's make another assumption: Xerxes subjugated the Babylonians by stealing and destroying the Bel-Marduk idol. Wouldn't he be inclined to do the same thing with the Greeks?"

Remi was already scanning Selma's report. "I thought I saw something. . . . Yes, here: Delphi."

"As in the Oracle at Delphi?"

"That's the one. Xerxes had his sights set on it."

Located a hundred miles northwest of Athens on the slopes of Mount Parnassus, the sanctuary of Delphi, dedicated to the God Apollo, was a complex of temples that included the Corycian Cave, the Castalian Spring, the Altar of the Chians, the Stoa of the Athenians, and the Temple of Apollo, where the Oracle resided, as well as numerous treasuries, stadiums, and theaters.

In ancient times as well as modern the temple housing the Delphic Oracle was perhaps the most frequently visited in the complex. Truth seekers from across the Mediterranean sought out the Pythia of the day, usually a local woman chosen to temporarily serve as the Oracle's earthly conduit.

Scientists had in the last few years relieved Delphi of its magical properties, suggesting the seemingly omniscient trance into which the Pythia would fall was in fact caused by methane, carbon dioxide, and hydrogen sulfide fumes leaking from the rock beneath the temple.

An attack on Delphi would have been in keeping with Xerxes' modus operandi, Sam and Remi knew. Pillaging Delphi would have been tantamount to rendering impotent the Greek gods, similar to what he had done in Babylon with Bel-Marduk.

Remi continued, "Right after he crushed the Spartans at Thermopylae, Xerxes sent a battalion of seven thousand men to sack Delphi. According to legend they were turned away by a timely rockslide sent by Apollo himself."

"Which may or may not be true, if I recall my ancient history correctly."

Remi nodded. "There's a lot of debate about that. Okay, let's continue the assumption train. What if Xerxes' raiding party wasn't turned back? What could they have taken?"

"The Pythia herself, but unless Bondaruk's looking for a skeleton, that doesn't seem likely. How about the Omphalos?"

The Omphalos, or "navel," was a hollow-cored pineapple-shaped stone that was said to have been modeled after a rock that Zeus's mother, Rhea, wrapped in swaddling rags to trick Zeus's father, Cronus, who in a jealous rage was bent on murdering the newborn.

Situated within the Delphic temple, the Omphalos allegedly allowed direct communication with the gods, but again scientists had since speculated that the hollow nature of the Omphalos did little more than funnel hallucinogenic gases into the Pythia's lungs.

Remi said, "No go. There are plenty of accounts of the Omphalos surviving the war. The problem is, who knows what the truth is? If the British had managed to steal the Declaration of Independence during the War of 1812, how anxious would the U.S. government have been to admit it?"

"True. What else?"

"There were plenty of treasuries at Delphi. Two in particular were said to have been centers of wealth: the Treasury of Argos and the Siphnian Treasury. They had some religious and cultural significance, but they were essentially small-time banks—gold and silver repositories."

Sam shrugged. "Again, it's possible, but Kholkov said Bondaruk was after a 'family legacy.' That sounds a little more personal than loot from an ancient bank robbery."

"Plus, he said, 'finish what was begun a long time ago.' Sounds like a mission of some kind."

Sam nodded and a yawn slipped out. "My brain is running out of steam. Let's call it a night and pick it up tomorrow."

———————

Thirty miles to the north, Kholkov stepped off the jet bridge and into the airport's concourse, powering up and checking his Black-Berry's voice mail as he walked. He stopped suddenly and peered at the screen. The three men with him did the same.

"What is it?" one of them asked.

In response, Kholkov simply grinned and walked to a nearby cluster of chairs, where he sat down. He pulled his laptop from his briefcase, powered it up, then tapped at a series of keys. After thirty seconds he muttered "Gotcha."

"You have them?"

"Not so smart after all, are we, Fargos?" he said under his breath. He looked up at his compatriots. "They're just south of us, in Bavaria. Let's go!"

CHAPTER 46

"A nd soon now you will enjoy my musical talent," the boat captain said in solid but heavily accented English. He throttled the engine back and the boat began to slow. "To your right you see Echowand—in English it is 'Echo Wall.'"

Along with the boat's other twenty passengers, Sam and Remi turned in their seats and looked starboard. They were aboard one of the eighteen covered electric passenger boats operated by the Königssee Boat Company. There were two types—a sixty-footer, which held eighty-five passengers, and Sam and Remi's model, an eighteen-footer that held twenty-five.

A quarter mile away through the early morning mist they could see a heavily forested cliff rising from the water. The captain lifted a polished flügelhorn from beneath the helm console, put it to his lips, and blew a few mournful notes, then went silent. Two seconds of silence passed and then the sound bounced back in perfect pitch.

The passengers laughed and clapped.

"Please, if you would, my trumpeting is not included in your fare this morning, and it is thirsty work. As you disembark, you may if you wish put *Trinkgeld* into my cup here or where you see them on

the bulkheads. I will divide proceeds between myself and my colleague in the mountains who answered my call."

More laughter. One passenger asked, "What is *Trinkgeld*?"

"Drinks money, of course. Thirsty work, the flügelhorn. Okay,
now we go on. Next stop, Saint Bartholomae's Pilgrim Church."

The ride resumed in near silence, the boat's electric motors making a soft gurgling hum. They glided along, seemingly suspended in
the mist, water hissing along the sides. The air was perfectly calm,
but chilled enough that Sam and Remi could see their breath.

They'd gotten up early, at six, and had a light breakfast in their
room before resuming work. Before going to bed Remi had e-mailed
a handful of former colleagues and acquaintances with three questions: At the time of Xerxes' invasion, what treasures did Delphi
hold? What was the current disposition of those treasures? Were
there any accounts of Xerxes making off with Delphic or Athenian
treasure?

Waiting in her in-box were a half dozen answers, most of which
simply opened doors to further questions and more what-ifs.

"Still nothing from Evelyn, though," Remi said now, thumbing
through her iPhone's e-mail.

Sam said, "Remind me: Evelyn . . . ?"

"Evelyn Torres. At Berkeley. She was the assistant curator at the
Delphi Archaeological Museum until about six months ago. Nobody
knows Delphi better than she does."

"Right. She'll get back to us, I'm sure." Sam snapped a few pictures of the scenery then turned back around to find Remi staring at
her iPhone. Her brow was furrowed. "What's wrong?" he asked.

"I was worrying about Kholkov showing up again and had a
thought: How many times has he popped up so far?"

Sam thought for a moment. "Not counting the Pocomoke . . .
there was Rum Cay, Château d'If, and Elba. Three times."

"Not in the Ukraine, not in Monaco, and not here, right?"

"Knock wood."

"Don't count on it."

"What's that mean?"

"I can't be sure, but if memory serves there are three things Ukraine, Monaco, and here have in common."

"Go on."

"I never used my iPhone in any of those places; we had the Iridium. I never even powered it up, and only did that here last night— no, that's not right. I checked e-mail when we landed in Salzburg."

"You're sure?"

"Pretty sure. Could they have bugged it?"

"Technically it's doable, but when could they have done it? It's never been out of your sight, has it?"

"Once. I left it at the B&B when we went to raise the Molch."

"Damn. The other times—Rum Cay, Château d'If, and Elba— did you just power it up, or did you connect to the Internet?" The iPhone could connect to the Internet in two ways, either through its built-in Edge network or via local wireless networks.

"Both."

"Kholkov could have installed a transponder. Every time you powered up or connected to the Internet the transponder tapped the iPhone's GPS and sent a ping back to Kholkov saying 'here.' "

Remi exhaled heavily, her mouth set. "Do you think they're—" She started to turn around but Sam stopped her: "We'll look when we're getting off. When was the last time you powered up? The hotel?"

"Right."

"I didn't notice anyone following us this morning."

"Me neither, but with these crowds it's hard to be sure."

"Unfortunately, Schönau's not that big. With a half dozen men they could have simply spotted us from a distance and watched us board the boat."

"What do we do?"

"First things first, we drag the riddles and the research to the burn folder," he replied, already doing so on his own. "Can't risk Kholkov getting his hands on it." As he had with most of their personal and household gadgets, Sam had tweaked their iPhones, adding a number of applications, including a quick-erase folder. Trying to open the folder without a password would instantly delete its contents. Once Remi had her data moved, Sam said, "Now we hope for a miracle."

"Which is?"

"That you're wrong about this. Problem is, that doesn't happen very often. Let me see your phone." She gave it to him. He got out his Swiss Army knife and went to work.

Sam, his head bent over the dissected iPhone in his lap, finally muttered, "There you are."

Remi leaned down. "Something?"

Using his knife's tweezers, he lifted a pinkie nail–sized circuit chip from the iPhone's innards. A pair of monofilamentlike leads trailed down to the phone's battery. "The culprit," he said. The good news was, the bug was set to transmit only when the phone was on; no signal ping would alert Kholkov that they'd found the device. Sam detached the leads and dropped the chip into his shirt pocket and started reassembling the iPhone.

Twenty minutes later, with most of the mist dissipating under a sun-filled blue sky, they rounded the Hirschau Peninsula. Saint Bartholomae came into view, its bright red onion domes glowing in the sun and the snow-veined granite of the mountains rising behind them. The meadow in which Saint Bartholomae's sat was on a forty-acre wedge of shoreline extending back to the forest. There were two dock areas, one for visitor arrivals and departures; the other, situated nearer the chapel, a covered boathouse. Strung out behind the chapel on islands of green lawn and meandering paths were a dozen wooden outbuildings, all rough-hewn and ranging from barn- to cabin-sized.

The captain circled the dock area once, waiting for another electric boat to disgorge its passengers, then headed in and glided alongside the pier. A crewman jumped across the gap, tied off the stern and bow lines, then swung up the boat's protective railing.

Scanning their fellow passengers for familiar faces, Sam and Remi disembarked, pausing to drop some *Trinkgeld* into the bulkhead cup.

"Didn't see anyone," Sam muttered as he stepped onto the dock, then offered his hand to Remi. "You?"

"No."

Theirs was the second boat of the morning to put ashore; the majority of the first group was still lingering in the landing area and around the gift shop, snapping photos and studying maps. Sam and Remi moved along the split-rail fence that encircled the landing, scanning faces before the crowd had a chance to disperse.

As they walked they could hear several tour guides starting their introductory speeches over the background babble:

"Originally built in the twelfth century, Saint Bartholomae was once considered the protector of alpine farmers and of milkmaids. . . ."

". . . find the interior floor plan is based on the Salzburg Cathedral and the exterior stucco work was done by famed Salzburg artist Josef Schmidt. . . ."

". . . until 1803 the hunting lodge adjacent to the chapel was the private retreat of the Prince-Provosts of Berchtesgaden, the last of whom . . ."

". . . After Berchtesgaden became part of Bavaria, the lodge became a favorite Wittelsbach hunting cabin. . . ."

Sam and Remi completed their circuit of the landing and ended up back at the dock. They'd seen no familiar faces. A half mile up the fjord, two more electric boats were coming around the peninsula.

Sam said, "We can wait here and check faces as each boat comes in or mix with the crowds and start hunting for clues."

"I'm not a big fan of waiting," Remi said.

"Me neither. Let's get moving."

They made their way into the gift shop, where they selected a pair of sweatshirts—one a pale yellow, the other a dark blue—from the rack, then a pair of floppy hats from another display. They paid for their purchases and headed to the restrooms to don their new clothing. If Kholkov and his men had been observing them from the Schönau docks, these rudimentary disguises, combined with the crowds, which had by now swelled to over two hundred, might provide Sam and Remi enough cover to move about anonymously.

"Ready?" he asked.

"As I'll ever be," Remi replied, tucking her auburn hair under her hat.

For the next twenty minutes they loitered around the landing area, taking pictures of the fjord and the mountains until Remi said, "Got him."

"Where?" Sam replied without turning.

"The boat that's circling, waiting to dock. Starboard side, fourth window back."

Sam turned and pointed his camera across the fjord and caught the incoming boat in the corner of the frame. He zoomed in, took a few pictures, lowered his camera. "Yep, that's Kholkov. I counted three others. Wait here."

Hat pulled low over his eyes, Sam strolled back toward the dock. "Hey, there, just a minute," he called to the deckhand who was getting ready to untie the docked boat. "Forgot the *Trinkgeld*." Sam held up a ten-euro note.

"Certainly, sir, go ahead," the deckhand said.

Sam hopped aboard, dropped the note and transponder chip into the *Trinkgeld* cup, then stepped back onto the dock. While in the bathroom he'd used the price stickers from their sweatshirts to affix a spare watch battery to the chip. The battery wouldn't power the transponder for more than thirty minutes, he suspected, but it would be long enough for their purposes.

He made his way back to Remi, who asked, "Think it'll work?"

"It'll work. They won't have a choice but to follow it. The question is, how will Kholkov handle it?"

———

Following the throng, half of whom were taking a guided tour, the other half on their own exploration, Sam and Remi made their way down the broad, white-graveled path toward the chapel. Back at the dock, Kholkov and his three companions were disembarking.

"You think they're armed?" Remi asked.

"I'd put money on it."

"We could find someone, see if there are any security guards."

"I don't want to put anyone in Kholkov's way. Who knows what he'd do? Besides, right now we're still a step ahead. No use in squandering that. Let's keep going, finish the job, find what we've come for, and go."

"Okay. So: the riddle. The first half we've solved," Remi said. "That leaves us with two lines: 'The Genius of Ionia, his stride a battle of rivals' and 'A trio of Quoins, their fourth lost, shall point the way to Frigisinga.' Something about that first line keeps nagging me."

"Such as?"

"Something from history. A connection I'm overlooking."

From behind them they heard a voice: "Pardon me, please . . . excuse me. . . ."

They turned and saw a woman on crutches trying to get past them. They stepped aside, and the woman smiled her thanks as she passed. Remi's eyes narrowed as she watched her move off.

"I know that look," Sam said. "Lightbulb pop on?"

Remi nodded, her eyes still fixed on the woman. "Her crutches. The one on her right is set a notch lower."

"So?"

"Put it another way: Her stride isn't 'a battle of rivals,'" she replied, her face lighting up. "That's it, come on." She hurried down the path to where it widened before the chapel and stopped at the fence, making sure they were away from prying ears. She hurriedly began tapping on her iPhone's screen. "There! Got it! You've heard of the Ionian League—ancient Greece, a confederation of states formed after the Meliac War?"

"Yes."

"One of the members of the Ionian League was the island of Samos—the birthplace of the 'Genius of Samos,' also known as Pythagoras. You know, the father of the triangle?"

"I'm still not following."

"The woman's crutches . . . one was shorter than the other. If you stretch your imagination they formed a scalene triangle—two unequal sides."

Now Sam caught on. He smiled. "Pythagoras was the father of the isosceles triangle—two equal sides . . ."

" 'His stride a battle of rivals,' " Remi quoted again.

"So we're looking for an isosceles triangle."

"Right. Probably marked by Laurent's cicada stamp. That leaves us with one line: 'A trio of Quoins, their fourth lost, shall point the way to Frigisinga.' "

Sam looked over his shoulder and scanned the crowds until he spotted Kholkov, who was strolling around the landing area. His cohorts wouldn't be far away. Sam was about to turn away when he saw Kholkov pull a BlackBerry from his pocket and study the screen. He jerked his head up, looked around, then gestured to someone in the crowd. Ten seconds later his three companions were huddled around him. After a brief conversation two of them turned and started jogging back to the dock. Kholkov and the other man headed for the chapel path.

"Took the bait," Remi said.

"But only partially. That's what I was afraid of. The question is, when will he realize the obvious?"

"Which is?"

"That he's got us trapped. All they have to do is stake out the dock and wait for us to come back."

CHAPTER 47

Quoin," Remi murmured, thinking aloud as they walked. "Three options: a wedge used to secure printer's blocks; wedges used to raise the barrel of a cannon; or architectural cornerstones. It has to be the last one. I don't see any printing presses or artillery."

Sam nodded absently, half his attention on keeping Kholkov and his partner in sight; they were halfway down the path to the chapel. Their heads swiveled this way and that, searching for their quarry.

Remi continued brainstorming: "A lot of corners around, but we have to assume it's not one of the wood buildings."

The split-rail fence on their left gave way to a hedge-lined *Biergarten* with umbrella-covered patio tables. A Bavarian brass band played an oompah folk song as onlookers clapped and sang along. Sam and Remi left the *Biergarten* behind and circled around the rear, lodge-like portion of the chapel to the north lawn.

"Cannon," Sam said, stopping in his tracks. "Sort of."

Remi followed his outstretched arm. Thirty yards away in the middle of the lawn was a waist-high stone pedestal. Mounted atop it was an ornamental bronzed sextant, a premodern navigation tool generally used to find the altitude of the sun above the horizon. Where most sextants were no larger than an opened hardcover book, this one was four to five times that size, measuring roughly four feet on a side. Its comically large telescope resembled the barrel of a blunderbuss.

Sam and Remi walked over. There were fewer people here; most visitors were sticking to the gravel paths, their attention focused on the chapel, the mountains, or the fjord.

"There's a plaque," Remi said. "It's in German."

Sam leaned down for a better look and translated: "Presented August of 1806 to Elector Maximilian I Joseph, House of Wittelsbach, member of the Confederation of the Rhine and King of Bavaria by Napoleon I, Emperor of the French."

"If that isn't a clue I don't know what is," Remi said. "Here, Sam, look at this."

He moved to where she had knelt down. The lower part of the sextant consisted of a vertical index arm designed to slide over a curved arc engraved with notches, each indicating one-sixtieth of a degree. A gap in the index arm showed the arc's current reading. It was set to seventy.

"Not a trio," Remi said. "Would have been nice if it'd been set on three."

Sam suddenly grabbed her arm and moved them around the pedestal, putting it between them and the chapel area. Through the arms of the sextant they could see Kholkov and his partner walking down the path toward the outbuildings nearer the trees.

"Maybe it is," Sam said. "Let's think outside the box: If the sextant is our cannon and the notches on the arc are quoins—the wedges—this part of Laurent's riddle is metaphorical."

"Go on."

"Remember the line: 'A trio of Quoins, their fourth lost, shall point the way to Frigisinga.' That suggests that a fourth quoin would complete the group. If you have a completed group, what percentage do you have?"

"A hundred."

"So each quoin would represent a quarter of the total. How many notches on the arc?"

Remi checked. "A hundred forty-two."

Sam mentally did the math:

142 / 4 quoins = 35.5
35.5 x 3 quoins = 106.5

He said, "Okay, so if we were to lift the barrel to a hundred six degrees . . ."

They both knelt behind the sextant and imagined the telescope angled upward to its new position. It was aimed directly at the forwardmost minaret atop the red-roofed onion domes.

"I guess that's what you call X marks the spot," Remi said. "Metaphorically, of course."

"Triangle marks the spot," Sam corrected. "Hopefully."

They hadn't taken ten steps back toward the chapel when a voice came over the loudspeaker, making an announcement first in German and then in English:

"Attention, visitors. We apologize for the inconvenience, but we have just been alerted of an impending storm. Due to expected heavy winds, we will be closing the park early. Please proceed immediately but calmly to the dock area and follow the instructions of park staff. Thank you."

Around Sam and Remi there came the babble of disappointed voices and mothers and fathers calling to children. Faces turned upward, scanning the blue sky.

Sam said, "I don't see any—"

"There," Remi said.

To the southwest a narrow wall of purplish black clouds were rolling over the peaks of the mountains. As Sam and Remi watched, the front seemed to roll like a slow-motion wave down the slopes toward the fjord.

Visitors began moving toward the docks, some trotting, some simply strolling. Staff members in light blue shirts acted as shepherds, gently encouraging stragglers and helping parents round up children.

"I don't know about you," Sam said, "but I'm not keen on—"

"Me neither. We're staying. Need to find a place to hide."

"Come on."

With Remi close on his heels, Sam headed for the shore, some fifty yards away, where a path led left, toward the forest, and right, toward the docks. They turned left and started trotting, passing a dozen or so visitors headed in the other direction. One of them, a man herding two toddler boys in green lederhosen, called out to them in German.

"You're going the wrong way! The docks are this way."

"Dropped my car keys," Sam replied. "Be right back."

A minute later they were inside the tree line. The path curved left, toward the outbuildings, but they kept going straight, ducking under the handrail and into the underbrush. After a hundred feet they stopped and crouched down beneath the boughs of a pine tree. Above, leaden clouds began rolling over the peninsula, blocking out the sun.

For the next twenty minutes they watched through the trees as visitors hurried down paths and across lawns toward the docks. A few minutes later they glimpsed one of the electric tour boats chugging up the fjord, passing two more coming down from the north, all three nosing their way through serrated whitecaps.

Slowly the cacophony of voices died away, leaving only the wind whistling through the trees and snow-muffled shouts of "all aboard!" from the dock area. The loudspeakers, which had been repeating the evacuation notice every thirty seconds, stopped broadcasting.

"Getting colder," Remi said, hugging herself.

Sam, having heeded the guidebook's advice, pulled their Windbreakers and knit caps from his backpack. Remi donned the clothes and pulled her hands into her sweatshirt's sleeves.

"Think they left with the others?" she asked.

"Depends on what Kholkov thinks we did. The safe bet would have been to wait for the last boat and look for us in the departing crowds."

"Still, something tells me we'd better assume the worst."

"I agree."

———————

They waited a full hour after the last boat had disappeared up the fjord. Filled with fat snowflakes, the wind was gusting heavily, shaking the tree canopies. Pinecones thumped to the ground and leaves skittered through the underbrush. Snow began collecting behind tree trunks and on the grass, but immediately melted as it touched the sun-warmed gravel paths, creating tendrils of steam that were whipped into tiny vortexes by the wind.

"Let's have a look around," Sam said. "Find someplace to warm up."

They picked their way back to the path and followed it inland to a clearing where they found a log cabin with a low-slung mansard roof and block windows. It was a long structure, measuring nearly a hundred feet, with a stairway rising up its rear wall to a door. Sam and Remi climbed up it and tried the door. It was unlocked. They pushed through and found themselves in a loft with a balcony overlooking the lower level. The interior was dark save what little gray seeped through the tarnished glass windows.

"It's not the Four Seasons, but at least we're out of the wind," Sam said.

"Comfort is relative," Remi said with a smile, brushing snow off her sweatshirt.

They found a warm corner and sat down.

———————

They waited another thirty minutes, enough time, they hoped, for any staff members who had stayed behind to catch a final boat back to Schönau. Whether any caretakers had stayed behind Sam and Remi didn't know, but they'd cross that bridge if it arose. Outside the wind had slackened slightly, giving way to heavy snow. Pine boughs scraped the sides of the cabin like skeletal fingers.

Remi jerked her head around, as though she'd heard something.

Sam mouthed, *What?*

She put her fingers to her lips and pointed toward the window. A few moments later Sam heard it: footsteps crunching through the snow.

Silence, then a thunk of a boot on wood. Someone was mounting the stairs outside. Sam got up, crept to the door, locked it, then returned to Remi. A moment later the doorknob gave a squeak, then a rattle. Silence again. The footsteps thumped down the stairs, then began crunching through the snow again.

A door on the lower level opened.

Remi huddled closer to Sam, who put an arm around her shoulders.

Footsteps again, this time a pair of them. They moved into the cabin and stopped. A flashlight panned over the ceiling, skimmed along the loft railing, then clicked off.

"Hello?" a voice called in German. "Park staff. Is anyone here?"

Remi looked at Sam, her mouth forming a question. He shook his head and mouthed, *Kholkov.*

"Anyone here? There's been a weather evacuation." Kholkov called in German again, then a few seconds later, "No one here. Let's check the other buildings."

More footsteps. The door banged shut.

Sam held his palm up to Remi, then put his finger to his lips.

A minute passed. Two. Five.

From below there came the faint scuff of a shoe on wood.

"They're not here," Kholkov said in English.

"What makes you think they're still here at all?" a second voice asked.

"It's what I would do. And I know how they think; they're too stubborn to let a little weather turn them back. Let's go."

The door opened, shut. Footsteps crunched through the snow and faded away. On hands and knees Sam crawled to the railing and peeked through. He turned and gave Remi a thumbs-up.

"My heart's pounding like a jackhammer," she said.

"Join the club."

"We're going to have to be careful about our footprints."

"So are they. In fact, let's use them while we can."

CHAPTER 48

They slipped out the door, climbed down the steps, and followed Kholkov's footprints out of the clearing, stopping every ten feet to look and listen. They were being overly cautious, they knew, but the Russian was a professional at this. There was a very real chance the man would double back and wait in ambush. Their best chance was to locate Kholkov and his partner and keep them in sight while remaining hidden themselves.

The weather was not going to make this easy. The snow was falling more heavily and the visibility had dropped to less than a hundred feet. Already Kholkov's footprints were filling in. After fifteen minutes of stop-and-start progress they reached an intersection of pathways. Left and right branches led to another pair of stucco/wood cabins, while straight ahead stood a barnlike outbuilding. Beyond that, barely visible through the falling snow, they could see the dark roof of the chapel's lodge.

To the left, a muffled thump: a door swinging shut.

Sam and Remi ducked off the path and dropped to their bellies in the undergrowth. Ten seconds later a pair of snow-blurred figures appeared on the path to their left, tromped through the intersection, and disappeared into the trees on their way to the other cabin. A minute later came the squeak of door hinges.

Sam slipped back onto the path, crept to the intersection, and looked right. He turned and signaled Remi forward. Together they hurried down the opposite path, to the cabin Kholkov had just left. They ducked inside and eased the door shut. Sam went to the window and knelt down to keep watch. Remi joined him.

After ten minutes Kholkov and his partner materialized out of the snow and turned right at the intersection, heading toward the chapel lodge. Within seconds the weather had swallowed them again.

"How long do we wait?" Remi asked.

Sam fished the brochure from his pocket and checked the tour map. "One more building between here and the chapel. Whether they've already searched it or not is anyone's guess."

"So we keep going and hope we see them before they see us."

"Maybe," Sam said, his eyes distant. "Maybe not." He dug through his backpack and came up with their camera. He called up the pictures on the LCD screen and began studying them one by one. "There." He handed Remi the camera. "I shot this while we were circling the dock."

It was a picture of the boathouse. Through its partially open barn doors was the white nose of a speedboat. "It's got to be for emergencies," Remi said. "I count two more behind that one."

In reply, Sam grinned devilishly and nodded.

"I know that look," Remi said. "The mental gears are turning. Let's hear it."

"A little MacGyver-inspired goose chase."

Remi said, "As ruses go, it's a bit transparent."

"I agree, but they'll still have the same the dilemma: follow, split up, or sit tight. They can't afford not to follow, on the off chance it's real. Either way, our odds are improved."

———————

They slipped outside, followed Kholkov's footprints back to the path, then turned left. Ahead the trail forked around the last outbuilding before the chapel. The fluffy snow had piled up quickly; three to four inches of it lay on the grass and the trees were shaggy with powder. Alpine spring had turned to winter wonderland.

Kholkov's prints went right, so they took the left path, then pressed themselves to the building's wall and slid down its length, ducking beneath windows and pausing every few feet to look and listen. They reached the front corner and stopped. Directly ahead lay the lodge portion of the chapel. To their right lay the split-rail fence, the meadow, and the path back to the dock landing. To their left they could just make out the sextant statue; beyond that the fjord, shrouded in snow and surface mist.

Remi stopped suddenly and tugged on Sam's sleeve to get his attention. She nodded with her chin at the wall behind them. With her palm against the wood, she mouthed, *Vibration.* He pressed his ear to the wall. From inside footsteps clunked on wood. Around the corner they heard the creak of a door swinging open. Sam peeked, then jerked his head back. He pressed himself flat against the wall. Remi did the same.

Moments later Kholkov and his partner appeared on the path on their way to the chapel lodge. Sam and Remi waited until they disappeared through the rear door, then sprinted ahead, dropped into a crouch, and duck-walked into the open-fronted firewood shed beside the door.

"Let's give them a minute," Sam whispered. "If they've already searched the chapel, they'll come out pretty quickly. If not, I'm going to make a run for the boathouse."

"And in the meantime, I'm doing what? Sitting here?"

"More or less."

"Forget it."

Sam gripped her hand. "Once I go, you block yourself in with this firewood and sit tight. Two of us on the move doubles our chances of being seen."

"Then you better keep up," Remi said and stood up. "You coming?"

Sam sighed. "I'm coming."

Hunched over, they took off at a flat-footed sprint, circling left around the chapel, careful to stay on the grass and off the gravel path. Within a minute they'd reached the transition where the lodge's wooden wall became the white stucco of the onion domes. They slid down this wall, following its curve to where it joined the shoreline path. They stopped. Down the path, not more than fifty feet away, was the boathouse.

The door was standing open.

Just inside the dim interior they could see movement. Kholkov stepped out, followed by his partner. They looked around, each pointing this way and that as they talked. Finally Kholkov pointed toward the landing and they headed in that direction. Sam and Remi waited until they were halfway down the path then sprinted forward and slipped into the boathouse.

Roughly the size of a two-car garage, it was divided into thirds by plank docks suspended by cables from the rafters. In each slip was an orange and white fifteen-foot Hans Barro work boat. The barn doors were closed and locked by a horizontal two-by-four cross brace.

Sam walked down the center catwalk, lifted the cross brace to its vertical position, and pushed the doors open a couple inches. A blast of icy air pushed through the gap.

"Check for keys," Sam whispered.

They checked each boat; there were no keys in the ignitions. "Guess that explains what Kholkov was doing in here," Remi said. "Cutting off our exit. It's either that or the staff keeps the keys in another location."

"Either way, something tells me he wouldn't have relied just on keys to keep us here."

In turn, Sam lifted each boat's engine hatch and checked the system under the glow of his LED microlight. In each case a wire had been removed from the engine's starter solenoid.

"Not cut," Remi said, looking over his shoulder. "Removed."

Clearly Kholkov was planning his own eventual exit strategy.

"Smart, but not smart enough," Sam murmured. From the time he'd been old enough to work a screwdriver, he'd been tinkering with things, starting with his mother's toaster when he was five years old, and both his degree and his work at DARPA had only honed his do-it-yourself skills.

"Keep a lookout," Sam said. Remi moved to the door and dropped to her knees, peeking through the gap between the hinges.

He climbed into the middle boat, clicked on his LED, then clamped it between his teeth and wriggled his way under the helm console.

The dashboard electrical system was a simple affair, the bundled cables hidden behind a plastic panel on the underside of the helm. In short order he traced the wires for the ignition system, the head-light, the horn, and the windshield wipers. Four snips from his Swiss Army knife's scissors and he had two seven-inch lengths of excess wire, both of which he stripped and noosed at each end. He spliced one into the engine's solenoid and pocketed the other.

"What else?" Sam whispered absently. "Something easy, but not too obvious."

Remi looked over her shoulder and shrugged. "You're asking the wrong gal. Any way you can rig something nasty for them?"

"Like a bomb? I wish. There's not enough here."

He kept looking. It took two more minutes, but he found what he was looking for: a bent brush arm inside the alternator. He adjusted the arm back to its original position.

Satisfied he'd found all of Kholkov's handiwork, he ducked back under the dash, found the ignition wires, then scraped away the insulation and let them dangle. He crawled back out and climbed onto the dock. It took only a minute to find what he needed hanging from a wall pegboard—a two-foot-long bungee cord with a hook at each end. He secured the cord first to the steering wheel, then to the throttle, which he pushed to its forward stops. Finally he untied the boat's bow and stern lines and let them drop into the water.

Now came the tricky part: the timing.

"How're we doing?" he asked Remi.

"See for yourself. No sign of them."

He crept back to the door and peeked out. The landing area was lost in the falling snow. He pulled Remi away from the door. "Soon as you hear the ignition spark, take off. Retrace our steps and we'll meet back at the woodshed."

"Right." Remi got into position beside the door.

Sam returned to the rigged boat and crawled beneath the helm console again.

"Cross fingers," he muttered, then touched the exposed ignition wires and gave them a twist. There was a spark, then a pop. Sam wriggled backward, jumped to the dock, raced for the door.

"Go," he rasped to Remi.

She peeked out, then darted into the gloom.

The boat's engines gurgled to life. Gray smoke burst from the manifolds and filled the boathouse. The water beneath the stern turned to froth and the boat surged forward, nosing through the doors and disappearing into the drifting snow.

"Sail true," Sam said, then turned and ran.

CHAPTER 49

He had taken three strides out the door when he heard a snow-muffled voice to his left shout, "There!" Unsure whether it was for the escaping speedboat or for him, Sam veered right, along the curve of the building, then sprinted onto the lawn in the direction of the sextant statue. If Kholkov and his partner were in fact after him he didn't want to lead them back to Remi.

When he saw the statue appear ahead, he dove into a headfirst slide that took him behind the pedestal. He flipped onto his belly and looked back the way he'd come. Ten seconds passed. He heard the sound of feet pounding on gravel. Through the blowing snow he saw two figures appear around the corner of the building and duck into the boathouse. Now the question was, how long would it take Kholkov to reverse his own sabotage? The solenoid wire would take less than a minute, but returning the flywheel to its proper position would be trickier. The longer it took, the harder their automaton boat would be to find.

One minute passed. Two minutes. An engine growled to life and revved up. After a few seconds it faded, moving out onto the lake. Sam got up, circled to the rear of the chapel, and found Remi crouched in the semidarkness of the woodshed.

"I heard," she said. "The question is, how much time did it buy us?"

"Ten, fifteen minutes at least. In this weather it'll take them at least that long just to find our decoy. Come on."

He helped her to her feet. They climbed the steps to the rear door and pushed through.

After the wind and snow, the relative warmth of the chapel felt like heaven. Compared to its grand exterior, the chapel was surprisingly simple, with reddish brown stone tiles, scarred wooden pews, and white walls bearing framed religious icons. Above their heads a balcony spanned the rear wall, while the vaulted ceiling was filigreed in light pink and gray paint. Tall mullioned windows on the side walls cast the interior in milky white light.

They made their way down the center aisle to the far end of the chapel to a narrow door. Through it they found a crescent-shaped room dominated by a spiral staircase. They started upward. After thirty or forty steps they found themselves at a wooden trapdoor secured by a sliding hasp and padlock. The padlock wasn't locked.

"Looks like somebody missed an item on the evacuation checklist," Remi said with a smile.

"Our good luck. Wasn't looking forward to defiling a Bavarian national landmark."

Sam removed the padlock and slid back the hasp bolt. He carefully lifted the trapdoor, climbed through, then helped Remi up and closed it behind them. Aside from what little light seeped through the shuttered slit windows, the octagonal space was dark. They clicked on their flashlights and began looking around.

"Here," Remi said, kneeling down. "Got something."

"Here, too," Sam said from the opposite wall. He moved to Remi and inspected what she was shining her flashlight on. Stamped into the heavy timber molding beneath the window, nearly obliterated by layer upon layer of paint and lacquer, was a cicada symbol.

"Yours the same?" Remi asked.

Sam nodded and they moved to the opposite side. A second cicada symbol was stamped into the wood. "Why two?" he wondered aloud.

"The line—'a trio of Quoins' . . . they must have meant it to apply to more than just the sextant."

It took them less than thirty seconds to find the third. The first two cicada symbols were situated near the front of the minaret, the third at the rear.

"Let's form it up," Sam said.

He crouched beside one of the stamps, and Remi did the same, then they extended their arms, each pointing at the other as well as the third stamp.

"Correct me if I'm wrong," Sam said, "but this is an isosceles triangle."

"It is indeed. But which way is it meant to point?"

"If we extend the lines, the two at the front would point at the lake and into the mountains. The third one points inland—behind us."

Sam lowered his arms as he sat down, back against the wall. His brows furrowed for a few seconds, then he smiled.

"What?" Remi asked.

"The last part of the line," Sam replied. "I knew something looked familiar." He dug into his pants pocket and came up with the Saint Bartholomae's tour brochure. He flipped through it. "There." He handed it to Remi. "Frigisinga."

Remi read: " 'Until 1803 the hunting lodge adjacent to the chapel was the private retreat of the Prince-Provosts of Berchtesgaden, the last of whom, Joseph Conrad of Schroffenberg-Mös, had also served as the Lord Bishop of Freising.' "

"I knew I'd read something about that during our research," Sam said. "I mentally misplaced it. The eighth-century name for Freising was Frigisinga."

"Okay, so this Schroffenberg-Mös fella was here?"

"Not just here. He lived here, and we've already been there."

They climbed back through the hatch and down the spiral staircase, then retraced their steps through the chapel and out the back door and started down the path toward the woods. Five minutes later they were back at the cabin in whose loft they'd first sought shelter. They stopped at the post-mounted plaque beside the front door.

Remi read: " 'Once served as the private hunting lodge and warming cabin for the last of Berchtesgaden's Prince-Provosts, Joseph Conrad of Schroffenberg-Mös.' "

" 'Formerly of Frigisinga,' " Sam finished.

They stepped inside. While most of the cabin was made of heavy timber, both the stanchion footers and the foundation, which rose eighteen inches from ground level, were constructed of blocked stone.

"Let's check the stonework first," Sam said. "Timber can be easily replaced; stone, not so much."

"Agreed. How are we on time?"

Sam checked his watch. "Fifteen minutes since our rabbit ran."

Knowing what they were looking for, they made quick work of the search, splitting up and walking hunched over along the walls, flashlights playing over the blocks.

"Grasshopper marks the spot," Remi called. She was kneeling beside a footer beneath the loft. Sam hurried over and crouched beside her. Stamped into the upper-left corner of the block abutting the footer was the familiar cicada stamp.

"Looks like we're going to have to do a little defiling after all," Remi said.

"We'll be gentle."

Sam looked around, then trotted over the open-hearth fireplace, grabbed a steel poker from the mantel rack, and returned. He went to work. Though the poker's end was slightly spatula-shaped, it was still wider than the gaps between the stones so it took a precious ten minutes of inching the block outward before together they could pull it free. Remi reached her hand into the alcove.

"Hollow spot around the footer," she murmured. "Hang on. . . ."

She lay down on the floor and wriggled her arm into the hole until she was elbow deep. She stopped. Her eyes went wide. "Wood."

"The footer?"

"No, I don't think so. Pull me out."

Gently Sam grabbed her ankles and dragged her away from the wall. Her hand emerged from the alcove, followed by an oblong wooden box. Hand clenched like an eagle's talon, her fingernails were sunk an eighth of an inch into the lid.

Silently they stared at the box for a long ten seconds.

Then Remi smiled. "You owe me a manicure."

Sam smiled back. "Done."

The heft of the box told them it wasn't empty, but they checked anyway. Snug in its bed of straw and enveloped in its oilskin wrappings was another bottle from Napoleon's Lost Cellar.

Sam closed the lid and said, "I don't know about you but I think I've had enough sightseeing for one day."

"I'm with you."

Sam stuffed the box into his rucksack and they stepped outside into the clearing. This far from the boathouse they wouldn't have been able to hear the sound of a returning speedboat, so they moved quickly but carefully, stopping frequently to hide and watch until finally they were back at the chapel.

"Almost there," Sam said. Remi nodded and hugged herself. Sam embraced her and rubbed his hands vigorously on her back. "We'll be drinking warm brandy in no time."

"Now you're singing my song," she replied.

They circled left around the chapel, following the straight and curved walls until they reached the front of the building. Sam stopped ten feet short, signaled for her to wait, then crab-walked ahead and peered around the corner. After a few seconds he pulled back and returned to her.

"Anything?" Remi whispered.

"Nothing's moving, but the door's partially shut. I can't tell how many boats are inside."

"How about the landing?"

"Nothing there, either, but with the snow—"

"Shhh." Remi cocked her head and closed her eyes. "Listen."

After a few seconds, Sam heard it: faintly, somewhere in the distance, came the buzzing of an engine. "Somebody's out there," Remi said.

"They wouldn't have just given up on the decoy," Sam reasoned. "They're either still chasing it or on their way back."

"Agreed. It's now or never."

After one last check around the corner, Sam motioned for Remi to move up. Hand in hand they broke from cover, sprinted to the boathouse, and ducked inside. In addition to their decoy boat, the right-hand boat was gone.

Remi jumped aboard the remaining boat and settled into the driver's seat while Sam set aside his backpack, then lifted the engine cover, quickly installed his makeshift solenoid wire, and bent the brush arm back into place. He closed the engine cover, shimmied under the dash and hotwired the ignition.

"Okay," he said, crawling back out, "let's—"

"Sam, the door!"

Sam spun. A figure was rushing through the boathouse door. Sam caught a fleeting glimpse of the man's face: Kholkov's partner. Turning, squaring up through the door, his hand came up holding a snub-nosed revolver. Sam didn't think, but reacted, snatching up the nearest object—a bright orange life vest—and hurling it. The man batted it away, but it had bought Sam the second he needed to leap to the dock and charge. He slammed into the man and they crashed back into the wall. Sam grabbed the man's gun wrist and twisted hard, trying to break the delicate bones there. The gun roared once, then again.

The man was a professional; instead of fighting the torque on his wrist, he went with it, twisting his body while swinging his left arm in a tight hook that slammed into Sam's temple. Sparks burst behind Sam's eyes, but he kept his grip on the man's wrist, then got his right arm inside the man's punching arm and wrapped him in a bear hug. Vision still swimming, Sam jerked his head back and slammed it forward. The head butt found its mark. With a muffled crunch the man's nose shattered. The gun clattered across the planks. With a grunt, the man levered himself against the wall and together they stumbled backward. Sam felt his foot step into empty air. He felt himself falling. He took a gulp of air then plunged into the water.

CHAPTER 50

The water enveloped him, so cold it momentarily stunned him like an electrical charge. Fighting his natural instinct to surface for air, Sam instead did the opposite. With the man still wrapped in a bear hug, he rolled over, flipped his legs straight up, and kicked, driving them deeper. The man was stunned, and with his shattered nose he'd hopefully been unable to snatch a last-second breath.

The man thrashed, punched wildly with his right arm. Sam took the blows and held on. The man suddenly stopped punching. Sam felt his arm between them. He looked down. Through the dark water and froth he saw the man's hand reaching under his jacket. The hand came out clutching a knife. Sam grabbed the forearm, tried to shove it sideways. The knife arced upward. Sam pushed off. The blade sliced through his shirt; he felt a sting as it sliced across his abdomen. The blade kept rising. Sam released his grip on the man's other wrist, clamped it around the man's knife hand. He sensed rather than saw the blade nearing his throat. He jerked his head back, turned it to one side. The tip of the knife skipped over the point of his jawline beneath his earlobe, pierced the upper curve of his ear, and sliced cleanly through.

A dozen years of judo had taught Sam the power of leverage. The man, having extended his more powerful right arm above his head, was at that moment at his weakest. Sam wasn't about to let the advantage pass. Left hand still gripping the man's knife wrist, Sam reversed his right-hand grip, cupped the back of the man's hand, then jerked down and twisted at the same time. With a dull pop, the man's ulna tore free from his wrist. The man's mouth flew open and he let out a muffled scream amid a stream of bubbles. Sam kept twisting, heard the grating of bone on bone. The knife fell away and dropped out of sight.

Sam rolled again, kicked downward. They thumped into the bottom. The man clawed at Sam's eyes with his left hand. Sam clenched his eyes shut, turned his head away, then drove his right hand up and palm-butted the man in the chin. The man's head snapped backward. Sam heard a sickening crunch. The man jerked once, twice, then went still. Sam opened his eyes. The man's own eyes, fixed and lifeless, stared back. Behind the man's head a jagged, triangular-shaped rock jutted from the sandy bottom. Sam let him go and he floated away, trailing tendrils of blood as he bumped along the bottom. After a few moments he disappeared into the gloom.

Sam coiled his legs and pushed himself off the bottom. He broke the surface beneath one of the plank walkways and laid his head back and gulped air until his vision began to clear.

"Sam!" Remi called. "Here, this way, come on!"

Sam paddled toward her voice. Draped in soaked clothes, his arms felt as if they were stroking through molasses. He felt Remi's hands gripping his. He grabbed the gunwale and let her help him aboard. He rolled onto the deck and lay still, panting. Remi knelt beside him.

"Oh, God, Sam, your face . . ."

"Looks worse than it is. A few stitches and I'll be back to my devilishly handsome self."

"Your ear is split. You look like a dog who just lost a squabble."

"Let's call it a dueling scar."

She turned his head this way and that, inspecting his face and neck and probing with her fingers until Sam reached up and gave her hand a reassuring squeeze. "I'm okay, Remi. Kholkov might have heard the shots. We better get moving."

"Right." She lifted the nearest seat cushion and dug around until she found a rag, which Sam pressed to his wounds. Remi gestured tentatively toward the water. Is he . . ."

"Gone. He didn't give me much choice." Sam sat up, rolled onto his knees, and stripped off his Windbreaker and sweatshirt. "Wait, the gun . . ."

"Already got it. Here." She handed him the revolver, then settled into the driver's seat as Sam untied the bow line. Remi turned the ignition and the engine rumbled to life. "Hold tight." She shoved the throttle to its stops and the speedboat surged through the doors.

"Look for an emergency kit," Remi said. "Maybe there's one of those space blankets."

Sam checked beneath each seat cushion until he found a large tackle box. Inside, as Remi had predicted, he found a rolled-up silver Mylar sheet. He unrolled it, draped it around him, then settled into the passenger seat.

Later Sam wouldn't remember hearing the sound of the other engine over the roar of their own—only seeing the white wedge of the speedboat's bow emerging from the mist to his left and the orange firefly winks of Kholkov's gun.

"Remi, hard right!"

To her credit, Remi reacted instantly and without question, spinning the wheel over. The boat slewed sideways. Kholkov's bow, which had been aimed directly at Sam's passenger seat, glanced off the hull and slid over the gunwale. Already ducking, Sam jerked his head sideways and felt the fiberglass hull skim over his hair. Kholkov's bow crashed through the corner of the windscreen, shattering glass and twisting aluminum, then crashed back down into the water. Sam caught a glimpse of the boat arcing away to the left.

From the floorboards, Sam asked, "Remi, you okay?"

"Yeah, I think so. You?"

"Yes. Turn hard left, go for five seconds, then shut off the engine."

Again Remi asked no questions and did as Sam asked. She throttled down, shut off the ignition, and the boat glided through the water until finally stopping. They sat in silence, the boat gently rocking from side to side.

Sam whispered, "He'll circle back. He'll assume we kept going in the same direction for a while."

"How do you know?"

"Natural instinct to panic and run directly away from him."

"How many bullets do we have in that thing?"

Sam pulled the revolver from his belt. It was a five-shot Smith & Wesson .38. "Two gone, three left. When we hear him off to our right, head left toward the shoreline. Go as fast as you can for thirty seconds, then throttle down again."

"Another hunch?"

Sam nodded. "That we'll run straight for Schönau."

"We'll have to eventually. It's either that or we hike for three days through the mountains in this snowstorm."

Sam smiled. "Or plan C. I'll explain later. Shhh. You hear that?"

Moving from left to right off their bow came the sound of an engine. After a few moments the pitch changed, echoing off the shoreline.

"Go!" Sam rasped.

Remi started the engine, jammed the throttle forward, and swung the boat to port. They drove for a count of thirty, then throttled back down and coasted to a stop. It was silent save the lapping of waves on the boat's hull. The wind had slackened to an almost dead calm; fat snowflakes began piling up on the gunwales and seats.

"What's he doing?" Remi whispered.

"Same thing we are. Listening. Waiting."

"How do you know?"

"He's a soldier; he's thinking like one."

Directly astern, perhaps two hundred yards distant, they heard an engine revving. Remi's hand moved to the throttle. Sam said, "Not yet."

"He's close, Sam."

"Wait."

Kholkov's engine kept coming, closing the distance. Sam pointed astern and to their left, then held his index finger to his lips. Barely visible through the falling snow, a ghostly, elongated shape glided past. They could see a man-shaped silhouette standing behind the wheel. Kholkov's head pivoted left and right. Sam raised the revolver and took aim, tracking the boat until it faded from view. After ten seconds Remi let out a breath and said, "I can't believe he missed us."

"He didn't. It was barely noticeable, a little pause when he turned this way, but he saw us. He'll double back now. Reverse engines. Take us backward—slowly. Quiet as you can."

Remi did so. After they'd covered fifty feet Sam whispered, "Slow ahead. Angle us back toward shore." He grabbed the eight-foot boat hook from its mount below the gunwale and peered through the mist. To their left he heard water lapping on rocks. "Okay, shut it down," he told Remi. "Ease right."

She did so.

Silence.

Off the beam the fuzzy, conical outline of a pine tree appeared, then another. Branches stretched out toward them like skeletal fingers. Sam snagged a larger limb with the boat hook, dragged them to a stop, and hauled until the hull bumped against the bank. The snow-laden boughs formed a canopy over their heads, drooping to within a foot of the lake's surface. Sam knelt beside the gunwale and peeked through the branches. Remi joined him.

From ahead and to the right came the revving of an engine. After ten seconds it stopped. A moment later, their boat started wallowing as Kholkov's bow wake reached them.

"Any second now," Sam whispered. "Be ready to move."

As if on cue, forty feet away Kholkov's boat drifted past, heading back toward the church docks. His engine was gurgling softly, just above idle. Then he was gone, lost in the snow.

"He didn't see us," Remi whispered.

"Not this time. Okay, let's move. Follow him. Five seconds of low throttle, ten seconds of glide."

Remi got back into the driver's seat and they pulled out from under the boughs, came about, and fell into Kholkov's wake.

For the next twenty minutes they continued their glide-and-throttle headway, always keeping Kholkov's engine noise directly on their bow, going silent when he did, moving only when his engine resumed. Their progress was slow, covering less than fifty feet at a time. Saint Bartholomae's docks drifted by on their right, the red-roofed onion domes seemingly floating in midair.

Directly off their bow Kholkov's engine spooled up and began arcing away to the left. Sam gestured for Remi to ease right, back toward shore. "Slow and easy." Kholkov's engine noise was moving toward the center of the lake.

"Cut the engines," Sam whispered, and Remi did so.

"He thinks we're hiding out or heading back to Schönau, doesn't he?" she asked.

Sam nodded. "He'll set up an ambush somewhere to the north. Unfortunately for him, we're not going to play his game."

The minutes slipped by. Five turned into ten, then into twenty. Finally Sam said, "Okay, let's keep going. Follow the shoreline south. Keep it just above an idle."

"Something tells me that warm brandy is going to have to wait."

"Would you settle for a roof over your head and a cozy campfire?"

CHAPTER 51

"Message from Evelyn Torres," Remi said, sitting down on the king-sized bed and kicking off her shoes. "Just a 'call me.' She sounded excited, though. She lives for this stuff."

"First that brandy I promised you, then Evelyn," Sam said.

"We're going to need clothes and essentials."

"Brandy, Evelyn, sleep, then shopping."

Since eluding Kholkov on the Königssee, they'd been awake and on the move for over twenty-eight hours. Heading south along the shoreline at a snail's pace, they reached the Obersee's Salet docks an hour later and disembarked. Sam opened the boat's scuttle cock, waited until a foot of water was sloshing on the deck, then pointed the bow toward the center of the lake and eased the throttle forward a notch. It disappeared into the snow.

Remi said, "We haven't exactly been low-impact tourists, have we?"

"Don't worry," he said with a wink. "We'll make an anonymous donation to the Saint Bartholomae's Historical Society. They can buy a fleet of speedboats."

From the docks they followed the gravel path inland for a half mile, then across the land bridge to the mouth of the Obersee proper, where they found another boathouse similar to the one at Saint Bartholomae's. This one, however, had an adjacent warming room. Inside they stripped down to their underwear, draped their clothes over coat hooks on the wall, and then found a kerosene lantern around which they huddled until nightfall when Sam started a small fire in the woodstove. They spent the remainder of the night curled together around the stove then rose at eight thirty, donned their clothes, and waited for the day's first boatload of tourists. They intermingled themselves with the crowds, strolled about for a few hours, and kept their ears tuned for any discussion of gunshots the previous day or a floating body having been found in the lake. They heard nothing. At noon they took the boat back to Schönau.

Once ashore they decided to err on the side of slight paranoia and not return to the hotel; nor would they use their rental car. Watchful for Kholkov and his men, they ducked into the nearest gift shop, then out the back door into the alley. For twenty minutes they picked their way away from Schönau's waterfront until they found a café on a secluded side street, where they called Selma.

At two o'clock a Mercedes from a Salzburg car service pulled up before the café and three hours later, after a scenic drive, during which Remi and Sam watched for signs of pursuit, they checked into the hotel under the names Hank and Liz Truman.

Fed and warmed by the brandy, they first e-mailed Selma the photographed symbols from the Saint Bartholomae bottle, then dialed Evelyn Torres at home.

"So why the sudden interest in Xerxes and Delphi?" Evelyn asked over a speakerphone after a bit of small talk.

"Just a little project we're working on," Remi replied. "We'll fill you in when we get home."

"Well, to answer your questions in order, at the time of Xerxes' invasion, Delphi was arguably the most sacred place in Greece. The

Pythia's predictions were sought for everything, from matters of state to marriage and everything in between. As for treasure, there wasn't much there of tangible wealth—a few treasuries, but nothing compared to the riches of Athens. Some scholars disagree, but I think Xerxes didn't understand Delphi's place in Greek culture. From what few oral histories I've read, he considered the Oracle a novelty, like a modern-day Ouija board. He was convinced the Greeks were hiding something at Delphi."

"Were they?"

"There've always been rumors, but there's no solid evidence to support them. Besides, you know the history: Xerxes' raiding party was turned back by the divine hand of Apollo—in the form of a well-timed rock slide. A few Persians got through and made off with ceremonial objects, but nothing of importance."

Sam asked, "Did anything of value survive the invasion?"

"The ruins are still there, of course. Some of the columns from the treasuries are in the Delphi Museum, as are some pieces of altars, stone friezes, the Omphalos . . . no gold or jewels, if that's what you're asking."

"Do you remember anyone ever nosing around about Delphi when you were there?" Remi asked. "Anything unusual?"

"No, not really. Just standard research requests from universities for the most part." Evelyn paused for a moment. "Wait a second. There was this one guy about a year ago . . . he was from the University of Edinburgh—the School of History, Classics, and Archaeology, I think. Weird character."

"How so?"

"He'd applied for a permit to examine the Delphi artifacts, and we granted it. There are rules for hands-on examinations—things you can and can't do with the objects. I caught him breaking one of the biggies—or almost breaking one, that is. I walked in on him trying to do some kind of acid test on one of the columns."

"Which columns?" Remi asked.

"The Karyatids. They stood at the entrance to the Siphnian Treasury at Delphi." Before either Remi or Sam could ask the next question, Evelyn answered it. "A Karyatid is a stone column—usually marble—in the shape of a robed Greek woman. The most recognizable ones are at the Athens Acropolis."

"What kind of test was he trying to do?" Sam asked.

"I don't remember. He had a jeweler's hammer and pick and some kind of acid kit. . . . I put it all down in my report to the board. I may still have a copy. Let me look while we talk."

They heard Evelyn moving about, then the rustle of cardboard and the shuffling of paper.

Remi asked, "What did he say when you caught him?"

"That he'd misunderstood the rules, which was bunk. I gave him the rules myself. He was lying, but he refused to say what he was up to. We ejected him and notified the guy's department chair at Edinburgh."

"No police?"

"The board decided against it. Lucky for him, too. The Greeks take that kind of thing seriously. He would have done jail time. I heard Edinburgh fired him, though, so that's something. I don't know what happened to him after that. Here's the report. . . . His name was Bucklin. Thomas Bucklin."

"And the acid kit he had?" Sam asked.

The sound of flipping pages came through the speaker. "This is strange," Evelyn said. "I'd forgotten this part. He was using nitric acid."

Remi said, "Why's that strange?"

"It's not a standard artifact test. It's highly corrosive. We don't use it."

"Who does?"

Sam answered. "Metallurgists. It's used to test for gold."

———

They talked for a few more minutes, then hung up. Sam opened his MacBook Air—one of the few things they'd brought along in his backpack from Königssee—and logged into the hotel's wireless Internet connection. There were almost two thousand hits for the name Thomas Bucklin. It took only a few minutes to narrow their search to the right one.

"Bucklin's written a number of papers on classical history, mostly focusing on Persia and Greece, but nothing more recent than a year ago," Sam said.

"About the time he got fired," Remi said, looking over his shoulder. "Are any of his papers available?"

"Looks like JSTOR has them all." JSTOR was a nonprofit online archive for scholarly work whose subjects ranged from archaeology and history to linguistics and paleontology. Sam, Remi, and Selma used the site extensively. "I'll have Selma download and forward them." Sam typed up a quick e-mail and sent it. Selma responded thirty seconds later: *Five minutes.*

Remi asked, "Any mention of what he's been up to since leaving Edinburgh?"

"Nothing."

Sam's e-mail chimed. Selma had found fourteen papers by Bucklin; they were included as pdf attachments. "Here's something interesting," Sam said. "According to Selma, Bucklin had been on a sabbatical from Edinburgh when he showed up on Evelyn's doorstep."

"So he was freelancing," Remi replied. "He wasn't there on behalf of the university. Who the heck is this guy?"

Sam stopped scrolling, his fingers frozen over the keyboard. He leaned closer to the screen and squinted. "There's your answer. Have a look."

Remi leaned over his shoulder. One of Bucklin's papers included a photo of the author. It was small, and in black-and-white, but there was no mistaking the mostly bald pate, fringe of orange hair, and black-rimmed glasses.

Thomas Bucklin was the lab-coated man they'd encountered in Bondaruk's private laboratory.

CHAPTER 52

Bucklin's papers were compelling, if not well received or widely circulated. According to JSTOR, Sam and Remi had been only the second party to purchase them since their publication. They had little trouble guessing the identity of the other interested party.

Sam forwarded the papers to his iPhone and gave Remi the Mac-Book, then they spent the next three hours wading through Bucklin's work. Not wanting to taint one another's conclusions, they waited until they were finished to compare notes.

"What do you think?" Sam asked. "Nutcase or genius?"

"Depends on whether he's right or wrong. There's no mistaking he's obsessed with Xerxes and Delphi. His version of the invasion didn't make him any friends in the academic world."

Through years of painstaking research Bucklin had come to an outlandish conclusion: that Xerxes' raid of Delphi had been more of a success than Greek historians admitted. According to Bucklin, in the weeks leading up to the invasion the keepers of the Siphnian Treasury devised a scheme to protect their wealth. Knowing no place would be safe from Persian plunder, the Siphnians melted down their stores of gold and cast it into a pair of Karyatids. When the columns cooled they were covered in gypsum plaster and put in place of the real columns that stood astride the treasury's entrance.

For reasons unknown the Persian raiding party did not fall for the ruse. On Xerxes' orders, a detachment of two hundred specially trained troops called Immortals fled with the Karyatids, intending to head north out of Greece before swinging east through Macedonia and Thrace and returning to the Achaemenid Dynasty capital of Persepolis, where Xerxes planned to melt down the Karyatids and have them cast into a massive throne, a memorial to his triumph over the Greeks that would sit in his Hall of a Hundred Columns for eternity.

Unbeknownst to the Immortals, word of their desecration of Delphi reached Sparta less than a day after the Persian raiding party left. A *phratra* of Spartan soldiers, roughly twenty-seven in all, gave chase, intending not only to recover the Karyatids, but also to avenge the brothers they'd lost at the Battle of Thermopylae.

They caught up to the Immortals in present-day Albania and cut off their easterly escape route. For three weeks the Spartans hounded the Immortals, chasing them north through Montenegro, then Bosnia and Croatia, before finally cornering them in the mountains of northwestern Slovenia. Even outnumbering them ten to one the Immortals were no match for the Spartans. The Persian raiding party was all but destroyed. Of the original two hundred that had left Greece a month before only thirty survived, these spared to serve as porters for the Karyatids.

The Spartan commander decided not to return home, not while Xerxes' army was still ravaging their country. The columns had become a symbol of Greece's survival, and the Spartans pledged to die rather than let them fall into Xerxes' hands. Not knowing how far the Persian invasion would advance, the Spartans headed north out of Slovenia, intending to find a place to hide the columns until it was safe to bring them home. The *phratra* was never seen again, save a lone soldier who stumbled into Sparta a year later. Before succumbing to his exhaustion and the ravages of exposure, he claimed that the rest of his comrades had perished and the Karyatids had been lost with them. Their location died with him.

"So that's the last puzzle piece," Remi said. "Or one of the last, that is. How Bondaruk and Bucklin found each other we may never know, but it's clear Bondaruk believes the story. He thinks Napoleon's Lost Cellar is a treasure map to the Siphnian columns. They're the family legacy he's trying to recover. Remember what else Kholkov said in Marseille about Bondaruk's motive: 'He's simply trying to finish what was begun a long time ago.'"

Sam nodded slowly. "The bastard wants to melt them down, just like Xerxes did. We can't let him get away with it, Remi. As archaeological artifacts, those Karyatids are priceless."

"Beyond priceless. It all fits: After the Battles of Plataea and Mycale, Xerxes abruptly hands over control of the army to Mardonius, and goes home—goes home assuming the Karyatids are on their way. Most accounts have him returning to Persepolis and starting a massive building program—including the Hall of a Hundred Columns."

"Where Bucklin claims he planned to display the throne. I'll give you one guess where Bondaruk plans to put his throne."

"The Persian playground in the basement of his estate," Remi replied. "It's sad, if you think about it. Xerxes died waiting for a prize that was never coming—a prize that meant relatively nothing to the Greeks—and Napoleon died waiting for his son to follow the riddles and recover the same prize."

"We might as well keep the streak alive," Sam said.

"What do you mean?"

"We make sure Bondaruk dies never getting his hands on the Karyatids. He'll be in good company."

———

At six the next morning Sam's iPhone trilled. It was Selma. "It's early, Selma," he said groggily.

"It's late here. Good news. We're getting better at this, I think. We've deciphered the code, but we thought you'd want first crack at the riddle."

"Okay, e-mail it to me."

"On its way. Call me later."

Sam shook Remi awake. She rolled over just as Sam's e-mail chimed. "Another riddle," he said.

"I heard."

He called up the e-mail and together they read the lines:

Man of Histria, thirteen by tradition
House of Lazarus at Nazareth
Son of Morpeth, Keeper of Leuce, the land that stands alone.
Together they rest.

"Any thoughts?" Sam asked.

"Ask me after coffee."

———

Having already unraveled two of the riddles, Sam and Remi now better understood the patterns Napoleon and Laurent had used to produce them. A patchwork of double meanings and obscure historical references, the solution to each puzzle depended upon the fusion of its individual lines.

By midmorning they'd gathered from the Internet the most obvious references for each line:

The first—*Man of Histria, thirteen by tradition*—likely referred to Histria, the Latin name for Istria, a peninsula between the Gulf of Trieste and the Bay of Kvarner in the Adriatic Sea.

The second—*House of Lazarus at Nazareth*—could have hundreds of meanings. The name Lazarus was mentioned twice in the Bible, once as the man Jesus raised from the dead, the other in the parable of Lazarus the Beggar. Nazareth, of course, was the childhood home of Christ.

The third—*Son of Morpeth, Keeper of Leuce*—was also too broad to nail down. Morpeth was a town in northeast England, and in Greek mythology Leuce was a nymph, the daughter of Oceanus.

The fourth—*Together they rest*—was the most ambiguous of all. Who were "they"? Did "rest" mean sleep or death, or something else altogether?

"Think about the last riddle," Sam suggested. "Napoleon and Laurent used a similar line—the 'Genius of Ionia' to reference Pythagorus. Maybe they're doing that here. We know the third line probably contains a place-name—Morpeth. Let's find out if Morpeth was home to any famous residents."

Remi shrugged. "Worth a try."

An hour later they had a list of a dozen semiprominent Morpeth "sons." None of them were immediately recognizable.

Remi said, "Let's cross-reference, see if there's a connection between any of the Morpeth names and the word 'Leuce.' Are any of them experts in Greek mythology?"

Sam checked the list. "Doesn't look like it. What else do we know about Leuce?"

Remi paged through her legal pad. "She was carried off by Hades, the god of the underworld. Depending on which version you go with, upon her death she was transformed into a poplar tree, either by Hades or by Persephone."

"Poplar tree . . . " Sam murmured, tapping on the keyboard. "The Leuce is a type of poplar." He checked his list of Morpeth names. "This might be something: William Turner, born in Morpeth in 1508. Considered by many to be the father of English botany."

"Interesting. So is the line about Turner himself, or about poplar trees?"

"No idea. What's the last part . . . 'the land that stands alone.'"

"My first thought would be island—they stand alone in the middle of water."

"My thought, too." Sam's Google search of "island," "poplar," and "Turner" turned up no revelations. "There're several references to a Poplar Island wildlife refuge in the Chesapeake Bay, but there's no connection to Turner—unless you count Tina Turner donating some money to the refuge, that is."

"Let's try the first line again—'Man of Histria, thirteen by tradition.'"

As they had with Morpeth, they generated a list of historical figures associated with the Istrian Peninsula, but like Morpeth, none of them were historically noteworthy.

They turned to the second line—*House of Lazarus at Nazareth*—and dug deeper, looking for more obscure references. "How about this?" Remi said, reading from the MacBook's screen. "During the Middle Ages, Christian religious orders used to oversee leper colonies known as Lazar houses."

"As in Lazarus, the patron saint of lepers?" Sam asked.

"Right. In Italy, the term 'Lazar' morphed into 'lazaret,' a quarantine station for ships and crews. The first recorded lazaret was established in 1403 off the coast of Venice, on the island of Santa Maria di Nazareth." She looked up at Sam. "That could be our Lazarus and Nazareth connection."

"We're getting warmer, but it can't be that easy," he said. "We're still missing the first line."

He did another Google search, combining and subtracting words until he came across a 2007 *National Geographic* story describing the discovery of a mass grave for bubonic plague victims who had been quarantined to protect Venice's uninfected.

Sam said, "The site was on an island in the Venice Lagoon called Lazzaretto Vecchio."

Remi flipped through her notes. "Vecchio . . . that's the modern name for Santa Maria di Nazareth. Sam, that's got to be it."

"Probably, but let's be sure."

Twenty minutes and dozens of search permutations later, he said, "Okay, here. I used the words 'island,' 'Venice,' and 'plague' and came up with this: Poveglia. It's another island in the Venice Lagoon, used to quarantine plague victims during the seventeenth century. The bodies were buried in mass pits, sometimes the living mixed in with the dead, or cremated in mass pyres. Estimates put the number of dead between . . ." He paused and his eyes went wide.

"What?" Remi asked.

"Estimates put the number of dead between a hundred sixty thousand and a quarter million."

"Good Lord."

"Something else: Before it was called Poveglia, it was Popilia."

"Why does that sound familiar?"

"Popilia is a derivation of *Populus*—Latin for 'poplar.' Poveglia was once covered in poplar groves."

"So on one hand we've got Poveglia, on the other Santa Maria di Nazareth. Both are solid possibilities. You're right: It'll come down to the first line of the riddle and our mysterious man from Istria."

"Either way, our next stop is Venice."

SEVASTOPOL

"I can tell by your tone the news is not good," Hadeon Bondaruk said into the phone.

"They're gone and one of my men is dead," Kholkov said. "We found the transponder chip from the Fargo woman's phone aboard one of the electric boats. How they discovered it I have no idea." Kholkov recounted the rest of the encounter at Königssee, starting with their arrival at Saint Bartholomae and ending with his losing the Fargos on the lake. "Somehow they must have slipped back into Schönau without us spotting them."

"Did they find the bottle?"

"I don't know."

"And where are they now?"

"We found a local that saw someone matching their description getting into a Mercedes. We traced it to a car service in Salzburg. We're on our way there now. We'll check the motels, the airport, the train stations—"

"No," Bondaruk said.

"Pardon me?"

"Every time we get close to them they slip the noose. I think it's time we step back and let the Fargos do what they do best. In the meantime, I want you to go ahead with your alternate plan."

"There are risks."

"I don't care. I'm tired of chasing these people all over Europe. You have a man in mind?"

"Yes," Kholkov said. "According to my sources, he's the only one with a family—a wife and two daughters."

"Get started."

"If he reports it rather than—"

"Then make sure he doesn't report it. Convince him that cooperation is his only way out. You can do that much, can't you?"

"I'll make the call."

CHAPTER 53

VENICE, ITALY

The water taxi pulled to a stop and Sam and Remi climbed out. Together they stared at the surrounding buildings.

"No matter how many times I see it, it always takes my breath away," Remi said.

Known to English tourists as Saint Mark's Plaza, the Piazza San Marco is in fact a trapezoid sitting at the eastern mouth of the Grand Canal. Famous for its pigeons and geometric "hopscotch" stone inlays, it is perhaps the most famous plaza in all of Europe, home to some of Venice's greatest attractions, many dating back a thousand years or more.

Sam and Remi turned in a circle, taking it in as if seeing it for the first time: Saint Mark's Basilica, with its Byzantine domes and spires; the Campanile, its three-hundred-foot bell tower; the imposing Gothic Palazzo Ducale, or Doge's Palace; and finally, directly opposite the basilica, the Ala Napoleonica, the one-time home of Napoleon's administrative residence.

Whether a coincidence or not they would soon know, but they

were keenly aware of Napoleon's connection to Venice and the Piazza San Marco, which he'd dubbed "the drawing room of Europe." In 1805, soon after Venice was named part of the newly created Kingdom of Italy, Napoleon ordered the Ala Napoleonica built after realizing his initial choices—the Zecca, or mint; the Libreria Marciana; and the Procuratie Nuove—were not large enough to accommodate his court.

It was nearly six o'clock and the sun was dipping toward the horizon over the roof of the Marciana Library. Some of the piazza lights had come on, casting amber pools on the arches and domes. Most of the day's tourists had left and the piazza was quiet save for the background babble of voices and the cooing of the pigeons.

"Who are we meeting?" Remi asked.

"The curator," Sam replied. "Maria Favaretto."

Before catching their two o'clock Lufthansa flight from Salzburg, Sam had called the curator of their destination, the Museo Archeologico, and introduced himself. Luckily, Signora Favaretto had heard of them. Their discovery of the lost diary of Lucrezia Borgia, the fifteenth-century Machiavellian political operator/seductress, a year earlier in Bisceglie had been front-page news in Venice, she told Sam. In fact, a former colleague of hers was the assistant curator of the Vatican Library's Museo Borgiano, where he and Remi had donated the diary. Favaretto agreed to meet them for an after-hours visit of the Museo Archeologico.

"Is that her?" Remi asked, pointing.

A woman was waving to them from inside one of the entrance arches to the Procuratie Nuove, in which the Museo Archeologico was partially housed; the rest was located within the Biblioteca Nazionale Marciana—the National Library of St. Mark's. Sam and Remi walked over to the woman.

"Signor Fargo, Signora Fargo, I am Maria Favaretto. It's my pleasure to meet you."

"Please call us Sam and Remi," Remi said, shaking her hand.

"And I'm Maria."

"Thank you for your help. We hope we aren't inconveniencing you."

"Not at all. Remind me again, what period are you interested in?"

"We're not positive, but none of the references we found are later than the eighteenth century."

"Good. I think we're in luck. If you'll follow me, please."

She led them through the arch, across a breezeway done in terra-cotta and cream tiles, and into the museum. They followed her past displays of Egyptian sarcophagi and Assyrian chariots, Etruscan statues and vases and Roman busts, Byzantine ivory carvings and Minoan earthenware jars.

Maria stopped at a wooden door and unlocked it with a key. They went down a long, dimly lit hallway. She stopped. "This is our not-for-public library. Given what you were asking about I thought the best person to help you would be Giuseppe. He doesn't have a title per se, but he's been here longer than anyone—almost sixty years. He knows more about Venice than anyone I know." She hesitated, cleared her throat. "Giuseppe is eighty-two and a little . . . odd. Eccentric is the word, I think. Don't let that worry you. Just ask your questions and he'll find the answers."

"Okay," Sam said with a smile.

"The reason I asked about your time frame is that Giuseppe is what you might call a throwback. He has no interest in anything modern. If it didn't happen in the nineteenth century or earlier, it doesn't exist for him."

"We'll keep that in mind," replied Remi.

Maria opened the door and gestured for them to step through. "Just press the buzzer on the wall here when you're done. I'll come back for you. Good luck." She shut the door.

The museum's library was long and narrow, measuring two hundred feet by forty feet. The walls were not walls at all, but floor-to-ceiling bookcases. They were twenty feet tall. On each of the four walls was a rolling wooden ladder. A single, ten-foot-long worktable and a lone hard-backed chair sat in the center aisle. Halogen pendants hung from the ceiling, casting soft pools of light on the green-tiled floor.

"Is someone there?" a voice called.

"Yes," Sam replied. "Signora Favaretto let us in."

As their eyes adjusted they could see a figure standing atop the ladder at the far end of the library. He was perched on the top rung, finger tracing along the book spines, occasionally nudging one inward or sliding one outward. After a moment the man climbed down and started shuffling down the aisle toward them. Thirty seconds later he came to a stop before them.

"Yes?" he said simply.

Giuseppe was barely five feet tall with wispy white hair that jutted out from his head at all angles. He couldn't have weighed more than ninety pounds. He stared up at them with surprisingly sharp blue eyes.

"Hello. I'm Sam and this is—"

Giuseppe waved his hand dismissively. "You have a question for me?"

"Um, yes. . . . We've got a riddle on our hands. We're looking for the name of a man, probably from Istria in Croatia, that might have a connection to either Poveglia or Santa Maria di Nazareth."

"Give me the riddle," Giuseppe ordered.

" 'Man of Histria, thirteen by tradition,' " Sam recited.

Giuseppe said nothing, but stared at them for ten seconds as he pursed his lips from side to side.

Remi said, "We also think he might have something to do with lazarets—"

Abruptly Giuseppe turned around and shuffled away. He stopped in the aisle, then stared at each wall in turn. His index finger tapped the air before him in the manner of a slow-motion conductor.

"He's cataloging books in his head," Remi whispered.

"Quiet, please," Giuseppe barked.

After two minutes Giuseppe went to the right-hand wall and pushed the ladder to the far end. He climbed up, plucked a book off the shelf, paged through it, then put it back and climbed back down.

Five more times he repeated the process, staring at the walls, conducting the air, and mounting the ladder before climbing back down and shuffling back to them.

"The man you're looking for is named Pietro Tradonico, the Doge of Venice from 836 to 864. Chronologically he was the elev-

enth Doge, but by tradition he is considered the thirteenth. Tradonico's followers fled to the island of Poveglia after he was assassinated.
They had some huts near the island's northeastern corner."

With that, Giuseppe turned and started shuffling away.

"One more question," Sam called.

Giuseppe turned, said nothing.

"Is Tradonico buried there?" asked Sam.

"Some think so, some not. His followers claimed the body after
his assassination, but no one knows where it was taken."

Giuseppe turned again and doddered away.

Remi called, "Thank you."

Giuseppe didn't reply.

"Did you find what you were looking for?" Maria asked a few minutes later when they came out. After they'd pushed the buzzer beside
the door it had taken her five minutes to arrive. During that time,
Giuseppe continued about his work as though they didn't exist.

"We did," Sam replied. "Giuseppe was everything you said he'd
be. We appreciate your help."

"It's my pleasure. Is there anything else I can do for you?"

"Since you're being so helpful . . . what's the best way to get to
Poveglia?"

Maria stopped walking and turned to them. Her face was drawn.
"Why would you want to go to Poveglia?"

"Research."

"You're welcome to use our facilities. I'm sure Giuseppe
would—"

Sam said, "Thank you, but we'd like to see it for ourselves."

"Please reconsider."

"Why?" Remi asked.

"How much do you know about Poveglia's history?"

"If you're talking about the plague pits, we read—"

"Not just those. There's much more. Let's have a drink. I'll tell
you the rest."

CHAPTER 54

"E xplain it to me again," Remi whispered. "Why couldn't this wait till morning?"

"It is morning," Sam replied, turning the wheel slightly to keep the bow on course. Though their destination showed no lights, its bell tower was nicely silhouetted against the night sky.

From above, Poveglia looked like a fan, measuring five hundred yards from its flared tip to its base, and three hundred yards at its waist where a narrow, walled canal bisected the island from west to east, save for a sandbar in the center.

"Don't get technical on me, Fargo. As far as I'm concerned, two A.M. is the middle of the night. It isn't morning until the sun comes up."

After drinks with Maria they'd managed to find an open boat rental office. The owner had only one craft left, a twelve-foot open dory with an outboard motor. Though not luxurious by any means, it would suffice, Sam decided. Poveglia was only three miles from Venice, inside the sheltering arms of the lagoon, and there was little wind.

"Don't tell me you bought into Maria's stories," Sam said.

"No, but they weren't exactly cheery."

"That's the truth."

In addition to having served as a dumping ground for plague victims, throughout its thousand-year history Poveglia had been home to monasteries, colonies, a fort and ammunition depot for Napoleon, and most recently in the 1920s, a psychiatric hospital.

In frightening detail Maria had explained that the doctor in charge, after hearing the patients complain about seeing the ghosts of plague victims, began to conduct crude lobotomies and gruesome experiments on the inmates, his own brand of medical exorcism.

Legend had it that the doctor eventually began seeing the same ghosts his patients had reported and went insane. One night he climbed up the bell tower and jumped to his death. The remaining patients returned the doctor's body to the bell tower and sealed the exits, entombing him forever. Shortly thereafter the hospital and the island were abandoned, but to this day Venetians reported hearing Poveglia's bell ringing or seeing ghostly lights moving in the windows of the hospital wing.

Poveglia was, Maria told them, the most haunted place in Italy.

"No, I don't buy the part about the ghosts," Remi said, "but what went on in that hospital is well documented. Besides, the island's closed to tourism. We're breaking and entering."

"That's never stopped us before."

"Just trying to be the voice of reason."

"Well, I have to admit it's very creepy, but we're so close to solving this riddle I want to get it done."

"Me, too. But promise me something: One gong from that bell tower and we're gone."

"If that happens you'll have to race me to the boat."

A few minutes later the mouth of the canal came into view. A few hundred yards down the shoreline they could see the dark outline of the hospital wing and bell tower rising over the treetops.

"See any phantom lights?" Sam asked.

"Keep joking, funny man."

He maneuvered the dory through the chop created by the lapping waves and they slipped into the canal. Sheltered from the seaward side, the canal saw little circulation; the surface was brackish and dotted with lily pads and in some places the water was only a few feet deep. To their right a brick wall draped in vines slipped past; to their left, trees and scrub brush. Above they heard the rasp of wings and looked up to see bats wheeling and diving after insects.

"Just great," Remi muttered. "It had to be bats."

Sam chuckled. Remi had no fear of spiders or snakes or bugs, but she loathed bats, calling them "rats with wings and tiny human hands."

Ten minutes later they reached the sandbar. Sam revved the engine, driving the bow onto the soil, then Remi got out and dragged the dory a few feet higher. Sam joined her and staked down the bow line. They clicked on their flashlights.

"Which way?" she asked.

He pointed to their left. "North end of the island."

They walked across the sandbar, then up the opposite bank to a dense hedge of scrub. They found a thin spot, pushed their way through, and emerged in a football-sized field surrounded by low trees.

Remi whispered, "Is this . . . ?"

"It might be." None of the maps of Poveglia had agreed upon the exact locations of the plague pits. "Either way, it's odd that nothing's growing here."

They continued across the field, stepping gingerly and shining their flashlights over the dirt. If this was the site of a plague pit, they were treading on the remains of tens of thousands of people.

When they reached the opposite tree line Sam led them east for a hundred feet before turning north again. The trees thinned out and they emerged into a small clearing filled with knee-high grass. Through the trees on the other side of the clearing they could see moonlight glinting off water. In the distance rang a gong.

"Buoy in the lagoon," Sam whispered.

"Thank God. My heart skipped a couple beats."

"Here's something." They walked forward and stopped before a block of stone peeking above the grass. "Must have been part of a foundation."

"Over there, Sam." Remi was shining her flashlight at what looked like a fence post on the right side of the clearing. They walked over. Affixed to the post was a Plexiglas-enclosed placard:

Ninth-century site of the followers of Pietro Tradonico, Doge of Venice 836 to 864. Remains disinterred and relocated in 1805.
—Poveglia Historical Society

"If Tradonico was here, he's gone now," Remi said.

" 'Relocated in 1805,' " Sam read again. "That was about the time Napoleon was crowned king of Italy, right?"

Remi caught on: "And about the time he had Poveglia converted to a munitions depot. If Laurent was with him, this is probably where they got their inspiration for the riddle."

"And they would have known where Tradonico's remains were sent. Remi, there was never a bottle here. The whole riddle was just a stepping-stone to send Napoleon Junior somewhere else."

"But where?"

The next morning at two minutes after eight Sam and Remi's water taxi stopped on a small side street two blocks east of Santa Maria Maddalena Church. They paid the driver, got out, and stepped up to a red door bordered by black wrought-iron railing. A tiny bronze plaque on the wall beside the door read, POVEGLIA HISTORICAL SOCIETY.

Sam pressed the buzzer. They heard footsteps clicking on wood and then the door opened, revealing a plump woman in a pink and yellow floral dress. *"Sì?"*

"Buon giorno," Remi said. *"Parla inglese?"*

"Yes, I speak English very well. Can I help you?"

"Are you the curator?"

"Pardon?"

"Of the Poveglia Historical Society," Sam said, smiling and pointing to the plaque.

The woman leaned out the door, squinted at the plaque, then

frowned. "That's old," she said. "The society hasn't met for five or six years."

"Why?"

"All that ghost business. All people wanted to know about was the hospital and the plague pits. The rest of its history was forgotten. I was the secretary. Rosella Bernardi."

"Perhaps you might be able to help us," Remi said. She introduced herself and Sam. "We have a few questions about Poveglia."

Signora Bernardi shrugged, motioned them inside, then led them down the hall into a kitchen decorated in black and white checkered tile. "Sit. I have coffee made," she said, pointing to the kitchen table. She filled three mugs from a silver percolator then sat down. "What do you want to know?"

"We're interested in Pietro Tradonico," Sam said. "Do you know if he was buried on Poveglia?"

Signora Bernardi got up, walked across the kitchen, and opened a cabinet above the sink. She pulled down what looked like a brown leather photo album and returned to the table. She opened the album and flipped to a page near the middle. Under a sheet of acetate was a yellowed sheet of paper bearing dozens of lines of handwritten notes.

"Is that an original reference?" Remi asked.

"*Sì*. This is the 1805 government census data of Poveglia. When Napoleon ordered the island annexed the government hurried to erase its checkered past."

"Which included the settlements established by Tradonico and his followers?"

"Yes, those, too. According to this, Pietro Tradonico and his wife, Majella, were buried side by side on Poveglia. When they were disinterred, their bones were stored together in the same coffin then temporarily placed in the basement of the Basilica della Salute."

Sam and Remi exchanged a glance. Here was the solution to the riddle's last line, *Together they rest.*

"You said temporarily," Sam said. "Does it say where the remains went after that?"

Signora Bernardi traced her index finger down the sheet, then flipped to the next page; halfway down the next sheet she stopped. "They were taken home," she announced.

"Home? Where exactly?"

"Tradonico was Istrian by birth."

"Yes, we know."

"Members of the Tradonico clan came and took the bodies to their village of Oprtalj. That's in Croatia, you know."

Remi smiled. "Yes."

"What they did with Tradonico and his wife once they reached Peroj we don't know. Does that answer your questions?"

"It does," Sam said, then stood up. Both he and Remi shook Signora Bernardi's hand, then walked down the hall and out the front door, where she stopped them. "If you find them, please let me know. I can update my records. I doubt anyone else will ask, but at least I'll have it written down."

Signora Bernardi gave them a wave, then shut the door.

"Croatia, here we come," Remi said.

Sam, who had been tapping on his iPhone, now held up the screen. "There's a flight leaving in two hours. We'll be there for lunch."

Sam's estimate was generous. As it turned out the quickest route was an Alitalia flight from Venice to Rome, then across the Adriatic to Trieste, where they rented a car and drove across the border and south to Oprtalj, some thirty miles away. They arrived in late afternoon.

Situated atop a thousand-foot hill in the Mirna Valley, Oprtalj had a distinctly Mediterranean feel, with terra-cotta pantile roofs and sun-drenched slopes covered in vineyards and olive groves. Oprtalj's history as an ancient medieval fort showed itself in the town's labyrinth of cobblestone streets, portcullis gates, and tightly packed, row-style buildings.

After stopping three times for directions, which came in either halting English or Italian, they found the town hall a few blocks east of the main road, behind the Church of Saint Juraj. They parked their car beneath an olive tree and got out and walked.

With only 1,100 inhabitants in Oprtalj, Sam and Remi were hoping the Tradonico family name would be renowned. They weren't disappointed. At their mention of the former Doge, the clerk nodded and drew them a map on a piece of scratch paper.

"Museo Tradonico," he said in passable Italian.

The map took them north, up a hill, past a cow pasture, then down a zigzagging alley to a garage-sized building painted in peeling cornflower blue. The hand-painted sign above the door had six words, most of them in consonant-heavy Croat, but one word was recognizable: TRADONICO.

They pushed through the door. A bell chimed overhead. To their left was an L-shaped wooden counter; directly ahead a twenty-by-twenty-foot room in white stucco and dark vertical beams. A half dozen glass display cases were situated around the room. Along the walls shelves displayed tiny sculptures, framed icons, and knickknacks. A rattan ceiling fan wobbled and creaked.

An elderly man in wire-rimmed glasses and a tattered argyle sweater vest rose from his chair behind the counter. *"Dobar dan."*

Sam opened the Croat phrase book he'd picked up at the Trieste airport, and opened it to a dog-eared page. *"Zdravo. Ime mi je* Sam." He pointed to Remi and she smiled. "Remi."

The man pointed a thumb at his chest. "Andrej."

"Govorite li Engleski?" Sam asked.

Andrej waggled his hand from side to side. "Little English. American?"

"Yes." Sam nodded. "From California."

"We're looking for Pietro Tradonico," said Remi.

"The Doge?"

"Yes."

"Doge dead."

"Yes, we know. Is he here?"

"No. Dead. Long time dead."

Sam tried a different tack: "We came from Venice. From Poveglia Island. Tradonico was brought here, from Poveglia."

Andrej's eyes lit up and he nodded. "Yes, 1805. Pietro and wife Majella. This way."

Andrej came out from behind the counter and led them to a glass case in the center of the room. He pointed to a framed wood-carved icon painted in flaking gold leaf. It showed a narrow-faced man with a long nose.

"Pietro," Andrej said.

There were other items in the case, mostly pieces of jewelry and figurines. Sam and Remi walked around the case, inspecting each shelf. They looked at one another, shook their heads.

"Are you a Tradonico?" Remi asked, gesturing to him. "Andrej Tradonico?"

"*Da*. Yes."

Sam and Remi had discussed this next part on the plane, but hadn't decided how to handle it. How exactly did you tell someone you wanted to gawk at their ancestor's remains?

"We would like to see . . . perhaps we could—"

"See body?"

"Yes, if it's not an inconvenience."

"Sure, no problem."

They followed him through a door behind the counter and down a short hallway to another door. He produced an old-fashioned skeleton key from his vest pocket and opened the door. A wave of cool, musty air billowed out. Somewhere they heard water dripping. Andrej reached through the door and jerked down a piece of twine. A single lightbulb glowed to life, revealing a set of stone steps descending into darkness.

"Catacombs," Andrej said, then started down the steps. Sam and Remi followed. The light faded behind them. After they'd descended thirty feet the steps took a sharp right and stopped. They heard Andrej's shoes scuffing on stone, then a click. To their right a string of six bulbs popped on, illuminating a long, narrow stone passageway.

Cut into each wall were rectangular niches, stacked one atop the other to the twenty-foot ceiling and spread down the length of the passage. In the glare of the widely spaced bulbs, most of the niches were cast in shadows.

"I count fifty," Sam whispered to Remi.

"Forty-eight," Andrej replied. "Two empty."

"Then not all of the Tradonico family is here?" Remi asked.

"All?" He chuckled. "No. Too many. The rest in graveyard. Come, come."

Andrej led them down the corridor, occasionally pointing at niches. "Drazan . . . Jadranka . . . Grgur . . . Nada. My great-great-great-grandmother."

As Sam and Remi passed each niche they caught glimpses of the skeletal remains, a jawbone, a hand, a femur . . . bits of rotted cloth or leather.

Andrej stopped at the end of the passageway and knelt at the bottom niche in the right-hand wall. "Pietro," he said matter-of-factly, then pointed at the niche above. "Majella." He reached into his pants pocket, withdrew a tiny flashlight, and handed it to Sam. "Please."

Sam clicked it on and shined it into Pietro's niche. A skull stared back. He shined it down the length of the skeleton. He repeated the process with Majella's niche. Just another skeleton.

"Nothing but bones," Remi whispered. "Then again, what were we expecting, that one of them would be holding the bottle?"

"True, but it was worth a try." He turned to Andrej. "When they were brought from Poveglia, was there anything else with them?"

"Pardon?"

"Were there any belongings?" Remi said. "Personal possessions?"

"Yes, yes. You saw upstairs."

"Nothing else? A bottle with French writing on it?"

"French? No. No bottle."

Sam and Remi looked at one another. "Damn," he whispered.

"No bottle," Andrej repeated. "Box."

"What?"

"French writing, yes?"

"Yes."

"There was box inside coffin. Small, shaped like . . . loaf of bread?"

"Yes, that's it!" Remi replied.

Andrej stepped around them and walked back down the passage-way. Sam and Remi hurried after him. Andrej stopped at the first niche beside the steps. He knelt down, leaned inside, rummaged about, then scooted back out with a wooden crate covered in Cyrillic stencils. It was a World War II ammunition crate.

Andrej opened the lid. "This?"

Lying atop folds of rotted canvas and half buried under spools of twine, rusted hand tools, and dented cans of paint was a familiar-looking box.

"Good God," Sam murmured.

"May I?" Remi asked Andrej. He shrugged. Remi knelt down and carefully lifted the box out. She turned it over in her hands, inspecting each side in turn, before finally looking up at Sam and nodding.

Sam asked, "Is there . . ."

"Something in it? Yes."

CHAPTER 55

Sam's iPhone trilled and he checked the screen. To Remi, he mouthed, *Selma,* then answered. "That's a new record. Took you less than two hours."

They were sitting on the balcony at the Grand Hotel Duchi D'Aosta, overlooking the lights of the Piazza Unità d'Italia. Night had fallen and in the distance they could see the lights twinkling in the harbor.

"We'd already decoded eleven lines of riddles and hundreds of symbols," Selma replied. "It's starting to feel like a second language."

After opening the box and confirming it did in fact contain a bottle from Napoleon's Lost Cellar, Sam and Remi had faced a dilemma. Clearly Andrej didn't know the value of what had been tucked away in his family's catacombs for the past two hundred–plus years. Still, they weren't about to give up the bottle. In truth, it didn't belong to them or to Andrej, but to the French people; it was a part of their history.

"This is a rare bottle of wine," Sam told Andrej.

"Oh?" he replied. "French, you say?"

"Yes."

Andrej snorted. "Napoleon disturb Tradonico grave. Take bottle."

"Let us give you something for it," Remi said.

Andrej's eyes narrowed. He stroked his chin. "Three thousand kuna."

Sam did the conversion in his head. "About five hundred dollars," he told Remi.

Andrej's eyes brightened behind his wire-rimmed glasses. "You have U.S. dollars?"

"Yes."

Andrej stuck out his hand. "We make deal."

———

Now Selma said, "I just e-mailed the riddle."

"We'll call you when we've got an answer." Sam hung up and checked his e-mail. Remi scooted her chair closer and looked over his shoulder. "A long one this time," he said.

> *East of the dubr*
> *The third of seven shall rise*
> *The King of Iovis Dies*
> *Alpha to Omega, Savoy to Novara, Savior of Styrie*
> *Temple at the Conqueror's Crossroads*
> *Pace east to the bowl and find the sign.*

"The first five lines fit the pattern," Remi said, "but the last is different. They've never been so explicit, have they?"

"No. This is the first time they've come out and said, 'go here' and 'find this.' We may be coming up on the finish line, Remi."

She nodded. "Let's get cracking."

———

They started as they had before, picking from the riddle what seemed like places and names. For "dubr" they narrowed the references to two likely candidates: Ad Dubr, a village in North Yemen, and *dubr*, a Celtic word meaning water.

"So something either east of Ad Dubr or east of some body of water. What's east of Ad Dubr?"

Sam checked Google Earth. "About eighty miles of mountains and desert, then the Red Sea. Doesn't seem likely. Up until now all of the locations have been in Europe."

"I agree. Let's move on. Try the 'King of Iovis.' When did he die?"

Sam checked. "No such person. Iovis wasn't a kingdom or a territory. Here's something. . . . We're grouping the words wrong—'*Iovis Dies.*' The original Latin for Thursday."

"King of Thursday?"

"Jupiter," Sam said. "In Roman mythology, Jupiter is the king of gods, like Zeus is to the Greeks."

Remi caught on: "Also known as the Jovian planet. So from the Latin Iovis they got Jovis, then Jovian."

"You got it."

"So try a search with 'Jupiter,' 'dubr,' 'three,' and 'seven.'"

"Nothing." He added and subtracted the search terms and again came up empty. "What's the fifth line?"

"'Temple at the Conqueror's Crossroads.'"

Sam tried "Jupiter" combined with "Conqueror's Crossroads," turned up nothing, then tried "Jupiter" and "temple." "Bingo," he muttered. "There are lots of temples dedicated to Jupiter: Lebanon, Pompeii . . . and Rome. This is it. In Rome the Capitoline Hill is dedicated to the Capitoline Triad—Jupiter, Juno, and Minerva. And here's the kicker: it's located on one of the Seven Hills of Rome."

"Let me guess: the third one. 'The third of seven shall rise.'"

"Yes." Sam found an artist-rendered map of how the area would have looked during Rome's peak. He turned the screen so Remi could see. After a few moments she smiled. "You see anything that looks familiar there?"

"You mean other than Capitoline Hill? No."

"Look due west."

Sam traced his finger across the screen and stopped on a blue serpentine line running from north to south. "The Tiber River."

"And what's the Celtic word for water?"

Sam grinned. *"Dubr."*

"If those were the only lines to the riddle I'd say we'd need to go to Rome, but something tells me it isn't going to be that easy."

Having assumed the last line—*Pace east to the bowl and find the sign*—would sort itself out whenever they reached their destination, they turned their focus to the fourth and fifth lines—*Alpha to Omega, Savoy to Novara, Savior of Styrie / Temple at the Conqueror's Crossroads*—and spent the next two hours filling their notepads and going in circles.

A little before midnight Sam leaned back in his chair and raked his hands through his hair. He stopped suddenly. Remi asked, "What is it?"

"I need the biographical sketch of Napoleon—the one Selma e-mailed us." He looked around, grabbed his iPhone from the nightstand, and called up the correct e-mail. "There," he said. "Styrie."

"What about it?" She paged through her notes. "It's a region in Austria."

"It was also the name of Napoleon's horse—or at least until the Battle of Marengo in 1800. He renamed Styrie to commemorate the victory."

"So the 'Savior of Styrie' . . . someone who saved Napoleon's horse. Are we looking for a veterinarian? Doctor Dolittle, perhaps?"

Sam chuckled. "Probably not."

"Well, it's a start. Let's assume the two previous phrases—'Alpha to Omega, Savoy to Novara'—have something to do with whoever did the saving. We know Savoy is a region in France and Novara is a province in Italy—"

"But they've also got a Napoleon connection," Sam replied. "Novara was the headquarters for his Department of the Kingdom of Italy before it was given to the House of Savoy in 1814."

"Right. Go back to the previous phrase: 'Alpha to Omega.'"

"Beginning and end; birth and death; first and last."

"Maybe it's talking about whoever ran the Department of the Kingdom of Italy first, then took over in 1814. No, that's not right. We're probably looking for a single name. Maybe someone who was born in Savoy and died in Novara?"

Sam punched different terms into Google, playing with combinations. After ten minutes of this he came across an encyclical on the Vatican website. "Bernard of Menthon, born in Savoy in 923, died in Novara in 1008. He was sainted by Pope Pius XI in 1923."

"Bernard," Remi repeated. "As in Saint Bernard?"

"Yes."

"I know this isn't it, but the only thing that comes to mind are the dogs."

Sam smiled. "You're close. The dogs gained their notoriety from the hospice and monastery at the Grand St. Bernard Pass. We were *there*, Remi."

Three years earlier they'd stopped at the hospice during a biking trip through the Grand St. Bernard Pass in the Pennine Alps. The hospice, while best known for ministering to the injured and lost since the eleventh century, had another claim to fame: in 1800 it had offered respite to Napoleon Bonaparte and his Reserve Army on their way through the mountains toward Italy.

"I don't know if there are any accounts of it," Sam said, "but it doesn't take much of a leap to imagine a grateful Napoleon handing Styrie over to the hospice's farriers. In the middle of a blizzard it would have seemed like salvation."

"It would at that," Remi replied. "One last line: 'Temple at the Conqueror's Crossroads.' Those mountains have seen their share of conquerers: Hannibal . . . Charlemagne . . . Roman legions."

Sam was back at the laptop typing. His query—"Jupiter," "temple," and "Grand St. Bernard"—returned an Oxford University article recounting an expedition to the site of the Temple of Jupiter at the summit of the pass.

"The temple dates back to A.D. 70," Sam said. "Constructed by Emperor Augustus." He called up the location on Google Earth. Remi leaned over his shoulder. They could see nothing but jagged gray granite.

"I don't see anything," Remi said.

"It's there," Sam said. "It may be just a pile of stones, but it's there."

"So if we look east of the temple . . ." Using her index finger she traced a line across the lake to the cliff along the southern shoreline. "I don't see anything that looks like a bowl."

"Not enough resolution. We'll probably have to be standing right on top of it."

———

"That's great news," Selma said when Sam and Remi called ten minutes later. She leaned back in her chair and took a sip of tea. Without her afternoon cup of Celestial Seasonings Red Zinger her afternoons tended to drag. "Let me do a little research and I'll get back to you with an itinerary. I'll try to get you on the first flight out in the morning."

"The sooner the better," Remi said. "We're in the home stretch."

"So if we're to believe Bucklin's story about the Immortals and the Spartans, then we're assuming the Spartans took the Karyatids through Italy into the Grand St. Bernard, then . . . what?"

"Then twenty-five hundred years later Napoleon somehow stumbles onto them. How or where we won't know until we make the walk from the temple."

"Exciting stuff. It almost makes me wish I were there."

"And leave the comfort of your workroom?" Remi said. "We're shocked."

"You're right. I'll look at the pictures when you get home."

They chatted for a few more minutes then hung up. Selma heard the scuff of a shoe and turned around to see one of the bodyguards Rube Haywood had sent moving toward the door.

"Ben, isn't it?" Selma called.

He turned. "Right. Ben."

"Is there something I can do for you?"

"Uh . . . no. I just thought I heard something so I came down to have a look. Must have been you talking on the phone."

"Are you feeling all right?" asked Selma. "You don't look well."

"Just fighting a little cold. Think I caught it from one of my little girls."

CHAPTER 56

There were two routes for reaching the pass, Sam and Remi discovered, from Aosta on the Italian side of the border and from Martigny on the Swiss side, the path Napoleon and his Reserve Army had followed almost two hundred years earlier. They chose the shorter of the two, from Aosta, following the SS27 north through Entroubles and Saint Rhémy, winding their way ever higher into the mountains to the entrance to the Grand St. Bernard Tunnel.

A marvel of engineering, the tunnel cut straight through the mountain for nearly four miles, linking the Aosta and Martigny valleys and offering a weather- and avalanche-proof route beneath the pass above.

"Another time," Sam said as they drove past and continued up the SS27. It would add almost an hour to their drive and with no way of knowing how long it would take to follow the riddle's last line, they erred on the side of caution.

After another thirty minutes on the switchbacking road they passed through a narrow canyon and pulled into the lake basin. Split by the imaginary Swiss-Italian border, the lake was a rough oval of blue-green water surrounded by towering rock walls. On the eastern shore—the Swiss side—sat the hospice and monastery; on the western shore—the Italian side—three buildings: a hotel-bistro, staff quarters, and a cigar-shaped Carabinieri barracks and checkpoint. High above Sam and Remi the sun burned in a cloudless blue sky, glinting off the water and casting the peaks along the southern shoreline in shadow.

Sam pulled into a parking spot at the lake's edge across from the hotel. They got out and stretched. There were four other cars nearby. Tourists strolled along the road, taking pictures of the lake and surrounding peaks.

Remi slipped on her sunglasses. "It's stunning."

"Think about it," Sam said. "We're standing in the exact spot where Napoleon marched when America was only a couple decades old. For all we know, he'd just found the Karyatids and he and Laurent were hatching their plan."

"Or they were worrying about how to get out of these mountains alive in the middle of a blizzard."

"Or that. Okay, let's find ourselves a temple. It should be on top of the hill behind the hotel."

"Excuse me, excuse me," a voice called in Italian-accented English. They turned to see a slight man in a blue business suit trotting toward them from the hotel's entrance.

"Yes?" Sam said.

"Pardon." The man stepped around Sam and stopped at the bumper of their rental car. He looked at a piece of paper, then the license plate, then turned back to them. "Mr. and Mrs. Fargo?"

"Yes."

"I have a message for you. A Selma is trying to reach you. She said it is urgent you call her. You may use the phone inside, if you wish."

They followed him inside and found a house phone in the lobby. Sam punched in his credit card number and dialed Selma. She picked up on the first ring. "Trouble," she said.

"We haven't had a cell signal since Saint Rhémy. What is it?"

"Yesterday when I was talking to you on the phone one of Rube's bodyguards—Ben—was walking around the workroom. I didn't think much of it at first, but it started nagging me. I did a scan on all the Mac Pros. Someone had installed a hardware keylogger, then removed it."

"In English, Selma."

"It's essentially a USB drive loaded with software that records keystrokes. You plug it in and leave it. However long it was installed it downloaded everything I typed. Every e-mail, every document. Do you think Bondaruk got to him?"

"Via Kholkov. Doesn't matter right now. Is he there now?"

"No, and he's late for his shift."

"If he shows up, don't let him in. Call the sheriff if you have to. When we hang up, call Rube and tell him what you told me. He'll handle it."

"What are you going to do?"

"Assume we've got company coming."

———————

They walked outside, grabbed their packs from the car, then circled to the back of the hotel and started up the slope. The grass was starting to green around the rock outcrops, and here and there they saw purple and yellow wildflowers poking up. When they reached the top of the hill, Sam pulled out his GPS unit and took a reading.

"You think they're already here?" Remi said, scanning the parking area with her camera's zoom lens.

"Maybe, but we can't second-guess ourselves. There are hundreds of people here. Unless we want to leave and come back later, I vote we push on."

Remi nodded.

Eyes fixed on the GPS screen, Sam walked south a hundred feet, then east for thirty, then stopped.

"We're standing on top of it."

Remi looked around. There was nothing. "You're sure?"

"There," Sam said, pointing beneath his feet. They knelt down.

Faintly visible in the rock was a chiseled straight line, roughly eighteen inches long. Soon they could make out other ruts, some intersecting, others moving off in different directions.

"Must be what's left of the foundation stones," Remi said.

They walked to what they guessed would have been the center of the temple, then faced east. Sam took a bearing with the GPS, picked out a landmark on the other side of the lake, and they headed back down the hill. At the bottom they crossed the road they'd driven in on and followed a path along the shore, past a stone block bistro fronted by a wooden walkway, then onto a rock shelf that ran along the water to a sheer ledge. Here they dropped down and followed a trail around a small cove to another flat area littered with boulders and patchy grass. Above them the cliff shot up at a fifty-degree angle. In the shade of the peaks, the temperature had dropped ten degrees.

"End of the line," Sam said. "Unless we're supposed to climb."

"Maybe we missed something back the way we came."

"More likely two hundred years of erosion turned whatever 'bowl' was here into a saucer."

"Or we're overthinking it and they were talking about the lake itself."

A gust of wind whipped Remi's hair across her eyes and she brushed it away. To Sam's right he heard a hollow whistling sound. He snapped his head around, eyes scanning.

"What's wrong?" Remi asked.

Sam held a finger to his lips.

The sound came again, from a few feet away. Sam moved down the face and stopped before a granite slab. It was ten feet tall and four feet wide. Two-thirds of the way up was a diagonal crack filled with yellow-green lichen. Sam stood on his tiptoes and pressed his fingertips to the crack.

"There's cool air blowing out," he said. "There's a void behind this. That top piece can't weigh more than five hundred pounds. With the right leverage we could do it."

From the packs he withdrew a pair of Petzl Cosmique ice axes and slipped them into his belt. Though unsure of what they'd find once they reached the pass, it had seemed unlikely the Karyatids were tucked away in a closet in the hospice. The most likely hiding place would be either in some high, hidden cranny or somewhere underground.

Remi said, "Next adventure, less spelunking, more tropical beaches."

"Anyone looking?" Sam asked.

They scanned the opposite side of the lake and the roads.

Remi said, "If they are, they're being careful about it."

"Do you mind playing ladder?"

"Have I ever said no to that?"

Sam slid his fingers into the crack and chinned himself up. Remi put her shoulders beneath his feet and he boosted himself onto the top of the slab. He turned himself around, his back against the slope. Next he jammed the pick end of each ax into the scree between the slab and the slope so the handles were pointing outward. He gripped a handle in each hand as if he was going to set dual parking brakes.

"Look out below."

Sam set his jaw, heaved back on the ax handles, and pressed with his feet. The cracked slab tilted outward, teetered for a moment, then toppled over. Sam's feet went with it. He spun himself onto his belly and crossed his arms, catching them on the ledge. The slab crashed to the ground, sending up a puff of dirt.

"What do you see?" Remi asked.

"A very dark tunnel. About two feet by two feet."

He dropped to the ground and they knelt beside the slab. He plucked the water bottle off his belt and dumped half the contents onto the face, washing away the dust.

Stamped into the stone was a cicada.

CHAPTER 57

They donned their headlamps and climbing harnesses, then Sam boosted himself up the slab and shined his lamp into the entrance.

"It's straight and level for ten feet then widens out," he said. "Can't see any ledges."

He wriggled feet first into the tunnel, then leaned over and helped Remi up. Once she was perched atop the slab he continued backing inside, Remi crawling after him until they reached the wide part, where he turned around. The ceiling was three feet tall and covered in "popcorn," tiny clusters of calcite.

Ahead a funnel-shaped hole in the floor was partially plugged by a stalactite. They saw no other openings. They crawled ahead and Sam peeked down the hole. "There's a platform about six feet below."

He rolled onto his back and kicked the stalactite until it broke loose from the ceiling. He shoved it away from the hole. "I'll go," Remi said, then scooted forward and slipped her legs through. Sam grabbed her hands and lowered her down until her feet found the platform. "Okay, feels solid." He let go, then a moment later dropped down beside her, reaching up and manhandling the stalactite into the hole after himself. With a grating sound it fell into place. He took a rock screw from his belt and wedged it between the stalactite and the edge of the hole.

"Early warning system," he explained.

Slightly canted, the platform was ten by six feet and ended at a ledge; over this they saw a thirty-degree diagonal chute. Under the glow of their headlamps it curved down and to the right.

Sam pulled a coil of nine-millimeter climbing rope from his pack, clipped a carabiner on the end, then dropped it over the ledge, letting it clink down the chute. After he'd let out twenty feet of rope the carabiner came to a stop.

"Another level spot," Sam said. "What we don't know is how wide."

"Lower me," Remi said.

He reeled in the carabiner and secured the rope to her harness. Feet braced against the wall, Sam lowered her down into the chute, letting out slack at her command until she called a halt. "Another platform," she called up, her voice echoing. "Walls to the left and directly ahead, and a ledge to the right." Sam heard her boots scuffing over loose rock. "And another diagonal chute."

"How wide is the platform?"

"About the same as the one you're on."

"Move against the wall. I'm coming down."

He dropped the coil over the edge, then lowered himself down until his feet touched the chute, at which point he dropped onto his butt and slid down to the platform. Remi helped him to his feet. The ceiling was taller, two feet above Sam's head, and dotted with inch-long "soda straw" stalactites.

Sam walked to the ledge and shined his headlamp down into the next chute. "I'm sensing a trend," he told Remi.

For the next fifteen minutes they descended, following a series of winding platforms and chute formations until finally they found themselves in a barn-sized cavern with a stalactite-spiked ceiling and walls covered in mottled brown-and-cream-colored flowstone. Barrel stalagmites jutted from the floor like gnarled fire hydrants.

Sam pulled a chem-light tube from his pack, cracked it, and shook it until it glowed neon green. He dropped it behind a nearby barrel so it couldn't be seen from the platform above.

Directly ahead lay a dead-end wall; to their right were three tunnels, each a vertical fissure in the wall. To their left a curtain of dragon's-teeth stalactites dropped to within a foot of the floor.

"We're at least a hundred feet underground," Remi said. "Sam, there's no way anyone could have gotten the Karyatids down this way."

"I know. There must be another entrance. Farther down the pass, I'm betting. Do you hear that?"

Somewhere to their left beyond the dragon's teeth came the sound of rushing water. "Waterfall."

They walked down the curtain, stopping to peek beneath it every few feet. At the midpoint they found a section of dragon's teeth had broken off, creating a waist-high gap. On the other side lay a four-foot-wide rock bridge spanning a crevasse; halfway across a thin curtain of water tumbled into the chasm, sending up a cloud of mist that sparkled in the beams of their headlamps. Barely visible through the waterfall they could see the dark outline of another tunnel.

"It's incredible!" Remi called over the rush. "Is it from the lake?"

Sam put his mouth beside her ear. "Probably snowmelt runoff. It probably won't be here in another couple months."

They walked back the way they'd come.

Somewhere in the distance came a metallic ping, followed by silence, then a series of pings as Sam's rock screw bounced down the chutes above.

"It may have just slipped," Remi said.

They crept back to the platform and stood still, listening. A minute passed. Two minutes, then an echoing voice: "Lower me down."

"Damn," Sam muttered.

The voice was unmistakable: Hadeon Bondaruk.

"How long do we have?" Remi asked.

"He'll have more people. Twenty, twenty-five minutes."

"He must think we're on the right track," Remi said. "He's come to claim his prize."

At that moment there was only a handful of people who knew this cave was the likely hiding place for the columns: Sam and Remi, and Bondaruk and whoever was with him. Bondaruk couldn't allow them to get out alive.

Sam said, "Then he's going to be disappointed. Come on."

They zigzagged their way through the stalagmites to the opposite wall and checked each tunnel in turn. Down the first tunnel and the middle tunnel they could see nothing but darkness. The third one jogged left after six feet. Sam looked at Remi and shrugged. She shrugged back and said, "Coin toss."

They slipped through the fissure and followed the bend. Remi tripped and fell; she rolled onto her butt, rubbing her knee. Sam helped her up. "I'm okay," she said. "What was that?"

An object on the floor glittered in her headlamp. Sam walked past her and picked it up. It was a straight, narrow sword about two feet long. Though heavily tarnished, spots of bright steel showed along the blade.

"This is a *Xiphos*, Remi. It was carried by Spartan infantrymen. My God, they were here." He shook himself from his reverie and they continued on.

The tunnel continued on for another fifty feet, turning this way and that until merging with a three-way intersection. "Left is the middle tunnel, I think. Leads back to the cavern," Sam said.

"No, thanks."

After twenty feet the tunnel began sloping downward, first gently, then more dramatically until they were sidestepping and groping the walls for handholds. The minutes ticked by. They turned a corner and Sam skidded to a stop, sliding a few feet before bumping into a wall.

"Dead end," Remi said.

"Not quite."

Where the wall met the floor there was a horizontal split. Sam crouched down and shined his headlamp inside. It was barely eighteen inches high. Cool air gushed from the opening.

"That might be the other entrance," Remi said. "I'll check it out."

"Too risky."

Behind them a voice echoed down the tunnel: "Anything?" It was Kholkov. In turn, two voices called back, "Nothing!"

"Bondaruk, Kholkov, and two others," Sam said.

"I'm going," Remi said.

"Remi—"

"There's less chance of me getting stuck. If I do we'll need your strength to get me back out. Don't worry, I'll just go in a few feet and see what there is to see."

Sam frowned, but nodded.

She took off her pack and harness. Sam knotted one end of the rope to her ankle and she dropped to her belly and crawled into the split. When she was up to her ankles Sam put his mouth near the opening and rasped, "That's far enough."

"Hold on, there's something just ahead."

Her feet disappeared and Sam could hear her scrabbling over loose rock. After thirty seconds the sound stopped. Sam held his breath. Finally he heard Remi's whispered voice: "There's another cavern, Sam."

He took off his own pack and belt, stacked them atop Remi's, then jammed the *Xiphos* between the packs. He clipped on the rope and gave it a tug. The bundle disappeared through the slit.

"Okay, now you," Remi called.

Sam lay flat and wriggled into the opening. The sides and ceiling closed around him, brushing his elbows and the top of his head.

Then, behind him, a noise.

He stopped.

Footsteps pounded down the tunnel, followed by the sound of boots skidding on gravel. A flashlight beam danced off the rock walls.

"There he is!" a voice said. "I've got them!"

Sam scrambled forward, hands clawing at the floor, boots pushing off the sides.

"You! Stop!"

Sam kept going. Ten feet away was another slit; silhouetted by her headlamp, Remi's head appeared. Her hands came into view, then a carabiner, at the end of her rope, clattered across the floor toward him. He grabbed, kept crawling. Remi began hauling the rope hand over hand.

"Shoot him!" Kholkov shouted.

There was a roar. The tunnel filled with orange light. Sam felt a sting on his left calf. He grabbed Remi's outstretched hand, coiled his legs, and shoved hard. He tumbled out headfirst, did a clumsy somersault, and landed in a heap. The gun roared twice more, the bullets ricocheting harmlessly through the slit just above their heads.

Sam rolled over and sat up. Remi crouched beside him and lifted his pant leg. "Just a crease," she said. "An inch to the right and you wouldn't have a heel."

"Small miracles."

She pulled the first-aid kit from her pack and quickly wrapped the wound with an elastic bandage. Sam stood up, tested the leg, and nodded his approval.

From inside the slit came sounds of crawling.

"We need to block it," Sam said.

He and Remi looked around the cavern. None of the stalactites was narrow enough to break loose. Something near the right-hand wall caught Sam's eye. He jogged over. He picked up what looked like a pole, but quickly recognized it for what it was: a spear. The hardwood shaft was amazingly well preserved, coated in a lacquer of some kind.

"Spartan?" Sam asked.

"No, the head is shaped wrong. Persian, I think."

Sam hefted the spear, sprinted back, and pressed himself against the rock beneath the split. "Turn around and go back," he shouted.

No response.

"Last chance!"

"Go to hell!"

The gun boomed again. The bullet thunked into the opposite wall.

"Suit yourself," Sam muttered. He popped up, cocked his arm, and jammed the spear into the opening. It struck something soft and they heard a gasp. Sam jerked the spear back out, then ducked down. They waited, expecting to hear their pursuer calling to his comrade, but there was only silence.

Sam peeked his head up. A man lay motionless a few feet inside the slit. Sam reached in and grabbed his gun, a .357 Magnum revolver.

"I'll take it," Remi said. "You've got your hands full. Unless you want to part with your poker." Sam handed her the revolver and she said, "It'll take them a while to get him out."

"Bondaruk won't bother unless he has no other choice," Sam predicted. "They're trying to find another entrance."

They looked around to get their bearings. This cavern was kidney shaped and smaller than the main one, with a twelve-foot ceiling and an exit in the right-hand wall.

Sam and Remi searched among the stalactites but found no other man-made objects.

"How many Persians and Spartans did Bucklin say survived?" Sam asked.

"Twenty or so Spartans and thirty Persians."

"Remi, look at this."

She walked over to where Sam was standing beside what looked like a pair of stalactites. They were hollow, their sides reaching up like flowstone flower petals. The spaces inside were perfectly cylindrical.

"Nothing in nature is that uniform," Remi said. "They were here, Sam."

"And there's only one place they could have gone."

They walked to the wall and ducked into the tunnel, which meandered for twenty feet before opening onto a ledge. Another rock bridge, this one only two feet wide, stretched across a chasm and into another tunnel. Sam leaned right, then left, checking the bridge's thickness.

"Seems solid enough, but . . ." He looked around. There were no stalactites to rope onto. "My turn."

Before Remi could protest, Sam stepped onto the bridge. He stopped, stood still for a few seconds, then made his way across. Remi joined him. They wound their way through a tightly packed forest of stalactites, then stepped into an open space.

They stopped short.

Remi murmured, "Sam . . ."

"I see them."

Caught in their headlamps, the Karyatids lay side by side on the floor, their golden faces staring at the ceiling. Sam and Remi walked forward and knelt down.

Cast with immaculate care, the women's golden torsos were draped in robes so finely detailed Sam and Remi could see tiny creases and stitching. On each woman's head rested a laurel wreath; each stem and leaf and bud was a work of art unto itself.

"Who moved them?" Remi said. "Laurent? How could he have done it by himself?"

"That," Sam replied, then pointed.

Lying beside the wall was a makeshift sled constructed of a half dozen overlapping shields. Made of lacquered wicker and leather, each shield was a five-foot-tall hourglass. They were bound together with what looked like catgut to form a shallow canoe shape.

"We saw one of these at Bondaruk's estate," Sam said. "It's a Persian *gerron*. Imagine it: Laurent, in here working alone for days, building his sled, then dragging each Karyatid across that bridge. . . . Amazing."

"But why leave them here?"

"I don't know. We know there's a gap in his biography a few years before he hired Arienne and the *Faucon*. Maybe Napoleon ordered him to try to get the columns out. Maybe Laurent realized he couldn't do it without help, so he left them behind assuming he'd return."

"Sam, daylight."

He looked up. Remi had moved farther down the wall and was

kneeling beside a shoulder-wide crack in the wall. The interior had collapsed and was choked with rock. A pencil-sized shaft of sunlight showed at the far end.

"Napoleon and Laurent might have come in this way," Remi said, "but we won't be using it to get out."

"Time to go," Sam said. "Let's go get reinforcements."

They found another opening, this one barely larger than the slit they'd come through earlier. At the other end was an alcove and another side tunnel, this one leading back in the general direction of the main cavern. For twenty minutes they picked their way along until finally they reached an intersection. To the left they heard the sound of rushing water.

"The waterfall," Remi said.

They crept down the tunnel to the mouth, stopping a few feet short. Directly across from them lay the dragon's-teeth curtain; to the left, the platform. They could just make out the glow of Sam's chem light on the wall behind the barrel stalactite.

"I don't see anyone," Sam said.

"Me neither."

They started across the cavern, angling toward the platform.

Sam saw the movement in the corner of his eye a split second before the gun roared. The bullet struck the stalactite beside Sam's hip. He ducked. Beside him, Remi spun, took aim on the charging figure, and snapped off a shot. The figure spun and fell, but almost rolled onto his side and started to rise.

"Run!" Sam barked. "That way!"

With Remi in the lead they sprinted for the dragon's teeth, through the gap, and onto the water-slick bridge. Never slowing, Remi crashed through the waterfall, followed by Sam. When they reached the far ledge Remi kept going, ducking into the tunnel, but Sam skidded to a stop and turned back.

"Sam!"

Through the waterfall he could see a figure running across the bridge. Sam dropped the *Xiphos* and the spear, scooped up a double handful of gravel, and tossed it across the bridge. A second later the figure crashed through the waterfall, his gun extended before him. His lead foot skidded over the gravel and shot out from under him. Eyes wide, his arms windmilling, he stumbled backward, his face upturned into the waterfall. He slammed back first onto the bridge. His leg slipped over the edge and he scrambled with his opposite leg, trying to find purchase. Then he was gone, screaming as he tumbled into the crevasse.

Remi appeared at Sam's shoulder. He picked up the spear, then stood up and turned toward her. "Two down, two to—"

"Too late for that," a voice said. "Don't move a muscle."

Sam pivoted his head. Surrounded by billowing mist, Kholkov stood on the bridge in front of the waterfall. His nine-millimeter Glock was pointed at them.

Remi whispered, "I've got one more bullet. They're going to kill us anyway."

"True," Sam murmured.

Kholkov barked, "Stop talking. Fargo, step away from your wife."

Sam turned his body slightly, still covering Remi's gun hand as he very slowly extended the spear toward Kholkov. Instinctively the Russian's eyes flicked toward the spearhead. Remi didn't miss the moment. Instead of raising the .357 to shoulder height, she simply lifted it to waist level and pulled the trigger.

A neat hole appeared in Kholkov's sternum; a red stain spread across the front of his sweater. He collapsed to his knees and gaped at Sam and Remi. Sam saw Kholkov's gun hand twitch, saw the Glock start to rise. Spear held before him, Sam charged onto the bridge. Kholkov's fading reflexes were no match for the spear's seven-foot reach. The steel head plunged into Kholkov's chest, then out his back. Sam leaned forward, wrenched the Glock from Kholkov's hand, then planted his feet and gave the spear a twist. Kholkov tumbled over the side. Sam stepped to the edge and watched him spin out of sight.

Remi walked up. "Couldn't have happened to a nastier person."

Back in the cavern, they picked their way through the stalactites, frequently checking behind and to the sides on their way back to the
platform. Bondaruk was nowhere to be seen. They half expected him
to step from the darkness of one of the tunnels, but nothing moved.
Aside from the distant rush of the waterfall, all was quiet.

They stopped at the platform. "I'll play ladder this time," Sam
said, then knelt down and formed a stirrup with his hands. Remi
didn't move.

"Sam, where's the chem light?"

He turned. "It's right over—"

Behind the barrel, the green glow of the chem light shifted.

Sam whispered out of the side of his mouth, "Run, Remi."

She didn't argue, but turned and started sprinting back across the
cavern toward the tunnels across from the dragon's teeth.

Ten feet in front of Sam, Bondaruk rose up. Like a cougar attracted
by a fleeing hare, he spun, raised his gun, took aim on her.

"No!" Sam shouted. He jerked up the Glock and fired. The
bullet missed Bondaruk's head, grazing past his cheek and slicing
through his ear. He screamed, turned, fired. Sam felt a hammer blow
in his left side. A wave of white-hot pain rushed through his torso
and exploded behind his eyes. He stumbled backward and fell. The
Glock clattered across the floor.

"Sam!" Remi shouted.

"Stop right there, Mrs. Fargo!" Bondaruk barked. He came out
from behind the barrel stalactite and stalked over and leveled his gun
with Sam's head. "Come back here!" Bondaruk commanded.

Remi didn't move.

"I said, come back here!"

Remi put her hands on her hips. "No. You're going to kill us
anyway."

Sam lay still, trying to catch his breath. Through the rush of
blood in his ears, he tried to focus on Remi's voice.

"Not true. You tell me where the columns are and I will—"

"You're a liar and a murderer, and you can go to hell. You may find the columns without us, but you're going to have to do it the hard way."

With that, Remi turned on her heel and began walking. Her unexpected defiance had the desired effect.

"Damn you, come back here!"

Bondaruk turned, bringing the gun to bear on her. Sam took a deep breath, set his jaw, then sat up. He raised the *Xiphos* above his head and chopped downward. The blade caught Bondaruk at the wrist. Despite having gone unused for two-and-a-half millennia, the Spartan sword still bore enough of an edge to sever bone and flesh.

Bondaruk's hand came off and dropped to the ground. He screamed and clutched the stump with his opposite hand. He collapsed to his knees.

Remi was there seconds later, kneeling beside Sam. "Help me up," he said.

"You need to stay still."

He rolled over, got to his knees. "Help me up," he repeated.

She did so. Grimacing against the pain, Sam straightened up. He pressed his palm into the bullet wound. "Is my back bloody?" he asked.

"Yes."

"That's good. Through and through wound."

"I wouldn't exactly call that good."

"Everything's relative."

Sam walked over to Bondaruk, kicked the gun away, then grabbed him by his jacket collar. "Stand up."

"I can't!" he gasped. "My hand!"

Sam heaved Bondaruk to his feet. "Mr. Bondaruk, how do you feel about heights?"

"What does that mean?"

Sam looked questioningly at Remi. She thought for a moment, then nodded grimly.

Sam began half dragging, half walking him across the cavern toward the dragon's teeth.

"Let me go!" Bondaruk shouted. "What are you doing?"

Sam kept walking.

"Stop, stop, where are we going?"

"We?" Sam replied. "We're not going anywhere. You, on the other hand . . . you're taking the express elevator to hell."

EPILOGUE

Remi pulled their rented Citroën into a tree-lined gravel driveway and followed it a hundred yards to a two-story white-stuccoed farmhouse with gabled windows framed by black shutters. She stopped beside the picket fence and shut off the engine. To the right of the house was a rectangular garden, its black soil tilled and ready for planting. A paving-stone walkway led through the gate to the door.

"If we're right about this," Remi said, "we're about to change a girl's life."

"For the better," Sam replied. "She deserves it."

Following the confrontation in the cave they'd spent two hours making their way back to the entrance, Remi climbing ahead, setting pitons and rock screws and taking as much of Sam's weight as she could. Sam refused to let her go for help. They'd come down together and they were going back up together.

Once outside, Sam made himself comfortable while Remi sprinted back to the hotel, where she called for help.

The next day they were at the hospital in Martigny. The bullet had missed any major organs, but left Sam feeling like he'd been used as a boxer's heavy bag. He was kept two days for observation and then released. Three days later they were back in San Diego, where Selma explained how Bondaruk and Kholkov had tracked them to the Grand St. Bernard. One of the security guards sent by Rube's friend had been approached days earlier by Kholkov and given an ultimatum: install the keylogger or see his two daughters kidnapped. Putting themselves in the man's shoes, Sam and Remi couldn't fault the choice he made. The police were left out of it.

The next morning they started the process of returning the Karyatids to the Greek government. Their first call went to Evelyn Torres, who immediately contacted the director of the Delphi Archaeological Museum. From there events moved rapidly and within a week an expedition sponsored by the Hellenic Ministry of Culture was in the cave beneath the Grand St. Bernard lake. On its second day inside, the team found a side cavern. Inside were dozens of Spartan and Persian skeletons, along with their weapons and equipment.

It would be weeks before the expedition would attempt to extract the columns from the cave, Evelyn reported, but the ministry was certain the Karyatids would safely find their way home and eventually be put on display at the museum. Before the year was out scholars the world over were going to have to rethink a good portion of Greek and Persian history.

Hadeon Bondaruk had died never laying eyes on his beloved and elusive Karyatids.

Once Sam was fully on the mend, they returned their attention to the Lost Cellar. According to the legend, Napoleon had ordered his enologist, Henri Emile Archambault, to produce twelve bottles of the Lacanau wine. Sam and Remi could account for only five: one lost by Manfred Boehm and destroyed, based on the Pocomoke shard found by Ted Frobisher; three recovered by them—aboard the Molch, at Saint Bartholomae's, and in the Tradonico family cata-

combs in Oprtalj—and finally the bottle stolen by Kholkov from the
Marder at Rum Cay and presumably delivered to Hadeon Bondaruk
at his estate, an issue the French and Ukrainian governments were
working to settle. For their part, Sam and Remi had already turned
over their bottles to France's Ministry of Culture, which had offered
an endowment of $750,000 to the Fargo Foundation. A quarter of a
million dollars per bottle.

One mystery remained: What had happened to the other seven
bottles? Were they lost, or were they somewhere waiting to be discovered, either superfluous parts of Napoleon's riddle or hidden
for their own safety? The answer, Sam and Remi decided, might
lie with the man who'd started the legend of the Lost Cellar, the
smuggler-captain of the *Faucon*, Lionel Arienne, whom Laurent had
allegedly hired to help stash the bottles.

As far as they could tell, Napoleon had been willing to trust only
Laurent with the task, and they'd gone to great lengths to ensure the
bottles remained hidden. Why then had Laurent enlisted the help of
a random sea captain he met in a Le Havre tavern?

It was a question that would take two weeks to answer. Their first
stop was the Newberry Library in Chicago, where they spent three
days sorting through the Spencer Collection, home to arguably the
largest gathering of Napoleon original source material in the United
States. From there they flew to Paris, spending four days and three
days respectively at the Bibliothèque Nationale de France and the
defense archives at Château de Vincennes. Finally, armed with a legal
pad full of notes, copies of birth and death certificates, discharge
documents, and transfer records, they drove west to Rouen, the capital of the Normandy province. There, in the basement of the provincial archives, they found the last link in the chain.

In September 1818 Sergeant Léon Arienne Pelletier, a decorated
veteran grenadier in Napoleon's Reserve Army and subordinate of
Arnaud Laurent during the 1800 Italian Campaign, was discharged
for reasons unrecorded and returned to his home in Beaucourt, 115
miles east of the port of Le Havre. Two months later he disappeared
from Beaucourt, resurfaced in Le Havre with a set of new identity

papers, and purchased a three-masted barque named the *Zodiaque*. The ship cost more than a sergeant could have made in eight lifetimes in the French army. He changed the *Zodiaque*'s name to *Faucon* and began smuggling arms and liquor up and down the coast, making modest profits and, astoundingly, not once running afoul of the French authorities. Two years later in June of 1820 Arnaud Laurent walked into a pub and hired Lionel Arienne and the *Faucon*. Twelve months after that Arienne returned to Le Havre, sold the *Faucon*, and returned home to Beaucourt, where he slowly but steadily drank and gambled away his fortune.

Why Pelletier/Arienne had chosen to reveal the secret on his deathbed neither Sam nor Remi knew, but it seemed clear that he, Laurent, and Napoleon were the only ones who'd known about the Siphnian Karyatids. Nor would they probably ever know how the three men had found the columns in the first place.

Selma's completed translation of Laurent's diary/codebook had solved two smaller riddles: Ten months after he and Arienne picked up the wine from St. Helena, having spent nearly a year secreting bottles around the world, they received word Napoleon had died. Heartbroken, but already enroute to Marseille, Laurent hid three bottles at Château d'If before returning to port. Of the other bottles, he'd said nothing.

As to why Napoleon's son, Napoleon II, never took up the quest his father had devised for him, this too was a source of despair for Laurent. From the time he returned to France with Arienne to his death in 1825, Laurent wrote Napoleon II dozens of letters begging him to obey his father's wishes, but Napoleon II refused, stating he saw no reason to leave the comforts of the Austrian royal court for a 'childish game of hide-and-go-seek.'"

Sergeant Léon Arienne Pelletier, it turned out, had one living descendant, a distant cousin named Louisa Foque. She was twenty-one and deep in debt after her parents had died in a car crash a year earlier and left her a thrice-mortgaged Beaucourt farmhouse.

"How do you think she'll take it?" Remi asked.

"Let's find out. One way or another her life is about to change."

They climbed out of the car and walked up the path to the front door. Remi pulled a leather cord and a bell tinkled. A few moments later the door opened to reveal a petite woman with light brown hair and a button nose.

"*Oui?*" she said.

"*Bonjour.* Louisa Foque?"

"*Oui.*"

Remi introduced herself and Sam then asked if Louisa spoke English.

"Yes, I speak English."

"May we come in? We have some information about your family—about Léon Pelletier. Do you know the name?"

"I think so. My father showed me our genealogy once. Please come in."

Inside they found a kitchen done in quintessential French Provincial: yellow plaster walls, a lacquered oak dining table, and a sage green sideboard displaying a few pieces of Chinoiserie pottery. Cheerful orange-checkered toile curtains framed the windows.

Louisa made tea and they sat down at the table. Remi said, "Your English is very good."

"I was studying American literature at Amiens. I had to quit. There was a . . . I had some family problems."

"We know," Sam replied. "We're very sorry."

Louisa nodded, forced a smile. "You said you have some information about my family."

Taking turns, Sam and Remi outlined their theory about Pelletier, the Lost Cellar, and their connection to the Siphnian Karyatids. Remi pulled a half dozen newspaper clippings from her purse and slid them across the table to Louisa, who scanned the articles.

"I read about this," she said. "You were involved?"

Sam nodded.

"I can't believe it. I had no idea. My mother and father never said anything."

"I'm sure they didn't know. Aside from Napoleon and Laurent, Pelletier was the only other person, and he kept the secret up until his death. Even then he didn't tell the whole story."

"No one believed him."

"Almost no one," Remi said with a smile.

Louisa was silent for half a minute, then shook her head in wonderment. "Well, thank you for telling me. It's nice to know someone in our family did something important. A little strange, but important still."

Sam and Remi exchanged a glance. "I don't think we've made ourselves clear," Sam said. "There are some bottles still unaccounted for."

Louisa blinked at them. "And you think . . . Here?"

Sam pulled out his iPhone and pulled up a picture of a cicada. "Have you ever seen this anywhere?"

In response Louisa got up and walked to the pot rack hanging above the sink. She pulled down a sauté pan and set it on the table before Sam. The handle was a thumb-sized steel rod. Set into its end was a cicada stamp. It was identical to the one they'd found in Laurent's crypt.

"My father found that in the attic a few years ago," Louisa said. "He didn't know what it was for so he used it to fix the pan."

Remi asked, "Do you have a basement?"

———————

While their research into Sergeant Pelletier had uncovered a number of surprises, it had also challenged one of their basic assumptions: that Laurent alone had placed the bottles in their hiding spots.

Having spent so much time consumed by the chase they'd begun to think like Laurent and Pelletier, and so it took them only fifteen minutes to find what they'd come for.

In the northwest corner of the basement beneath a wall next to the root cellar they found a block bearing the cicada stamp. As usual, Sam did the prying, Remi the probing. Louisa stood behind them with a flashlight.

Remi slid her hand out of the hole and got to her knees. "Seven," she said.

"Oh, my Lord . . . " Louisa breathed. Remi scooted aside so the girl could kneel down and look for herself. "How long have they been there?"

"A hundred and ninety years, give or take," Sam replied.

"What happens now?"

Remi smiled. "Louisa, you're rich. You pay off the farm, go back to school, and live happily ever after."

———

Hand in hand Sam and Remi walked out the front door to their car. "We got eleven bottles out of twelve," Remi said. "Not bad."

"Better than not bad. Think about it: Those bottles survived a trip around the world, the fall of Napoleon, and two world wars. I'd call that miraculous."

"Good point. I have to say, I feel a little let down."

"About?"

"The end of the adventure," Remi said wistfully.

"The end? Not on your life. Patty Cannon's treasure is still out there, and we've got most of the Pocomoke Swamp left to search."

Remi laughed. "And after that?"

"After that, we pick a spot on the map and go."